PRAISE FOR TISH COHEN AND

The Truth About Delilah Blue

"A beautifully written, finely wrought, race-to-the-end novel about finding your family, finding a life, and finding yourself. Tish Cohen is the next great thing in women's fiction."

—Allison Winn Scotch,
New York Times bestselling author of
The One That I Want and *Time of My Life*

"Tish Cohen knows how to slide us into a story, letting us imagine we might know the pathway. But we are wrong because she is a wonderful story teller and will surprise us at every turn. She has created a cast of characters who are filled with delicious human frailty and love. If you think you know anything about parental love and misguided choices, think again. Cohen peels away the layers of families and human desires and leaves us with a world of hope."

—Jacqueline Sheehan,
New York Times bestselling author of
Lost & Found and *Now & Then*

"What is more wrenching for a girl than being separated from her mother? In this engrossing novel, estranged parents navigate narrow lines of legitimacy in the aftermath of an awful twelve-year family separation. It is impossible to turn away from these damaged yet engaging characters as they struggle to either erase or face the past. Cohen, who writes with clarity, wit, and warmth, is brilliant in her penetration of the family layers, presenting all sides of the drama by allowing each character to be the star of their own show. This is a book that won't be set aside until the last page is turned."

—Randy Susan Meyers, author of
The Murderer's Daughters

THE TRUTH ABOUT DELILAH BLUE

Also by Tish Cohen

Town House
Inside Out Girl

THE TRUTH ABOUT DELILAH BLUE

A NOVEL

TISH COHEN

HARPER PERENNIAL

NEW YORK • LONDON • TORONTO • SYDNEY • NEW DELHI • AUCKLAND

HARPER PERENNIAL

This book is a work of fiction. The characters, incidents, and dialogue are drawn from the author's imagination and are not to be construed as real. Any resemblance to actual events or persons, living or dead, is entirely coincidental.

HarperCollins books may be purchased for educational, business, or sales promotional use. For information, please write: Special Markets Department, HarperCollins Publishers, 10 East 53rd Street, New York, NY 10022.

FIRST EDITION

Designed by Aline C. Pace

Library of Congress Cataloging-in-Publication data is available upon request.

ISBN 978-0-06-187597-7

10 11 12 13 14 OV/RRD 10 9 8 7 6 5 4 3 2 1

For Max and Lucas

THE TRUTH ABOUT DELILAH BLUE

Prologue

June 6, 1996

The smell of asphalt and dandelions and the last days of school made the air tingle with summer promise: fireflies in applesauce jars, bare toes in the sand at Kew Beach, and leisurely decisions at the ice-cream truck about whether or not to chocolate dip. The afternoon heat had stilled the city. Other than the sprinkler clucking and whirring from across the road and the *Young and the Restless* theme song wafting from the window next door, the entire neighborhood of Cabbagetown had fallen silent.

She was meant to wait inside. But when the sun finally burst through the salt-stained curtain of winter, you took notice. Even at eight years old, you knew to plunk yourself in its lap, wrap its edges around your waist like a favorite sweatshirt you left on the streetcar and thought you might never see again.

Sitting on the driveway with dirty-blond hair covering her face, Delilah Blue Lovett played a game with herself—held a shard of broken glass over her thighs until she couldn't stand the pain, then checked to see if she'd blistered.

Ian grunted a warning from the front porch. "No more yelping. That neighbor lady of yours will start up again."

They both watched as Mrs. Del Vecchio's plaid curtains snapped shut.

"When's my dad coming?"

Ian appeared to be wearing the same ripped T-shirt and expensive-looking black jeans he arrived in the day before, when her mother introduced her new friend as a "mixed-media artist with talent that is, honestly, nothing short of genius." Delilah didn't care what sort of skill the man had. He'd spent so much time in the Victorian house's only bathroom that morning—shaving his already bald head to perfection—that she'd had to sneak out back in her nightgown and pee behind the cedars. He pried the cap off a bottle of beer. "Not until five."

"Can we call him to come get me now?"

"No way. Your mother said you're hers until five."

"But she's not here."

"Hey, it's no picnic for me either. You don't see me whining."

She climbed up off the pavement, tossed her glass shard into the bushes, and wandered to the road's edge. "I wish I could see his house from here. I wish I could fly."

He sucked from the bottle and swallowed. "Don't waste your time wishing, kid. You'll never have the goddamn wings."

It irked her.

Delilah raced up and onto the porch, through the smell of beer, and up to her room. When she came back down she was wearing, over her T-shirt, the sparkly wire wings from an old fairy costume.

She rummaged through the crawlspace beneath the back porch and emerged with an armload of broken bricks, which she toppled onto the driveway before piling them up into a messy wall two bricks deep. Satisfied with her base, she found a long plank of wood and propped it against the buttress like a ramp, all the while conscious of the weightlessness and movement of the wings on her back.

After hopping on her squeaky red bike, Delilah coasted out onto the driveway and wound a slow circle around the makeshift ramp. The wings were fluttering now; she could feel them.

Ian laughed. "It'll never work."

Delilah gripped her handlebars, stood up, and pumped her pedals as hard as she could. Her circle widened as she raced around and around the driveway, picking up speed, wings flapping behind her in the hot breeze, bike rocking from side to side from her effort. The back tire skidded out on a few of her turns. Once the sun got in her eyes and she nearly lost control of the bike.

"Be careful," said Ian.

She whizzed past. At the end of the driveway, she turned sharp and raced back toward the bottom of the ramp. The board buckled and thumped under the weight of her tires.

Then nothing but silence as the bike sailed into the air. As if all of the city had stopped, held its breath. No roaring bus engines, no keening cicadas, no honking cabbies. Even

Delilah herself seemed to be frozen in time, standing up on her pedals, whitened fists gripping the handlebars, her face euphoric. Proud.

"Look!" shouted Delilah as Ian started off the porch toward her. "I'm flying!"

One

SEPTEMBER 4, 2008

The only thing that stood between Lila's naked body and twenty-seven art students was a stiff brown robe that reeked of every petrified model that had come before her. The freshman boys were the worst, she'd been warned, particularly during the first term. They slumped behind easels and art boards, eyelids drooping with the malaise of seasoned artistes, but the moment you dropped the robe, they were horny little ten-year-olds, hunkered down behind the sofa ogling a tattered copy of *National Geographic*.

Until this morning, it had seemed the perfect plan: earn a fine arts degree—an utter waste of paper as far as her father was concerned, and an even greater waste of money—through osmosis by memorizing every word that falls off the professor's tongue while a roomful of students at L.A. Arts scrutinizes and interprets her every inflamed hair follicle, every peeling fingernail, every pore, every scab; then hurry off to reenact the entire lecture in the dirt-floored cellar back home. The paychecks would be paltry, but it wasn't as if she had mouths to feed or rent to pay. She needed enough to keep her in oil paint and canvas, maybe even a pair of boots that weren't covered in childish doodles.

Lila had not, she now realized, in a dizzying show of poor timing, given enough thought to the absoluteness of her scheme. She'd prepared herself for the exposure of body parts customarily kept under wraps, but hadn't delegated a moment's consideration to her feet. Now, standing on the dirty floor, without the weight of her boots to tether her delicate frame to the ground, she felt so feathery light it was terrifying. As if her bones were made of balsa wood. As if, were the entire class to blow hard enough, she might be swept up and out the window.

A student with razored bangs and a thrift-store blazer shot Lila a predatory grin. She pulled the robe tighter, horrified to find his eyes fixed on her chest. She gave him the finger but not before her heart came loose and snapped against her ribs like a wet towel, taking with it any bit of resolve she'd mustered.

It was a terrible plan.

What had she been thinking? No dream was worth this. There were people perfectly happy working at In-N-Out and babyGap and Rodney's Liquor. She could be a barista. Anything. Normal people did not show their tits to achieve their career goals. Lila glanced at the studio door. The professor hadn't arrived yet; she could go home and rethink things. Come up with a better strategy—one that shrouded her in opaque layers from ankle to chin.

"You must be the new model." A tall male, an older student, stood in front of her, arborescent and congested in his plaid shirt and low-slung jeans, with messy brown hair quivering under the overhead vent. Rectangular black glasses slipped low on his nose and he nudged them up with a pinkie finger. He wasn't appealing at first glance. But his mouth saved him, wide and uptilted at the edges as it was. It gave him a certain look. Knowing and careful. Jaded. Amused.

"I'm Adam Harding." He sniffed with great importance, then undid his authority by wiping his nose with the back of his hand. "The TA here. So if you have any questions or whatever."

The model's area was hard to miss, raised as it was on a wobbly plywood platform. The wall directly behind the dais was gussied up with ornate millwork and crown molding. It was fixed with a towel bar, two rusty pulleys, and a long rope, obviously acrobatic paraphernalia for models to use in striking atypical poses. There was a Louis XIV chair done up in faded velvet, a circular platform that could spin the model like a lazy Susan, and a red plastic milk crate stocked with different-colored linens, fake flowers, an antique bowling pin, and a few pieces of plastic fruit dented from years of use. Lila tucked long, coppery hair behind her ears and shrugged. "I guess this is the place."

"It's where the magic happens." His eyes sparkled with something resembling innuendo. Her disgust must have been obvious because he attached himself to her elbow. "God, did that sound dirty?"

She pulled away. "It did, kind of."

"I meant art-wise. You know, where creation begins and

all that. Have you done this before? You look on the young side."

She stared down at her feet, which had taken on a sickly blue pallor in the frigid air-conditioning. Fiona, the gray-haired, kimono-wearing model who had tried to befriend her in the office a few days prior, had asked Lila to go for coffee so she could fill her in about the job. Uneasy about having a tête-à-tête with someone she barely knew, Lila claimed to have another commitment. Fiona had left her with a warning: You're never modeling for the first time. Not even the first time.

To Adam, Lila said, "I'm twenty and yes. I've modeled tons. Down in Laguna. And the greater Laguna area."

He nodded his approval, then pulled a bottle of NyQuil from his pocket, uncapped it, and sucked it back. After inhaling what must have been half the bottle, he burped softly into his hand. "In case you're worried, no one audits classes here. No spectators."

Was he kidding? It was the first thing she'd researched—whether she could sit in on classes as an observer. Had the answer been different, she'd be fully clothed right now. "Good."

"I'm moving to New York as soon as I graduate next spring. Much better place to make it as an artist."

He was interfering with her exit plans. If this went on much longer the professor might arrive and blow her chance. "Cool."

Adam began to tug on the ropes and pick up the props one by one, tossing each in the air and returning it to its rightful bin as he explained that she should make use of the trappings as she saw fit. As if to reinforce the sturdiness of his setup, he leaned down on the chair's seat and gave it a good shake before plopping down on it. She didn't like the feel of his eyes searching her narrow chin, her cheeks, her brow. "What?"

He stared a bit longer, taking in her thin skin maybe, the circles beneath her eyes, or the reddish dye in her messy layers, before looking away. "Nothing."

Liar. Something about her had struck him, she could tell. It made her hate him. It made her want to run. She moved toward her backpack.

A sharp voice called out, "Welcome to Life Drawing 101, people."

Damn.

The professor breezed in with an armful of books and paintbrushes. He dropped the load onto his desk and turned to face the class. He was more mosquito than man, with jutted elbows and hunched shoulders that careened toward his lowered head in such a menacing slope his nose could end only in a stinger. "My name is Julian Lichtenstein. Yes, *that* Lichtenstein. Roy was my second cousin." Displeased by the excited whispers that spread across the class, he barked, "My celebrated cousin may have found star status with cartoonish spoofs that might better have graced the walls of a child's clubhouse than the Museum of Modern Art, but you'll find I do not subscribe to his style. Fame, in my opinion, is a sorry rascal, a fraudulent measure of an artist's place in the world."

Lila stood up taller. Fame was something she craved more than life itself. Desire bubbled up her esophagus and burned the back of her throat. To have her work dissected by critics, bringing rise to comments like "stealthy," "astringent," and "absolute." Not because she deserved it. Not because she needed the flashing cameras of the paparazzi. Not because restaurant owners might lead her to a special table near the back where an appropriate hush would fall over the other diners as they realized whom they had as a neighbor. No. While these things had their appeal, what Lila really wanted was for Elisabeth to see her daughter's face in *Vanity Fair* magazine one day and say to herself, "My God. I've made a terrible mistake."

"Mister Lichtenstein is something of a tongue-cramper," the professor continued. "Feel free to call me Lichty."

Lila didn't have time for nicknames. The man was blocking her path to the door.

Her father had made his tuition-paying stance perfectly clear years ago. A business degree was a worthy pursuit Victor Mack was willing to fund. After all, if she worked hard, *really* hard, she too might—if she got lucky—grow up to sell articulated human skeletons, paper gowns with plastic belts that fell off, and gynecological stirrups that didn't need to be cloaked in oven mitts to hospitals and medical schools as he did. An art degree, on the other hand, was designation without a purpose; the supernumerary nipple of post–secondary education.

So far, hers had been a profitless pursuit. Not only did drawing and painting leave her with little time for such homely activities as part-time jobs to accumulate college funds, but her severe self-censure meant that most of her creations did not survive the emotional crash that came once the trance of artistry faded, when the dirt beneath her feet grew damp and cold, and the bulb strung from the rafters revealed fatal errors in her work.

Her pieces were never as good as she imagined them, never lived up to her intentions. The moment she stooped to retrieve a dropped pencil, her subjects' eyebrows, noses, and ears scuttled about and realigned themselves. When she paused to sneeze, elbows crooked at peculiar angles. In a blink of an eye, perfectly rendered hands wizened and curled into spiky appendages that could only resemble hoof picks.

As such, most of her works were issued the ultimate punishment. Graphite on paper received death by ferocious crumpling. Acrylic on foil was finger-clawed beyond recognition. Nasty ends, both. But it was oil on canvas that faced the most savage decree by far: death by Swiss Army knife.

As it stood, she had very little to show for her hours of labor. For now, *Vanity Fair* would have to wait.

Lichty's mustache twitched as he looked over his students, ranging from a pair of sun-scarred surf types to a navy-haired girl whispering into a cell phone. If, over the summer, the man had dreamed of discovering a Rembrandt or a Gauguin in this year's crop of freshmen, that dream had just crumbled to dust like a fallen watercolor patty. He sighed and slipped behind his desk.

Now. She could bolt. Two seconds, maybe three, and she'd be gone.

Lichty instructed the students to tape drawing paper to mason board and pull out the graphite pencil sets and pliable erasers from the recommended supplies list. Just as Lila scooped up her backpack from the floor beneath the blackboard and started around him, he asked, "Where are you going, Model?"

"I was just . . ."

"And why aren't you Georgie Ketonis?"

In a different situation, she might have had a clever answer. Something like, "You'll have to take that up with a higher source," or "My boyfriend asks me that all the time." Instead, she scratched her nose. "I'm Lila Mack."

"I specifically asked for Georgie today."

"I was just given a classroom and told to change."

He wiped imaginary bangs off his face. "Any tattoos?"

"No."

"Lewd piercings?"

She shook her head.

"Fashionable bikini waxes? I insist models be in their natural human state."

This was getting far too gynecological for her taste. She muttered, "How about we do a pap smear?" It came out louder than intended, and a few nearby students giggled in shocked delight.

Lichty looked at her sharply. "What did you say, Miss Mack?"

It was far too early in her career to make enemies in high places. "Nothing. I'm in a natural state."

He spun around. "Good. You'll do for now. Get paper taped to boards, people. We'll be paying particular attention to highlights today. No hard edges; you'll see the body is made up of shadow and light, not the blackened outlines of a coloring book. I consider myself to be a classicist, a strict disciplinarian. You'll learn to do it right before you go Warhol on me."

Lila's theory exactly. It wasn't until she'd learned skeletal structure that she allowed herself to draw muscles. And it wasn't until she understood muscles that she allowed herself to draw flesh.

She let her bag drop to the floor.

"It is in this class you will finally learn to see as adults. A child does not draw what is in front of him, but what he believes to be in front of him. His images come from memory, perceived understanding. The eye sees what the mind knows. It was in 1895 that English psychologist James Sully heard from a child, 'First I think, then I draw my think.'" Lichty leaned across his desk. "Let me be clear on this . . . There will be no *thinking* in my class."

Brilliant. Lila was no longer capable of leaving.

Some students were poised, ready with sharpened graphite pressed to paper. Others were still taping paper to mason board, or digging supplies out from backpacks or small art boxes. Lila glanced at Lichty, whose expression immediately changed. He looked back at her with something nearing a smile, lifted his brows, and cocked his head, eyes blinking shut as he did. It was the sign she'd dreaded. Time to drop the robe.

It isn't porn.

Art modeling was a noble profession. So said Fiona the model. Gone were the days when the only females willing to shed their vestments in the name of art were prostitutes and masked Victorians. It was the twenty-first century now. Women could shed their vestments in the name of just about anything. Or nothing at all.

As long as their medical supplies salesman fathers didn't find out.

After sucking in a deep breath, Lila unbelted, let the robe slip off her shoulders, and clamped her eyes shut. She moved into her pose.

Air rushed at her skin from every direction. So much so, she felt weightless again, hovering about a foot off the floor.

She felt her nipples harden and closed her eyes, mortified. They say being blind makes your other senses sharpen. It may have been true, but so did stripping off your clothes in front of a roomful of strangers. Lila was first hit by scents so strong she could taste them. The fresh rubber of new erasers. The bitter snap of unused graphite. The stale robe at her feet.

Every sound clawed at her eardrums with ragged nails. Excited whispers from the jock types in the far corner. The rustling of denim. From the right, a bored sigh. Closer, across from her left kneecap, a muffled cell phone.

To dull her senses, she focused on her pose. It was one she wished she were drawing. A pose she'd try to re-create at home later with a vinyl skeleton swiped from her father's supplies closet. Hands clasped behind her head to widen the upper back, a slight twist to the right to bend the spine, one leg leaning inward to hide parts she was not yet brave enough to expose.

Lucky for her, the skeleton had no such modesty.

A few giggles erupted from close by. Then soft footsteps drew near and stopped. She opened her eyes to see Lichty's menacing stinger—nostrils barbed and cavernous and amplified to the point of absurdity by its nearness to her own—staring back at her.

A smile unfurled beneath his nose, his mouth tightened with amusement, giving him the expression of someone hard at work on a candy, trying to crack away the peppermint shell before the chocolate center melted away. "Is this your first time modeling, Miss Mack?"

"No."

"I see. While enthusiasm is a quality I prize in my studio,

I ask that my models refrain from disrobing while I'm still explaining the day's lesson. A naked body can be somewhat distracting. In the future—should there be a future for the two of us—you'll keep your more clandestine bits under wraps until I've instructed you to do otherwise."

The roving chuckles erupted into a collective bark of laughter. Lichty shot the class a disapproving look, silencing the room in an instant.

"Sorry." She snatched up the robe and wrapped it around her torso, never more humiliated in her life. "I thought when you nodded—"

"You'll find, as far as human evolution goes, I'm fairly sophisticated. I don't tend to communicate my desires in bobs and grunts. When I want you to drop robe and pose, I'll simply ask for it. Are we clear?"

"Yes." A hot flush spread from Lila's forehead down to her abdomen.

"Resume your pose."

She didn't move.

"Drop the robe and pose, Miss Mack."

And so she did. Mercifully, the room filled with the chorus of graphite stroking plump white paper.

"Begin with light, airy strokes, people. Stay away from strong lines. We want to build up our drawing. Be selective in your notice. A man with a pencil takes all that is in front of him no matter the result, but an artist takes only what he needs." Lichty wound his way between the students and scrutinized Lila's body as if it were a vase filled with wilting flowers. "Pay careful attention to model's rib cage," he boomed. "Prominent, near masculine in its musculature, its implied athleticism. Now look to model's shoulders and biceps. In relation to the ribs, you might expect the upper arms to be robust and sturdy. Don't let your mind fool you. The comparative scantiness of her arms may be disappointing to future lovers, but offers the artist a delicious lack of balance."

Lila dropped her arms and stared at him in disbelief. "What?"

"Model does not speak!" Lichty's voice echoed off bare walls. "Return to your pose." When she did, he addressed the class. "Look for the unusual and play off it, people. Don't be tempted to skip over the birthmark on her right hip. Draw it in all its geometric vulgarity."

This she could not argue. Doctors back in Toronto had said it would shrink. Or, rather, she would grow and the espresso-colored stain on her hip would not—the old optical illusion thing. But this particular birthmark—this nevus, this ambitious vascular lesion—had kept pace, galloping alongside her growth spurts like a determined Labrador chasing a Buick. These vigilant blood vessels never slept, not even through the excruciating summer between seventh and eighth grades when Lila sprouted three inches in sixty-one days and woke up each morning with bones that drummed and moaned from another California night spent growing.

The Arabic called birthmarks *wiham*. "Wishes." According to folklore, these *wiham* represented a desire the mother had while pregnant—one that went unfulfilled. Which made some sort of sense, as her mother was an artist and the birthmark was shaped like a jagged eraser. Not much of a wish, Lila supposed. Not unless you needed to make something vanish.

Then again, other more ominous legends said a birthmark was the physical embodiment of a mother's greatest fear.

Another forty-five minutes of being dissected in the name of art and the naked was over. Lichty dismissed the class and sauntered over to Lila, she was dead sure, to inform her she was not to show foul mouth nor malformed body in his studio again. As she swathed her invisible bruises in the robe—never had a piece of unwashed clothing been more adored—the man looked at her and blinked. "There's a quiet sadness, an ethereal sort of sufferance, to you I find appealing. The challenge you offer to these students is to not only recognize the pain that pulses just beneath the surface of your skin, but to capture it in a way that makes the observer wince."

He might as well have kicked her in the gut. Her wind was gone, her chest hurt, and she gulped for whatever oxygen she could swallow. How dare he presume to know her like this? It was one thing to criticize her frame, another thing entirely to x-ray her soul and assess what he saw.

He continued, "I have a multimedia class at ten tomorrow morning in the music building, north wing. Studio three-F. An usual place for a studio, so plan to get lost your first time."

Lila's shout came out as a whisper. "No."

"You can't?"

"I won't."

He was clearly a man unaccustomed to hearing the word no. His eyebrows arched skyward. "Am I to understand you are refusing to do my class?"

"No. I'm refusing you." She spun on her soon-to-be-booted heel, feeling Adam's eyes on her as she snapped the changing-room curtain shut.

Two

Victor Mack leaned over his desk, swiped silver hair from his eyes, and stared down at the half dozen powdered jellies. Straight from the oven, the girl at the store had assured him through her cottony lisp.

He poked at one and watched the dough submit and spring back again. No longer warm, but seemed fresh enough. He'd never liked powdered jellies himself—messy creatures with a tendency to relieve themselves atop one's trousers if one wasn't nimble with a napkin. Other than being propped in two neat rows of three, the arrangement of pastries was less than aesthetically pleasing with holes pointed every which way to Tuesday. Victor reached into the box and shuffled the donuts around until the vulgar little assholes were hidden from view.

Seemed the gentlemanly thing to do.

The treats weren't for him. Genevieve was her name. Not insanely young, somewhere about the tail end of her forties—an energetic, capable type with a tidy brown haircut, lips shaped like tulips, and melon-colored hospital scrubs to match the lips. She was the kind of woman who knew how to make a man feel as if he mattered. Always remembered his coffee. Always stocked his cream.

Gen managed the front desk of the Fairfax Institute, a psychiatric facility in Santa Monica he'd been calling on for years. She'd celebrated her birthday a few weeks back, and he'd walked in just as her coworkers presented her with a powdered jelly—her favorite, she announced just before she blew out the candle.

He would swing by after calling on a potential client not far from there, some hotshot new group of chiropractors looking for exam tables, machinery, skeletons—the works. He'd practically sealed the deal over the phone. Stopping by was really just a formality. By two-thirty that afternoon he should be handing in a signed contract worth about $75,000 with a commission of nearly five grand. It was the kind of order he needed to reinstate his position in the company. He glanced at the brass plaques on the wall above the filing cabinet. Top salesman at RoyalCrest Medical Distributors seven years running, a streak that ended only when Blair Austen and his kamikaze closing tactics joined the team two years prior.

Anyway, Gen. Victor would be in a good mood by the time he arrived, his briefcase fat with the chiropractors' contract. He'd pull into the driveway, coast past the facility's ochre stucco facade, with ivy that scrabbled up from the ground and swallowed the entire south side of the building, along the narrow laneway to the best parking spot in Los

Angeles: a spacious, almost silky-smooth concrete pad conveniently sprawled out beneath a row of tall, but crowded, queen palms all graceful and green and bushy. If he arrived well after noon, they would shade his pristine and sporty 240Z—circa 1973, before Datsun morphed into Nissan—like a dream.

He would leave his briefcase and contract in the car. Totter inside with his box. Set the donuts on her reception desk and ask her to eat dinner with him. They still did that, didn't they? It had been a while for Victor. He didn't mind admitting he was out of practice. Anyway, it didn't have to be dinner. Coffee would work just as well. There was just something about the soothing creases at the corners of Genevieve's smiling eyes he couldn't get out of his head.

He was a sucker for a female. It had always been that way. Growing up in north Toronto, the only child of a medical researcher father and librarian mother, with no cousins to speak of, Victor had but the most fleeting contact with girls. He saw them at school and in the playground, but it was as if they were a different species entirely. He could never relate to them with any sense of ease. When a girl plopped down next to him in the school cafeteria and asked if he'd pass the ketchup, an alarm sounded in his head. *Danger! You're talking to a girl!*

How easy life might have been if he'd had a sister to normalize—maybe even taint—the gender. Surely he'd never have married Elisabeth. He'd have been able to keep his thoughts in order the first time she flipped her curls out of the way to get a good look at him that night at the pub. Or giggled the way she did, with the tip of her tongue trapped between perfectly square white teeth.

How different his life might have turned out.

And then there was Lila. From the moment she pushed her tiny fingers out of the pink swaddling blanket in the delivery room and gripped his index finger, he'd felt it. His new reality: that he'd spin the world the wrong way on its axis to do what was right for her, no matter what the cost.

What he hadn't fully considered, all those years ago, was what his love would cost his daughter. And that his remorse would grow and mature as she did. For some fool reason, he'd expected it to fade.

He stood up and crossed the room, bent his fifty-three-year-old frame down, and pulled open the bottom drawer of his file cabinet, stared at the rows of ties lining the drawer. Victor kept a log of which tie was worn on which sales call, and once a tie had completed the rounds, it was retired to his bedroom at home for everyday use. Sometimes Lila swiped them and used them to hold back her hair while painting, but Victor didn't mind. By that time they'd served their purpose.

Ties were to a salesman what a necklace was to a woman. A finishing touch. An expression of personality, of success. It was Victor's trademark. Lila teased him about it, laughed and called him a dandy, a glamour boy. He didn't mind. She was still a child, far too young to see the importance of not letting your clients see you in the same tie twice. It kept his image fresh, and made for easy chitchat before he pulled out the product catalogs and laid his signing pen on the table. Keeping track of the ties wasn't easy—then again, the important things in life never were.

Pale gray paisley caught his eye—the silvery shade should complement his graying beard. A birthday gift from his assistant earlier in the year, this one had never been worn. He pulled it out of the drawer and slipped it around his neck. It was a tie he'd been saving for a special day. Today seemed about right.

HE DIDN'T MARCH through the doors at Fairfax feeling quite as elated as he'd hoped. One of the Starkman sales reps had beat him to the chiropractors. The rep, Margie Kwinter, serviced them so well, in fact, that all they needed from Victor was the box of free RoyalCrest mugs he'd set on the reception desk when he walked in. Then, after battling the multiheaded, fire-breathing beast that was crosstown traffic in Los Angeles at noon on a Tuesday, he found his favorite Fairfax parking spot occupied by a filthy teal moped with a sticker that read CAUTION: BLIND DRIVER.

There was no justice.

After parking on the street—too close to a team of orange-vested city workers jackhammering a hole in the sidewalk for his comfort—and after a final check in the rearview mirror, he gathered Gen's donuts and made his way past the construction, hoping his daughter had had the good sense to at least consider the glossy program from Connelly School of Business Management he'd left on the kitchen table that morning.

The combination of velvety silence and cool air that met him as he stepped inside invited him to pause for a moment and collect himself. Best not to appear at Gen's desk all leaky and swollen with heat before uttering the words, "Eat with me tonight, please." He followed the curved wall that led to reception and waited patiently as Noreen, the part-time girl who covered Gen's lunch breaks and sick days, folded an elderly patient into his wheelchair and told the orderly where he should be taken. Once Noreen settled herself back in her chair, she glanced up at Victor and smiled.

"Well. Mr. Mack. Did you have an appointment with purchasing?" She shuffled through her book. "I don't have anything written down here."

"No, not today." He peered past Noreen to the rows of colored files, expecting to find Gen kneeling down with a stack of patient records on her lap, but found the area empty. Not unusual. Gen was ambitious. She'd been taking nursing classes at night and had been assuming duties more directly related to patient care. "Will you please page Genevieve for me?"

Noreen looked surprised. "Genevieve?"

"That's right."

"But Gen's gone. Her big trip to Greece, remember? She showed us the brochure for that villa in Santorini. The place with the little blue gate." She reprimanded Victor with a cluck of her tongue.

Of course. There'd been a backpack-laden donkey climbing a hill in one of the photos, and he'd teased Gen about donkeys being used as cabs. They'd had the discussion not five days ago. He'd spent the weekend imagining her walking, bikinied and sunburned, along the beach with black sand, and trying not to imagine her falling for one of the local men. It wasn't possible he'd forgotten. And yet he had.

"You do remember, don't you?"

"Of course. Idiotic of me." He stepped backward lest she see the hot flush spreading up from his collar. "You know, I think I was looking at next week in my agenda. My assistant must have left it open to the wrong spot. My fault for not checking first."

"Did you want to leave a message for when she's back?"

"No. Thanks. No message."

He wandered outside and leaned against the stucco facade, blinking into the midday glare and trying for the life of him to fathom where the hole in his memory had come from.

Three

Lila marched up the winding road, her cutoffs doing little to shield her legs from the merciless afternoon sun. To make matters of roasted flesh worse, it was possible the sole of her left boot was worn clear through and her kneesock was all that protected her foot from the sizzling griddle that was Rykert Canyon Boulevard.

The city bus didn't penetrate this area. It made the one stop at Rykert Canyon and Moreland Street, then chugged off in the opposite direction. Since her first day of high school, Lila had skidded up and down the dust-covered hills to and from 71 Palo Verde Pass in her slippery-soled boots, never once succumbing to mounting paternal pressure that she consider footwear with better traction.

She turned the corner, relieved to be shaded by a stretch of elegant and towering Eucalyptus trees, with their hairy bark and leathery gray leaves. Vines weighed down the branches and tickled the pavement, and Lila slowed down to weave in and out of them as if they were beaded curtains. The hill, parched from a long summer, sloped straight up on this side of the street, so front doors and peeling wooden gates fronted directly onto the asphalt. Houses across the way—houses like her own— sat so low on the hillside they were mostly unseen, crouched beneath the road as if hiding from view.

Life hadn't always looked like this. In 1996, she'd been another girl entirely. She was Delilah Blue Lovett, living with her charismatic, free-spirited mother in the gingerbread neighborhood of Cabbagetown in Toronto. Behind a vermillion front door that closed with a muffled thump that mimicked her mother's faint French-Canadian accent. She had a curlicue-trimmed portico where a broom and a brass tub full of umbrellas stood ready to shelter her. She had Sunday-night dinners at her grandmother's house in Mississauga. She had the asthmatic Russian son of the opera singer next door to spy on, and sleepovers with her best friend down the street.

Life hadn't been perfect, but it had a certain ticktock. She could count on birthday parties with kids she'd known since kindergarten and cousins she'd despised since birth. The school was 793 footsteps there and back if you were careful not to step on any cracks—she was always vigilant about her mother that way.

Then her memory became a blur. Her parents stopped speaking and her life would never look the same. Her father buckled her into a lumpy seat on a 737 bound for Disneyland and said a long weekend on her own should give her mother the quiet time she needed. Who was Lila to argue? She was eight years old and on her way to meet Cinderella.

Turned out a weekend away from her only child wasn't enough. Elisabeth Lovett, and her long, russet, corkscrew curls, her caramel skin, and her laugh that sounded like tinkling bells, needed more. So Victor bought a ramshackle cabin in the Hollywood Hills, enrolled his daughter in the local public school, and said he'd never liked the name Delilah. It had been Elisabeth's overly whimsical choice and it was too much for California. He announced it was time for a nickname and Lila would do just fine.

It was at this moment the freshly christened Lila had an idea. While they were on the subject of inappropriate names, the thought of enduring another year with the nickname "Shove It" (or Lovett's oh-so-imaginative and quick-witted cousin, "Hate-It") made her feel sick to her stomach. Victor's smile had nearly split his face. He patted her small hand, and said it was the perfect time to tackle their problematic surname and he happened to have one standing at the ready: Mack. He said it would honor his Mackinnon ancestors from the Isle of Skye, off the west coast of Scotland. She thought about it. Short, snappy, easy to spell. Seemed it would do just as well as any.

Then there were twelve birthdays without phone calls, twelve Christmases without cards, too many missed bedtimes to count; it was as if having a mother never happened. As if Elisabeth, and the liquid click of her lighter, the sweaters and T-shirts that slipped off her shoulder when she giggled, the flirtatious uptilt in her voice that turned her sentences into questions, had never existed at all.

After a while Lila stopped waiting. After a while it sunk

in. Hope turned to numbness turned to disbelief—a coating that had grown so deep and crusty Lila could etch her name in it.

There was a game Lila used to play with herself: Had She Been Less of a Mother. Had Elisabeth been, say, a forensic accountant instead of an artist, would the absence of her clay-softened palm on Lila's cheek have stung quite so much? If her voice hadn't been rendered slightly rutted by cigarettes, would her bedtime lullabies have been quite so hypnotic? And what about her impossibly tiny ears? Had they been large and lumpy, would it have been less magical when she tucked that halo of hair behind them and leaned closer to hear what Lila had to say?

The answer was always the same. To have a mother like Elisabeth, and then lose her—not because she was struck by a car or swept out to sea by a dangerous current, but because she wasn't sufficiently enamored by you to hang around—it left a hole in who you were. You became one of those people who radiated worthlessness. You became a living, breathing, walking—and in Lila's case, drawing, painting, getting naked—tragedy.

But that didn't mean Lichty, or anyone else, for that matter, was allowed to notice.

There was a flash of movement on a driveway up ahead. Lila slowed and feigned interest in her boots. Danica Seldin was climbing out of her Alfa Romeo convertible and gathering a few shopping bags from behind her seat, her glossy white ponytail falling forward. Typical Danica, all fit and beach ready in Lycra shorts, a tight white T-shirt, and flip-flops.

They'd started going to school together when Lila and Victor first moved in. Before her mother's rejection had wormed its way into her flesh, rendering her so broken that her cracks scared off the other children, Lila had looked to Dani as a possible replacement for her best friend back in Toronto. Dani had worn hand-knotted string bracelets on one tanned ankle and a faded navy T-shirt that read CRAIG'S SURF SHACK in cracked letters across the chest. Her teeth were so white they could have been made of sugar, and the other kids crowded around her on the first day of school because her dad, Craig Seldin, had won a skateboarding competition Labor Day weekend and had been interviewed on TV.

Even to the newcomer with the fledgling name, it was clear Dani was the school's reigning goddess and all the other kids followed her into class with the aim of sitting as close to her as possible. But the teacher had other ideas and assigned Lila the coveted seat next to Dani, then asked her to stand up and tell the other students where she was from.

You're not from Canada, Victor had informed her the night prior—the first of many "lessons" he would teach her. "Americans," he explained, "love other Americans. They never fully accept northerners as one of them. If you really want to fit in, you'll tell the kids you're from Seattle."

So, tugging on her freshly cut bangs, she did. Turned out Victor's advice worked. At recess, Dani sidled up to her and told her there was a famous skate park in Seattle. Said she was lucky to come from such a place and wondered if Lila had a skateboard. When Lila told her no, Dani offered to teach her to long board on the weekend. Lila didn't know or care what a long board was—she had a friend.

Or so she thought. On Saturday morning, when she was preparing to go to her new buddy's by scrubbing her navy T-shirt against a rock so it would look as distressed as

Dani's, Victor came out of the house, sat down beside her on the porch steps, and informed her it wasn't safe to go off to the home of a strange family. Anything could happen. This wasn't Toronto, he explained. This was America, and people had guns. In spite of his daughter's insistence that Dani's parents were neither armed nor dangerous, Victor said they couldn't know for sure. He said it was best not to get too chummy because guns and molester-type habits wouldn't be spread out on the dining-room table for her to examine. No, he said. She could see her new friends at school and that was enough.

Lila begged to be allowed at least to run to Dani's house and explain lest the girl think she was being stood up. But Victor said there was no time. He was taking her to Universal Studios and wanted to get there before the lines got too long and the day grew too hot.

On Monday, she raced up to Dani at school to explain her father wouldn't let her go, but the damage was already done. Dani, who had likely not experienced much in the way of rejection, refused to acknowledge Lila's existence. And so, living in California became a never-ending string of paranoid declarations, arrested friendships, and conciliatory family outings.

Now, with arms full, Dani caught sight of Lila and bumped the car door shut with her hip. She glanced quickly, hopefully, toward the house, before conceding that escape was not an option and forcing a smile. "Hi, Lila."

Lila wanted to slap her. "Hey. Haven't seen you in, well, forever." She felt herself square her shoulders in an effort to appear more substantial. Less flimsy.

"You look good," said Dani.

Dani's older brother, a surfer, had surfaced from the

house, wearing nothing but faded plaid shorts, blond chest hair, and a leather necklace. Kyle pulled a couple of heavy paper bags from the trunk. They chinked as if filled with booze. Grinning, he reprimanded his sister. "Lila doesn't look good. She looks great." He winked, then trotted back up to the house.

The compliment unnerved Lila and she chose to ignore it. "So what are you up to these days, Dani? Running your dad's surf shop?"

"Nah, that's more Kyle's thing. I'm up at Pepperdine studying sports psychology."

"Wow." Of course Dani was in college. What kind of twenty-year-old wasn't in college? "You'll be Dr. Seldin."

"It'll be Dr. McAllister. Remember Mark McAllister from high school?" Dani held up one hand and flashed a modest diamond ring. "We just got engaged."

Lila examined it. "Pretty."

"Mark's at Pepperdine too."

"Nice."

"What about you? Where do you go?"

Nowhere.

I go nowhere.

Correction—today I went somewhere. Didn't work out because I'm too broken for my own good. So tomorrow I'll get back to my intensive program of going nowhere.

"I've been taking a bit of time off to figure things out. Working on my painting and stuff."

Dani's discomfort was visible. How embarrassing to have asked such a nonachiever where she goes to school. It was the equivalent of asking the fat lady at the grocery store when she was due. Dani flashed a patronizing smile. "Good for you."

Kyle was back. "We're having a party." He pulled two cases of beer from the trunk and turned to face Lila. She felt his glance roam over her legs. "You should come hang out."

Dani laughed. "Lila Mack doesn't lower herself to attend lame-o parties, Kyle. She's the tormented artiste, right Lila?"

Lila didn't answer, stuck, as always, between being offended and flattered by this reputation her peers had bestowed upon her.

"Come on, Lila," said Kyle. "I'll make sure you have a good time."

Kyle was attractive. Not many women would argue. To imagine spending time anywhere near such a male was to have a tingle shoot from Achilles tendon straight up the center of your spine. Even Lila wasn't immune to the chemical reaction. Yet she backed away. "Thanks. But I have this thing to go to. With my dad."

Dani marched—rubber shoes slapping against her heels—toward the ivy-tangled wooden gate that led up to the brick cottage. "Okay. Good luck with . . . what you're doing." With a sorrowful look back at Lila's legs, Kyle fell in line behind his sister.

IF THE NEIGHBORING Hollywood Hills homes, many of them suspended on stilts as thin as uncooked spaghettini, had ever taken notice of the wooden house squatting at their knees, they didn't let on. Maybe the primitive carpentry unsettled them, reminded them that they too, but for the grace of a few million dollars, might have wound up with window frames that weren't square, carpenter ants that gnawed on their tibias, and indoor paneling that reeked of unwashed sheets. Or it could be that they kept their noses up to prove they actually do have a decent view of the Pacific. If the weather was clear and the air quality tolerable.

The Macks' two-bedroom cabin had no such panorama. Whoever had built it, some eighty years prior, either required nothing more than a place to hang his rifle during hunting season, or had an aversion to glorious vistas, prompting him—or her—to position all the windows facing directly into the hilltop. The structure seemed convinced, like a young boy hiding behind his mother's skirt, that by burying its face in dead grasses and exposed Eucalyptus roots, it was completely hidden from view.

Lila couldn't have loved it more.

She tugged open the front door. "Dad?"

"Lila? That you?"

There he was in a kitchen chair in his blue suit, rapping his fist against the tabletop and staring out the window. In front of him was a box of donuts with greasy splotches on the lid. Lila flipped open the lid and pulled one out. "Soggy. Were they sitting in your car all day?"

He snapped the lid shut and sat back in his seat, obviously worked up about something. "You're not going to believe it."

"Believe what?"

Standing up, grim faced, Victor buttoned up his suit jacket, then smoothed his hair and motioned for her to follow him outside, his polished brogues lapping softly against the brick floor as he marched, toes pointed outward and knees slanted in.

"What? Where are we going?"

"You'll see." He started up the cement steps that led to the road.

"Why all the secrecy?"

"You'll see."

After trotting up the rest of the steps, he stomped across the gravel parking pad to where a white Prius sat tucked close to his beloved car. With eyes averted as if it were simply too painful to look, he waved toward the driver's-side door. "Did you ever?"

The parking pad was built too wide; an open invitation for neighbors and their visitors to squeeze their cars right next to her father's 240Z. This car was his most beloved possession, and the tiniest ding or scratch inflicted by a careless driver drove him to madness. As long as she could remember, no matter what the weather, he'd parked in the very farthest corner of the lot at the mall, in the spot even the mall designers probably mocked. Not only that, but he always positioned the car on a diagonal, lest anyone intrepid enough to join them out in the badlands considered parking nearby.

It wasn't a good time for Victor's invisible car drama. She itched and crawled and ached to stand under a scalding hot shower and cleanse her skin of the afternoon's humiliation. Instead, she peered closer to where he was pointing, to a spot just to the left of the door handle. "What am I looking for?"

"This. See this?"

"That speck?"

"White paint. From the Prius. I've calculated the trajectory of its passenger door. And if you look closely, you'll see chipped paint on the edge of the Pruis's door—exactly the same height where it struck mine. And it's much bigger than a speck."

"You need to stop obsessing and come back inside."

He leaned over at the waist and ran a finger along the side of the car. "*Jesus.* The metal is damaged. Dented right in! It'll have to be punched out, buffed, probably even painted." He began scrubbing at the car door with the heel of his hand, his jacket sleeve brushing against the paint.

"Dad!" She reached out to stop him. "Your jacket."

He examined his now grimy cuff. "It's not too bad. The cleaner should be able to get it out, don't you think?"

"Hopefully, but you should be careful with it. It's your leading-man suit, remember?"

It was twelve years ago, a short while after they'd arrived in California. They were late for a movie in Westwood—*Beethoven*—to be followed by burgers and shakes at Hamburger Hamlet. Victor was not yet familiar with Los Angeles and had parked the Datsun—in its more pristine, prespecked days—too far away and, with only ten minutes to spare before the film began, he had taken hold of his daughter's hand and begun to jog.

Even through the eyes of an eight-year-old, Victor looked overdressed, marching flat-footed the way he did along the city streets on a Saturday, dressed in his impeccably cut navy suit and white shirt, with jacket tails and chartreuse tie flapping behind him as he rushed. But Victor was Victor—ever the preener. No occasion was too casual to risk being underdressed. Besides, he'd lost weight from jogging through the hills and was thrilled he could fit into the indigo Hugo Boss he hadn't worn in years. It played up his blue eyes, his brand-new California tan.

He'd slowed down at an intersection, unsure if they were headed in the right direction. As they waited for the light to change, a couple dressed in matching pastel T-shirts, carrying maps and cameras, stopped and whispered to each other with great excitement. They moved closer and the husband said to Victor, "I know you."

Lila would never forget the way her father's hand squeezed hers, tighter than ever before. Her knuckles pinched into one another painfully and she tried to pull away, but couldn't. "We're in a hurry," Victor said curtly.

The wife, a heavily built woman with short, umbrella-shaped hair, said, "You were in that movie. *Pretty Woman*."

They'd thought him a film star. From that moment forward, he and Lila had joked about the suit, calling it his leading-man suit.

It wasn't until the couple had toddled off in a haze of disappointment that Lila had asked, "What about *Beethoven*?"

"I'm trying to find the theater."

"Are we lost?" Lila had asked.

"We most certainly are."

"How lost?"

He looked up at the hills, then across town in the direction of the Pacific, before staring up at the sky. He squinted as a snarl of dark clouds crept in front of the sun, not quite blocking out the light. The look on his face was one Lila would never forget: horror and relief. Guilt and sorrow. He bent over to pick her up and started marching in the opposite direction. "Wonderfully and terribly lost."

NOW, STANDING ON the parking pad in his desecrated suit, Victor nodded. "I remember."

"Come. Let's head back inside and I'll pour you a nice drink."

He smiled, reached for her hand, and clasped his leathery fingers around it. Another father might pull his daughter near, wrap his arms around her, and mumble loving words into her hair. Not Victor. Physical closeness had never been listed in his emotional catalog. The man loved her, she had no doubt about it, but his emotions overwhelmed him. Embarrassed him. He patted her hand, then dropped it.

With her father waiting in the living room, Lila wandered into the kitchen, a long galley boasting plywood cupboards with red plastic knobs and matching red tiles on counters and walls. The rust stain in the big white sink paid homage to a tap that hadn't stopped dripping since they moved in, and a few of the floor bricks were cracked so deeply it seemed as if weeds might burst through at any minute. She loved the cabin's unrefined feel. From the moment they'd first set eyes on it, it was that kind of house. Inside out. Backward. Askew. A favorite T-shirt you pulled on in the dark.

She reached for a handful of ice cubes, dropped them into her father's favorite glass, and drained what was left of the Balvenie Doublewood over the ice. With nothing but about a half inch of single malt scotch in the bottom of the glass, she looked around the room for another scotch to top it off with. There was really no choice. The only remaining scotch in the pantry was the watery-looking Dewar's. It would have to do.

There was a knock at the door. Holding her father's drink, Lila opened it up to find an angry-looking man on the stoop. He was vaguely familiar—in his mid- to late thirties, bald on top with what remained of his hair curled down to the shoulders of his PLANET ORGANIC T-shirt. Eying the scotch glass in her hand, he grunted and said, "That explains a few things."

"Can I help you?"

He held up a two-page note, handwritten and stapled. "Did you leave this under my wiper?"

She recognized her father's elegant script. The note was unsigned. "You're the owner of the Prius?"

"Do you realize it's full of threats? I could take this to the police and have you people investigated."

She reached for the note. "What kind of threats, exactly?"

"Could have you arrested even. My lawyer wants to have a look at the letter."

"You do realize you dinged my father's car? It's vintage. Original paint."

"So your father wrote the note? Good to know for when I'm filing the deposition."

"He's just a little sensitive about his vehicle. If you could give his car a bit of distance, it'll make life easier all around."

He stuffed the note in his pocket. "I'm hanging on to this."

"Just, please, next time you're in the neighborhood—"

"Most other folks welcomed us with wine or flowers. Your father threatens my hybrid."

She looked from his bald spot to the house next door and back again. The one with the dog that woke them up before six that morning. And every morning for the past week. "You're the new neighbor?"

"Keith Angel, and believe me, I'm regretting this move as much as you are right now." He started walking toward his property. "Tell your father no more notes."

"No more dings. And while you're here, can we do something about the barking? I'm not getting any sleep."

"Don't drink if you aren't sleeping," he shouted back as he hiked up the incline onto his property, huffing with effort. "People don't realize alcohol's a stimulant a few hours later. It'll actually wake you up."

His dog, a slender red-and-white animal with a curly tail and pricked ears, yipped and danced as he crossed his yard.

"No, it won't," Lila called before downing her father's scotch and choking on the biting taste. "I'll already be up from your dog!"

SEPTEMBER 8, 1996

She couldn't have known it would be her last September in Toronto, those stifling days and cool nights back in 1996. It was a Sunday. Delilah was eight, sitting cross-legged on a wooden bench inside a darkened bus shelter near the west end. A pair of headlights lit up her father's impeccably trimmed beard as he trotted farther and farther from the stalled car in an effort to get a good cell signal, motioning for his daughter to stay exactly where he'd placed her. She shivered in the thin blouse and jeans she'd worn for an afternoon of picking apples and running through corn mazes at a fall fair north of the city; but Victor had refused to allow her to wait in the warmth of the car lest someone driving with his eyes shut plowed into the trunk.

Even after hours of feeding handfuls of mystery pellets to donkeys in Schomberg, and chasing his daughter through a haunted barn in his white button-down shirt, pressed jeans, and loafers, Victor managed to look just as crisp as when he picked her up from her mother's that morning. He slipped his phone into his pocket. "Can't get a decent signal. Let's go find a phone." He scooped up his daughter.

Victor began marching forward, then paused in front of the stalled Datsun. Scanning the barren, industrial surroundings, he wondered aloud, "You think the car is safe here?"

"Safe from what?" Delilah asked.

He didn't answer. Just shook his head and started down the street. "We'll be quick. Nip into the nearest restaurant or bar so I can call your mother before she gets the police involved, then we'll call for a tow truck."

"Are kids even allowed in bars?"

"The alternative is spending the night in that bus shelter."

Delilah ran her fingers along the prickly edge of her father's beard. "Don't worry, Dad. I won't tell her about your bar."

"It won't be my bar," Victor said with a sigh. "Though I suppose we can keep it quiet. Let's not rile your mother over nothing."

The first place they happened upon had a rooftop neon sign of a woman in a miniskirt who bent over, exposing her neon bottom, then stood back up again with an "oopsie" kind of smile, before repeating her indiscretion over and over again. When Delilah asked if this was a bar with a phone, Victor grunted and kept walking.

After another two blocks of closed tile showrooms and electrical parts dealers, the sidewalk lit only by the glow of a rusty moon, Victor led them up the steps of a place called Hogan's, which, from the outside, appeared innocuous enough with its phony log cabin construction and cedar-shingled roof. A western-themed menu was displayed behind glass at the entrance, and the only thing lit up in neon was a small purple cowboy boot beside the door, which was fashioned out of splintered planks.

They stepped inside to hear U2 playing on a jukebox by the empty dance floor. "Sunday Bloody Sunday." A tired older woman with eyes lined in kohl pencil, dressed in a flowered blazer and peasant skirt, leaned against the bar, trying to attract the attention of a baby-faced biker. Behind the bar stood an elephantine man with a mustache protruding like charred tusks beneath a bulbous trunk nose. He pulled beer glasses from a mirrored shelf and polished them, his vigorous scrubbing causing great gelatinous waves to thunder down his T-shirt. He looked up and nodded as they passed.

"Sweet mother of God," whispered Victor. "We've stepped into A Confederacy of Dunces.*"*

"What's that?" Delilah asked.

Without answering, Victor led them to the back and began feeding coins into the pay phone. Delilah slid into an empty booth and eyed the mess on the table—a near-empty plate of nachos and two sweaty glasses containing about a half inch each of swampy brown liquid. She rested her chin on the dirty table and poked one of the liquor glasses with her finger. The dregs of the cloudy liquid sloshed and burped against the sides of the glass. She looked up to see a young boy staring at her. A tall, weedy waitress with crowded teeth and a chin that jutted out like an open cutlery drawer kept rushing past him, gathering up dirty dishes, and ordering him to go back out to the car and tell his daddy she'd be out in just a minute.

He was more fetus than boy, as if his features hadn't had sufficient time in the womb to fully develop and, after a premature birth, he'd been pickled in a jar of vinegar in the hope that his nose and cheekbones would ripen into a fully human face. He blinked slitted eyes. "I'm Deak."

She didn't much feel like sharing her name. Most kids laughed when they heard it so what was the point? She nodded toward the dirty glass in front of her. "How much will you give me if I drink it?"

"You're not going to live to see your own titties grow."

"Give me five dollars."

"It has food floating in it. And anyways all I have is a quarter." He dug in his front pocket and held out a grimy coin.

"Fifty cents and I'll do it." She picked up the glass. Her tongue darted out and touched the lipstick-stained rim.

Deak slid his money back into his pocket and made for the door. "Okay. Forget it."

"No, wait. I'll do it for a quarter."

"Deal. But you have to drink it all."

Delilah wrapped both hands around the greasy tumbler as if warming her fingers on a steaming cup of cocoa. Bringing the glass close to her face, she stared into it, humming tunelessly for a few moments, before tipping back her head and pouring the lumpy sap down the back of her throat. She slammed the glass on the table and swallowed, then stretched out a hand and waggled her fingers. "Pay up."

Four

Not even ten A.M. and the day was filthy with heat. A slender woman in an antique lace skirt, white tank top, and battered ballerina flats meandered along the avenue and stopped, her posture so plumb the top of her head may well have been strung from the sky. She looked around at the streetscape—sun-bleached up above, fading into a dingy potato-colored haze closer to the ground—blurred just enough that she thought her eyes had gone funny and tried to blink the neighborhood back into focus.

With bronze hair wrapped into a braid and enormous black sunglasses shielding her eyes, she ducked under an awning and peered through the window of a gallery. Her ninth that week. Third that morning. Last in West Hollywood. After one final drag, she dropped her cigarette to the sidewalk, pushed her sunglasses up onto her head, and waded into the watery darkness of the shop.

The gallery assistant looked up from his *People* magazine and appraised her from his perch behind the desk. As elegant as was her gait, there was something sensual about the swing of her limbs, the rocking of her hips. As she passed him by, she eyed him. It felt like being snapped with a rubber band and he sat up taller, sucked in his belly.

She stopped. "Are you the owner?"

"Me? No, I'm his assistant."

She moved on.

Life-size sculptures crowded the center of the room, with drawings and paintings lining the walls. Prices varied from the $47,000 bronze sculpture of an old man the assistant dusted just prior to the woman's arrival, to the series of inexpensive pencil sketches the gallery owner's pampered niece had eked out last month at college.

The woman wove her way through the statues, looked up briefly to ask the price of a small lithograph. When the assistant told her she frowned, looked again. "You're not charging enough. It's insulting to the artist."

When he shrugged, she moved toward the walls. She looked moneyed, the assistant thought to himself. Had that thrift-store patina of the very rich. Only those living paycheck to paycheck pulled out their finery to check out the gallery. The others, the ones that might drop a hundred thousand dollars in an afternoon, were nearly impossible to spot. Her scuffed ballet shoes raised his hopes, creased as they were by years, possibly decades, of use. Every suburbanite and her sister owned them these days, but the assistant knew only the very fashionable, and, hopefully in this case, very flush, had been wearing them all along.

She drifted closer to his desk, staring all the while at the art lining the long brick wall. She passed the corner and came upon the graphite sketches. For a moment she appeared unimpressed. Not surprising—the assistant was certain the owner's niece was a talentless hack. He wondered if he should speak up lest she think he had bad taste; let her know that the display was nothing more than nepotism and that she'd be better off checking out the pricier pen and inks on the opposite wall. He was, after all, on full commission.

The woman moved closer to one of the sketches and her posture changed. Stiffened. She turned, pale-faced, toward the assistant. "What do you know about this nude?"

Five

Lila stood in front of the mirror in underwear and a sports bra and stared at her face, puffy and red from a rough October night.

In spite of its breezy locale high up the hillside, in spite of visible slivers of the sky where the cabin walls weren't flush with the ceiling, in spite of adventitious air streams that inevitably accompany such primitive construction, the Mack house wrapped itself around the squirming heat and held it down as if forcing an apology. As soon as the late-afternoon sun settled across the roof shingles, they worried and throbbed with the swimmy waves of a highway mirage, heating up the living quarters well into the night. The brick floor that ran throughout, probably installed with the intention of cooling overheated occupants, instead digested the soaring temperature and enveloped the family with an inescapable degree of closeness. In cool winter months, this intimacy was homely and sure. In the heat of California autumn, it grew yeasty and thick, making the simple act of falling asleep a formidable task.

And then there was the Angels' dog, who'd been up serenading the canyon much of the airless night. There had been three glorious acts: a beseeching episode of wailing just after one o'clock; another, more fed up installment of what sounded like a jilted teenage girl weeping into her pillow around four-thirty; and then the crescendo—a frenzied climax of groaning and warbling that started up around five-forty, just as Lila began to drift off again.

As for her school situation, something had to give. Student loans were out of the question. Victor had flat-out refused to allow her to submit one piece of personal or household information to the government, citing immigration red tape that still hadn't been cleared up since they'd moved from Canada. Besides, he'd said, coming out of art school hip-deep in debt was like starting a race with not one but two feet encased in cement.

So now the only other means of funding even a church basement art class was filling out an application—and actually getting hired—at someplace like Mel's Drive-in or Book Soup or anyplace else that would require regular attendance and would take her further and further away from her mother opening up that most excellent issue of *Vanity Fair*. Lila now realized she'd made a grave mistake quitting her modeling gig. She realized she had little choice but to put on a repentant face, go to Lichty's studio, and hope like hell he'd let her get naked in his class again.

She squared her body and examined her upper arms. What had Lichty called them? Scanty. Unbalanced. Disappointing to future lovers. She balled her right fist and flexed her bicep. The elongated muscle leaped into action, forming a hardened knoll that was only somewhat reassuring. She dropped her arm to her side.

There was a scuffle in the yard, followed by a high-pitched wail, then silence. There, not three feet from her window, stood a large coyote, sandy gray tail tipped with black. One enormous, feathery ear stood erect, the other drooped at half-mast, having been chewed up in a long ago brawl. The gold eyes didn't blink. While coyotes were rampant in the hills, this particular canine, notorious for his mangled ear, had simply become known to the locals as Slash.

Mythology portrayed coyotes as either heroic—with heart and even a sense of humor—or clever, impulsive, and greedy. Slash lived up to the latter by finding a way into even the most carefully bungeed and locked trash cans. If you tried to beat him by putting your trash out the morning of pickup, it was as if he knew it was Thursday, waiting in the bracken to dart out, not when your front door slammed shut and you might still hear the outdoor tussle, but once you turned on the shower, climbed in, and lathered yourself up with soap.

Cunning to the core.

As if mocking her, the wild dog stared back and shook the bloodied limbs of the headless hare he held between his teeth. She reached for her discarded boot on the floor behind her and hurled it through the open window. "Out of here! Go!"

The animal blinked at her calmly, then loped away into the bushes.

"Lila? What's all that screaming?"

"Nothing." She threw on a tank top and shorts and padded to her father's doorway, watched him smooth his hair in the mirror, then lick his thumb and use the saliva to paste his locks to one side. Seven-thirty A.M. and the man was all decked out in a gray suit, Egyptian cotton shirt, suspenders. The flesh under his eyes looked puffy and sore.

She yawned into her hand. "Did the dog keep you up too?"

"Only half the night. The other half it was the heat."

"I heard you snoring sometime around two, Mister."

He thrust his chin upward and fussed with his collar. "I've half a mind to steal it."

"Steal what?"

"The Basenji. Deserves a better home than living out back in a half-buried rain barrel. The breed originated in the Congo. Was used by the Pygmies as a hunting dog. It's not suited to living outside in the winter. Even in Southern California. The nights can be quite cold. Gen used to have one."

She squinted. "Since when do you know about Pygmy hunting dogs and who is Gen?"

"There's quite a bit you don't know about your old dad."

"Like what? He was a warrior in the rain forest in a past life?"

"Like he did a project on the breed in his last year of high school because his extraordinarily attractive science teacher was a breeder and he thought it would impress her."

"Ah. Well then. On the basis of pubescent efforts toward love that was ultimately doomed, your Basenji facts are allowed."

"It's one of the only dog breeds known to have no bark."

"Why bother when you have far more annoying sounds at your disposal?"

"They can only mate during one thirty-day period each year because—"

"No." She covered her ears. "Please. No canine gynecology before I have my coffee."

With an impish expression, he turned to face the mirror over his dresser. "Who knew I raised such a lightweight?" A green tie hung loose from his neck and he picked up one end and wound it around the other. When she saw he'd left the narrow end too short, she moved to help. Positioning herself behind him, she wrapped her arms around the front of his neck and began looping the silk around itself into a triangular knot.

The dog crowed again from next door.

"I did a bit of research," Lila said, smoothing his now-perfect knot. "The neighborhood bylaws say no excessive noise between eleven and seven."

He let out a long tired breath. "If only you would throw these research skills into learning the value of a good business education. You can do anything with a business degree. You don't have to follow in my footsteps. Start an arts-based business. It's the best damned foundation for almost any career."

"Dad . . ."

"I mean, look how you've spent the last few weeks. Holed up in the cellar all day every day. You're wasting your life."

"I'm working."

He grunted in disbelief. "Working? What kind of work?"

"Painting."

"Well at least show me what you're working on. Where do you keep these paintings?"

She pushed her toe into a snag in the rug. "I don't."

"Don't what?"

"I work like crazy on them. I just don't keep them. Not yet."

"You destroy them?"

"For now."

He seemed distressed, wiping his forehead and looking around. "I just don't want you to turn out like . . ."

"Like?"

He exhaled. "No one. But I'd feel better if you'd show me a painting." He slid the business school brochure along his dresser until it lay in front of her. "Better still if you looked at this."

Ignoring it, she picked up a pair of silver cuff links and set about adjusting his cuffs. "Don't worry about me. I'm working on a plan."

"Plan. I'd like to hear more about this—"

The dog let out a long, plaintive wail that sounded sickeningly human.

"You know that dog's a Basenji," Victor said. "The only breed in the world that doesn't bark. Comes from the Congo, you know, once used as a Pygmy hunting dog. Extremely unsuited to spending its nights outdoors. It can be quite cool at night in Los Angeles."

Lila studied her father, searching for a sign he was joking. But Victor just blinked, sincere as anything. It was then that she noticed his shirt collar was rumpled on one side.

"What?" he said.

"Nothing. It's just . . . you just told me about the Basenjis. Then you told me all over again."

He edged closer to the foot of his bed, dropped down onto the folded duvet, and pressed his mouth into a defiant frown. "Pass me my black shoes," he said in a quiet voice.

Lila stood frozen for a moment, unsure what to say. She searched the situation for reason. Had she not reacted appropriately the first time around? Was he testing whether she'd been listening? Was age catching up with him and this was a sign of senility?

"Pass me my goddamned shoes!"

She jumped up to grab a pair of black loafers from his closet and held them up as a question. When he nodded, she set them on the floor by his feet and watched, mute, as he slipped them on.

The Basenji yapped twice.

Of course. Her father was sleep deprived. Sleep deprivation could do terrible things to the mind. Confusion, memory problems. Hallucinations, even.

She sat on the bed and pressed her hand over his. "I'll go next door and get them to quiet their dog. Threaten them with animal services. Things will get back to normal once we both get a full night's sleep."

EVERYTHING ABOUT THE neighbors' house was weighty and thick, like a bunker. Tiny cypress-framed windows were sunk deep into pinky-brown adobe walls. Planks of dark wood, held together with hammered iron straps, formed the arched front door. No wonder they let the dog screech and bray. Living in this fortress, they probably couldn't hear it. When Lila rapped twice with the twisted knocker, the animal started trumpeting again from out back.

Chinking and clinking sounds, then the door flew open to reveal a woman in her early forties with long, muscular legs and wispy brown hair pulled back in a knot. Her freckled face was devoid of makeup, and papery lines fanned out from the corners of her eyes. Her shorts appeared to be army issue, as did her black boots, and her sleeveless LIVE GREEN T-shirt was tied tight at the waist. "Yes?"

The trumpeting out back twisted itself into high-pitched squealing.

"Hey. I'm Lila. From next door."

The woman looked toward a dark room as if a pot were about to boil over or a child about to fall off a change table. Lila hoped it was the first. "Corinne. Can I help you with something?"

Yip. Yip yip yip.

Lila shoved her hands in her pockets and raised her voice to be heard over the noise. "We need to figure something out. About this barking. Or whatever."

The woman wiped loose hairs off her face, then pushed her upper body through the door and cocked her head, listening. "I can barely hear it."

"I can. So can my dad. It doesn't stop. It *never* stops."

With eyes roving Lila's body, the woman laughed. "Something tells me you're not an animal lover."

Lila looked down at her abbreviated skirt, wondering how her fashion sense had managed to make such a statement. It wasn't as if the mini was made of fur. "I just think you should bring your dog inside. At night anyway."

"Anaïs is very happy where she is."

"Dogs are social animals. They need to be around peop—"

"Honey, I know what dogs need. We're from Arizona.

We've lived in the desert. We've raised orphaned wolf pups in our own kitchen."

Lila tried to look past her.

"We released them once they were grown."

Lila glanced back toward the cabin and noticed her father at the window. She stood up taller. "Basenjis come from the Congo. They shouldn't be sleeping outside. They're equator dogs."

"Since you seem to be so interested," Corinne said, crossing her arms and moving closer, amused, "the breed adapts very well to colder climates. Even as far north as Alaska."

A detail Victor failed to share. "Still, your dog is disturbing the whole neighborhood."

"And yet you're the only one complaining. The same family who left a threatening note on our car."

"Look, my dad's not sleeping. And when he doesn't sleep, he gets—"

A telephone rang from deep within the house and Corinne backed inside. "You take care now." The door thumped shut and the backyard exploded into yelps and yodels.

Lila tugged her skirt down closer to her knees and pressed her face into the closed door, shouting, " . . . confused!"

Six

Around ten o'clock that morning, after a final check in the mirror, Victor slipped his signing pen into his briefcase and made his way toward the elevator with plans to drop in on a West Covina medical clinic run by a husband and wife. There'd been an issue two weeks prior whereby they'd run out of gloves and sterile needles. The Guzmans were long-time clients and Victor had promised to deliver the shipment himself to save time. But when he arrived, Rona Guzman had turned up her nose at his supplies. Insisted she'd asked for nasal swabs, alcohol wipes, and specimen containers.

It was never Victor's style to argue with a client. In spite of his irritation, he'd smiled politely, arranged to have the new order filled the next day, and tucked the unwanted supplies into the back of his car. Chalked the whole thing up to overwork on the part of the Guzmans.

He heard papers being shuffled and stacked as he walked past his boss's corner office. Douglas Siniwick was already halfway through his day, starting as he did at five A.M. so he could "get his thoughts straight" before the phones started ringing and his assistant started bursting in looking for signatures and flight confirmations. At six-foot-five, his college quarterback frame appeared comical behind his modern desk, as if the glass desktop were sitting directly on his knees. Douglas looked up when Victor passed, his fair skin toasted pink and peeling at the tip of his nose. "Vic, do you have a minute?"

Victor stopped. "Can it wait until later? I've got an important call this morning. Two, actually."

Douglas pulled a file from a credenza behind his desk and motioned toward a chair. "Come on in, big guy. And shut the door behind you."

THE FOURTH FLOOR of L.A. Arts' visual arts building was dark. Empty too but for the back of someone's head at a studio entryway. Lila nearly turned around when she realized it was the teacher's assistant, Adam Harding. He pressed a notice to the door with one elbow while tearing a piece of masking tape with his teeth. The sign said class was canceled due to the heat. "Hey," he mumbled through the tape.

She dropped her backpack to the floor, took the roll of tape from him, and stuck a short curling strip on each of her spread-out fingertips.

"Thanks." He took a piece and affixed the top of the poster. "Lila, right?"

She nodded, tearing more tape. "Are Lichty's classes canceled too?"

"The whole school."

"Is he still here?"

"Not sure. Check his office if the studio is empty." When she didn't answer, he added, "I don't mind classes being canceled. Midterms are going to suck and I need time to study."

She'd kill to have a problem like midterms.

"One more semester and I'm out in the real world. Scary as hell."

"Yeah, well. You and millions of other college grads."

The muscle in his jaw bulged and he chanced a quick glance at her, saying nothing.

She shrugged. "Sorry, but it just doesn't sound that bad. Try taking your clothes off in front of a roomful of people your own age. Nothing will seem scary after that."

"You get nervous?"

"Only to the point of having to swallow my own vomit."

"Huh. Well you look pretty darned good to me."

The TA leering at the art model? She dropped the tape to the floor. "Do you even hear yourself?"

"What? No—"

"*Jesus.*" She scooped up her bag and marched down the hall.

SHE SLIPPED THROUGH the studio doors and closed them behind her, hoping Adam wouldn't come after her. "Asshole," she muttered under her breath.

Behind her, she heard a ticking sound. She spun around to find Lichty staring at her, clicking a ballpoint pen. A wicked smile unfurled across his face. "Well, Miss Mack, to what do I owe this foul-mouthed outburst?"

Lichty. She was completely unprepared now. And why did he have to click that pen? It sounded as if something was about to explode. "Uh . . ."

"As eloquent as ever, I see." He set the pen on his desk, picked up a stack of essays, and slid them into his valise. "I'll have to ask you to take your games and go. This is a place of learning, not a kindergarten playground. Besides that, we had a conversation, about you and me and places you are not permitted to enter in the futu—"

"I made a mistake," she blurted out. "I never should have quit. I wasn't thinking. I was new."

"New?" He touched one hand to his chest. "Well, now I am shocked. Correct me if I'm mistaken, but I believe you said you'd modeled before."

"I did. I have. Lichty, I came to say I'm sorry. I realize now how badly I need this job and I'm asking you to forget what happened."

He appeared amused. Like a cat that's just come upon a three-legged mouse. "I'm afraid I never forget. If I'm known for nothing else, it is my unfailing memory."

"Forgive, then. Please."

Silence. Then, "No model has ever walked out on my classes."

"Why would they? You're the best. Everybody knows it."

"Don't patronize me."

"I mean it."

"Posing in my classes is a thing models aspire to, not a thing they escape from."

"I know. Think of all they can learn while they're standing there."

His face changed. With one tilt of his head, he was at

once surprised and vindicated, as if he'd been wondering for years whether the models take in what he is saying in his classes. "You're telling me you want to model again so you can learn from me?"

The wetness beneath her scanty arms spread now. A hot trickle ran down her side. How to answer this? Anything she said could infuriate him, send him into a haughty tirade about how models should be focused on the pose and nothing else, for how—if a model is taking internal dictation—can he or she possibly offer the students the most of a particular posture? Her answer would likely determine her future with Lichty.

She decided to go with honesty. "Yes."

He huffed out a bit of air and nodded, assessing her. "Interesting." Then he reached for his leather case and started toward the door.

"Lichty?"

He spun around.

"May I come back?"

He disappeared into the hall. A few moments later, she heard him call, "I have a nine-fifteen watercolor class in the morning. I'll change the schedule with the office. Don't even think about being late." And he was gone.

LILA DROPPED ONTO the stool by the blackboard and let herself spin in slow circles. So Lichty had a heart. Somehow, knowing this made her feel better about baring herself again. As if at least one person in the room might be, if not on her side, at least not 100 percent against her.

She kicked out at the floor to spin herself harder and watched the windows, cupboards, blackboards, speed past in a blur.

She'd never been alone in a real studio before. The first day there'd been at least a dozen students by the time she'd arrived. Now, sitting on one of the student stools, she stopped spinning and focused on seeing the room as they did. Did any of them realize that day, as they yawned and scratched and shaded her scapula and highlighted her pubic bones, how she envied them?

She crossed the room to the slatted cabinet that housed the mason boards, the paper. Like the students had so many times before her, she slid her hand inside one of the shelves and pulled out a board. Right away something feathery and multilegged skittered across her fingers and she dropped the board on the floor with a silent shriek. The back of her hand was sticky.

Lila moved closer. Deep inside the shelf, stretched across the far corner, was a dense tangle of threadlike webbing. A black spider hung from the center. Its shape was both graceful and deadly—smooth inky abdomen polished to a sheen, long front and back legs with shorter, tidier legs in the center, red hourglass shape on the underside of its round belly.

A black widow.

Her fifth-grade teacher had had a fear of them and had brought in photos of one her husband found living in their mailbox. Lila stepped back and burrowed her sticky hand into her T-shirt.

A brush with death. Though people didn't actually die from black widow bites. There were hospitals, there were antidotes. Maybe this was more a brush with agony and panic followed by a quick scramble to find someone to administer the cure. She was entranced by the arachnid. Beautiful and terrible, delicate and revolting.

Quickly, before her subject developed stage fright and scuttled off into the gaping seams of the cabinet, Lila pinned paper to board, grabbed a pencil from Lichty's desk, and—leaning the board against the shelving—peered into the shelf and started to sketch with only the light from the window to guide her.

The spider was blacker than black. Her outer shell appeared plastic, hard, as if it might make a sickening crunch under your shoe. The only real way to depict her menacing curves was to leave slices of white paper untouched to show the highlights. Lichty would hate this, Lila thought to herself. Nothing gray about this subject. Nothing soft, shadowy, open to interpretation. The black widow may have had nothing more sinister planned for the day than repairing the tear in her web or pushing a giant sac of babies out her swollen belly, but her very form demanded respect. You were drawing horror in cold, hard black and white.

Lila heard footsteps behind her and looked up, stiffening when she saw Adam walking toward her. He held up a black bag. "You took mine."

"Oh. Sorry." They exchanged backpacks. "You're done with your posters?"

"Ran out of tape. And paper. Plus I lost my Sharpie."

"Excellent progress."

He looked at her art board. "Lichty has a thing about people using the supplies when he isn't here."

She looked up at him. "What . . . You're going to tell on me now?"

"No. I just don't want you to get in trouble."

"I was about to leave."

Renderings of herself, as well as other models, dotted the walls, and she bristled when she realized he was looking at the drawing tacked above Lichty's desk, a closeup of her shoulder, hair draped across her skin, only a sliver of her downward-turned face visible. It was exquisite, actually. A private moment. This was done by the Indian girl with the navy hair, a quiet and a sensitive artist Lichty singled out the first day for her ability to zoom in on the real charm of a pose.

"You'll get used to it," he said.

"What?"

"Their interpretations." He pointed to another drawing. "Surfer dude did this one. I can tell. Shows you with Jessica Rabbit breasts and hips so narrow you should be unable to walk." Then he nodded toward another Lila. This one was padded around the middle. The nose was longer too. "Remember that older woman? She had short, grayish hair?"

Lila nodded. "So they're not really drawing me."

"More like the you they see through their own crap. And noncrap. The model can offer whatever pose she wants; it will never be interpreted the same way by two students."

"Are they all female?"

"The models? No, why?"

She shrugged. "You said she."

"No. We've plenty of guys. I've even modeled here. I fill in sometimes when a model doesn't show."

"It doesn't bother you?"

"Nope. Makes me feel good about my body." He sniffed and stretched his neck from one side to the other as if to prove it. "If you ever need a model, I'm happy to pose."

"No. I'm good."

"Whatever."

Hoping he would take the hint and leave, she went back

to her drawing, sharpening the edge of the spider's front leg. Instead of sensing her desire for privacy, he moved closer and peered down at her work, and she tried to lean forward to block his view. "I don't really like people to see my drawings . . ."

"You're good."

The praise felt wonderful. She allowed herself a quick glance at him. With a nonchalant sniff, she asked, "You think?"

"You could be a student here."

"Yeah. Well. I'm not."

"Money? Because you could try for a scholarship."

"I'm not that good. They'd never take me."

"You never know, right?"

"No. Sometimes you really do know."

He said nothing, just pulled out his bottle of NyQuil and twisted open the lid, sipped hungrily. "I'm going to New York."

She turned her pencil around to erase a tiny mistake. "So you said."

"Right. Sorry." He burped into his hand, then stuffed the bottle in his bag. "I say it twice and now you think I'm this self-centered jerk who loves his own stories so much he can't keep track of what he's said to who."

She couldn't resist. "Whom."

"Perfect. Now you're thinking, 'Linguistic ignoramus.' "

Trying not to smile, she said, "Actually, the who/whom thing wasn't a deal-breaker for me, but 'linguistic ignoramus' . . . You don't actually expect me to move past that one."

He hoisted his bag onto his shoulder and started to weave backward, clumsily, toward the door, then half squinted, half smiled. Stopping, he tipped his head to the side. "Wait. Did you just ask me out?"

"No. Good-bye, Adam."

"It didn't come out right—what I said back there in the hall. It sounded creepy, but I just meant your pose was so thought out; you challenged the students the way other models should but usually don't. It's good. It's why Lichty just told me to schedule you for more than half his classes."

Taken aback by his honesty, Lila stared down at her drawing and said nothing. By the time she looked up to thank him, he was gone. She returned to her drawing. Not one minute later, she heard a muffled cough behind her and turned, expecting to find he'd returned.

He hadn't.

In the center of the room was a tanned woman in her early forties, maybe late thirties. Not especially tall, but the way she stood, hunched over herself, hands squeezing each other for support, and clutched to her chin—it was as if she was waiting for a blow. The woman said nothing at first, but inched a bit closer. Coppery curls hid part of her face, and her eyes—round and hoping, like a child's—blinked furiously.

It was the same woman in the flowered mini Lila had seen on her way in. The secretary was giving her a hard time, something about nonstudents not being allowed to wander through the halls. Lila might not have recognized her but for the fact that she wasn't wearing a bra beneath her gauzy blouse.

"If you're looking for Lichty, class was canceled," Lila said.

"Pardon me?"

"Try him tonight. He has a sophomore class at six-thirty."

The woman's lips flattened together as if suppressing a smile. Then she pressed fingertips to her mouth and a near-silent sound escaped. Almost a whimper or a gasp. Like the sound a child might make if you woke her up too early. Not the response Lila was expecting. Finally, the woman spoke. Her voice was husky and near the point of breaking. "He dyed your hair."

"What?"

"Looks like mine."

Lila's hand reached up and touched her messy braid. Was her hair dye that obvious?

"Delilah."

She hadn't heard the name in so long.

Delilah.

It wasn't a question or a greeting.

It was a statement.

The woman stepped closer. "It's me. Your mother."

The art board slipped from the shelf and struck Lila in the knee. For whatever reason, Lila looked back to the spider, but she too had been startled by the intrusion and scuttled into a gap in the cupboard. Suddenly, with no sense of how she got there, Lila was on her feet.

Her mother. Her. Mother. Lila's memories of her were hazy. Thick and murky and choking, like the smoke that settled over L.A. after a week of wildfires. Yes, she could see it was her. Or a tinier version of her. It was the movie-climax moment Lila had wished for, but it wasn't that moment at all. Instead it was strange, sticky like the web. And she could smell her own body odor. That would never happen in the movies.

Lila wanted to back up, hide. Get naked in front of the class. Anything to give herself a moment to drum up the requisite joy. Where the hell were her emotions?

The last time Lila saw Elisabeth's face was the night before moving away, when her mother dropped her at Victor's for a sleepover. Lila tried to wave, but Elisabeth hadn't looked up—her last memory of her mother was the side of her jaw seen through a dusty car window.

And now. Standing here, shorter than me. So much shorter than me.

It was time to speak. She'd stood, stunned, too long. "Wow" was all that came out.

Elisabeth started to laugh and cry at once. "Do you know how long I've waited to hear your voice? My God, look at you. How you've grown. Last time I saw you, you didn't come to my breast."

"I feel like a giant."

"You're beautiful." Elisabeth moved forward and hugged her quickly, stiffly, then moved back as if worried she might scare her daughter away. "I saw the nude."

"Nude? Of me?"

"I couldn't believe my eyes. I'd been to every student gallery in town and there you were, right there at the back of a dumpy place on Melrose." Elisabeth stepped forward again, took Lila's hands. "Delilah, sweet baby. It's been forever. Forever . . ." Elisabeth was crying now. Real tears and crumpled face and exposed teeth.

Something metal crashed to the ground in the storage closet and Adam Harding emerged from the doorway looking sheepish and apologetic. He held up a stack of poster paper and a fresh roll of tape. "I'm not even here. Just carry on with your moment like this never happened." After offering up a clumsy half bow in apology, he ducked his head and marched out of the room.

"I can't believe it's you," said Lila. "Here."

Her mother reached out to touch her face. "Don't tell me you lost faith in me?"

Lila was silent. Of course she lost faith in Elisabeth. It had been twelve years. Faith had petered out, sputtering and coughing, somewhere around year five. She looked into her mother's green eyes, blinking and full of emotion.

The someday she'd waited so long for was here in front of her. She had to take special care of this moment; it was flyaway and delicate and shone like a bubble stretched so big they were standing inside it. One wrong move and it would pop. They would never see it again. She was meant to say something joyous and affirming. Something like "Never" or "I knew you'd come for me someday." Instead she hiccupped and watched as the bubble burst. "Actually," she said, "I kind of did."

Seven

Victor stared through the glass door in the lobby. The plastic bin in his arms held the shrapnel of his career: a handful of stacked salesman awards, a few photos and baubles that had decorated his desk, a heavily thumbed copy of Napoleon Hill's *Think and Grow Rich*. The good pen he saved for signing contracts, the shoe-shining kit Lila had bought him for Christmas the year Victor turned forty-nine, and, on top, eighteen carefully rolled-up ties.

It had been vital to him, as he packed up in stunned silence, that he exit with the utmost decorum. He'd nodded to whichever salespeople happened to be in the office, winked at the administrative assistants, and set the box between his feet so he could shake hands with Douglas and thank him for all the years of employment.

Blair Austen, with his butternut squash–shaped body

that caused his thighs to rub together, and his great fleshy swag of a neck, complete with razor nicks and burns—for who could properly shave an empty sack of skin?—was to assume not only Victor's corner office (he'd seen the boxes beside the jackal's desk), but all of his accounts.

Including Fairfax.

Including Gen.

The thing is, Douglas was right. Victor had been having trouble with his memory. Arrived at an appointment on time, but found himself at the wrong address. Arrived at the right address, but on a Saturday. What he hadn't realized was that other people were catching on. Still, it was normal, wasn't it, to forget a few things in your fifties? Surely the Guzmans having to close early because of one misunderstanding was not something to get fired over. Siniwick was overreacting.

Blair Austen and his hard-sell approach made other people, people with more mannerly conduct, appear ineffectual and disposable—that was the real problem.

Lila wouldn't be home yet—she'd said something about heading down to an art supplies shop off Sunset Boulevard that stocked a special type of canvas or paper or some such thing. Victor hadn't really been listening. Or, if he was going to be honest, he had listened perfectly well. Then he'd promptly forgotten.

Then again, the art store mightn't have been far from home. Lila could be back by now. He couldn't bear the thought of going home and finding her sitting at the kitchen table, smiling up at her father and seeing the failure in his eyes.

He was hit with guilt so strong it turned his stomach. The girl didn't deserve such a father. The thought of telling her he'd been fired—ousted by his own mind—the proof of deteriorating to such a degree rocked him with shame.

And if it was a case of Fate stepping in, getting even with Victor Mack for choices made, well, that wasn't fair. The past was, as they say, the past.

A UPS courier carrying a large box trotted up the steps toward the door, and Victor pushed it open with his back, watching as the young man with the cheery pink face, razored hair, and brown shorts that revealed chubby knees hurried through. Nodded his thank you. Victor turned and watched him rush into the open elevator. "I had no choice," Victor called as the elevator doors glided shut.

Squinting into the morning sun, Victor started down the boxwood-edged walkway that led out to the street. On the sidewalk he stopped in front of the RoyalCrest Medical Distributors sign—a low-lying structure with raised stainless-steel lettering that Douglas had had installed a few months prior—and stared into the traffic racing past on La Cienega Boulevard. Everyone rushing, everyone needed somewhere.

He walked to his car, settled his box in the steaming trunk, and opened the windows to let the heat escape. The steering wheel was too hot to touch, and after starting the engine, he shaded the wheel with the sun visor and blasted the fan. Waiting for the car to cool, he thought of Genevieve. She would be back now from her big trip, sitting at the front desk, pursing her lips the way she did as she shuffled papers, and glancing toward the window now and again in the hopes that a bird might finally discover the feeder she'd placed in the bleak hospital garden. If Victor were there, he'd crack a joke about California birds being picky, insisting upon nongenetically modified sunflower seeds or low-fat peanuts. It would have made her smile.

Once the steering wheel was comfortable to touch, he pulled onto Lammens Road, exceptionally busy for the middle of the day. As he approached the light at La Cienega, intending to make his usual right turn and head for home, he reconsidered.

There was no reason to turn right.

So he felt like his chest, his ego, his life, had been rammed with a Mini Cooper. It was no reason to avoid Genevieve. He slipped into the left turn lane and hit his blinker, inching forward in a line of three cars, hopeful he'd make the light as he watched the first car turn left.

Seeing Genevieve had even more appeal now. She would be supportive without showing pity. She'd pat his hand, offer him coffee, tell him things would turn out fine. Knowing Gen, she'd even offer to pay for lunch, given the circumstances. But Victor wouldn't allow it. He was still a man. He could still buy a woman a plate of spaghetti.

The second car in the lineup made it through the turn and Victor inched forward again.

Gen had been married before. To a man named Zig. He'd been a crack golfer, apparently, before dying suddenly of some disease Victor couldn't recall. But that was a long time ago. Nearly a year and a half. By Victor's calculations, it was the perfect time to swoop in. Gave her enough time to mourn, realize this really was her new life, but not so much time that she got swept away by another suitor. He couldn't afford to face any competition. He wasn't sure he'd measure up.

Especially now.

Another break in oncoming traffic and the Volvo coupe ahead of Victor swung into action, made the turn, and disappeared into westbound traffic. The light turned yellow. Victor pulled farther into the intersection and strummed his finger on the wheel. Finally, oncoming traffic obeyed the light and stopped. Just as the light turned red and he started to make his turn, two cars came out of nowhere, clearly running the light, one overtook the other, honking wildly, and they both careened through the intersection like maniacs. Victor slammed his foot down on the brake, narrowly avoiding being T-boned, his heart hammering in his chest.

The shock of it disoriented him.

The light was red now. Victor sat in the middle of the intersection, frozen, unable to remember what he was meant to do in this situation. There was a rule, but it eluded him. Should he execute his turn? Back up? One shouldn't be in the middle of an intersection on a red light. At a standstill. He glanced hopefully in the rearview mirror only to discover that backing up was not an option—there were too many cars lined up behind him. The light on La Cienega turned green and now traffic approached from both sides. Horns wailed and honked as Victor struggled to organize his thoughts. To breathe. He needed to act, to do something to get out of the way. But what? Everything had happened too quickly for him to react.

More honking, then traffic veered around the Datsun, people shouted out their windows at him, honking, crowding, coming at him from left and right.

A few more minutes of panic and the lights changed again. Sweating now, Victor made his left, dodging down the first side street, where he pulled to the curb, turned off the engine, fought to calm his pounding heart. He dropped his head onto the steering wheel and exhaled while the sun coming through the windshield seared the back of his neck.

Eight

When a child spends a lifetime, or close to it, waiting for one specific moment, something magical and faraway with the power to set her entire world straight, she imagines that someday from up, down, and sideways. She thinks of the moment taking place here or there, the clothes she'll have on, what song may or may not be playing on a fortuitously placed stereo. She pictures the weather; wouldn't have to be perfect—a raging thunderstorm can provide a theatrical, you-and-me-against-the-world sort of backdrop. And she thinks about what she will say. Oh, the witty and poignant things she will say!

But there's a fact about someday that you can't possibly understand until it has settled upon you. Someday was doomed the moment you wished it into existence. You've already ruined it. By imagining it even once, you've created an expectation someday cannot possibly live up to.

About an hour later, Lila and her mother stood on the roadside looking down upon the cabin. Elisabeth raised one arm to shield her eyes from the sun and her blouse shifted to bare a tiny shoulder wrapped in relaxed muscles and toasted skin. There was a raw physicality to the woman that Lila had forgotten. Her sensuality and comfort in her own limbs was what you noticed before anything else. She moved with near-liquid ease. "So this is where you've been all these years?"

"This is it."

Her mother squinted down at the hillside and frowned into the late-afternoon glare. "Is that a pile of steak bones?"

"There's a coyote."

Elisabeth sucked the back of her teeth in disapproval. "This place isn't fit for a child."

"I chose it." She hadn't, though. Victor's boss had come across the private sale while visiting his great aunt all those years prior. But something unexpected happened on the drive home with her mother. The numbness Lila had been filled with, the bubble of the moment she'd floated inside of back in the studio, had been replaced by something else. Anger. She watched her mother cringe.

"I'm sorry," Elisabeth said quickly. "I don't mean to insult the place. Must have been fun to grow up around such urban wilderness."

Lila nodded, pointing out the bridge over the cactus growing in the dry riverbed. "I used to play Three Billy Goats Gruff down there with a housekeeper's daughter who didn't speak English. And there's this impossibly tiny in-ground Jacuzzi—it's hard to see because of the bushes—

where Dad used to let me take bubble baths under the stars. I used to think they were winking at me. Later Dad told me it was the smog swirling around."

"Ironic. After you left, I used to wonder who turned out the stars. Here they were, watching over you the whole time."

Lila didn't answer. It was as if her mother felt *she* were the wounded party. "So why now? Why come now, just like that?"

Elisabeth smiled, cupped her hands around Lila's cheeks. "I came to see my girl, Delilah Blue. Why else would I be here?"

A car drove past and Lila realized she should say something, anything. But banal objects kept catching her gaze: bits of trash trapped beneath some bushes, a rogue daisy that should never have survived the summer's drought, dog shit parched to white next to the mailbox where she'd waited for letters—certain if she put enough force into waiting they would come. She grew to despise the ugly mailbox, the way it stood, head cocked, at the edge of the parking pad, untroubled by the twenty foot drop that loomed behind. When the little door hung open, the mailbox looked foolish, like a drunken frat boy showing his tongue to prove he'd swallowed a goldfish whole.

Her mother appeared as entranced as she was by the mailbox, staring as she was at the faded letters that spelled out MACK. "This is yours?"

Lila nodded.

Elisabeth stared at the stick-on name. She pressed a balled-up tissue to her mouth. "Mack. All this time . . . Mack."

Lila nodded. "Dad changed it. And I go by Lila now."

"Lila Mack." She giggled sadly, tears flowing again, head shaking from side to side. "Lila Mack."

"Lila's just easier. And Mack . . . Dad said it was Grandma's maiden name. Or Mackinnon was. That Grandma was the last Mackinnon, and when she married the name died. He said she was gone now so we could honor her memory this way. With Mack."

"It was the name he wanted to give you if you'd been a boy. Did he tell you that?"

"No."

"I never thought of it. Not once in twelve years."

Lila couldn't resist. "If you'd called I'd have told you."

Elisabeth turned away, dabbed at her eyes with the tissue. After a moment, she turned back, more composed. "So, Miss Lila Mack, where's the front door?"

Lila pointed to the other side of the cabin. "Are you—do you want to come in?" She glanced down at the plaid curtain flapping through the open kitchen window. "Dad's home early, I think. His car's here."

"No." Elisabeth pressed another kiss to her cheek. "And I don't want you to tell him I'm here. Not yet, okay?"

Lila shrugged.

"We'll meet in the morning like we talked about. After that, you can tell your dad."

"Okay."

"And, sweetheart, there's no pressure. You can call me whatever you want. Mum, like you used to. Or Elisabeth. It's been so long and I realize you're feeling quite shocked right now."

Lila half laughed. "Just a bit."

"Then why don't you call me Elisabeth for now? Then, later, who knows?"

"All right. Elisabeth."

"Your head will be much clearer after a good night's sleep." Her mother pulled her close again. "I've spent every moment of every day loving you. You just remember that."

Her mother had loved her?

Near impossible to fathom. One didn't cut off all ties with a person they'd spent every goddamn day loving.

How could the woman stand here and lie to her face?

Elisabeth climbed back into her car, her face almost level with her daughter's knees now. She reached for Lila's hand and gave it a squeeze. "You won't disappear will you?"

"Why would I do that?"

Elisabeth smiled sadly and whispered, "I'll see you in the morning."

And just like that her mother was gone. They would reconvene the next day over coffee and toast in a sidewalk café, blinking out the rosy morning light with grapefruit and strawberry jelly. Eighteen percent cream between them to help if things got weird. Lila would keep her thoughts focused this time. Try to keep her mind off the bits of trash skittering by on the street—and whether beige was such a great choice for the nearly new cowboy boots she'd bought the other day as it looked too much like fresh canvas and might just fall victim to inadvertent doodling—and firmly attuned to the situation.

There's a thing that happens to a child who grows up thinking her mother doesn't want her. That child can't help but hold this knowledge like a cavity way at the back of her mouth. It's ugly and tastes bad and convinces her she is unlovable to the core. For who could fall for someone whose own mother can't stick around? But instead of turning against her mother, the child reveres her.

After all, this mother is nothing if not discerning.

There might be one day in high school, early on in twelfth grade, perhaps, when the English teacher is away and the substitute turns on one of those TVs on the tall rickety stands so the class can watch the Angels game. The girl with the rotting tooth might sit up a little taller when she recognizes the bird logo on the opponents' chests. It's the Toronto Blue Jays and they're playing at home. In Toronto. The child can't help but scan the faces in the crowd, nor can she help holding her breath when the camera settles, for just a moment, on the reddish-haired woman holding a hot dog with mustard in one hand—even though the mother despised mustard and, the child is fairly certain, never watched baseball.

Look, the child might say to the class. That's my mother. The kids roll their eyes until the girl insists it's where she comes from. That Toronto is her home team and that her mother is a fan. That part is a lie, but she's already in so deep it seems necessary. The girl then refuses to take her eyes off the game, marveling the whole time about the minuscule odds of such a sighting. The class marvels as well, which makes the girl feel important. There is also a feeling of justification. Of course her mother doesn't have time to contact her. She is busy. She is on television! There must be dozens of home games over the course of a year, repeating themselves year in, year out.

In bed that night, alone in the dark, the girl knows she was wrong. But reliving the sighting is so delicious that she decides to languish in it until she falls asleep. And for a few more years after that.

Nine

It started with words going missing. Victor would be sitting across from a client and would suddenly lose the word "shipment." But not in the same way as other slips of the tongue, where you could search your mind, wait a moment or two, and welcome the word back into your mouth with a blush and a smile. This was different. Shipment. As if the word, maybe even its meaning, had never existed for him at all.

He'd driven straight home and parked the car, oddly more shaken by his ill-timed mental lapse than by the breakdown of his career. No, that wasn't quite right. More that his temporary inability to reason confirmed what Siniwick had, apparently, suspected for some time: that Victor was crumbling apart.

The sky was drooping with a heavy cloud cover that offered the air below a reprieve from the relentless sun. Probably wouldn't last. Before long, the cloud would dissipate and the heat would once again rush through as if an oven door had been opened. Victor marched toward a clump of bougainvillea rioting up the stem of a basketball hoop that backed onto a ditch. Idiotic place for a hoop, Victor thought. Every missed shot meant the ball would tumble down a gulley to the cul-de-sac about five hundred feet below. Though, he supposed, any child learning the game under such exhausting conditions would develop an accurate shot mighty quick.

Victor would get up early tomorrow to prepare cover letters and résumés to send to every major medical laboratory, medical supplies outfit, and retirement center in the greater Los Angeles area, none of whom he expected to hear back from. It was his age. Might as well have been emblazoned across the top of his bio—Aging fast! Not a day younger than fifty-three!—complete with a high-resolution photo of his creased face. Who could miss the obvious? He graduated college in 1978.

He could just hear the responses. *We're not looking to add to our sales team right now. It's a tight economy. We'll keep your résumé on file and give you a call should our needs change.*

He thought about setting out to see Gen again. But the crosstown drive spooked him. If he, a man who had long considered himself a highly skilled driver, was capable of losing his senses in the middle of a simple turn at a simple intersection, anything could happen. So what was he to do? Call her up and ask her out, inform her she'd have to pick him up because driving over to her place gave him the willies? Out of the question. He'd have to come up with a better way.

He continued on with nothing much to look at but

scorched brown bushes and a yellow sign warning of even more twists in the road. After a while, he veered down a freshly paved street to his right. If nothing else, the tarmac was softer beneath his dusty brogues.

A few minutes later, he reached an oversize stop sign at a three-way intersection. A silver Nissan 350Z, the pricy modern evolution of his own 240Z, pulled up alongside him and the passenger-side window rolled itself down. The young man behind the wheel, looking purposeful and corporate in a gray suit and close-cropped hair, leaned toward him. "You wouldn't happen to know the quickest way to Mulholland Drive, would you?"

"Nice car."

The man glanced at his clock. "Thanks."

"What kind of mileage do you get with these new ones?"

"I'm running a bit late. If you could point me toward Mulholland . . . ?"

Everyone was in a hurry. Victor was going to miss being in a hurry. If he'd known it was a temporary state, that it would skitter away from him before he was done with it, he'd have had a bit more respect. Not wasted time bitching and groaning about traffic and meetings that ran late and clients who made outrageous demands on his time. It was the hurry that made you important. It was proof that you were needed somewhere. By someone. Proof that you weren't starting to disintegrate.

Then again, at this moment, here was someone needing his help as he stood, dusty and sad, in the gravel. Pride shot through Victor's veins like epinephrine. He tugged up his pants and squinted at the street sign, which only revealed the name of one of the roads, Rykert Canyon. He wasn't about to let this moment pass too quickly. Glancing down at the young man, Victor said, "What sort of work do you do?"

"Financial planner."

Victor smiled. "Ah. I'm in sales. Or was. Though it wasn't money I sold, more like Vacutainers and surgical masks to hospitals and doctors."

The guy looked interested in something other than his clock for the first time. "So you're in a period of adjustment?"

Victor reached up to smooth his hair. "I'm open, yes. You could say that. If the right opportunity presents itself." He wouldn't mind selling financial products. Sure as hell would be easier on the back than lugging around cartons of disassembled human skeletons. Perhaps things might turn out all right after all. Maybe with his experience he was more employable than he gave himself credit for.

The guy pulled out a card and handed it to Victor. WEST COASTINVESTMENTS,INC.,MATTHEWNG,INVESTMENTPLANNER. "Maybe after my appointment, we can chat."

"Certainly. I could make some time this afternoon." Victor thumbed the card, imagining his own name on the front. Investment planner. Had a certain impressive ring to it. "I'll give you a call in about an hour and a half. That sound okay?"

"Sure. And in the meantime, check out the Web site, WCI.org."

"Good idea. Never hurts to be prepared."

"Read up on our Senior Advantage line of products. I'm advising all my aging clients to stay out of high-risk investments and I'll tell you the same."

Victor stared at him, blinking as reality settled over his mind like a film of canyon silt. Matthew Ng had no interest in hiring him. He wanted to sell him investments for the aged. Saw Victor as a man wrapping up his life, with no greater goal than making sure he has sufficient cash to pay for orthopedic socks, maybe even an electric scooter. So stupid to think he was looking to hire a balding wanderer with sand on his shoes and sweat on his brow.

Outrage at Siniwick, at this cool financial planner, at the goddamned hazy rules for left turns at traffic lights, and most of all at life for being so easily charmed by his ex, churned in Victor's belly and rose up his chest like bubbling, belching, burning lava. To top it off, he couldn't remember the name of this person staring up at him.

"So," said the boy with no name, "how about those directions to Mulholland?"

Victor leaned his forearms on the passenger-side door. "You won't get anywhere fast on Mulholland."

"Why's that?"

"Fucktard of a road bends and twists itself around so tight, it eats breakfast out of its own asshole."

As the car roared away, a cloud of dust scrabbled up Victor's Italian wool pants, and he heard the word "prick."

Matthew Ng! Victor stood up straight and smiled. Matthew Ng was his name.

SEPTEMBER 8, 1996

Two hours after the car stalled, Victor pulled onto his ex-wife's narrow, leafy street in Cabbagetown and slowed to navigate past the parked cars lining the right side of the road. Things hadn't gone well on the phone in the bar. Elisabeth had all but told him he was the cause of Delilah's bad grades and theatrics. She'd insulted his parenting skills, his ridiculous attempt at a crosstown shortcut, even his choice of vehicle, declaring forty-one-year-olds didn't drive around in vintage sports cars.

The tow truck driver hadn't helped matters. He showed up an hour late without jumper cables, which was all Victor wound up needing. The guy flagged down a silver Lexus, its bald driver rushing home for Sunday-night dinner after a day on the golf course—poor soul attempting an ill-timed shortcut—and begged him for a jump-start, something Victor could have done himself hours before. That is, if he weren't so worried about blowing up his child by connecting the wrong wires.

He pulled the car into the shared driveway of Elisabeth's elegant house—a slender Victorian with bricks painted a gleaming white, rafters stained black to match the roof, and a front door done in high-gloss blue. From the street, the house appeared tidy and spare; it wasn't until you stepped up onto the porch and were greeted by the metal aardvark statue painted in the colors of the desert and the enormous firefly made of coat hangers and the purple child's handprints stamped all over the floorboards that you realized you were looking at the home of someone who appreciated whimsy. The light over the front door seemed to wink as he ducked his head to pass beneath the feathery red Japanese maples lining the verandah, Delilah sleepy in his arms.

Footsteps pounded against the floor inside the house, the front door flew open. Elisabeth stood taller in outrage, in the usual bare feet, undershirt with no bra, paint-splattered black leggings, hair streaming out from behind child-size ears. Sexy and animal, even in anger. Under the porch light, Victor could see deep vertical lines forming along her upper lip. If he'd been brave enough, or stupid enough, to point them out, Elisabeth would probably attribute these to him as well. She stabbed her cigarette into an ashtray on the radiator just behind the door and reached for her daughter, hauled her inside as though her ex had been dragging the child toward the mouth of a grizzly.

"Two and a half hours late, Victor," she snapped, pressing Delilah's head into her abdomen, back into the womb. "Two and a half hours. Do you know what I've been going through?"

"Sorry. There was an accident on the highway, so I took what turned out to be a terrible shortcut, and wouldn't you know the car died over by the meat packing plant, where there is absolutely no cell reception and don't get me started about the smell. The ground reeks of blood from the slaughter—"

He stopped. It wasn't until now Victor noticed a few pseudo-artsy types lounging on the sofas, all wearing grimy, wrinkled T-shirts to mark them as angst-ridden souls so tormented by their own brilliance they were unable to contemplate anything so banal as throwing a load into the wash; as poverty-stricken beings who navigated such dank and narrow passageways leading down from their garrets, it was impossible to stay clean. But most of all, as beings who were far too superior to give a damn, and if society didn't like it, society could just suck it.

But Victor had been around Elisabeth's friends long enough to know to look closer, past the smears of paint on the grimy cotton to the tiny embroidered polo player over the left breast. Or the expensive detail of ticking-stripe broadcloth affixed to the shirttail. These dedicated artists Elisabeth surrounded herself with didn't live in garrets. They were mostly wealthy trust-fund babies from Forest Hill or Rosedale who called themselves artists, but spent most of their days lying around somebody's living room smoking pot.

Typical Elisabeth. Invited anyone she pleased home to mingle with their daughter. Elisabeth's standards were loose—she might have only known a man twenty-four hours but if she met him in an art gallery, if his khakis were covered in paint, if his shoes were Cole Haan, he was to be trusted.

And if history had proven nothing else, it had proven Elisabeth's judgment to be dangerously lax.

"You're entertaining again on a night you have Delilah?

But Elisabeth had already turned away. She watched, openmouthed, as her daughter staggered across the living room and, with impressive drunken drama, draped herself across an overstuffed armchair. The stoned-looking guests shot exhausted greetings to Delilah, who was strung out sideways in the chair and groaning.

"What's wrong with her?" Elisabeth said. "Is she sick?"

"Is that a bong on the table?" Victor craned his neck to get a better look and the tubular apparatus vanished from view. "How long have you known these characters?"

"I'll thank you not to denigrate my friends."

Delilah announced, "I'm drunk. Deak says I have backwash."

"My eight-year-old daughter's been drinking?" Elisabeth squeaked.

"It's not what it sounds like," said Victor. "We had to run into a bar to use the phone. It was a perfectly decent place, more of a restaurant really, one of those western-themed—"

"You took my child into a bar, let her get drunk, and you're describing the cowboy theme?" asked Elisabeth, curling back her upper lip in disbelief. "Are you kidding me?"

Victor stepped onto the threshold and clapped at Delilah, pointed up the stairs. "You go off and get ready for bed, Mouse. Daddy loves you."

"Don't tell her what to do under my *roof," Elisabeth said, lighting another cigarette with shaking hands. "And don't call my daughter Mouse."*

Delilah squeezed her eyes shut and pointed herself toward the stairs, feeling the air in front of her as if she were suffering from not only the deathly grip of backwash, but sudden-onset, alcohol-fueled blindness. "Night, Mister."

"Look," Victor said to Elisabeth, "this could have happened to anyone. I stopped someplace to use the phone and you know our girl. She likes to shock . . ."

Elisabeth backed him out of the house. "First of all, this is the second time she's gotten into drink with you. She got into vodka at your house last year. And second," she hissed, "she's not our girl. She's mine."

"We'll see about that."

"What a joke—you going for joint custody right now. You think I won't bring this up at the hearing? You think this is going to help your case?"

"That's ridiculous! She didn't even know it was an alcoholic drink. She just downed the dregs of someone else's Coke and there happened to be rum in it. Don't start up about this. She could just as easily have done it with you."

"Oh." She laughed angrily. "I doubt that."

"Be reasonable, Elisabeth. This is Delilah we're talking about."

He couldn't argue that he was the perfect father—he wasn't. He'd made too many mistakes to count. More than his ex-wife knew about even, if you counted the time Delilah slipped away from him in the sporting goods store and hid herself in the center of a display of hockey jerseys. Nine and a half minutes of absolute hell before Victor heard her giggling. And the afternoon he'd fallen asleep on the sofa and awakened to find she'd unscrambled the porn channel and was watching two undressed women pretend they couldn't get enough of their middle-aged boss on the boardroom table. Then there was the time he was tucking her into the infant seat in the Datsun and bumped the girl's head on the doorframe. The kind of thing that could have happened to anyone, but not the kind of thing you told your ex-wife.

But he cared more about Delilah than the beating of his own heart. He'd lie down and die before endangering her in any way. It was Elisabeth she wasn't safe with.

"I just can't trust you," she said. "Again you've proven it."

Victor laughed angrily. "Me? I think we both know which one of us almost—"

The door slammed shut.

Ten

The house was too still. Lila knew he wasn't home the moment she stepped inside and stood blinking in the darkness. She wandered back out and down the gravel path behind the house, past the overgrown bushes, to check the wild and weedy area that led down to the street below theirs, then climbed back uphill around the north side of the property, past the miniature pool, to where the old green shed leaned for dear life against the hillside. She tugged open the squeaking door and blinked stupidly into the dark. "Dad?"

Slashes of sunlight from splintered planks made dust particles dance and bob. A long shredded cobweb swung down from the door frame, and when something brown and hairy scurried across the dirt floor, Lila backed outside and slammed the door shut.

Next door the dog started braying. Not bored staccato cries. More like inside out, scare-away-the-old-man cries. She looked toward the heavily treed south side of the property, where their lot abutted the new neighbors'. It was dense with half-dead underbrush and had no fence. She marched across the dirt and scrambled up the stony rise toward the property line, staying low when she heard snuffling and scraping. On her hands and knees, she crawled closer and peered through some piney branches, shrinking down again fast. The dog wasn't braying at her dad. There was a coyote in the yard. Slash.

She looked up again. The foxlike Basenji, red with a white blaze that stretched from muzzle down to chest and belly, was dancing around the intruder, stamping white feet and furrowing its wrinkled brow in an effort to drive the coyote away. Not the most brilliant move, perhaps, but a valiant effort. Lila willed the dog to back off before Slash became fed up.

It seemed the coyote had no interest in the pert little dog. He had his snout rammed deep in a food dish and was so transfixed on eating, he was propelling the dog bowl clear across the deck. Once the dish flipped over onto the grass, empty, the animal inspected the ground for remnants and, finally, turned his attention toward Anaïs.

Lila stood up and charged into the yard, waving her hands and growling like a lunatic. Slash looked up, then bolted, gliding off into the brush with his black-tipped tail tucked low against his hocks.

THE DATSUN WOUND down a narrow bend in the road and sped through a shaggy and tangled tunnel of leafy trees. This stretch of road looked like a back alley, with weathered garages and faded fences and ancient homes opening right onto the road on both sides, many of them looking as if they'd grown there, sprouting up from the ground along with the thistles and periwinkle and feathery, soot-covered grasses.

Normally she wouldn't put this much effort into chasing down her father. If the man wanted to take a walk, let him take a walk. Today was different. Could have been the encounter with the coyote, or the shock of seeing Elisabeth, but Lila had a bad feeling sitting in her lower spine. Probably meant nothing, but it seemed Victor had been gone for a while, and she would never forgive herself if something had happened and she'd sat at home eating a bowl of Cap'n Crunch. She had been combing the neighborhood for forty minutes and had just pulled to the side of the road so she could think about what to do next, when she saw a well-dressed man clutching a travel mug.

Victor.

Lila turned off the engine and watched for a moment. Victor was staring across the road at a mother and daughter coming out of the painted clapboard store that stocked fresh salmon, radicchio, and organic cleaning products for canyon residents who preferred not to make the trek down into town. The mother, a young woman in peasant dress and leather sandals, and a girl with long sandy hair, a floral shift, and flip-flops, lifted a few bags into the wicker baskets on their bicycles and stooped to unlock the chain that linked their tires.

Still staring, unaware that his daughter had pulled up behind him in his beloved brown car, Victor stood and watched the child, smiling. He took a step toward the road. A black Ferrari raced past him, shooting dust up his pant legs. Undaunted, he waved his arms to get the little girl's attention, then stepped onto the hot pavement.

"Dad!" Lila was out of the driver's seat and running toward him. She caught his elbow just as a navy SUV swerved around him, horn blaring. Lila guided her father back to the safety of the shoulder. Confused, he allowed himself to be led, but glanced from his daughter to the girl across the road.

"What were you thinking? You walked right out onto the road!"

"That bike. She shouldn't be getting on it."

"What are you talking about? You don't even know her."

"It's just . . . I don't know." Victor watched as the mother and daughter pedaled away. He reached up and rubbed his jawline, looked at his daughter as if she'd just arrived. "I'm not sure what happened. The light was in my eyes, I think."

"Why did you wander so far, anyway? You must be starving." She took the stainless steel cup from his hand.

"I could use a sandwich. Bacon, lettuce, and tomato might be nice."

She led him to the car and debated telling him about Elisabeth. After all, to whom did she really owe her allegiance—to the woman who couldn't be bothered to make a phone call for over a decade or the man who'd been there for every scraped knee, every nightmare, every Christmas morning? It seemed traitorous to keep quiet.

But then he did it. Stiffened when she handed him the keys. As she made her way to the passenger-side door, he stood at the rear bumper, holding them as if they'd been dipped in acid. "You drive, Mouse."

"Me?"

He climbed into the car. "Why so shocked? You have a perfectly good license."

It was an unwritten rule in their household. As long as Victor had a pulse, he drove. Period. It had taken Lila two full years of begging before Victor had allowed her to drive the car, and the experience had been so fraught with warnings of devaluing a pricey car and hard-to-find vintage parts it had nearly turned her off driving for good. She could thank the city of Los Angeles for her perseverance. Had she lived in a city more conducive to walking, she'd have given up. "I don't get it. Are you sick?"

"No."

"Then what's going on? You never want me to drive."

"Just tired."

She went around the other side and climbed in. There was no telling him about Elisabeth now, not with him behaving so oddly. "Okay, Mister. But no snide comments about my driving. Promise?"

He didn't answer.

"You make me nervous and then I make mistakes."

"Siniwick fired me this morning."

"What?"

He nodded.

"From your job?"

"Yes, from my job."

"Why? You were salesman of the year all those times."

"Who knows?" His hair had slipped away from his spreading bald spot, over which he carefully gelled it each morning, and fallen over his eyebrows like overgrown bangs. With eyes large, troubled, he gathered the strands off his face and hunched his shoulders. It killed her when he did this. He looked like a young boy. "The reps they bring in keep getting younger and younger. I don't suppose they like having an old toad like me around."

"But that's ageism. We can sue."

"No one's suing anyone. I'll find another job."

It wasn't a good time of life to be unemployed. Victor was far too young to retire and far too old to stand much chance of landing a decent job somewhere else. "Well, they must have given you some kind of severance."

"Surprisingly decent, since they said they had 'cause.' "

"What does that mean? You did something to justify it?"

"It's just some term they use so they don't have to compensate when they weed out the over-fifties."

She knew what being fired meant for a man like Victor. Being ousted from his station of provider of authority; donor of electricity, salad dressing, and Q-tips—even if he sent his semi-loyal subject skittering down the street to get them; king of decreeing the lawn to be mown or the trash to be banished. To take away his power was to crush such a monarch. All he had left was his easily distracted shaggy-haired serf and his splintering citadel.

"Age isn't cause, Dad. Maybe if we call a lawyer . . ."

His face grew pink as he stared at her. "No lawyers. I don't need some pompous prick who thinks he's better than me digging into my affairs."

"What affairs? You were fired."

"And you can bet he'll charge me three hundred fifty dollars an hour to do it!"

"Okay, Dad. Settle down. You'll get another job. A better

job. We'll do up your résumé. We'll put you through practice interviews. Everything will be okay. You'll see."

It was barely perceptible. As she shifted the car into gear and pulled onto the road, Victor's hand, ever so slowly, reached for the door handle and gripped it hard as if bracing for impact. "Dad!"

Eleven

Morning took years to come. Anaïs's yowling had begun around two A.M., and a chorus of overexcited and probably unneutered males joined in just before four o'clock. When the commotion didn't stop, when the dogs didn't pipe down after Lila's countless pleas through her bedroom window, when she realized Anaïs was likely not spayed and was in heat, maybe even in danger as she was significantly outnumbered by her frenzied group of suitors, Lila had finally tugged on a pair of rain boots and marched outside in the dark, barreled into the neighbors' yard to chase the males up and onto the road.

There was no sleep after this, especially with thoughts of Elisabeth swirling around her brain and butting heads with worry about Victor's state of mind and sudden lack of a job, so Lila had parked herself in the darkened living room, wrapped herself in an old afghan, and curled into a ball.

Lila had left Toronto unexpectedly, with plans to stay with Victor for just one night. Eighteen hours, twenty if Victor brought her home late, which was his pattern. As such, she'd brought none of her favorite things: not the unfinished paint-by-number of the smiling dolphin, not the well-laundered teddy bear her grandmother had given her when she graduated from kindergarten, not the photo album she kept under her bed with class photos, Christmas photos, photos of ants from her pithy stint as an entomologist—a career path that ended abruptly when Lila held a magnifying glass over a worker ant on the sidewalk to get a look at his antennae and accidentally fried him to death.

As a result of her hasty overnight packing, the only photos she had from her other life, the only photos she had of Elisabeth, were in an old album of Victor's, stashed on a bookshelf in the living room.

She'd flicked on a light, pulled out the book, and flipped to the second-to-last page to the photo she loved most. Five by seven, glossy, with a thin white border all around. Lila was about five or six—all giraffe limbs and bony joints in her sleeveless dress—nothing soft or cuddly about her. But Elisabeth, propping her daughter up in front of a canvas, encouraging her young child to paint for the camera, snuggled her around the middle as if she were the most huggable child on earth.

This photo used to taunt her. Look at what she'd had, then lost. But now the photo angered her. Who might she be now, had she grown up with such adoration and confirmation of her worth? This seemingly good mother who later turned around and abandoned any interest she had in her child. Did she really have it at all?

Now maybe the lingering questions would be answered. If nothing else, life would finally make sense.

LILA LEANED INTO the wind on Sunset and marched toward the awning of Le Petit Four with hair whipping and snapping in her wake. The morning's nebulous mixture of stratus and fog had worked itself into an irritable tempest that sent sidewalk debris skittering up her legs. Not only that, but the temperature had plunged. Felt more like January. Los Angeles January.

Lila didn't mind the cooler air today. It had given her reason to pull on an oversize navy turtleneck, one that Victor had tired of a few years back, and fraying Levi's cutoffs. For the occasion, she'd dressed up her feet. She'd pulled on the cowboy boots she'd found at Goodwill for $32.75 a few days prior. They were nearly new. Soft and sandy suede and full of the new person she promised herself she'd become: a proper person who draws on paper rather than self.

She came upon Book Soup and its plein air bookshelves, magazine covers flapping in the wind. Not wanting to arrive at the café before Elizabeth, she paused and pretended to flip through a copy of *National Geographic*. She studied an ad for an animal rights group without really seeing it. Another two, three minutes and she would be sitting in front of her mother. Her stomach lurched and she regretted the extra cup of black coffee.

She'd made a decision on the way over. This was not going to be an ooey-gooey, you're-back-in-my-life meeting with her mother. First of all, Elisabeth could take off at any minute, not to resurface again for another twelve years. So it was best not to get too close. Second, she had already proven herself to be reprehensible as a parent—the most untrustworthy person in Lila's life, really. So what this brunch was about was getting answers, ingesting a little protein, and protecting herself from further hurt. But not necessarily in that order.

It was time. Lila left the safety of the magazine rack and continued along the sidewalk in a fog, crossing side streets without looking, barely noticing the car that screeched to a halt when she stepped out in front of it.

Answers, caloric sustenance, emotional distance. Lila repeated it silently as she marched.

Then there she was, right where she said she'd be, at the far end of the patio, all expectant and glowing under the canopy of dazzling yellow umbrellas that sheltered the outdoor tables. She could have been anyone, glancing up the street, flicking cigarette ashes onto the sidewalk: a recently jilted woman wondering if her blind date would ever show; an empty nester waiting to meet her girlfriends for baby green salads after yoga class; an aspiring screenwriter with 110 pages of hope trapped in a rubber band, waiting to slip it to a B-list actor on his way to the restroom.

With her curls gathered into a loose knot, with lips glossed pink but a face otherwise free of makeup, in a flamboyant, beaded turquoise jacket and an ankle-length, snug white skirt, Elisabeth looked up and waved, then clapped her hands over her mouth in excitement. Lila snaked through the tables to her mother, unsure what to do when she got there. No need to worry, Elisabeth was already up and gathering her close. Lila had to work to soften her body—stiffened from years of distance—and allow herself to be hugged by the woman who birthed her.

It overwhelmed Lila, the sensation of being held so close. It seemed a lifetime since she'd felt it. Victor had never been a hugger and, other than the odd coworker of Victor's who reached over his desk to muss her hair on days she accompanied him into the office, she'd grown up with very little human touch. Now, with the strength of her mother's hand cupping the back of her head, Lila stared down at Elisabeth's flowered mules and tried to lose herself in the strange sensation of closeness.

There was a show she'd seen recently on TV about newborn panda bears and how zoologists in Japan don't name the impossibly tiny cub until she reaches six months of age in case the cub doesn't make it. All too often the mother inadvertently flattens her offspring. In order to ensure the blind, hairless, squalling, and bawling infant has the best possible chance, the cub might spend up to half her time in an incubator. But not swaddled in receiving blankets like a human. They slip her into a large pocket made of panda fur. Right away, the panda stops screaming because she believes she is being pressed against her mother's chest.

Lila too was silent.

Elisabeth's hair smelled like Alfred Sung perfume—her old standby. Breath mints. Cigarette smoke. Lila gulped it in as if she might take back her entire childhood in Toronto. It was a good smell, a sweet and dirty smell, and brought her back to her old green daisy comforter and sheets, her Holly Hobbie doll, tramping through the ferns and mossy logs in the Rosedale woods to spy on people who had cushioned patio furniture and gardeners and pools, the sofa in her mother's painting studio from where she used to watch Elisabeth—paint brush in one hand, cigarette in the other. It brought back sliding down the thinly carpeted stairs in a sleeping bag, and getting her head stuck in the painted metal banister while spying on Elisabeth's friends. Watching *Degrassi Junior High* reruns way too young and drinking milk from a bag rather than a carton. But most of all, her mother.

Answers, caloric sustenance, emotional distance.

Lila pulled away from the hug. It hurt her mother, she could see in Elisabeth's curled lip. Hurriedly, Lila said, "It's so good to see you."

Elisabeth's eyes were moist. "I was sure I'd dreamed you into being yesterday." She stood back and stared hard, as if to keep her daughter from vanishing once again. "I still can't get over you. So lovely. All grown up and tall and strong. I was thinking last night that, if I'd passed you on the street, I would have known you, I'm sure of it."

"Me too," said Lila. "I'd know you too." It was true. Elisabeth hadn't aged a day. Same wild hair, same round green eyes, same delicate jawline and wide mouth. Same year-round caramel skin, faintly dusted with freckles, that suggested she'd spent a year somewhere exotic and beachy. The lines at the corners of her eyes might have deepened but only enough to make her smile hit you harder in the gut.

Mumbling awkward observations about the weather and the traffic, they lowered themselves into the slatted wooden chairs and Lila realized, for the first time, there was a small girl at the table with eyes so blue they could have been snipped from the sky. Long, white-blond hair whipped around her face like blanched snakes, clearly a source of irritation as she kept reaching up to try to tame it. Near-black eyebrows and lashes seemed to belong to another person entirely. She wore what appeared to be a private school uniform: carefully pressed white blouse, gray cardigan, and pleated navy skirt. In between self-consciously rearranging her silverware, and attempts to force her hair behind her ears, the child stole awestruck glances across the table at Lila.

Lila waited in silence for an introduction that didn't come.

"I just can't believe I'm here with you again," said Elisabeth, pulling a package of Tylenol from her purse. She took two tablets and washed them down with ice water. "I think my whole system's in shock. Delilah, sweetie, you look a little pale. You want a painkiller?"

"That's how I always look: washed out and in need of ibuprofen."

Elisabeth threw back her head and laughed. "You're so funny." She looked at the girl. "Kiki, didn't I tell you Delilah was funny?" The girl appeared to be suppressing a smile and nodded.

Lila started to ask who she was, but Elisabeth interrupted. "It's a lot to take in, I know. Did you say anything to your father?"

"No. But I will today. Dad and I don't keep secrets from each other." Except, of course, those pertaining to standing naked in front of strangers. Jesus, she thought, what a hypocrite I've become.

"You can tell him after breakfast. I just wanted a little time with you first."

Lila nodded.

"We have so much to catch up on. It's going to feel strange for a while, and that's okay."

"Yeah."

"I worried about the coyotes all night. Can't somebody get rid of them? It doesn't seem safe to have them right in your yard like that."

"You get used to them, living in the hills. And anyway, they were there first, right?"

"Still. I'm your mother. It's been my job to worry since the day you were born."

Lila stared at the tablecloth and willed herself not to comment about Elisabeth's lengthy hiatus from said job description.

There were many times, in recent years, especially, when she had sat in front of the computer, heart thumping, went to Google, and dared herself to type in Elisabeth Lovett. It wasn't a terribly uncommon name, and, not surprisingly, a good many matches came up. There was the realtor in Florida—she held the coveted www.elisabethlovett.com URL, where she showcased glorious estates on the waterways in Fort Lauderdale and Hallandale. There was a musician, a self-published parenting author with an Amazon listing and shabby-looking Web site, and some swim meet stats for some Elisabeth Lovett from Ireland. On the first page of Elisabeth Lovetts, these were the regulars, though sometimes the order of their placement differed.

In all honesty, Lila really didn't want to know what it was that had proven more worthy of her mother's time and energy. It might hurt too much to learn her mother was hawking her sculptures and paintings to investors from Dubai. Or that she'd given up art entirely to raise her brood of quintuplets and was blogging her way through the toddler years. It was like Victor always said:

Never ask a question unless you're prepared to hear the answer.

Every time, she signed off before clicking through to page two.

Lila looked up at her mother, determined to say something innocuous. "You know what they say about worry. Not healthy. Good thing you took a decade off."

Elisabeth took a moment to adjust her blowing hair and smiled brightly. Too brightly. Her eyes filled with tears she blinked away.

Lila couldn't have felt worse. *Answers, caloric sustenance, emotional distance.* A waiter, in his late twenties and so striking he could only be an aspiring actor, came by to take their orders. RYAN, said his name tag. Elisabeth composed herself quickly, ordered hot chocolate for the girl and mimosas for the two of them. Ryan looked up from his pad and smiled at Lila. "I hate to be a drag, but I need to ask you for ID."

Lila wrinkled her nose. "Don't have it with me. Sorry."

"She's twenty-one," said Elisabeth, reaching out to squeeze his forearm. "I'll vouch for her. I am her mother."

Ryan blushed, laughing. "Yeah, that might not meet California code . . ."

Elisabeth's tongue darted out to wet her lips and she tilted her head, allowing her curls to fall forward and blow against her cheek. It was as if she'd turned up the charm factor to full. "It's a very special occasion."

"It's okay, Mum. I'll have orange juice."

"Not so fast. Ryan looks like he's the kind of guy who breaks a few rules now and then."

"Argh . . . you're killing me," he said.

She was rubbing his wrist now, her dimples peeking in

and out from behind her hair. "Come on, honey. It's a quiet morning. Your boss will never know."

"All right. But I'll bring her OJ and if anyone asks, both mimosas were for you."

One thing was certain, the woman knew how to get what she wanted. A gene that skipped over her daughter completely.

"You're a darling," she called after him.

As Ryan walked off, grinning like a man smitten, the little girl turned her face to the sky to analyze a growing bright spot in the clouds, where the sun was attempting to push its way through. With a determined brow, she set about undoing the buttons of her cardigan, pulled it off, folded it carefully, and draped it over the back of her chair. She tested the sweater's stability and, once confident it wouldn't slip to the ground, she turned around. The wind had fortuitously switched direction, which offered her busy hands a reprieve from hair taming. They sat, clasped but ready, on the edge of the table.

Lila could wait no longer. She leaned down close to the child. "What's your name?"

Scorching red splotches flared up on the girl's cheeks. With careful annunciation, in a voice more suitable to a fifty-nine-year-old smoker, she replied, "Kieran Scarlett Lovett-Moore. Scarlett is spelled with two T's and Moore is my father's last name, but he never sees me because Mummy says he 'has a hard time appreciating the magic that is a child.'" She dabbed her mouth with the corner of her napkin before setting it back on her lap, then resumed studying Lila as if the older girl were made of rutted dinosaur bones held together with a series of supports and wires and Kieran was determined to make it worth the price of admission.

"How old are you?" asked Lila.

"Seven and two-thirds. As of yesterday."

"Seven and two-thirds. Well. I guess it doesn't get much closer than that to eight."

Kieran stared at her with a solemn face. Lila noticed dark circles beneath the child's eyes. "Actually, it does."

Lila didn't have a casual comeback for this. She turned to Elisabeth. "Are you watching her for a friend?"

"I guess it's as good a time as any to tell you. You have a baby sister. Half sister, I suppose."

Lila tried not to appear shocked. How had she missed this possibility? Probability. It had been so many years; it made perfect sense for Elisabeth to have wanted another child. She'd always been a young mother. Only twenty-three when she'd had Lila. Forty-three now.

It didn't mean Lila had been replaced.

It didn't.

"Kieran was born close to your birthday, Lila. November twenty-ninth. I tell you, it makes me feel young again to have one so small."

Some sort of answer was required. Fast. "Wow. That's fantastic. A sister." She stared at Kieran's folded sweater and did her best to appear thrilled. "This is good. Really good news."

"I sleep in your old bed," said Kieran. "Only I have new sheets because yours made me sweat." She pushed her hair out of her face again and offered up a partial apology. "The daisies were pretty, but I need to sleep in cotton because it breathes."

It was ridiculous how much this irritated Lila. She couldn't fathom which was worse—the child taking over her bed or insulting her sheets or having rules about breathability. Stupid to be upset. What was the girl to do—sleep on a straw mat? The bed was sitting there, empty. And if the fibers didn't breathe, they didn't freaking breathe. But somehow, having those daisies back took on enormous importance. Lila turned to her mother. "Did you keep my sheets? I'd love to have them again."

"I kept everything. Don't you worry."

Lila shot Kieran a look that meant, but hopefully didn't convey, that she'd won. She cleared her throat. "So Kieran, do you go to school?"

"We call it grade three back home, but if I say that here, no one plays with me at recess. Now I call it third grade."

"And now they play with you?"

"When the teacher makes them." The girl turned her attention to her blouse and smoothed away nonexistent wrinkles. She added under her breath, "Which doesn't even count."

"It's your own doing, Kieran," said Elisabeth. "The teacher shouldn't have to get involved. There are twenty-one kids in your class. If one child doesn't want to play, you go play with someone else."

"That's what I tried to do on Friday, but they were playing on the big rock and that's out of bounds."

"For God's sake, Kiki, be a child. Children need to imagine and dream. They need to wonder. Try things and fail. Even if it means stepping over the property line now and then."

Kieran didn't reply, as busy as she was with controlling her hair in the wind, which had circled back again. She reached into a small purse, pulled out a plastic headband and slid it onto her head. "I don't want to get a detention."

Lila chuckled. "I had so many detentions that any day I went home at three-fifteen felt like a half day."

Kieran tried to hide her disapproval. She stared at her big sister a moment before croaking to her mother, "She doesn't look *anything* like her pictures."

Elisabeth explained. "Kieran was expecting blond hair."

"I've been dying it for years."

"I like it. Makes us look more like mother and daughter."

Lila nodded.

"Your little sister has grown up surrounded by photos of you. The mystery of Delilah Blue. Always wanted to know your favorite foods. Your favorite color. Your favorite television shows."

Lila looked at the child. "I definitely watched *Barney*—that big purple dinosaur. Is that still on?"

"I'm too old for *Barney*."

"There were always people dropping by to chat about you," Elisabeth continued. "At night we said prayers for you. I think you're rather like a celebrity to her." Elisabeth reached out and pulled Kieran's short bangs out from beneath the plastic band. "Fix your bangs, sweetie." Elisabeth smiled apologetically. "She has her father's forehead."

"Don't." Scowling, Kieran reached up and fingered her bangs.

"That's it," said Elisabeth. "Much prettier that way."

Lila looked away.

A girl without a mother spends a lifetime watching other girls being mothered. On TV and at school, in the neighborhood and at the mall. She sees them being kissed.

She sees them being grounded. Criticized. She sees the girls complain about curfews, become embarrassed when mothers trail into the school with forgotten lunch bags or homework binders. The girl without a mother of her own will always look away. That way the lie she will tell herself—that hers is a life that is freer—is easier to believe. That she is the lucky one.

Lila grinned. "Do you remember that time you got me safety scissors for school?"

"How could I forget? I woke up the next morning to find you'd cut off the top of my hair. I looked like a balding actuary."

Laughing, Lila sipped from her water. "I felt so terrible, I cut off my own."

"Yes, but yours wound up being cute with that teensy short fringe. It was edgy and Queen Street cool. Once I evened it off."

Ryan returned with the drinks order, rested the tray on the table. "Here we go," he said, setting the hot chocolate a safe distance from Kieran's fingers, and the orange juice in front of Lila. As he set both mimosas down in front of Elisabeth, he added, "And two glasses of champagne for you. The juice is freshly squeezed." He smiled at Kieran. "And don't you go sneaking a sip, Missy. Then I really will get fired."

The warning was totally unnecessary, Lila thought. Kieran getting into champagne would never happen before it was legal—if it happened at all. As Lila willed the waiter to leave, Elisabeth held out a camera and asked Ryan, "Would you mind taking our picture? I'd like to remember this day."

"Sure." He waited as they squatted beside Kieran's chair

and fumbled to put their arms around one another. Steadying the camera, Ryan asked, "So what's the special occasion?"

A flash of light.

Elisabeth nodded toward Lila. "This is my eldest. I haven't seen her since she was eight years old."

"Well," said Ryan. "This *is* a special day."

"Most special day in my life," said Elisabeth. When Ryan left, Elisabeth reached forward to pat Lila's hand. "Did you see the way he looked at you just then? I think he has a crush on you."

"On me? Try you."

Elisabeth smiled to herself, sat back in her chair, and held this information close to her chest. "Don't be ridiculous. He was definitely interested in you. He's a real sweetheart, don't you think?"

"No. Yeah, but I don't really date much."

"Seriously? Delilah, love is one of life's great pleasures. It isn't something you want to miss out on. Especially at your age."

"I'm not good with guys."

"What about girls? Surely you have some friends."

"I was friendly with the girls at school. But that was kind of it. I don't know. I guess I'm a bit of a loner."

Elisabeth frowned. "So how do you spend your time?"

"I paint, draw, that kind of thing."

"What sort of subjects?"

"People mostly."

"So you study them rather than mix with them."

Lila laughed. "I guess."

"Well, I am relieved to hear you're doing something with all that talent."

A woman walked by with a *Vanity Fair* magazine in her arms and Lila smiled to herself. It hadn't taken a double-page spread to bring back Elisabeth after all. "I am. It's been kind of tight, moneywise, so I'm working as a model at L.A. Arts, where you found me, and absorbing, rather than earning, a fine arts degree. I have nothing better to do while standing in front of the class, so I take mental notes of everything the prof says while I'm there, then come home and get to work."

"Brilliant. What a smart daughter I have. All you really want is the instruction. In all these years, no one has ever asked to see my degree. I graduated with honors too. I suppose all that work was a bit of a waste."

"It's not a waste. I remember your work being wonderful," said Lila.

Elisabeth broke into a wide smile and ran her hand down her neck. "I don't know. Sometimes I think my style is too . . . infantile. It isn't expressive enough."

"It is," said Kieran. "You always say that but it's not true."

Elisabeth pressed thin lips together and studied the child. "See now, I can't tell if you're being sincere."

"I am."

"You're sure?"

"Yes."

"Then I thank you."

"So why come all the way out here now?" asked Lila.

"I just knew art would lead us to you. We came here about five months ago and rented a little apartment. The psychic said to head west, and I thought to myself you'd be college age now and it might be worth combing all the student galleries for your work. That's how I came across the nude on Melrose."

"Melrose? The L.A. Arts student gallery is on Beverly."

"I know. I'd actually just been there a few days before. It was divine justice, I guess. I'd been checking out so many galleries and it was such a hot day. I almost didn't go in because the place was so upscale; I figured your work couldn't possibly be in there. Not yet. Not with you being only twenty." She stopped. "I'm sorry, dear, if that sounds like an insult. It's just reality. You're still so young is what I mean."

"No, I get it."

"Good. Anyway, there was the nude. The gallery assistant said it was done by the owner's niece in her first class at L.A. Arts and they were showing it just to please her. Wasn't worth displaying if you ask me—the girl has a long way to go in terms of understanding light—but I'm thankful it was there. I saw that birthmark on your hip and knew it had to be you. Took a bit of hunting but eventually I found out the sketch was from that class."

"But why were you looking for my work in galleries in the first place? Why didn't you just call?"

Elisabeth didn't seem to have heard. "Bethany Richards was the student's name. It's hanging in my living room back at the apartment. Wildly overpriced, but of course I had to have it. I'll show it to you when you come over." She laughed. "I have to say, even with the shock and excitement, part of me was disappointed. I'd imagined my daughter as the artist rather than the model. Because of what they say—those who can, do."

Lila forced a smile. Their second meeting and she'd already disappointed her mother.

"Turns out that was a good thing, because I'd never have recognized your name. Plus it shows your dedication. It isn't everyone who is willing to go to such lengths to succeed. I'm quite proud of you, Delilah."

"Don't tell Dad, okay?"

"He doesn't know?"

Lila shook her head. "And he never needs to."

Elisabeth sipped from her drink and continued, "I'd offer to pay for your education myself, but all the years have left me rather broke. My paintings still sell, but not for a whole lot. Your grandmother left me a tiny inheritance and then there was some money the Web site brought in, but it's been many years and life in either city isn't cheap."

"Grandma died?"

"I'm sorry, sweetie. Five years ago."

Lila was silent a moment. "I'm confused. You came to L.A. months ago and searched through galleries for my work."

"I did."

"Why didn't you just call me? And why did a psychic have to tell you to head west?"

Elisabeth's expression changed. She stared at Lila, sad. Quiet. A gust of wind played with the edge of her collar, and she leaned forward and took Lila's hands. Held them tight. So tight Lila's knuckles were being crushed. "You don't know what happened, do you?" asked Elisabeth.

"What do you mean?"

"What did your father tell you?"

"About what?"

"About him taking you out here. About me being gone from your life."

Terrible to have to say it. Forget anger and blame. Right now Lila wanted to just forget and forgive. Just lose the dozen years of limbo and hurt. "I don't know."

"Delilah. You can tell me. It's okay."

"Just that you were busy. Needed some space. Didn't have time and stuff."

Her mother looked away for a moment, closed her eyes, shook her head. "At least he didn't say I was dead. That was my biggest fear."

"Why would he—"

"*Such* a monster, your father. I mean, I knew it. It's what the lawyer said he'd tell you. That I didn't want you."

Lila didn't answer, but felt her muscles weaken. Liquefy. Either that or the patio had buckled beneath her chair and she was sinking lower and lower into the ground. Now that the moment was here, Lila didn't want any answers. What was she thinking, wanting to know why? Why was a terrible question—one people should never ask. She knew that now, and wanted only to clap her hands over her ears and run.

Elisabeth touched her cheek with one hand. "Baby, your dad lied to you."

Lila held her breath.

"I never washed my hands of you. I dropped you off for a sleepover expecting to see you the next morning. But then your father decided to take you to Florida. To Disneyworld. Did he ever actually take you there?"

Lila thought back to that Saturday in September. "Not exactly. First he said Florida, but when we lined up at the gates, it said Disneyland. He told me we weren't in Florida and that I must have misheard him—he'd said California. I figured I was just so excited I got it wrong."

"You didn't get anything wrong, baby doll. He was trying to hide his tracks."

It sickened Lila to ask. She was terrified that she already knew the answer. "Why?"

Kieran leaned forward over the white tablecloth, fingers pressing her white hair to her neck, eyes the size of swimming pools. "Because you were kidnapped."

Twelve

A trio of badly dressed males, caught in that simian state between their teens and their twenties—backward baseball caps and drooping jeans only serving to broadcast their lack of maturity to the world—thundered past Victor on the sidewalk. He moved to the side, instinctively smoothing his tie, watching them tumble, shove one another, and carry on like baboons into a music store.

Not that Los Angeles was known for its pedestrian traffic, but Victor was painfully aware that he was the only one on the sidewalk who was alone. The suited woman up ahead might be by herself, but her briefcase kept her from being truly alone. The balding jogger across the street was kept company by not only his headphones but by the blood thumping purposefully through his veins.

He'd had a promising line on a job that morning. Just

after Lila left to meet a "very special person" for breakfast, he'd had a return call from the head of a retirement home on Sepulveda Boulevard. Sounded like a simple enough job, sitting in an office every day pressuring guilty relatives into springing for the larger room, the private room, for their aging loved one. His conversation with the female manager had gone reasonably well, until she'd said she'd like to check out a reference before committing to a face-to-face interview and could he provide the name and phone number of his former supervisor.

So that was that. Siniwick wasn't going to have anything good to say about Victor's abilities. And, when interviewing for a senior sales position, was there any potential employer in the country who would not want to check his references? Victor Mack's job prospects were abysmal.

He should be angry. Frustrated. Brimming with fight. But Victor was feeling anything but. What he felt, to the marrow of his bones, was unadulterated relief. With a new job came pressures and schedules and left turns he wasn't sure he was up to anymore. For the first time in his life, he was without a goal or plan of any sort.

It had been depressing earlier, sitting in the cabin waiting for Lila to come home from wherever she'd gone off to. He'd hopped a bus and headed down to Sunset, where his aim could be simple: find himself a cup of coffee. Maybe even a nice toasted bagel. Poppy seed with cream cheese.

He wandered along in the late-morning sun, and, finding himself at the window of a pet store, Victor stopped to watch a playpen full of puppies leap and dart and pounce upon one another in a deep bed of newspaper shavings. All sharp teeth and pleading eyes, hopping around a steaming pile of excrement.

One pup, white with a brown head, saddle, and tail, seemed to feel he owned a green rubber bone, the only toy in the pen. He pulled himself out of the canine action and settled in the far corner for a good chew. Fascinating that the others didn't object. A black pup—far too snub-nosed for Victor's liking—stared at the play toy, his tiny tongue throbbing with desire, but he didn't dare approach. Another one, clearly the runt, waddled over to the corner only to be chased away by the saddled leader.

In spite of this dog's ears being too small for his blunted head, his nose being dotted with a sickly pink, the base of his tail being tied up in mats, this pup was very clearly the managing director of the bunch.

Victor had never considered a dog before. He marched into the tiny shop, set his mug on the counter, and headed toward the window. He leaned over and plucked the pup from the playpen. At first the animal stared down at his chew toy and watched, helpless, as his opportunistic siblings pounced upon it, snapping and snarling at one another as each tried to claim ownership. Victor prepared himself for the coming tantrum, maybe even a hostile nip in the abdomen. This was, after all, an alpha dog. But the little beast forgot about his bone and began to scrabble up Victor's body. If he didn't know better, Victor might have thought the animal to be attempting a badly executed sort of canine embrace.

So light, he thought, as he headed for the cash register and tried to control the squirming dog by pressing it close to his chest. And the smell. He hadn't anticipated such a milky sweet scent any more than he'd anticipated the pup might actually take to him—straining as it was toward his face. Suddenly the muzzle was at his chin, all wet nose, soft fur, darting tongue. As the pup licked his tidy beard, Victor did everything he could to suppress the smile that threatened to pour across his face.

"That'll be enough now," he gently scolded the pup, who placed both paws at his collarbone and stared at Victor, yipping right back at him. Victor felt himself smiling and he scratched behind the dog's ears with one finger.

He set the tiny dictator on the counter in front of the clerk. "I'll take this one," said Victor, pulling out his wallet. "How much?"

The clerk, a tall bony male with long hair and a tattooed forearm, set down his papers. The tag on his shirt read THEODORE. "You want to buy this puppy?"

Victor slapped a credit card on the counter. "You take Visa?"

Theodore looked around, as if needing assistance. "Yeah, it's just that . . . don't you want to know anything about it first? People usually spend a bit of time with a pup. It's a big decision."

"Not for me."

"This one's a Maltipoo."

"A what?"

"A cross between a Maltese and a poodle. People like them because they don't shed a lot. And they train fairly well."

Victor considered this, nodded. "That'll be fine."

The dog wandered too close to the edge of the counter on Victor's side. When Victor did nothing to stop it from tumbling to the floor, Theodore scooped it up and held it to his chest while the pup chewed on his finger. "Have you had a dog before, sir?"

"No. Do you have some sort of box I can put it in? It's a long walk home."

Theodore knitted his brows together, processing the odd request. He backed up, the puppy still in his arms. "You know, I'm just going to check something with my manager. I'll be right back."

While he was gone, Victor busied himself collecting a few cans of puppy food, a black leather leash, and matching collar. Then a brush and comb set. Feeding, walking, grooming; these acts would offer some shape to his days. After setting his loot on the counter, he thought for a moment, his chin still tingled from the puppy's soft tongue. A youngster needed a toy, did he not? Victor spun around and picked up a rubber bone just like the one in the playpen, added it to the pile, and waited for Theodore to return with his pet.

No longer would he be faced with wandering the hills, the dales, of the Western Hemisphere all by his lonesome. With a dog by his side, he'd be positively brimming with purpose. Didn't even need a job. He had a decent severance. Should last him if he was careful with it.

Theodore did return, but with an older woman in tow. A broad, busty female with the shoulders of a garbage truck. Her hair was as short as Victor's and she blinked at him through funky metal glasses. "I'm Sandra, the manager here. I understand you're interested in buying a puppy?"

He pointed at the dog in Theodore's arms. "This one here."

"And is this something you've been thinking about for a while?"

"What's this all about? I just want to pay for my dog."

Sandra motioned for Theodore to step aside. "I'm afraid we can't sell you a dog today, sir. Buying a puppy is an enormous decision and we have to feel certain you're . . . ready for it."

Victor could feel the vein in his temple throb.

"Our breeders trust us to place their dogs in good homes."

"If my home is good enough for me, it's good enough for a dog."

"You live in a house, do you? I mean, as opposed to an apartment."

"Yes. A house. And I'll protect him from coyotes, if that's what you're worried about. I'll build one of those . . . one of those . . ." He searched his brain, the word just slightly out of reach. His hands formed the shape of a barrier, an enclosure, while his mouth tried to wrap itself around the word. "F-f . . ." It started with an F. What the fuck came after the F? He turned to the side, all these eyes staring at him made it impossible to think. Sweat dampened his back. "It's hot in here. Is there some goddamned reason you keep it so hot?"

Sandra's eyes grew soft. She knew. Hadn't spoken with him for longer than two minutes and already she saw his mind for the dried up piece of Swiss cheese it was becoming. Victor watched as she told Theodore to put the dog back in the playpen and stay close by. Just in case.

If she hadn't told the fellow to stay close, if she hadn't had that look in her eye when she said "just in case," Victor might have walked out, disappointed. But it was clear this Sandra person thought him a faulty pistol, capable of misfiring at any moment. He was to be feared. Pets were to be protected. God only knew what he might do—smash a fist through an aquarium! Tip over the parrot cage! Unleash the tarantulas!

He hated the look on her face. Patient. Understanding.

Nervous. He hated the way she inched herself closer to the phone. "You think you can judge me, just like that? You think you fucking know me?"

Sandra's hand was on the phone now. "I'm going to have to ask you to leave, sir."

He shot a look at the playpen. His pup was standing, tail wagging, paws pressed into the mesh siding, his affection for Victor not dampened in the slightest by the outburst.

Sandra picked up the phone. "Sir? I'll ask you to leave one more time and then I'll call the police."

With a longing glance at the puppy, Victor Mack shuffled out of the pet shop and out to the curb, where he stared up at the underbelly of a low-flying plane and tried to think of the word for those metal or wood or—who the hell knew, maybe even vinyl—enclosures that wrap themselves around a property. When an elderly woman in a polyester pantsuit set down her shiny black pocketbook next to him so she could slide a few envelopes into a mailbox, he asked her. What did he care what she thought? He was never going to see her again. "Fence," she replied in a way that was surprisingly nonjudgmental. She wished him a nice day, picked up her purse, and headed into the bank next door.

He looked toward the sky, where he imagined Fate hid itself away, and gave it the middle finger. "Fence!"

Thirteen

It took a minute for Kieran's words to have meaning. They were too big, titanic. Throbbing as they lurched up over her head, burst through the yellow umbrella, mushroomed toward the sky. These words were epic, unfathomable. While Lila struggled to make them fit into her ears, into her brain, her fingertips pricked and sparked with lack of oxygen.

Her mother started to speak, but the roar of an overhead plane—working extra hard to penetrate that huge cloud of words—blocked it out. Lila sat back in her seat and watched Elisabeth's lips move, wondering if she could make her mother vanish all over again.

Was it years later or just minutes? Elisabeth had risen and wrapped herself around Lila. Only this time Lila wanted to run right from the start. She couldn't take any amount of closeness just now. Couldn't take that black-lashed child staring at her like she was a charred wreck on the side of the freeway. The pastel buildings, billboards, palm trees, and buses of Sunset Boulevard warbled and bobbed, and the sun—having finally broken through the clouds—flashed white in her eyes as she was rocked back and forth, in and out of the glowing yellow shelter of the umbrella. Flashes of white, then yellow, then white, then yellow. It was feverish and nauseating. People stared. The waiter touched her shoulder, asked if she was all right.

Lila pulled away from it all. Moved away from the table and mumbled something about the restroom. She entered the restaurant nearly blinded by glare. Fumbled her way inside and reached the toilet just in time to drop to her knees, wrap her arms around the bowl, and throw up that morning's coffee.

SHE'D BEEN IN the bathroom too long. Not that it mattered. Surprisingly little mattered once your reality had exploded like this, into millions of invisible flakes of ash and horror and vomit swirling above the city. Could be what smog was made of—the incinerated remains of lives like her own. Lila rinsed her mouth, her face in icy water, then stood leaning on the sink, staring at the mirror, watching water trickle down her chin and into the neck of her sweater.

Her hair. Her dyed hair.

It was their first month in Los Angeles. They'd just moved into the cabin, unpacked what little they had, when Victor piled her into the Datsun—bought for a steal from a couple going through a divorce—and drove down to La Cienega where he pulled up in front of storefront complete with rotating barber pole and sign reading HOLLYWOOD HAIR. "Time for haircuts," he announced.

Lila had been impressed with the sign. "Is this where movie stars get their hair cut?"

Victor caught sight of the faded Elvis bust in the window and smirked. "Not likely. But it seems as good a place as any." Before opening the door, he looked down at her. "I thought we'd try something new. Short hair all around."

Her hands flew up to her head. "I'm not getting my hair cut short."

"You've got nice features, a long neck. Short hair would look perfect on you."

"I'm not having short hair, and you can't make me."

"We'll see about that." Victor opened the door and waved her inside, where a rotating fan with colored ribbons tied to it blew hot air in their faces. Lila entered, sucking angrily on a blond pigtail. While her father dropped into a spinning chair and announced he'd like his wavy hair buzzed off—he would later return to his longer layers, accusing the ultrashort hair of being too prickly against his pillow—Lila parked herself at a child-size table loaded with stacks of white paper and old coffee cans full of markers, crayons, and pencils and began to scribble with fury. It would be another few years before she would see footwear as paper.

Once her father had been sheared, the stylist, a leathery woman closing in on sixty, her long hair an unruly combination of dun gray and nicotine yellow, with a polished stone strung around her neck from a chain, gestured toward Lila. "And your daughter? Is she having a haircut today as well?"

Victor smiled. "I'd like to have her hair cut short, but she isn't too excited about it."

The woman, whose beaded bracelet read KRISTINA, laughed. "Little girls—they all want to look like princesses nowadays." She wandered over to the kids' corner and touched Lila's hair. "You like your hair long, sweetie?"

Lila nodded. Kristina squatted down low and set an oversize magazine on the kiddie table in front of her. "Why don't you look through this and see if you don't find a hair-style that makes you happy."

Sulking, Lila flipped through the pages. After a few minutes, she held the magazine over her head. "I changed my mind. I do want a hairdo." The center spread was a photo set against the backdrop of London. A waiflike woman stood in front of a double-decker bus holding the leash of a whippet, who was straining to get to the Standard poodle across the street. The woman was dressed sixties style in a cropped jacket, slim pants, and flats, her copper hair carved into an edgy bob.

"Perfect," said Victor, both pleased and surprised. "Very classy."

"Just the color." She stood up and handed the book back to Kristina. "My same long hair but this color."

Kristina objected, pointed out the perils of chemical processing at the tender age of eight and demarcation lines once her hair started to grow in. Besides that, she said, the girl was going to look like Pippi Longstocking with her small white face and big eyes.

But Victor insisted. His daughter would have the color she wanted and he'd bring her in for regular upkeep until she was older and able to dye it herself. He lifted Lila up, swung her onto a booster seat on a swiveling chair, and asked if someone could get the child a lollipop.

Sickened by the memory, Lila turned to the toilet and threw up again.

Someone banged at the door. The man asked if she needed any help. She didn't answer. Didn't move until she heard the jiggle of keys. Until the manager himself poked his head in and asked if she was okay.

Lila reached for a paper towel and scrubbed her face until it burned. "If I said, 'No, I'm not,' you'd regret asking pretty damn quick, wouldn't you?"

When he said nothing, she pushed past him and headed back to the table where Elisabeth looked relieved to see her.

"I was getting worried," she said when Lila sat. She set her fingers on Lila's arm and Lila edged it away.

"How do I know this is even true? I mean, here it is twelve years later, and you show up in an empty classroom and you have this new kid and you make this crazy accusation. I mean, how do I know what Dad did or didn't do? And how do I know you're not just making it up to excuse yourself from dropping out of my life? "

"I know, sweetheart. It's hard to fathom that anyone is capable—"

"Yes! It is. It's impossible to fathom," Lila said too loudly. From the corner of her eye, she saw her own hair, the russet color touched up just three days ago from a drugstore kit, snapping in the wind and captured it in her hands, tucked it all into her thick turtleneck where she didn't have to look at it. "Dad's not like that. He would never do anything to hurt me. Plus he's no criminal. He won't even let us put the trash out on the wrong night."

"It was a custody thing. It's all very complicated."

"He said you didn't want me."

"No, no. Baby, never would I have given you up. *Never.*" Elisabeth kissed Lila on the forehead again before settling back into her seat. "I did what any mother would do if someone stole her baby. I moved heaven and hell to find you. It was the career I never wanted. I gave up seeing friends, I gave up exercise, I gave up doing normal things. My life became looking for you."

Lila stared at the ragged threads where she'd scissored her shorts.

"I worked with a child find agency, with the Canadian government, the American government, even the British government because your father has relatives there. I worked with Interpol and private detectives. I hired psychics and tarot card readers. I asked the universe for a sign. I even wrote a letter to Oprah begging her to put me on her show, to air your photo."

"My picture was on *Oprah*?"

Elisabeth smiled sadly. "No. But I tacked up posters all across Florida when he said you'd headed there. Nine years ago I had a Web site made: www.findDelilahBlue.com."

"It's red and white," Kieran explained with a sniff. "Should have been blue."

A Web site made it much worse. Made it real.

"Web site, T-shirts, buttons," said Elisabeth.

Lila thought back to all those hours hunched over the computer, daring herself to look past the first page on Google, never even thinking to search her former name. Why would she? Delilah Blue Lovett didn't exist, as far as she'd known.

Kieran reached in her purse and pulled out a wallet. From that she pulled out a plastic sleeve. From that she removed a carefully folded piece of paper, opened it, smoothed it, and set it on the white tablecloth and started to read, "Name: Delilah Blue Lovett. Born: December 16,

1988. Last seen: early morning, September 21, 1996, wearing a denim skirt, T-shirt, and fairy wings, getting into her noncustodial father's tan Datsun 240Z in Leaside, Toronto. Distinguishing marks: rectangular birthmark on right hip."

"What is that?"

"The most recent missing child poster," said Elisabeth.

Lila looked at Kieran. "Can I see it?" Sure enough, across the top, in block letters, it said MISSING. Below that was Lila's school photo with an age-enhanced picture of how she might appear today. Looked nothing like her; Lila still had her natural dirty-blond hair, for one. But still.

It was proof.

She'd been abducted.

Kieran continued. "Eyes: Blue. Hair . . ." She eyed Lila's copper strands and said accusingly, "Bl-ond."

"How did you know I was wearing the wings?"

Elisabeth shrugged. "Your dad's neighbor was out walking his dog before sunrise. Saw the two of you getting into the car. He and your dad chatted a bit. Victor told him you were off to Florida and you showed him your wings. Said you were going to fly. It seemed an important detail for the poster, so people would look for an especially imaginative sort of child."

Again, nausea rushed Lila's body, leeching from her stomach and spreading all the way to tingling scalp, fingers, toes. She looked away a moment and focused on breathing, not retching. Suddenly there was a pen in her hand and it started scribbling on her thrift-store boots. She didn't have the strength to stop it, no matter how much she adored them. She laughed falsely and searched for something to say. "I still have them. The wings. In my closet. The wires are broken in places. I stab my hands sometimes when I reach for my shoes."

"I was the one who bought them for you." Elisabeth rubbed Lila's arm. "Never dreamed they'd fly you away from me."

"Was I a milk carton kid?" Lila asked.

She nodded. "Only a few dairy companies do that these days, but yes. Your face was on milk cartons, in Walmart stores, on the back of delivery trucks, you name it. There was even an outdoor media company in Florida who put your face on a billboard. I did local talk shows. A news conference. Pleading for someone to notice you, help bring you home where you belonged. It's not easy to find one little girl in such a big continent. Like a penny in the sand."

Lila leaned forward to keep her stomach from flopping out onto her breakfast plate. She stared down at her boots, which, at that moment, were all that felt real.

"Your mother became quite famous from it, wouldn't you say, Kiki? For a while there, anyway."

Kieran nodded. "Mummy was on TV."

"Every scrap of attention mattered. It meant your photos got out there one more time. It just takes one person—the right person—to see you. To recognize those big blue eyes and pointed chin, that look of wonder on your face, and call the police or write in through the Web site. Just one person." She slapped her thighs. "Well, doesn't matter now. It didn't happen that way. All that matters is it happened. Finally, finally, *finally*, I found my baby girl."

Lila shook her head in disbelief. "It's so much. I can't even think straight."

Elisabeth stood up and smoothed out her skirt. "That

mimosa went straight through me. Delilah, sweetheart, would you keep an eye on your sister? I'll be right back."

Keep an eye on your sister. Six words—ordinary instructions from mother to daughter. Six words other children had heard a thousand times over—a maternal directive that might have another daughter rolling her eyes or whining out loud. Not Lila. To Lila it was something akin to winning the lottery. Admission to a club she'd been ejected from in another lifetime and had coveted ever since.

Suddenly, it was intoxicating, having her mother back, and she tried to sound casual in her reply. "No problem. I'll watch her."

Fourteen

Later that day, with Victor tucked quietly in his room, Lila poured herself a glass of water and padded into the dining room, settled herself at the computer. She hesitated before typing in www.findDelilahBlue.com. What came up on the screen made her gasp. She pushed her chair back and tried to focus on her breath.

The banner across the top was black with FIND DELILAH BLUE LOVETT in tall, thin brushstrokes. Beside the words, scattered on the left side, were childhood photos of a dirty-blond Delilah. Of Delilah with a teacher. Delilah with sawed-off bangs on Elisabeth's lap. Yes, even Delilah with sparkly lavender fairy wings. Photos so unfamiliar to Lila it made her sick just looking at them. As if she'd been followed, tracked. As if she'd left impressions behind she never knew about.

Red buttons in the shape of maple leaves marched

across the page, as if identifying Lila as a Canadian might shrink the vastness of the planet, given that she could have been anywhere on it. Each red leaf was clickable. One said ABOUT DELILAH BLUE. Another said HELP FIND, another said NEWS AND UPDATES. She clicked on this last one and up popped a new screen with a list of imagined sightings. One in North Carolina at a gas station. Several in Toronto. One in Bayfield, Ontario, in front of a yellow bookstore, another in Wales, England, getting onto a bus. But these were old listings, some from ten years back. They ended on November 14, 2003, with a sighting of a teenage girl leaving a museum in San Francisco. So close. She clicked on the ABOUT DELILAH BLUE button, shifting her chair forward, sitting up taller, as if improved oxygenation would make this easier. A huge photo came up. Her face took up the entire frame, with wisps of long, stringy hair blowing across her eyes—huge from this close up. This Delilah wasn't looking at the camera. Her small pointed chin had tipped her face to one side. It appeared as if she was speaking with someone, in a playground perhaps, someplace so exciting that the child hadn't noticed the windblown hair in her eyes.

It wasn't a photo she remembered any more than it was a day she remembered. But that wasn't what had her stomach in cramps. Something about the photo—maybe the feeling of movement long stilled, maybe the look of sureness in her eyes—had the faraway, lost-hope quality of a memorial photo in the local paper. When a child has suffered the most terrible fate of all. The type of picture that would be accompanied by a second photo showing a group of weeping schoolchildren placing flowers, notes, and teddy bears on the sidewalk in front of the mourning family's home.

A hot, gravylike haze enveloped her, moved in close,

pressed on her from every which way. As if the world had evaporated and nothing solid was left underfoot. Pinpricks of light marched in from her periphery, and she realized she was holding her breath. She should breathe, she knew that. Any idiot would. But she refused, feeling her consciousness ebb and shudder and loom large enough to see too far, beyond where time begins and time ends. It was too far a journey for such a broken passenger. She wasn't up for it. The room in front of her melted into a soup of swirling colors, sounds, matter.

She closed her eyes. Instead of losing consciousness, Lila turned to her left and vomited for the third time that day.

LATER, VICTOR SAT at the kitchen table nudging corn niblets onto his fork. "Where did you get this corn?"

"Green Giant."

He pushed the forkful into his mouth and raised his brows. "I hope you bought more. It's delicious."

The light was too bright in the kitchen. The entire house had been growing ever brighter over recent months. When they first moved in, Victor used only pink-tinted lightbulbs, claiming it made for a cozy ambiance. But his aging eyes had other ideas about mood lighting, prompting him to seek out stronger and stronger bulbs until the rooms kicked you in the retina when you entered. They were now living in a 7-Eleven.

In the nine hours since she'd left her mother, her father had been restless. He'd paced the length of the house repeatedly, tried without success to nap twice, insisted on watching the airing of the original black-and-white Audrey Hepburn film *Sabrina*, and made a half dozen phone calls about getting some kind of fence installed. When she asked why, he'd refused to elaborate. Thankfully, the evening air seemed to have stilled him.

Her stomach was empty, free of convulsions. It was as good a time as any to confront Victor. She dropped into the vinyl chair across the table and wrapped her arms around her knees. "Dad."

No response.

"Dad."

Victor looked up. "Have you seen a box of powdered donuts? Said GENEVIEVE on the lid?"

"It said nothing on the lid, and I threw them out weeks ago."

"They did not say nothing. They said GEN."

"Who is this Gen anyway?"

"She's the one who likes the powdered jellies."

Lila sighed. She wasn't prepared to get into drama about donuts. "I need to talk to you about something else. Do you know who I was with today?"

Victor pierced a series of niblets with the tines of his fork and slid them off with his teeth. "I do not."

"I was with Mum."

He stopped chewing. "Your mother?"

"Yes. You remember her. Reddish-brown hair, about five-foot-six. Big smile. Gave birth to me."

"She's here? In L.A.?"

"Yes."

Pushing his chair back from the table with a scrape, he leaned forward, eyes darting from the window to his daughter's face. From the way his chest rose and fell it was clear his breath was coming fast and furious. "Where is she now?"

"I don't know. Her apartment, I guess. She came to find me yesterday."

"Where? Where did she come find you?"

Not at art school where I had just finished begging to pose nude. "Nearby."

He jumped up, went to the window, and looked out into the dusk light. Once assured she wasn't lurking in the bushes, he spun around. "I don't feel right. I can't breathe. Or swallow." His hand went to his chest and he allowed his daughter to lead him back to his chair. "I need a drink maybe."

She grabbed his empty juice glass and filled it with tap water. When she set it in front of him, he waved it away. "Something stronger. There's a new bottle of Balvenie. In the cupboard."

"What is it? Your heart?" She glanced at him, worried, as she uncorked the bottle and sloshed dark amber liquid into a shot glass, spilling it all over the table.

"Careful." He mopped the scotch with his napkin.

Okay. The man wasn't dying. In the history of heart attacks, there couldn't be one person who, in the throes of cardiac arrest, contemplated sucking scotch out of the corner of a paper napkin to ensure he got his money's worth. "You're panicking. Just take a few breaths and calm yourself."

He tossed back the drink and tapped his glass on the table. When she poured him a refill it vanished just as quickly.

"Feeling better?"

He didn't answer. Just stared at his shot glass and breathed in, breathed out.

"Fucking hell. *Fucking* hell. It had to happen. I knew it had to happen."

"She says she's been looking for me, Dad. All these years. And that's not all."

He got up again and crossed the room, dropped his bearded jaw into one hand.

"She says you took me. Just like that. Just ran away with me and disappeared."

The dog started braying outside and Victor looked through the window. "Damn neighbors."

"Is it true?"

Yip yip yip.

"Dad."

Silence.

She lowered her voice to a near whisper. "Tell me what happened."

He looked at his daughter, blinking. When soft strands of hair fell in front of his eyes, he nudged them to the side and shrugged, his shoulders limp, his expression that of someone who'd accidentally set the toaster on fire. He sucked in a deep breath and said nothing.

SEPTEMBER 12, 1996

Graham Trent was Victor's oldest friend. Though these days, not much remained of the overweight jokester with a distaste for school and an appetite for the stage. After wasted years spent lining up for auditions alongside his starry-eyed mother, and never securing much more than a back-to-school flyer for a national drug store, Graham grew serious about his studies. He secured a job selling vinyl windows and doors, and eventually put himself through law school at the prestigious and historic University of Toronto.

Now, at forty-one, sitting behind a polished wooden desk with leather inlays, his graying hair still long enough to graze his collar, Graham reeked of success. Framed degrees and certificates lined his walls; photos of his young wife and partner, Kelly, decorated bookshelves packed with family law journals; and industrious assistants and articling students buzzed in with files needing his immediate attention.

"You're right," said Graham, unwrapping a stick of Doublemint and popping it in his mouth before tossing one onto the desk in front of Victor. Graham grinned. "The courts have favored Elisabeth. The woman knows how to work those dimples. Just like she sweet-talked you back in the day, she charms these judges. Maybe you should work on your girlish smile."

Victor ignored his friend's attempt at humor. "I walk around every day now terrified for my child's safety. I'm up half the night. I'm seeing a therapist. I have shortness of breath. I'm telling you, I can't take this. I even asked Elisabeth if I could move back in—at least then I'd be able to control what's happening in the house."

"Come on. You may not like your custody arrangement, but things aren't as bad as that."

"You know she left Delilah with some stranger the other week? Another one of these weirdo artsy losers she drags home. She meets him the day before at some art soiree and leaves her eight-year-old alone with him while she goes out to pick up Thai food. The guy answers the phone—I could hear him sucking on a joint—and actually questions me before letting me speak to my own daughter. You believe that? The guy could have done anything to her."

"Seriously?"

"And you know how she justifies it? She met this jerk at the AGO and assures me he's okay because he's a patron. *He tells her his family made some whopping donation to the gallery and she invites him back to her place for dinner."*

"Always looking for her prince," said Graham, shaking his head. "Clearly she thought you were her ticket at one point."

"Turns out all I did was make her hunger for more. Pharmaceutical sales didn't cut it. My bonus checks stopped looking good once she discovered trust-fund boys. Nice padded bank accounts remove all the risk, not to mention the waiting."

"Well, she is single now. She has every right to look for moneyed men."

"You're missing the point. She gave this guy full access to her child and she'd known him a few hours."

Graham winced as he processed this information.

"So the next day Delilah starts yapping about how cool he is because he paints all night and drives a Porsche Carrera. Then she tells me she saw him naked in her mother's studio when she came downstairs for a glass of milk. Turns out Elisabeth was sketching him."

Graham groaned.

"And she let Delilah walk home from a friend's house alone last week. It was after dark. 'You have to let kids be kids,' she tells me. 'Give them freedom.' Said the world is full of loving people and that I was the lousy parent for not trusting the human race!"

"The human race? Man, tell her to spend a day at the courthouse. That'll set her head straight."

"The child doesn't even have a bedtime. Apparently setting a schedule for a child is something akin to corporal abuse. And Delilah's sleeping bag smells like cigarette smoke." Victor pulled a tiny bottle of aspirin from his suit jacket and popped two pills without water.

"Sure, but—"

"This is a woman who left her toddler alone in a wading pool in the backyard while she ran inside to 'adjust' a painting. Remember? You've got to get me a better deal. Get me full custody and she has visitation."

"It won't happen." Graham's phone buzzed. He held up a finger to Victor and answered his assistant's question, then leaned back in his chair and stared at his friend. "These are definitely examples of poor parental judgment, I won't argue that. I wouldn't want her watching my kids—should Kelly agree to have any—but it's damned near impossible to take custody away from a mother unless she's flat-out abusive. Or addicted to crystal meth."

"Yeah? How about last June? How about when she almost . . . Jesus, I can't even say it. I get heart palpitations just thinking about it."

"We've discussed that to death. I'm prepared for Elisabeth and her potential accusations."

*"*False *accusations."*

"False accusations."

Victor felt a flush rise up his neck and into his cheeks. "It's just like every other time Elisabeth has messed up. Never her fault."

"What about Delilah? Is she ready yet to talk about what happened?"

"Doesn't remember a thing. Doctors said that was the brain's way of protecting the psyche and it's probably best for us not to say anything."

"How long has it been?"

"It was June."

Graham twisted his mouth to one side, lost in thought. He stared at Victor. "If we had a witness, we could un-

dermine the judge's confidence in Elisabeth. Tilt the favor toward you."

"It's her word against mine and that scares me to death. The woman's as smooth as they come. Just tell me I'm not going to get my access reduced if she piles on the lies."

"Won't happen."

"And if it does, what's my worst-case scenario?"

"Vic, it won't happen."

"Just give me the what if. Please."

Grant let out a long breath. "You could lose unsupervised access."

"Which means?"

"You'd see Delilah in a government-regulated supervised access center for visits of an hour or two at a time."

Victor rubbed his forehead. "No sleepovers? No outings? No holidays, even?"

"Stop doing this to yourself. That's not *going to happen. It's not even a consideration."*

Victor's stared at the wall and whispered, "I couldn't live that way. I swear to God, I couldn't."

"Victor, I've known you forever. You tend to . . ." Graham crossed his legs. "How do I say this nicely? You tend to get a bit paranoid when it comes to Delilah. Remember when she was a baby? You took her to the emergency room the first time she spit up."

"Screw you, Graham."

Graham laughed. "I'm sorry, buddy. But you need more in your life than your kid and your work. You need a distraction. Try golf. Might help you sleep."

"Full custody and my daughter living to see her twenty-first birthday would help me sleep. I can't take the stress. It's impossible to fight Elisabeth. I'm telling you, I might do something crazy."

Graham's assistant poked her head in. "Sorry, Mr. Trent. But it's nearly noon. You have to be in court . . ."

"Right." Graham stood up and reached for his valise. Shooting his friend an apologetic look, he began packing his case with legal pads and files. "I have to go. But call me tomorrow. We'll talk some more. Nothing rash in the meantime, okay? Things are going to work out fine—you'll see."

Victor nodded, waving his thanks as he rose and headed toward the door.

Graham called out, "Hey." Victor turned around. "I know it's tough. But if we get the right judge on Tuesday—believe me, a hard-nosed judge like Judith Lewicki would not succumb to Elisabeth's charms—we'll get you a lot more face time with your daughter."

"And if we get any other judge?"

Graham pulled on his trench coat. "The very worst that will happen is things stay as they are now."

Fifteen

Victor spun around and surveyed his beloved kitchen as if saying good-bye. As if the staleness of cupboard doors that creaked and copper pipes that dripped had served him well and he no longer needed their backing. As if the front door no one could find and the windows that burrowed into the center of the earth had accomplished exactly what he'd hoped and he and they were sharing a private moment, a surreptitious wink wink, nod nod.

"It's true," he said. "I took you away from your mother."

A fly landed next to what was left of the puddle of scotch, jerked itself closer, and washed its front legs in the pricey liquid. They both watched as the insect completed its toilette and flew away, satisfied.

Lila couldn't react right away, so unashamed was Victor's admission. She dropped into a chair and tried to form a thought—any thought. When nothing came, she forced herself to stare at the one chipped red tile at the edge of the counter. Eventually, she whispered, "Why?"

Victor seemed to be preparing his reply, blinking and nodding his head as he was. Then, without warning, he up and walked out of the room. "It's a rather long story."

She hurried after him. "Believe me, I've got time."

He headed out onto the porch, around the house, and down to the laundry room, where he tugged balled-up sheets from the dryer. After kicking the metal door shut, he marched wordlessly back up to the house. Once he was in his room, he spoke. "I'd prefer to discuss this in the morning. You know what I'm like at the end of the day."

"How could you? I mean, that's something a criminal would do. Something you read about and think, *How could he?* Regular people don't abduct their children."

"My stomach's been bothering me all evening . . ."

"You should see her. She's so sweet and loving and, oh my God, she's lived through so much. My face was on milk cartons!"

He dumped his sheets on the stripped bed and rubbed his belly. "Bloat, I think."

"I knew she was good." Lila sank into a chair. "Even when I really hated her, like around Christmas or my birthday, I think, deep inside, I knew it was impossible for her to have walked away from me. It's like I could feel her. That mother-and-child thing—you never lose that connection."

He started tucking the fitted sheet over his pillow-top mattress. "I don't know why they make these mattresses thicker than the sheets these days."

"How can you talk about your bed right now? Why did

you do it? Was I being beaten? Abused? You must have had a reason. A pretty freaking big one."

"I did."

She waited.

He rubbed his eye sockets with forefinger and thumb. "Custody isn't always a simple issue."

"You lost custody?"

"No. Not quite."

"Then what?"

He peeled the sheet off the mattress corner and started over. "Blasted thing's sideways."

"Put the stupid sheets down! I have a right to know what happened!"

He stammered, "I-I just—I need a minute to think."

Her cell phone vibrated inside her pocket. She flipped it open to see a strange number: 213 area code, but whom? And it hit her. Her mother. Feeling enormous again, she dug through her pocket to find the napkin where she'd scrawled Elisabeth's number and, sure enough, it was the same. How many times had she dreamed of this event? A phone call from her mother. She'd wished and wished. She'd stared at first stars of the night, she'd extinguished birthday candles, she'd blown dandelion puffs.

Eying Victor, she debated what to do. This was not the moment to bring Elisabeth into the room. Still. Lila had waited too long for this phone call to happen. She flipped open her phone and wandered into the hall. "Hi."

"Sorry, sweetheart. I wanted to make sure I didn't dream you. I'm going to seem crazy for a while."

"Me too."

"And Delilah?"

"Yes?"

"There's something else. I need to give you the heads up before it happens. Baby, the police are going to be involved. My lawyer wants to bring them in before your father does something illegal, like hopping on a plane and fleeing the country. I couldn't bring myself to tell you earlier—you'd already had such a shock. But the police could arrive as early as tonight."

She peered back into Victor's room where he was staring down at his mess of bedding. Her father, in jail? It would kill him. "Could we wait on that?"

"I know how upsetting it is, but you have to understand the gravity of the situation. Your father committed a very serious crime. There is no way for it to go unpunished."

"Wait. Just another day. Please."

"Delilah, I really don't think—"

"I'm begging you. I need to hear his side before things blow up."

Silence. Then, "Okay. Only because I love you so much. But don't let him talk you into anything foolish, like jetting off to Belize or something."

She looked at her father, a twisted sheet now wound around his lower half. "No. I think we're safe on that front."

"All right, baby. I love you. Sleep tight."

She snapped the phone shut and returned to the chair.

"Was that Elisabeth?"

Lila nodded.

He said nothing for a moment, just allowed his eyes to search his daughter's features while his own face drooped so low she nearly didn't recognize him.

In reality, there was a great deal about her father she didn't know. That he was an abductor, for one. A man willing to do something most people would never even contemplate. And once he'd succeeded with that, he was perfectly fine with telling his daughter her own mother rejected her and letting her grow up feeling unworthy of any love that wasn't his love.

"Dad, you really need to start talking."

"Mouse, I think it's best we put an end to this discussion. I'm not quite prepared to talk about the past just now."

Her fury came out in a half gasp, half cough. "Oh. Okay." She backed toward the door. "Sure. I mean, why muck up a perfectly lovely night with something as bothersome as this? It was only a kidnapping. A one-time thing. I should just move on, right?"

"I know how it seems. All I can ask is that you trust me."

She stared at him in stunned silence, too many emotions swirling around inside of her to think straight herself. Trust him? Trust him?

"Besides, it's getting late," he said. "You know I don't think clearly this far into the evening . . ."

"Yeah. Right. By all means get into bed. Lose yourself in a good book."

"Now, now. Let's not get sarcastic." Victor unwrapped the sheets from his torso and threw them onto the mattress. He looked at her, pleading. "I'm going to need help with this bedding."

All the years of living with him, being cared for by him, being fed and clothed and shod by him, did none of it count? How many times had he made her bed when she was young? Or gotten up in the middle of the night to soothe her from a terrible dream? Was it not something like deposits of goodness into an account—was he never allowed a withdrawal?

Maybe. But this one was so big it left him damn near broke.

"Mouse?"

Her lungs felt small. Miserly sponges with little room for trivialities like oxygen and lifeward impulses. "You know what?" She forced herself to her feet and walked away. "Make your own bed."

SHE WANDERED OUT into the night and up to the road. After a few moments she dropped to the ground and arranged herself cross-legged in the dirt. A mosquito settled on her leg and she swatted it away. Incidences of West Nile had been increasing in California in the past few summers, and reports kept insisting autumn was the wrong time of year to get bitten. Though this year's numbers were nowhere near 2005's—there'd been nearly eighty cases in Los Angeles County alone that year and mosquito samples had nearly doubled from the year prior.

Or something.

It was wrong to have a head full of statistics at such a time. To be worried about a disease she'd never catch. There was something almost minuscule about her, despite being eleven feet tall whenever her mother appeared. Why did her mind do that—cloud the brain with minutiae the moment her world started spinning backward on its axis?

She heard a snuffling sound from across the road and looked up to see an overturned trash can, its useless bungee cord flung into the middle of the road. Behind it, Slash stood staring at her, his platinum legs splayed wide to accommodate the refuse at his feet. The look on his face was one of sarcastic triumph. He stood perfectly still as he gazed at her, determined that she not threaten the decomposing bounty spread out before him.

In spite of her best efforts to remain motionless and unthreatening—the front door was, after all, a good distance away and the animal could easily overtake her should he so desire—she felt a tingle in her nose. Holding her breath didn't ward off the sneeze. It was fast, ferocious, and echoed off the canyon walls like the Basenji's yelp.

The sound spooked him. Slash dropped down and crammed half-eaten drumsticks and chicken wings into his mouth. She could smell the barbecue sauce. He didn't stop at two or three, but attempted to hold some ten to twelve bits between his teeth. Then he loped off into the darkness without leaving a single scrap of rancid poultry behind for the other creatures of the night.

As soon as he was gone, she raced down the hill to the safety of her cellar, with its buzzing fluorescent light, ancient washer and dryer, and dirt floor. It was cool inside, and smelled like moist earth, rot, and water. Like Tide with bleach, and rags soaked with turpentine, and every color of oil paint imaginable. Like cobwebs so old they'd blackened and solidified and become a permanent part of the ceiling beams.

She stared at the canvas stretched out on the floor—about nine feet wide and nearly seven feet tall, a rhythmical splattering and pouring of barely controlled chaos, into which, if one looked carefully, could be seen the fragile profile of a helpless woman—and thought the four months she put into it may have resulted in the first piece of work she wouldn't destroy.

She planned to photograph it, buy one of those black portfolios real artists carry, and haul it around to a few galleries in the vain hope of securing representation one day. Make up for time lost. Another surge of fury washed over her. Victor took that too, the art career that might have started years back. There'd been a collector in the barbershop that day so long ago. He'd wanted to buy Lila's doodle—the one she'd been working on while her father had his hair buzzed off. But Victor wouldn't hear of it. He ushered her out into the parking lot with the doodle tucked beneath his arm. Which now made sense. He couldn't have an art prodigy bringing the "Mack" family under the microscope of the L.A. media, hungry to report on the next sensation. Serious art talent at eight years old was something the world took notice of. But now too many years had passed. Talent at twenty didn't cause quite such a stir, did it? She was one of thousands of artists with big dreams and little cash.

How much different might her life have been?

Then again, maybe nothing would have come of it. Big things didn't happen to people like her. Wait, strike that. Big things *did* happen to her. After all, thanks to her father, she was now the victim of a kidnapping! How many people could claim such a thing? It was the kind of incident you read about. The kind of happening that transforms regular people into those who leave you squeamish, those you secretly congratulate yourself for not being and vow never to get too close to lest the misery soil your existence like graphite smudged on the heel of your hand.

One thing was certain: No one could ever find out. She didn't want her photo to be in the *L.A. Times*—God, no. A story like this could travel. *USA Today,* maybe even *O* magazine. Tabloids, newsmagazines, publications in Canada. She actually *looked* like the victim of some horrific crime, a big-eyed twerp, prey, all pathetic and leggy, circles under her eyes as if Victor kept her chained to the water heater in the cellar. It would be easy to believe, given her lack of dermal melanin.

Her painting gazed up at her, unimpressed with the transformation that had taken place. Tiny, jagged hyphens in cerulean blue yawned and turned away, nudged cadmium yellow light in the ribs and jeered. The mixture of alizarin crimson and manganese violet and phthalo blue she'd worked so hard to get right and smeared across the lower right side of the painting in an effort to show the cold (but not too cold—if you looked closely there was hidden warmth) world this woman inhabited actually got up and marched off the edge of the canvas and under the dryer like a never-ending trail of ants.

Lila couldn't take the disinterest. Not from her own creation. Not today.

Forget the portfolio.

She reached up to the shelf behind her, flicked open a paint-spattered Swiss Army knife, and dropped down onto her knees. She crawled to the top of the canvas, stabbed the knife through the linen and into the dirt, and slowly, precisely, slashed her painting into ribbons.

Sixteen

Going to a dance club the same day she learned she was kidnapped turned out to be a colossal error in judgment.

Back in the damp of the cellar, with curls of shredded canvas at her feet, Lila had decided that she, her father, and the stainless-steel blade in her hand all needed a bit of distance. She'd changed into a miniskirt and off-shoulder sweater—red for the feeling of having been infused with a quart of someone else's iron-rich, heated-to-boiling blood—swapped her new cowboy boots for the comfort of her doodled pair, and driven along Sunset to the Cathouse—a gritty little club a few blocks away from L.A. Arts that the students had pretty much claimed as their own, even going so far as to strike up a deal with the owners to paint the interior as they saw fit. Ceiling, walls, tables, chairs, and ductwork were spattered, graffitied, crosshatched, and finger painted. Rumor had it that one wall had been stamped with bare torsos, and if you looked closely, you could see the imprints of navels, nipples, hip bones, and chest hair.

It was as if an enormous gallery boasting art of every style and method and talent level imaginable, exposing motivations good, evil, and depraved, had been gathered in a vessel and held over a flame, shaken like Jiffy Pop, then poured over the nightclub and left to cure.

Lila had wandered inside a few times before working at the school, but she'd felt like an impostor and quickly skittered back to the dismal acceptance of her cellar. It wasn't as if there was a rule about who could or could not enter the club. But still. Now she felt qualified to walk past the humping cherubs that decorated the doors and into the frenetic interior.

The intention was to swathe herself in music that would thump against her flesh and through to her organs. To sip alcohol from a badly washed glass and vanish into a herd of people who thought they needed an escape from their own existence. Of course, the need to escape was subjective. These kids might be running from schoolwork, lousy jobs, or money stress. Dating complications, maybe. Lila felt fairly confident in her status as sole abductee in the room.

Refusing to be held back by California lawmakers, Lila waited next to a group of rowdy girls at the bar, and watched the bartender set their drinks one by one on the counter. When no one was looking, she picked up the tallest glass—one filled with clear bubbly liquid and ice—and slapped a ten in the puddle where the drink had been.

It wasn't in her to steal.

Armed with what turned out to be vodka and 7-Up, Lila

wormed her way through thrashing, grinding bodies on the dance floor to a rickety staircase—more of a fire escape, really—that led to a loft, and found an unoccupied table with a view of the action on the main level. She sat, settled her bag by her feet, and tipped carbonated alcohol down her throat, loving the way her head started to whirl almost immediately.

Staring up at the dusty pipes that snaked across the ceiling, she thought for a moment. Her last name. Mack. It couldn't possibly be legal. Come to think of it, weren't they living in the country unlawfully? She was smuggled in with a fake ID, for Christ's sake. Would she be deported if she went back to Lovett?

Who the hell was she now?

She watched human shapes move around in the dark down below. Every single one of those lurching bodies had a name. No matter how abandoned, dejected, wasted, broken, slutty, drunk, or otherwise messed up, they all had names. Tears blurred her vision and she scrubbed them away with her sleeves.

Two beers clunked down onto the small round table to her left, followed by a male body.

Adam Harding. Lila looked away fast.

"Lila. Is that short for something?"

She shrugged, praying he would sense her mood and go sit elsewhere.

"Mind if I join you?"

"Actually, I'm not staying—"

Too late. The beers were on her table and he was already pulling a stool way too close and straddling it. He grinned and slid a beer in front of her. "The other day. Wow. I'm so sorry."

She shifted away. "Doesn't matter."

"I mean, here you are having this huge drama with your mother and there I am stuck in the closet. I didn't know what to do. If I stay in there, I'm a creep who's listening to this totally emotional reunion between long lost relatives. And if I come out, I interrupt, and very possibly annihilate, the moment." Before sipping his beer, he pulled the NyQuil from his jacket pocket and took a few big gulps that stained his lips greenish black. "But then I tripped over an easel and fell on my ass."

"Seriously. I'd forgotten all about it."

"Anyway. I apologize."

"What's with the medicine? You're sick?"

"Allergic to paint fumes. I've been on this stuff for three months now and I'm much better. Forget antihistamines. The 'Quil is all you need to keep the air passageways open."

"So you take it all the time? Even when you're not painting?"

"The way I see it, I can take the NyQuil and live. Or not take it and probably live." He shrugged. "I can't take that kind of chance." He tilted the bottle in her direction. "Want to try?"

"Nah." She shook her head and stared down at the crowd. "I don't care much if I live."

"You always this cheery?"

"If I told you my twin died yesterday, would it make you feel like a jerk?"

"Holy crap." He put his hand on her back. "I'm so sorry."

Again, she moved away. "Are you always this pawsy?"

"I wasn't making a move on you, Lila," he said, carefully enunciating each syllable. "I was expressing sympathy for your loss."

"Well don't. I don't have a twin."

He blinked at her, silent.

She felt her boot stick to the floor and examined the underside. "Perfect. I stepped in gum."

"I can fix that." After a long swig of beer, he pulled a package of Clorets gum from his pocket and popped a few pieces into his mouth, chewing hard. He motioned for her to give him her boot and, after she set her still booted foot on his thigh, he spat out his gum and pressed it into the flattened bubble gum. "It's the best way to remove anything gummy from a surface. Fight sticky with sticky." Once green and pink had morphed into a pebble-spackled brownish gray, he attempted to peel it off, only to have small wads crumble to bits in his fingers.

"Nice," said Lila, pushing her hair out of her face and leaning forward for a closer look. "You've made it thicker. And uglier."

"Yeah. We're going to need some peanut butter." His eyes locked on to the miniature silver pen drawing Lila had scrawled on her heel a few weeks back. A man's head, in profile. In spite of the unusual canvas, the diminutive size, the complete lack of shading, there was no mistaking the man's sorrowful expression. Adam looked up at her. "Wow."

"It's nothing."

"Believe me, *that* is not nothing."

"Just some guy on the bus."

He crossed his legs in front of him. Tilting his head up toward the ceiling, he said, "Draw me."

"Can't."

He laughed. "You can draw some guy on a bus but not

the guy who puts this kind of vain effort into liquoring you up, insulting you, and wrecking the sole of your boot? Come on. A little respect for the underdog."

"Sorry. No pen."

"And if I were to pull one out of my pocket?"

She shrugged.

"Okay." He looked at his watch. "Whatever."

"Did you actually have one? A pen?"

"Would it have made a difference?"

"No."

Adam drank again. "Is it hard for the guys you date? They take you out then drop you off to strip for a bunch of other guys?"

"My boyfriend doesn't mind me stripping for other guys. He kind of gets a sexual charge out of it."

He grimaced. "Sounds like a keeper."

"I don't have a boyfriend."

He stared at her a moment, leaning back in his seat. "See now, I don't take offense. You're feeling tender. You've had a major upheaval in your life with your mother showing up like that. Who wouldn't lash out? You're deflecting and I actually think that's healthy. Feel free to have another go."

"Nah. You've taken all the fun out of it now."

"Had you had much communication with her before she showed up like that?"

She pushed her beer toward him. "I don't want this. I'm more of a Boone's Farm kind of girl."

"Seriously?"

"No."

"My mom died when I was six," he said. "So I know all about growing up without one. It sucks. The worst is the week before Mother's Day at public school. All those flowerpots and poems and paper hearts kids have to make. And, like, halfway through the week, the teacher remembers you have no mother and suggests you address yours to a grandmother or an aunt. You've been there, am I right?"

"I should go home now." She rooted through her bag for her keys. "My father wasn't feeling well. I never should have left."

"You know, the school can probably recommend someone for you to talk to. There are ways you can get free therapy. I can get some information for you, if you want. I help out in the office now and then."

"I don't need therapy, okay? *Jesus.*"

"I'm just saying." He leaned over the table. "And I'm always around if you ever want to talk."

She cast him a sardonic glance. "Or draw you nude?"

"Should the need arise. The two are not mutually exclusive."

"I'm confused. Are you trying to hit on me or be my BFF?"

His mouth twitched. "I appear to be striking out in the therapist-cum-friend arena. I might make more headway as a letch—at least that draws a smile. So I'm totally open at this point."

"Good to know. What else you got?"

"That's about it. The 'Quil, the gum remedy, the odd kindness-gone-ugly."

He pushed aside his empty bottle and sipped from hers. "Is it working even a little bit?"

"No."

"Good. It's a system that rarely fails me." He shifted his weight and nearly fell off his stool. Righting himself, he said, "Whoa. Dizzy."

"Are you drunk?"

"Not on one beer." He leaned against the table, swaying. "I'm no lightweight. You should know that. Don't want to scare you."

She pulled her bag from the floor and set it on her lap. "I'm really just hoping you don't vomit in my purse at this point. Anything else would be a bonus."

He smiled, rocking back and forth. "I think you're developing quite a thing for me." He stood up and staggered to the right, reaching for the wall to stop himself from falling. "I'm going home before I say something you regret."

She pulled him back to the stool and leaned him on the table. "Adam, you're completely plastered. How did you get here? Did you drive?"

He nodded.

"Well, you can't drive home."

"I can. Car's electric."

"Yeah, that helps. Do you have a friend we can call? A family member?"

He laid his head on his arms and smiled, eyes closed. She liked the curvy line of his mouth, like a flattened-out W. "See? Already you want to meet my family."

Jesus. He was a mess. She reached into his backpack and pulled out the cold medicine. Right there on the bottle it said, MAY CAUSE MARKED DROWSINESS; ALCOHOL MAY INCREASE THE DROWSINESS EFFECT.

No wonder he was wasted. She helped him to his feet and wiggled herself beneath one of his arms. "We've got to get you home before you pass out. Where do you live?"

"On a futon in my divorced sister's sunporch. If you can call that living."

"Address?"

"It's the house we grew up in. My sister and her ex bought it from my mother before she died. After the divorce, Wendy rented out my bedroom to a computer student who's never home. Until I make it in New York and start sending home the bucks. And I will, believe you me."

"Adam, focus. What's the address?"

"3414 South Pomona."

"I'm taking you home."

"Geez." He put his arm around her for support. "You got it real bad."

THE COOL NIGHT air sobered him enough that he was able to lift his weight off Lila's shoulder and walk upright. Yawning and swaying, he followed her up a hilly side street.

"You should come with me," he called out. "My cousin has this third-floor walk-up in Soho. She's going to Europe for a year and said I can stay for free if I take care of her sphynx."

They entered a gravelly parking lot dotted with weeds, beer bottles, and chirping crickets. Lining the lot were a series of dejected storefronts: a variety store, a Laundromat, and a porn shop—all with barred windows.

"What's a sphynx?" she asked as they wound their way through the parked cars.

"You know, those grayish-pink cats—all skinny with no hair?"

She made a face.

"I know. Scary-looking at first, but you get used to it."

"What'll you do there—besides not brush the cat?"

"There are zillions of little galleries everywhere. In New York, they're way more open to new faces in the art scene. And if I can't get signed to a gallery, I can still sell my stuff on the street. You just set up a little stand on Prince Street and watch all the tourists scramble for your work. That's how my cousin made it. She does nothing but bare tree branches and she had them screened onto T-shirts. They sold so well, her oil paintings started to take off. "

"Cool." She pulled out the keys to Victor's car and opened the passenger-side door. "It's my dad's car, so promise you'll shout if you get nauseous."

"You should come with me. We could be roommates."

She helped him lower himself down into the seat, covering his head so he didn't concuss himself on the way in. Still, he bumped his forehead. "I'm thinking guzzling that stuff every day isn't such a great idea," she said. "Maybe you should switch to DayQuil."

He leaned back against the seat and closed his eyes. "Never. They put uppers in it. That's the difference. DayQuil makes your heart race."

She closed the door and went around the front of the car. When she climbed in, he was gone. She spun around to see him lying in the hatch area, knees touching the roof, staring up at the sky. "What are you doing back there?"

"I need to lie flat. I swear to God I'll hurl if I have to look out the window."

She started the car. "Okay, but keep your knees down. I'm not getting pulled over on top of everything else this week."

"What else happened?"

"Nothing."

"Oh, your mother. Right. Where was she all these years anyway?"

"Don't want to talk about it," she sang.

"Okay, pretty girl. It's your wounded psyche."

The exit was partially blocked by a few poorly parked cars. Rather than risk scraping the Datsun, Lila drove toward the adjacent lot, which appeared to sit a bit lower down than the first. As she attempted to guide the Datsun down what she imagined in the dark to be a gentle paved slope, the front end of the car dropped from underneath her and landed with a great crash about two feet down, killing the engine and leaving her hanging forward from her seat belt toward the steering wheel. The car's back end was stuck on the upper lot and both her feet were stamped down hard on the brake. "Oh my God! It was a total cliff!"

Adam's curled body had also slid forward and now rested against Lila's seat back. He groaned.

"What do I do now?" squealed Lila. "We're stuck."

"I think I'm hurt. My nose is making clicking sounds."

"My dad is going to kill me."

Adam leaned closer and pushed against his nose. "Do you hear that?"

She spun around and squinted. "Maybe you should stop poking it."

"Just check yours. See if it clicks."

"I'm a bit busy up here, Adam. What should I do? Let the back end drop? I have to, right? We can't go backward."

"Why did I get in the car with you?" He was silent a moment, his fingers traveling across his face. "Wait . . . what?" He reached forward to adjust the rearview mirror. "Holy crap, my nose is totally bleeding. Take me to Cedars-Sinai. You broke my freaking nose!"

"How was I to know this would happen? It's dark out and where was the cement barrier? There's supposed to be a barrier, right?"

"It's not that hard to spot. I can see—very clearly—this lot's down in a ditch."

"Which is why you should be in the front seat instead of back there with the surgical gloves and cartons of specimen containers."

He pulled a few boxes closer and examined them. "Vaginal scopes? What the hell goes on back here?"

"Hold on to your nose. We're going down."

There was no alternative but to let the back end of the Datsun crash to the ground. Then pray like hell the car started. With one foot clamped hard on the clutch, the other stamped down on the brake, she shifted into neutral and, holding her breath, eased her foot off the brake. The car rolled a few inches, then the back end smashed down hard.

Adam howled from behind her.

Lila turned the key in the ignition, relieved to hear the engine rattle, thump, then roar to life. The radio station had changed. Joni Mitchell's smoky voice crooned in the background. "It's working!"

She spun around to find him crawling toward her. Blood stained his upper lip. "You're going to bleed all over the upholstery."

"Heartless." He stared at her, blinking. "Yet validating."

After turning off the engine, Lila trotted around the rear to open the hatch. "Climb out."

He flipped himself onto his side and slithered to the back, keeping his face upturned to the sky and pinching his nose to stop the bleeding. "It's nothing," he sniffed, lifting his shirt to reveal a dark red scrape across his ribs. "I'm lucky I didn't puncture a lung from all the paraphernalia back there. What the hell are you doing driving around with a box of tourniquets? And what's a"—he tipped a narrow box on its side—"Vacutainer?"

Something about Adam's smile—equally arrogant and apologetic—reminded her of Victor when he asked for help with his sheets. Her father had been having more and more of these moments of confusion. There had been many perplexing conversations and they couldn't all be chalked up to a sleepless night or a failed career. The Basenji, stepping out in front of an SUV, needing donuts for somebody named Gen. Maybe his reaction about the abduction, his refusal to discuss it, was just another episode. She couldn't know for certain that he was being obtuse. She couldn't know what was going on inside his head at that moment. That moment itself, with all its inherent stress, might have set off another episode.

She felt her pulse quicken. That was it. It had been the dementia talking. And she'd left him alone with his confusion. Didn't give a thought to how lost or scared or terrified he might be.

Whatever her name, she was a terrible daughter.

Was it Alzheimer's? Surely Victor was nowhere near old enough to succumb to such a disease. He had been increasingly forgetful this past year, but until recently any episode had been trivial. Losing his keys and finding them in his pocket. Misplacing his glasses and she'd find them in the car. Nothing alarming. If anything, these past episodes had been amusing. She'd teased him. Could Alzheimer's strike out of nowhere and take out a perfectly healthy man in the middle of his life?

Surely it wouldn't hit now, just when she needed him—and his answers—most. "That's it," she said to Adam.

"That's it? What does that mean?"

"You need to find your own way home."

"You're deflecting again. You're feeling stunted by your mother's sudden reappearance and instead of taking me up on my generous offer to listen, you're running me out of the car."

She had to see her father now. He'd slept for a few hours and might be himself again. There had to be a good reason for what he did. He took her by mistake, maybe. He took her under some gross misunderstanding. Victor, for all his brusqueness, was a decent man. "Just go. Okay, Adam? Will you please just get out?"

"How will I get home?"

An old man pushing a grocery cart full of newspapers shuffled past, his cheeks and mouth sunken from loss of teeth, his ancient back gnarled into the shape of a comma, a garbage bag wrapped around his shoulders like a scarf. Adam's eyes followed him, widening in horror. "I could be killed."

"You have to go. Please."

"But I can't drive."

"Walk out to Sunset." She pulled a twenty from her bag. "Wave down a cab."

"You shouldn't be alone, Lila. You need a supportive shoulder to lean on. You need to explore your ambiguity about your mother's unexpected emergence. You need to make sure you don't use this sudden upheaval to sabotage your own existence." He pulled a tissue from his pocket and stuffed the corners up his nose. "Besides, this is L.A. Getting a cab could take all night."

"I'm sorry. I'll see you in class."

He climbed out and, still pinching the bridge of his nose, watched, as she sped away in the night.

BACK AT THE cabin, Lila paused at Victor's door. His breathing was deep, regular. Sure. There was no way she would sleep tonight without speaking to him. Her thoughts were racing in every direction and she needed to do something, anything, to streamline them. Turning the knob, she slipped inside his room and tiptoed across the shadows. She stood at his bedside and willed herself not to cry.

He hadn't managed to make his bed after she left, but laid out the fitted sheet like a folded tortilla and climbed inside. But the elastic edges had pulled the top end down on to his head like a puckered hood that was stapled to his eyebrows. At the other end, his legs stuck out, bare from the knees down, with slippers still on his feet.

The top sheet lay twisted and useless on the floor. Proof he'd been having an episode. She was a monster of a daughter to leave him this way. He looked like a man completely unloved.

She went to her own room and gathered her quilt, laid it out over him, and pulled the fitted sheet off his face. She'd make his bed properly in the morning, tuck the top sheet in extra tight, just the way he liked it. As she dragged the chair closer to his bedside, he opened his eyes and reached for her hand.

"Where've you been, Mouse?" His cloudy eyes searched her face.

"I need to talk to you, Mister. So much has happened, I don't know what's what anymore. I'm just confused and, I don't know, lost. But here's the thing. You're a good man. You wouldn't have done it without a damn good reason. There must have been a misunderstanding. I don't really know. I don't really care. All I want right now, and I can't promise it will stay this way—for all I know I may not speak to you in the morning—is to see you as you. The man who raised me. The one who used to bounce me on his knee and push me too high on the swings and slip me the olives from his martini."

His mouth stretched wide and the look in his eyes grew tender. As if it was what he too wanted. To return to a less complicated time.

"Dad, I guess what I'm saying is I love you. I shouldn't, but at this moment I love you in a way that is scaring me. Do you hear me?"

He clenched her hand tighter.

She moved closer and waited, not daring to breathe. "Earlier, you were having another moment of fuzziness, right? When you said you wouldn't tell me why you took me. I've been thinking it's probably time to get you to a doctor for this. It's happening too often and I think I've heard there are ways to slow down the progression if it turns out to be Alzheimer's."

"No doctors."

"Why not? This was two episodes in one day. I'm pretty sure—"

He let his hands fall onto the thin white T-shirt covering his chest. "What happened tonight wasn't an episode. I was perfectly lucid. I didn't want to discuss what happened in Toronto."

"And now?"

"Nothing has changed. I'm sorry if what I did hurt you. But what's done is done and I don't care to discuss the details."

"You're sorry if it hurt me? Of course it hurt me! You took away my childhood. You told me she didn't want me. There's no 'if' in this equation and I deserve to know more."

"It's not a good idea. But what is . . ." He struggled to get out of the quilt and onto his feet. " . . . is getting myself to the toilet. I'll never get back to sleep with a full bladder."

The bathroom door clicked shut. With her lips pressed into a furious knot, she made his bed, fluffed his pillow, and adjusted her quilt. Then she stomped to the kitchen and stared at his empty chair, worn from years of sitting at the head of the table. The toilet flushed. The indifference, the ordinariness of water hurtling through pipes in the wall, whooshing and banging, was too much. She reached into the pantry for the spare can of corn niblets, opened it up, and dumped the contents into the trash.

Seventeen

Lichty's classroom smelled like blood. Lila sniffed the air, trying to determine where he'd stashed the body—or perhaps where he stored the blood he sucked from his models—and determined the odor was coming from the metal gurney he appeared to have rolled out of the morgue and into his classroom. It was for her and no, the icy surface wouldn't be warmed with a white sheet. That kind of nicety was reserved for corpses. Shivering models were expected to just deal.

Once on top of the gurney, she would be allowed any pose she liked, so long as her body reflected loftiness. Maybe even a bit of superiority. Both were doable. So long as the wheels of the cart remained firmly locked, she'd give Lichty both altitude and attitude. The students had a good clear view up her nostrils and into her cerebral matter. And, if she wasn't dainty about her stance, straight through her vaginal pipeline, along her fallopian ductwork, to the gumball machines that foolishly released an unfertilized child as a monthly option. After all, one didn't come across a family brimming in such moral riches every day. It would be a shame not to continue the family line.

Turned out a good night's sleep had done nothing to improve her father's chattiness. Nothing this morning from him but another apology for what he'd done and a whole lot of silence when it came to explaining it. She had noticed, however, while he was waiting for his toast to pop up, that he peered out the window and scoured the vicinity for police presence.

After dropping her robe—the blue silk dressing gown that had long been hanging in the back of her closet, unloved and unworn until today—she climbed up onto the table and squatted like a cat to make sure the gurney was stable. It was surprisingly so. Then she stood and pressed her ankles together, bent her knees. With her head close to the ceiling, she twisted from the waist, assuming a pose she'd been thinking about for days: one where the muscle fibers on one side of her body would be different in action and shape from those on the other side. This would give the trapezius—typically drawn as a flat sheet—a swollen, bunched form that was sure to challenge the students. Fairly certain she'd achieved it, she stared across the ceiling at the lights. The longer she stared, the more she appreciated their closeness, their warmth. It was what she needed today—to come to class, pose. Made her feel almost normal.

"Wipe the look of stupefaction from your face, Model," said Lichty from across the room. "If I wanted my class to sketch the vapid emotions of a cheerleader who's misplaced her pompons, I'd go down to the football field and drag her back by the bleached-blond ponytail."

He spun around and wrote the word "Crux" on the board. "Today we look up to the adult face as seen from the eyes of a newborn. The face holds in it all we need to know about becoming a human; as such, it is the infant's preferred sight. The child needs to connect with mother for her very survival. But the human face contains more than just a source of food and comfort for baby. It holds the feelings she will mask and the injustices she will suffer and the hopes she will dare not dream. She looks to it to determine the very crux of life itself."

As the students turned to their boards, glancing up for quick visual references, Lila became painfully aware that she should not have undressed. She could have been, if not fully clothed, at least wrapped in the robe. Shame spread across her flesh like a hot rash.

"And despite the fact that our brazened model insists on showing us her everything this morning, I'll ask you all to refrain from sketching anything below the clavicles." Lichty peered down at a black-haired boy in jeans and flip-flops. "For those of you unfamiliar with 'big words,' I am speaking of Miss Mack's collarbones."

She felt her cheeks redden and caught sight of the delicious pile of blue silk on the floor. Did she dare? "Um, Lichty?"

His head snapped around as abruptly as if the wall itself had spoken.

"If I could just break pose for a second to put on my robe. I didn't know we'd be doing just the face."

"Absolutely not. It is precisely the tension between your exposure and your humiliation, combined with no small amount of fragility, that gives us such a forbidden peek beneath the surface today. I'm fascinated to see how it will manifest on paper. The models I use most often express subtle nuances of emotion in their poses and the challenge for them is to bare themselves—if you'll excuse the pun—to interpretation. It's a rare model who decides, with a tilt of her chin or a blush on her breastbone, what we should see. What she wants us to deal with."

Yes, people. See what I'm feeling. And while you're at it, check out www.findDelilahBlue.com and a few of those age-enhanced missing child posters. They're dog-eared but fun. Bonus points if you can dig up a festering milk carton with my face on it. And once you've sucked the essence from that, spend a few minutes trying to get an answer from my abductor—the man I thought was my one and only ally.

Then go ahead and deal. Any way you can.

Lichty called out from across the class. "Only the face, people. You show me a breast or a shoulder, and your work goes into the recycling bin."

There was no sign of Adam.

Which was, of course, not her problem. She hadn't set out to meet up with him the night prior, she hadn't suggested he mix medicine with alcohol, and she certainly hadn't been under any obligation to deliver him home to beddies.

She had, as they say, her own shit.

Lichty bent down to correct someone's work, then stood up and boomed, "Light bounces off faces from every direction, which only serves to muddy what the model is or is not showing you. It is your job as observer, as artist, to find what lies beneath. Not all is what it seems."

It wasn't as if she left Adam in such a terrible area. West Hollywood wasn't bad. There were—what?—six hundred murders last year? In a town of fourteen million, what were the odds one chalk outline would be his? Besides, who could stand the smell of NyQuil long enough to off him? Even a murderer had to have standards.

As the students continued to draw, Lichty wandered back toward the sinks, where he clapped his hands. "That reminds me." He pointed to a sketch next to the window. "Did anyone of you do this drawing Adam pinned up? If so, I'd like to speak to you after class."

Keeping her face absolutely still, Lila's eyes shifted enough to see Lichty pointing to her black widow spider drawing. Adam taped it to the wall. In spite of everything, a little thrill shot through her body. She wondered what Lichty wanted. To punish her because he could somehow sense she'd used pilfered supplies, maybe.

Unless Adam told. No, Adam wouldn't tell.

Where was he?

She couldn't help herself. "Has anyone seen Adam today?" she asked.

"Model does not speak!" boomed Lichty.

The students, if they responded at all, answered in shrugs and uninterested frowns. What did they care about the paint-sensitive senior with the lopsided glasses and the one-way ticket to New York City?

"I have to admit I was wondering the same thing myself." Lichty peered out the window and down to the courtyard. "In nearly four years, he's never missed a class."

An image of Adam lying faceup on the porn shop door-mat, newsprint-covered windows behind him, appeared on the ceiling, first in grainy pixels, then in distressing clarity. His glasses had been knocked clear over to the Laundromat, as useless to him now as the twenty-dollar bill she'd rammed into his pocket. The killer's knife had pricked Adam's chest and sliced it open, nicking the medicine bottle on the way down. The dark green of the tincture then mixed with the deep red of his blood, and it was a case of mixing opposite colors on the color wheel. What resulted would be a dead neutral. Color theory in action.

She was accessory to a murder. And there were thirty minutes of naked left before she could do a thing about it.

Once the bell rang and the students began packing up and trickling out into the hall, Lila jumped off the gurney and hurried into the changing stall to dress. She had to go looking for Adam. But before driving out to his place, she'd cruise past the parking lot and look for signs of a struggle. Pools of neutral fluids dried to near black by the morning sun. As she swung her backpack over one shoulder, she passed Lichty's desk and remembered the spider drawing. She paused.

Clearly annoyed, the man ignored her, kept grading assignments from another class.

"Sir?"

"Mm?"

"It was me."

"I've no time for cryptic communication, Miss Mack. Please decipher."

"The drawing you mentioned. It's mine."

He looked up, silent. After glancing from her face to the spider and back again, he dropped his red pen and intertwined his fingers while Lila prepared for security to arrive and oust her from the building for using school supplies. "It's very good," he said.

"Thank you."

"How long have you been drawing?"

She shrugged. "Ever since. Always."

"Any formal instruction?"

She shook her head.

Leaning back in his chair, he considered the sketch again, squinting into the late-afternoon sun. "Strangely enough, I see why you excel at modeling. You understand form, you understand how to see. Do you have a portfolio?"

No. She didn't. Nor did she have more than two or three lousy pieces of art to show for herself, with her tendency to destroy each piece as fast as she created it. And damned if, just last night, she hadn't destroyed her very favorite. "Yes."

"Bring it in next class. I'd like to see it." Packing his papers into his valise, he stood up and pulled on his cardigan. "We've had a scholarship mix-up and you may wind up a contender."

Scholarship. It was too much to hope for.

"Sir?"

He spun around, still buttoning.

"I'll need more time. To get things ready."

"How much more time, Miss Mack? An artist should be ready when opportunity knocks."

"I can have it ready in two weeks."

Eighteen

Victor lay in the tub trying to drain the now lukewarm bath-water by pressing the lever beneath the faucet with his big toe. He didn't know how long he'd been submerged, only that his digits had started to wizen, the once steamy water had assumed his own body temperature, and he needed out.

Then again, maybe he didn't.

He knew this day would come. He'd known that from the start. His goal had never been to keep Lila from her mother forever. More to keep her mother from Lila until the child was old enough to be safe.

That much he'd accomplished.

The move was always going to lead to this. Someday he would be found out. But he'd imagined himself reacting differently. Self-righteous. Angry. Telling his daughter he had no choice. That she wasn't safe with her mother. That he did it for her.

Only, he didn't do it for Lila. He did it for himself.

What he hadn't anticipated was the look on Lila's face when she asked—how could he? How could he tell her Elisabeth didn't want her?

Nor did he have an answer. All he had was shame. Remorse. Exhaustion.

And Elisabeth. He didn't need to see her to know he'd broken her. Time after time he'd imagined himself in the position of left-behind parent. It had been the theme of many nightmares. Even in his own nocturnal productions, Victor didn't suffer the loss as valiantly as Elisabeth. The very fact that she had survived proved it. She was the bigger man.

It was easy now that Lila had grown up so strong and beautiful, so safe, to assume Victor didn't have to do what he did. That he could have handled things in a more traditional, if not more lawful, manner. But that was all hindsight, and hindsight wasn't just twenty-twenty. Hindsight wrapped everything in sunshine. It got in your eyes and made a positive outcome appear inevitable all along. Made any impulsive move appear outlandish.

Victor knew, to his waterlogged toes, things might have turned out different. As sorry as he was for the pain he'd caused Elisabeth, Lila, he wouldn't erase his actions.

Except for one. It was their first night in California. They were still down in Anaheim, wandering around the never-ending Disneyland parking lot looking for the rental car and Delilah—it would be another few days before she would become Lila Mack—trailed behind him, still working on an enormous lollipop made of spiraled, multicolored rope candy. She'd asked if they could call her mother when they got back to the motel room. Because Elisabeth worries, she pointed out.

"She does, does she?" Victor had tried to keep the irritation out of his voice. His ex-wife didn't like *not* having Delilah around. Yet she was perfectly fine with Victor not having her.

"Can we call her when we get to the motel, Dad?"

"It's too late back east. After one in the morning."

"But I want to tell her about Pirates of the Caribbean. All the fireflies."

"Your mother's fast asleep by now."

"She won't mind if we wake her up for fireflies. And she's going to worry I'll miss school on Monday. We should tell her I won't."

He marched to the end of the row of vehicles and found himself completely disoriented, staring out at the sea of cars, SUVs, and minivans, most of which had out-of-state license plates. They'd gone too far. They were in the Kanga section. Eeyore was what they needed. Taking Delilah's hand, he started back the way they came. "I was thinking we could stay on in California for a while."

"I don't want to. I hate it here." She trotted behind him, pulling her lollipop out of her tangled hair. Her eyes were so enormous, her face so young. "There're no fireflies."

He stopped, irritated. "You just said you wanted to call about the fireflies."

"Those were fake. I mean no real ones."

"I'm sure the real fireflies have better things to do on a Saturday evening than hang around an amusement park. I'm sure there are plenty of real ones if you know where to look."

"Like where? Where are the real ones?"

The night was hot and his button-down shirt was glued to his back and the burger he'd wolfed down earlier was howling in his belly. Worse, much worse, was the stress of what he'd done, the guilt, the fear all day that the police would be waiting at the next cotton candy cart. The way every woman inside the park with coppery-red hair had morphed into Elisabeth, and he kept smelling her perfume. Kept hearing the thin wail of sirens in the distance. Who would think Anaheim would have so many sirens? It made him snap. "I have no idea off the top of my head. Maybe in people's backyards or in the mountains by the lakes. It's not exactly a thing I've spent much time researching!"

A battered pickup truck full of rowdy teens careened down the aisle and he pulled Delilah close to his legs as it passed.

"I didn't see any fireflies at the motel," she whispered.

"It was afternoon when we checked in," he said, spinning around and searching for Eeyore's hangdog face. "Who sees fireflies in the afternoon?"

"I would." Delilah wrapped her lips around her sucker and sobbed. "I would see them if I was home. If I really tried."

How could he have done it? How could he have lost his patience at the very moment she needed his support?

"That's it," he'd roared. "Not another word about fireflies. We've just had a wonderful day at Disneyland. Do you know how lucky you are? Do you know other kids would kill to come here? Everyone loves California, the beach, the hills, the weather. They had three hundred forty-five days without rain last year. Do you think that happens at home?"

There. The Eeyore sign. Victor picked up his daughter and walked toward it. "Your mother needs a break. She's starting art school and needs some time to herself. I said I'd help out by taking you off her hands. Pardon me if I thought you'd appreciate it."

Her hair, tears, blew straight back in the warm wind. "She doesn't want me?"

Victor stopped, stood still for a moment and despised himself for taking his stress out on Delilah. "Now that's not what I said. A break is what I said."

"How long?"

"We'll see."

Slower now, he walked toward the rental car, the red metallic paint of which twinkled beneath the lamppost. He opened the back door and buckled her in, squeezed her knee awkwardly. "I know it's not what you expected, but we're going to have a great time together here. I've landed a new job—one where I stand to make a lot of money. I'm going to make things good for us here. Trust me."

Delilah had set her head back against the seat and yawned. He would never forget the look of utter faith in her eyes when she whispered, "I trust you, Daddy."

Now, suspended in the cloudy bathwater, he couldn't think of one good reason such a father should live. Inch by inch, he allowed himself to sink beneath the surface, holding his breath and staring up at the world that throbbed and drifted above his face. He could see a wash of pink wall tiles, a rippling mass of gray that was the cheap plastic shower curtain he'd been meaning to replace. But what mostly drew his eye was the undulating square window of blue sky that dazzled and danced before him. Fate looking in at him, cheering him on. Perhaps even nudging Death as if to say, "This fool is yours now. Enjoy."

He could hear nothing but the muffled squeak of his own worn-out body parts shifting against the enamel. About half a minute passed and the need for air took over. He fought it, feeling the pressure in his chest and head build.

There was no reason to keep going. He was of no use to anyone. If anything, his presence butchered Lila's life even further.

Pressure turned to pain. His fingertips tingled. His field of vision began to narrow. This was it. It was right and just. The turbid end to a turbid existence. Lila would not have to wonder how to move forward with such a father. What kind of life to remake with this monster of a man.

He'd never told her she was right about the fireflies. Once they were settled in the cabin and he started working at RoyalCrest, he'd asked around. Not one person had seen a single firefly in California. Eventually Lila had stopped looking. It was as if she had forgotten she'd ever seen one at all.

Searing pain in his lungs as a few bubbles escaped his nose.

Lila.

She would come home to find him lifeless and swollen in the tub. She would scream, pull him out, soaking her boots with his bathwater and postmortem release of bodily fluids. Shaking, she would dial 911. Probably lean over and throw up in the toilet—her stomach was never up to much in the face of trauma.

With a mighty gasp, he burst up to sitting, water streaming from his nose and face. He coughed and gagged. Blindly, he reached for a towel and came up with nothing but a washcloth. He used it to wipe his face, then sat very still.

The room grew marginally dimmer as thin clouds

passed over the sun. He could just imagine Fate rolling its eyes, shaking its head. Things had looked so good there for a moment.

After several painful near misses, Victor's wet toe finally took purchase on the shiny lever and nudged it downward. A belch, a glug, and a gurgle, and the murky water began to lower.

From outside the bathroom door, silence thundered. There was the rattle and hum of the dryer, the sound of a car idling somewhere up the street, and the tick of the wall clock in the kitchen.

He would never, from this moment forward, do anything else to pain his baby girl. His every breath, every moment of lucidity, would be toward restitution.

Nineteen

South Pomona was a steep, winding road, snarled and matted overhead by weeping gum trees. And even though number 3414 was close to the bottom where the bungalows were more modest, the road was still vertical enough that when Lila parked, she turned the steering wheel sharply away from the curb to direct the backs of the tires into the sidewalk. She tugged on the parking brake for good measure, but as she reached for the door, the vehicle began to creep backward. The car had popped out of gear and rolled toward the curb. Again, she shifted into first, only to have the gear pop and the car thump against the curb.

Clearly, the nosedive into the porn shop parking lot had rumpled the car's innards. Victor would go ballistic if he found out.

She couldn't trust an eight-inch curb to hold the car on such an incline. The only solution was to park perpendicular to the road, so she backed the car across the street and pulled into Adam's gravel driveway and, ducking under the vines that hung down from the trees like cobwebs, headed to the front door with hopes of finding him alive.

The house was one of those quaint 1920s Hollywood bungalows—the kind with arched doorways and window frames painted navy blue or apple green, and Spanish tile on the porch. The trees and bushes and roses barely survived one another, intertwined and choked as they were from decades of fighting for attention. No sounds came from inside the house, other than maybe a parakeet chirping from a back room. She rang the doorbell and waited, reaching down to pat a brown cat—this one complete with fur—that appeared from the nearest garden and wound itself around her calves.

Finally a shuffling came from behind the wooden door, locks swished and clicked, and the door swung open to reveal Adam in a holey T-shirt, little boy pajama bottoms with dirt-stained knees, and a striped bathrobe that appeared to be a favorite scratching surface of the cat, who shot past Adam's feet and disappeared down a hallway. Adam's nose was puffy and purple, phthalo violet, to be exact. He blinked as if it hurt. God, he *had* been beaten up.

"Hey," he said with a grunt.

"Hi!" She forced an unnatural brightness into her voice. "Missed you at class today."

He pulled an oily paint rag out of his pocket and wiped his forehead with it. His glasses were knocked sideways in the process and he pushed them up with his index finger, then chugged from his NyQuil.

"So look at you. You clearly got yourself home okay."

"Got home. Not sure about the okay part."

"Seriously? You look good. Really good."

"Hangover."

She closed her eyes in relief. She hadn't nearly killed him after all. "The NyQuil's got to help with that."

He made a face as if she were insane to expect such miracles. "It's one little bottle."

"Yeah, but what a bottle, right?"

He turned around and disappeared, leaving the door open. Unsure what to do, she stepped inside and followed him through a navy dining room, then a kitchen as small as a cookie, to a sunken, glassed-in room at the back. It resembled a summer porch with white beadboard ceilings, a heavy overhead fan, and French doors he kept open to the yard. Maybe so the cat could wander in and out as it pleased.

The sunlight was dazzling back here, it bounced off the white windowsills and gritty plank floor. Painted canvases lined the walls, the floors, in some places three canvases thick. Two easels held half-finished works in acrylic, and an enormous oil painting leaned against the inner wall, completely blocking the doorway to another room. This one was of a nude female—a woman with long, lanky limbs and pixie-short blond hair—leaning against a glassed doorway and smiling at something. Someone. At dawn or dusk, from the look of the furry blue shadows and grainy, barely there light. Actually . . . Lila looked from the French doors back to the painting. It appeared to have been done in this very room.

She was Lila's polar opposite. Tanned to Lila's pale. Dainty to Lila's awkward. This woman's assuredness was absolute, where Lila's was nonexistent. Not only that, but she probably had an identity that wasn't purchased from the trunk of someone's car.

"She's stunning," Lila said.

He glanced up at it, then away. "Yeah."

"A model from school?"

"Nah. Just my ex. Excuse me a minute? I'll put on some clothes." He padded down the hall.

His ex? She looked like she could grace the cover of a magazine. Hard to imagine a girl like that with Adam Harding. She looked like someone you'd see on a yacht in Nice, all athletic and carefree with her arms flung over the shoulders of George Clooney.

Coming into Adam's workspace had been a mistake, she could see that now. Not only did she not come close to measuring up to the girl in the painting, but his studio made envy bubbled up her esophagus like bile. There was no dirt floor, no washing machine that only ran a permanent-press cycle, no dryer that screeched when tumbling a full load, no buzzing fluorescent bulb, no sound of footsteps thumping from above. And though she couldn't know for certain, probably no subterranean silverfish that snaked across his feet while he worked.

"This is my latest," he said. She spun around to see he'd returned, still barefoot but wearing faded Levi's and a white T-shirt, his hair and face damp and smelling like Ivory soap. Standing on a paint-spattered drop sheet, he pointed toward a sky blue canvas taller than he was; a piece depicting empty window frames that floated in the air without context, each one farther in the distance until the one at the center, the tiniest one, had blackness where the glass panes would have been. "I'm not quite done," he motioned to the upper-right corner. "But almost."

Lila didn't love it right away. Though somewhere deep inside, she suspected her judgment was born of envy. "Nice."

"There's this designer who needs some art for her lobby. Nothing too out there, you know? More like nudes that are not too overt. Some sort of ironic statement for her denim line. She's a friend of my sister's. Ever heard of Norma Reeves?"

Lila felt her eyes widen. "You're going to sell to her?"

"If she's crazy enough to like my work. Hey, you should come with me to the meeting. Slip a piece of your own into my shipping crate and see if she wants it."

"Is this another ploy to get me to paint you naked?"

He sucked from his medicine bottle again. "Or if you want to pose for me, that'd be cool too. Doesn't seem right to ask my sister to strip down."

"You should sell the designer your ex-girlfriend over there."

"No. That's being picked up this aft. You want to help me wrap it?" When Lila didn't object, he gathered a huge spool of brown paper and a roll of shipping tape and motioned for Lila to help him lay the painting out on the floor. "Her brother's coming for it in his pickup. This was my surprise engagement gift to her, believe it or not. I painted it from a photograph I took early one morning."

She stared at the girl's face as she held up the top of the painting so Adam could roll out the spool beneath the frame. "What's her name?"

"Nikki." He pulled paper across her face and secured it with tape, then motioned for Lila to scoot down to the other end of the canvas while they repeated the procedure on her feet. "Nikki Ireland. She's a business major over at Connelly."

Her father must be proud, Lila didn't say. All that remained of Nikki was her torso: full breasts, soft belly, and a whisper of blond pubic hair where modesty had her legs crossed tight. "So what happened?"

He sat back on his knees. "You really want to hear this? I know you're not big on sharing."

She rolled the paper across what remained of Nikki's lower half, leaving nothing but pale nipples exposed. It seemed rude to stare, and Lila worked hard to tape down the paper without looking. "I do." There was no way Adam walked away from a girl this beautiful.

"We'd been engaged a month, living together in her apartment for nearly a year. It was last May and I was supposed to be at school. She'd been out a lot in recent weeks, but that didn't strike me as too weird. There was this guy at Connelly—fancy kind of guy. The type that wears these pastel dress shirts, even to school. You know, tangerine-striped button-downs that he always tucked into ironed jeans."

She nodded. Sounded like something Victor would have worn if he were twenty years younger.

"Anyway, I wasn't feeling great—some kind of stomach bug—and I left school early. Only I couldn't get into the apartment. Door was locked from the inside. Then I saw the tasseled loafers beside her sandals on the mat in the hallway. She was tidy like that; didn't want 'the streets of Los Angeles' on her kitchen floor. I knocked and knocked, but she couldn't hear me." He paused to lay a sheet of paper over Nikki's nipples, then looked up. "The AC unit is in the bedroom. You can't hear the front door from there."

"Ouch."

"Yeah. I moved out that night and he moved in three weeks later."

Together, they taped down the last sheet of paper and he asked if she would help haul the painting to the front door. As they shuffled along the dim hallway, straining under the weight, Lila asked, "Do you love her still?"

He kicked the front door open with his foot and they set the enormous parcel down on the porch, leaned it against the house. "I'd cut off my hands to have her back." Dropping onto the porch rail, he folded his arms across his chest and stared at Lila. "I told you mine—you tell me yours."

Behind him, at the edge of the yard, was a rock garden. Cheery black-eyed Susans and pulpy sedum sprung up in clusters around large stones. The garden had just been watered; a hose lay limp on the dried-out lawn and the flower heads were still heavy with shining droplets. At the flowers' feet, beside the hose, lay a hefty pile of freshly pulled weeds. There was an old sign on the fence behind the garden, partially obscured by a shrub that had grown through the pickets from the neighbor's side. She leaned to the right and saw it read DEEDEE'S GARDEN.

Lila thought back to Adam's mud-stained pajama bottoms.

Even in his state, he'd been tending his mother's garden.

Because a child without a mother hangs on to whatever remains. The spiky armor of the weeds might puncture your flesh, the hair dye might sting your scalp, but that wasn't real pain. It was proof your mother used to exist, and amounted to nothing compared to her absence. A paper cut versus a severed limb.

She reached for his hand and turned it over. His palm was scratched and dotted with tiny red sores. Barely making contact with his skin, she traced around his wounds with her finger, then took a tissue from her pocket and pressed it over the cuts.

"Did you wash these out?"

"Yes."

"Sometimes the prickles get in beneath the surface. You have to scrub them good."

He nodded.

Still holding his hand, she pulled him down to the welcome mat where she arranged herself in front of him, cross-legged, her knees nearly touching his. With her eyes cast down at her scribbled boots, she told him. About the move. About the barbershop. About growing up believing her mother didn't want her. Learning she did. Her father's refusal to explain the abduction.

As Lila spoke, she felt herself lighten. The sensation was dramatic. As if she were being bled of the murky, leaden fluid, the liquid wretchedness, that had weighed her down far too long, and now her body could take flight. Levitate into the air, as if wearing her fairy wings again, and get tangled in the overhead branches. She found herself grasping Adam's bare foot, lest the weightlessness take her away from his soft presence for even a second.

Finally, she stopped speaking and looked up. His eyes were still bloodshot, but the brightness of the sky and the whiteness of his shirt made the pattern of his irises as clear and intricate as kaleidoscopes. It was impossible to look away.

She wasn't sure what to expect from him—maybe a lame joke to cut the tension or maybe the requisite platitudes. Something like, "It'll all work itself out. You'll see." Perhaps a bit of wondering out loud about what kind of person her father might be or insistence that he was sorry for what she was going through.

But Adam did none of these things. To her relief, he placed his hands on either side of her face, pressed his forehead to hers, and said nothing at all.

Twenty

The trouble with California was that it wasn't level. Victor stood back, squinting into the early-October glare, and evaluated his progress. Ten wooden posts, the kind you'd use to stake your tomatoes, stared back at him, arranged in a largish, sloped rectangle beneath a shade tree. It hadn't been easy to hammer them into the rain-starved hillside, that was for bloody certain. Like spearing a boulder with a toothpick. He'd never built a fence before, but the plan was to set up the posts, join them with horizontal slats, then wrap the interior with chicken wire. Problem was, in trying to find a good place to sink his posts on the downward incline, he'd set some of them too far apart. His slats were too short to reach from one post to the next.

After repositioning the errant posts and affixing the slats, after testing the entire structure for strength, after installing his rudimentary gate, Victor leaned over, careful to press his tie to his shirt, and dug through his toolbox for his staple gun. Assured it was loaded, he took the roll of wire and stapled it to his first post. Nasty business, he soon discovered. The force of the staple gun dislodged a few of his stakes, and the edge of the chicken wire cut into his hands. Besides that, tiny jagged rocks and tough scrubby grass dug into his knees.

Some forty-five minutes later, he stood up, wiped off his trousers, and blotted his brow with his tie. It was an ancient Pierre Cardin with a herringbone pattern he'd never liked anyway. Made him dizzy. His white shirt clung to his wet back, and he desperately needed a glass of water. But, looking down upon his handiwork, he felt a rush of pride. The thigh-high pen might be a bit crude in its craftsmanship, and it might be lacking in finishing touches like fence caps and a gate that actually hung straight, but it would serve its purpose. It would keep a dog in and, with any luck, predators out.

He was ready. He'd called to check what day the manager was off. Fridays. And now that he knew what was expected of him—a little charade where he pretends to debate his commitment to raising a pet—now that he had a safe pen, he shouldn't have any problem heading back down the road and bringing home his puppy.

But not today. Had to be a Friday.

A flash of movement next door caught his eye. Someone, a woman, was bent over a table in the backyard. He'd never seen her before. Must be the new neighbor. Nothing too stylish about her bare feet, sleeveless tan blouse, and garish-looking skirt.

She marched toward the back door, vanished for a bit,

then came back out with what appeared to be a plate of food. She set it down on the table and peered out at the scrubby hillside as if a few dozen dinner guests might be hidden in the prickly brush. Once or twice she paused to adjust her visor or swat away a fly, but mainly she remained focused on the vegetation.

There was something commanding about her movements that attracted him. Made him picture her fussing over the dinner table at Thanksgiving, good-naturedly slapping at little hands—or big ones—that reached out to grab a sliver of hot turkey. The image made him smile.

She sighed and removed her visor, tossing it on the table. Then, as if someone might be watching, she ran one hand over her smooth brown hair, held back by a clip.

Victor frowned, picking his way across his property to get a better look. Could it be? He climbed the weedy knoll that led up to her yard, careful to lean over and brace himself against the ground as he went. As he got closer, he broke into a smile.

Gen.

Hiding himself behind a screen of dying tree trunks, Victor gave himself a good dusting off. He tucked in his shirt and rolled his sleeves up to hide the dirt stains, then spat in one hand and ran it over his trim beard. With pounding heart, he steadied himself and tried to think of what to say. Comment on her new home, perhaps. Or ask about things back at . . . what was the name of that place?

He could see through the twigs that she was leaned over now, making kissing sounds and waving something in the air. He stepped out of the brush and onto the edge of her yard, stopping for a moment to pick a handful of yellow wildflowers swaying at his feet. As he gathered them into a pleasing arrangement, he saw an animal emerge from the bushes.

It was a coyote.

Victor stepped forward, "Watch it there!"

Without turning, she shushed him. "Quiet! You'll scare him." She got down on one knee and held out what appeared to be a steak bone. Kiss kiss went her lips.

He watched as the coyote—the scrappy one who got into everyone's trash, his back grizzled with silver as if he were part of the dusty earth, his nose too small and his ears too large—wove back and forth in an effort to get close to the meat without getting close to the woman. He kept his black-tipped tail low against his hocks as if anticipating disaster.

"I think you should get inside," said Victor. "That's a wild animal."

"Shh!"

The coyote stepped into the yard now, slinking lower as if crawling beneath a city bus. As thin as he was, his coat gleamed with health. His yellow eyes were intent on the offering as he inched closer, lost his nerve and raced back to the bush, then crept close again.

"Here, sweet thing," said Gen. "Come baby." Without taking her eyes off the animal, she called out, "Justin, you getting this?"

"Yeah."

It wasn't until now Victor noticed a teenage boy on the back deck. He stood perfectly still with a camera pointed toward his mother.

Kiss kiss.

The coyote stopped to consider things, planting his front feet wide and bobbing his head side to side. Then, in a movement so fast Victor barely saw it happen, the coyote darted close, snatched the steak, and loped up the hill and into the brush. The back door slammed shut and the boy and the camera were gone.

The woman spun around, smiling at Victor. "Did you see? What a beautiful animal!"

Staring at the close-set brown eyes, the upturned nose, the chin so sharp it threatened to pierce the skin, Victor's spirits sank. This wasn't Gen at all. Not even close. A blue jay cried from somewhere behind him, and he realized it was his turn to speak.

Instead, Victor started back to his own yard. He threw down the flowers and called back. "You might want to clear away the dead brush at the edge of your property. It's a goddamned fire hazard."

THE PHONE WAS ringing when he stepped into the kitchen where Lila sat eating tuna salad, scraping the metal bowl with her fork as she scooped up each mouthful. He shot her a look that reprimanded her for not jumping up to answer it—blasted thing hung on the wall just above her head—and she motioned toward her food. Victor snatched up the receiver. "Yes?"

"Is this Victor Mack?"

"It is."

"Bob Rittenberg here from Air King Heating and Cooling. I'm calling about the résumé you sent in."

Lila's boot began tapping against the table leg. Victor nudged her, pointed toward the phone, and held a finger to his lips to shush her. "Oh, yes."

"Are you free to come in for an interview? We're looking for a senior sales rep for the Valley and you seem to have a good deal of experience."

"Senior sales rep you say?"

"That's right. I'm going out of town for a few weeks, but does two o'clock on the thirtieth work for you?"

"Just a minute, let me check." Victor pressed the receiver to his stomach and waited a full minute before returning it to his ear. "No. I don't think I can make it." He didn't need to look up. He felt his daughter's shocked stare boring through the back of his head.

"Oh. Okay then. We have a district meeting on Monday, so that's out. What about the Tuesday following? The seventh."

"I don't think so. But thank you for your interest." He hung up the phone and leaned against the wall.

"They had a job for you?"

"They did."

"And you turned it down?"

"I did."

"Is there something wrong with this employer? Like they pay their staff in mittens? Or their units are built by seven-year-olds chained to fire hydrants in Pasadena?"

"Air King is a perfectly reputable outfit. I am simply choosing not to go back to work, that's all. I choose to retire."

Lila took a long sip of water, then took her dishes to the sink. "Is this another episode of confusion I should be concerned about? Because I'm not sure the financial arithmetic adds up."

"Adds up fine."

"Because I might not always be around, you know. You can't count on me to support us forever."

Victor couldn't help it. The laugh snuck out. "You finding eventual employment and paying for me in my elder years is not part of my plan, rest assured, my darling Mouse."

She appeared to mull this over. "I might not even live anywhere close. Just so you know. I could wind up with a cat, living in New York."

"I wouldn't advise that. Cat hair is inexorable the way it drifts through the air and works its way into everything. It will demonize these paintings you refuse to show me."

"They have hairless cats just like they have barkless dogs, and I'll show you a painting. Eventually."

"Yes, well. It's the eventually that has me worried. Time passes very quickly and before you know it, everyone your age will have degrees and careers. They'll pass you by and you'll have no real marketable skills. Believe me, I've seen it. And your future—"

"My future?" She shook her head, incredulous. "I don't even have a real past, or a real name—how do you expect me to build myself a future?"

"What are you talking about? You have a name."

"A legal name!"

He sucked on the side of his cheek. "It's legal enough."

She laughed angrily. "Is that what you told yourself when we boarded the plane? That it was legal enough?"

"Don't get glib with me on this. I told you I had my reasons. Is it so impossible to believe I knew what I was doing? That it was for your own good? My God, does everything have to be opened up and examined to death in this world today? Can you not just trust me on this?"

With an exhausted sigh, she dropped her bowl in the sink and stared down at it. "I'm trying—really trying—to be patient here. What I'm asking for is perfectly reasonable. I want your side of the story so I don't wind up hating you for what you did. Mum can't believe the way you're . . ." Lila stopped. Victor's face had drained of its color and he bent forward, leaning on the vinyl chair for support. "What's wrong, Dad?"

"You've spoken to your mother?"

Lila spoke slowly. "*Yes.* I told you. Mum's here in L.A. I saw her the other day, remember?"

"This day . . . I knew it would come."

She watched as he rubbed his jaw, trying to pick his way through the plaque building in his mind. As angry as she was, the confused expression on his face—a look that was appearing more and more frequently—made her feel like weeping for him.

"Dad, you need to see a doctor."

He stared at her. "No doctors."

"But—"

"No doctors!"

His eyes weren't the same when he vanished from his own mind. They became the eyes of an old man. They opened too wide in an effort to see through the neuro-sludge and, in doing so, exposed spidery veins creeping toward the irises. Pink rims. Water that threatened to spill onto his cheeks, perhaps from tear ducts that burst from such desperate attempts to see life clearly again. The glaring light overhead revealed the skin beneath his eyelids to be papery and transparent. Bloated blisters beneath his eyes. His existence had never seemed so fleeting.

As he crossed the room to pull open the curtain, then peer outside and look for the cops, just as he'd done the other day, she walked up behind him, wrapped her arms around his middle, laid her head on his shoulder, and squeezed him with equal parts fury, frustration, and sadness.

God, she was a selfish bitch for what she was thinking.

This gunk that was cruelly coating his brain was not only stealing away her father. If the truth about her past didn't come out soon, it too would be gone forever.

Twenty-One

The end of California summer stretched itself across the early days of October. The hills were baked to brown in most parts, scarred with dusty trails and clogged with bushes so parched they snapped from the stirring of a sparrow's wings. With any luck, if the fires that raged in areas surrounding the city didn't get too greedy, if the Santa Ana winds behaved, if the temperatures cooled down; the hills overlooking L.A. would soon be woken up, slapped on the cheek by their long-awaited friend—the winter rain. Soon, paper-thin blades of grass, in Veronese green no less, would work their way through the trampled tangle of baked straw that covered the hills and the state would once again be rioted with life.

Her mother had been back in her life nearly a week; it had been the best and the worst seven days of Lila's life.

Heaven to luxuriate in having a mother again. Hell to deal with Victor at home while coming up with excuses for his silence. As long as Elisabeth believed the conversation between Lila and Victor was about to happen, she was willing to wait. But the moment she realized her ex-husband-turned-child-abductor was refusing to cooperate would be the moment she dialed 911. The excuses Lila had come up with had grown from reasonable (Dad wasn't home last night) to downright lame (Dad had a bad day; he's feeling a bit fuzzy just now).

Walking along Melrose Avenue, Elisabeth and Lila listened to the sky—usually sleek and silent and blanched to near white, but now dingy brown and cramped with bloat—grumble and belch overhead. It was the way Lila loved the rains to come on, with threats and warnings and days of false starts.

"I hope you didn't mind me stealing away your afternoon," said Elisabeth as she folded up her sunglasses and tucked them into her canvas bag. "It's just that it's been so long, you know? I didn't realize how much I adored waiting for you outside your school until it was gone. Little things like that are the things that really get you."

Lila hadn't touched her mother yet. She'd allowed herself to be touched, hugged, but hadn't had the nerve to reciprocate. Now, seeing the look on Elisabeth's face, she reached over and stroked her mother's cool brown shoulder. It was like touching lightning. Elisabeth looked up. It startled her too.

"It's okay." Lila pushed her hand into her back pocket. "I'm glad you came."

"Me too. Someone stopped to ask me directions to the Wallace Stuckey building. He thought I was a student."

"Or maybe a teacher."

Elisabeth stopped and frowned. "Now why would you say that?"

"No reason. I just . . ."

"There was absolutely none of that sort of submissiveness or reverence—not even the slightest bit—that people use with teachers. I'm certain he thought I was a student."

"You're right. I mean, I'm sure you're right."

"Actually, I wouldn't have minded if he'd asked me out. He was darling."

Lila exhaled rather than laughed.

Elisabeth walked ahead a bit, her gait so smooth she might have been on ice. They came to a pretty shop with peach stucco. VERY DEAR, said the sign. Beneath the smooth arch of the window stood a silver mannequin wearing slim black pants, gleaming ankle boots, and a crisp, white trench coat. Elisabeth sighed as if it were an outfit she'd been eying for months. Who knew? Maybe she had. "Classy, don't you think?"

"Definitely. You'd look good in it. Try it on."

Elisabeth lit a cigarette. "Forget it. You know what 'very dear' means? Very expensive. I'm afraid I'm destined to be a window shopper only." She sucked on the cigarette, then exhaled slowly. "Did you get an answer from your father yet?"

"It's been a crazy week. Soon, though. I promise."

"Has he explained anything at all? I mean, what does he have to say for himself?"

"Not much." Two girls came out of the store, both clutching enormous bags overflowing with silver tissue. Lila moved aside to let them pass. "He's been having these spells. Plus not sleeping. It's been a rough couple of months, actually."

"I wouldn't be surprised if it's Alzheimer's. Early onset."

"That's kind of what I was thinking. But he hates doctors. Refuses to go."

Elisabeth looked at her, amused. "Of course he doesn't go. The man's been surviving on illegal documents for over a decade. If anyone dug into his files too deeply, they'd find out Victor Mack doesn't exist. Have you ever known him to see a doctor?"

"I don't know. Maybe not."

"What about you? Did he take you to doctors?"

Lila ran her fingers along the edge of her shorts. "I've always been healthy."

Elisabeth laughed angrily and sighed. "The lawyer warned me about that. Doctor. Dentist. Eye doctor—we'll need to book them all. Please tell me you're on the pill."

"The pill? I really don't have any need for—"

"Baby, your dad's fudging to buy himself time. He could even be making travel plans. My lawyer is breathing down my neck about this; I really think we need to act now."

"I need a few more days. It's just, it's hard to know what's going on with him right now."

Her mother half laughed, half grunted. Then she shook her head. "I should just hold my tongue. Even with what he's done, I don't want you to get stuck in the middle. I've never wanted to be one of those parents who gains ground with her children by denigrating their fathers. That kind of thing is damaging to young people."

"I guess."

They strolled along once more, this time in silence.

"So tell me more about this psychic," Lila said after a minute or two. "It's wild she told you to come west."

"I met her back in Toronto. Amelia was her name." She rolled her eyes, reddened. "You'll probably think this is crazy."

"No, I want to hear."

Her mother hesitated, still unsure.

"Seriously. I'm into that kind of thing."

"Well, I was just walking up Amelia's driveway—I don't have the gold Mazda anymore. Not with all it cost to look for you. I've been using the subway. Got myself a Metropass and it gets me around well enough. Kind of embarrassing at my age, but that doesn't bother me. Of course, here I had no choice. I leased the little Toyota."

Lila nodded. "What happened with the psychic?"

"Right. I walked up her driveway. She lives just off the Danforth in a narrow place with a shared driveway. Remember? Just like in Cabbagetown. The kind where you knock off your side mirrors every time you back out, but—if I'm going to be honest—hers isn't nearly as charming as ours." She paused and Lila worried the story had gone off-road again. Paranoia from living with Victor in recent days, she supposed. But Elisabeth continued, "So, walking up the driveway, I got to thinking about the way you used to sit on the hot pavement in your shorts and leather sandals and draw all over the driveway with that big fat sidewalk chalk. And how you refused to use the white chalk because it reminded you of school. Then I knocked on the screen door, and the moment Amelia let me in, she said, 'Who's the young girl with the blond hair?' I knew right there to trust whatever she said. And she told me you were out west."

"That's incredible."

"She didn't know where, exactly. But the more she went

on, the more apparent it was that she was seeing palm trees. And hot sun. Never-ending sun, she said."

"She got that right. Other than today."

"Then she said you looked very different. Your dyed hair, I suppose. I figured he'd either have cut it off or colored it. Not exactly necessary, if you think about it; it's not as if I knew to come here before now."

"Are you planning to stay in L.A.?"

"I'd like to." She smiled. "Especially now. But beyond selling the odd painting or sculpture, I'm not really earning anything. It takes me a long time to finish a piece of work these days. I'm not one of those artists who keeps pumping them out."

"No? I always imagined you working away at it."

Elisabeth blushed, touched her throat. "Don't forget the years have been stressful. Some years I managed a watercolor or two, or maybe a small figurine, then other years, well. It's not the number you produce—it's what you sell them for."

"I guess. I just can't imagine not painting all the time. I finish hundreds, I just don't keep them. One day, I like to think, I'll have enough confidence that—"

"To be honest, what I became very good at, and grew to love, were the media interviews. All the activity surrounding your disappearance made your mother something of a star. One time I popped into Pharma Plus for vitamins and caught two older ladies whispering and staring at me. They actually came up to me and said they'd seen me on Citytv. Can you imagine? It was like being a celebrity. I thought for a minute they were going to ask for my autograph."

They strolled past a coffee shop, through the delicious scent of fresh-roasted beans. "But speaking to the press isn't a skill that would translate into many positions, other than maybe newscaster. And I'm too old to start up with that." She turned to her daughter, studying her face. "You could, though. You have the presence, the looks. The camera would love you."

Lila laughed at the suggestion. "I'd be terrible. I'd blurt out the wrong thing. Draw on my clothes."

"Don't be too quick to dismiss it. There's a reason so many people chase fame. It feels damn good to be a celebrity. I'd be lying if I said I didn't miss the attention."

Lila tried to make sense of it. Her mother came to *enjoy* being interviewed about her abducted daughter? And missed the attention once it died away? She supposed it was possible to become so entrenched in the job of looking for someone that it becomes part of your makeup. Even people kept captive could feel anxious or displaced upon their rescue. She'd seen it on TV. "Maybe."

Elisabeth stopped at the corner of a short street called Bitter Cherry Drive and pointed toward a grand two-story Georgian mansion with thick columns stretching from roof to ground. Black shutters flanked massive windows, and vines scrambled up the whitewashed bricks. Iron fencing buffered it from the street, but the imposing gates had been left open. The front yard was a gravel courtyard lined with riots of trees and tropical shrubs.

"Wow," said Lila. "Nice place."

"It's not mine. Belongs to a friend I met when we first arrived. It's converted to apartments inside; the rooms are mostly rented out to artists. There's a photographer and a few students. Worth about four million, if you can believe it."

They walked into the courtyard, gravel crunching beneath their feet. "Incredible."

"I have a little deal with the landlord. I get half-price rent in exchange for art lessons. He's a very talented individual, but he's struggling a bit with his creativity. We think working in another medium might be just the jolt his subconscious needs. What he doesn't know is he could also use the sort of stability a female brings."

"So you're dating?"

"Not for now. But we'll see. I would definitely consider it." She pointed toward a pond in the center of the courtyard, where a concrete statue held an urn on one shoulder. "The fountain comes on after dark. It's set up on a timer."

"Pretty glamorous place to live."

"I suppose so."

Elisabeth pointed to a tree at the far edge of the property. "It grows oranges. Kieran loves picking them, but I never let her eat them. Nothing serious, but her hands break out in these tiny red bumps. The itching makes her crazy and I refuse to use those corticosteroid creams on a child. On myself either. People are always looking for that quick fix. Well, I never used that stuff with you, not even with the eczema you used to get each winter. No, it was oatmeal paste for Delilah Blue and it's oatmeal paste for Kieran Scarlett."

Lila imagined, rather than remembered, her mother standing at the kitchen counter of the Toronto house, stirring oatmeal in one of the deep cobalt bowls from her childhood. "Must be why I love oatmeal."

Elisabeth's face broke into a smile. She linked her arm through her daughter's and led the way toward the house. "Come. Let's go upstairs."

THE INSIDE OF her place had the sorrowful stillness of an apartment that had sat empty for too long. One that had seen too many residents come and go to waste any energy on absorbing the personality of any particular person. The curtains were gathered so tight that they seemed more intent on keeping in the dark rather than blocking out the light, and the minimalist futon-sofa-and-black-TV-stand decor allowed the stains on the battered carpet to become the only real focal point in the room. If Lila had hoped to gain any insight into whom her mother had become in the years since they'd parted, it wasn't going to come from this lifeless space.

"The furniture came with it." Elisabeth yanked back the curtains. "Amelia said I wouldn't be here long, which gave me such hope. Of course, now I hope she's wrong because I don't want us to be apart." Staring at Lila, Elisabeth set her hands on her hips. "Now what can I get you? A cup of tea?"

Lila nodded. "I haven't had tea in years." It was so different with Elisabeth. So easy. With Victor, she had to fight for her place as child of the family. He had always needed his daughter to pick up grapefruit juice from the store, top up his scotch, soothe irate neighbors who found notes on their cars. With Elisabeth, she could just stand back and let her mother be the parent. Take Lila for breakfasts on Sunset, brew her tea. It felt delicious.

She followed her mother and dropped into one of two vinyl chairs squeezed into what was probably not meant to be an eat-in kitchen. Just as she kicked off her boots, settled back in her chair, and tucked her feet beneath her, Lila felt a small, demanding presence. She turned to find Kieran standing, calm and silent, right behind her. "Kieran! Where did you come from?"

"From the babysitter."

"Just across the hall," said Elisabeth. "Works out well because Kieran can run home as soon as she hears our door thump shut."

Kieran blinked. "I go there after school some days."

Lila looked down at the girl's outfit. Same as at the restaurant: trim white blouse, pleated skirt, kneesocks, and oxford shoes. "Must be some fancy school."

"Just the local public school," said Elisabeth as she set the kettle on the stovetop. "That's just Kieran's way of expressing herself, right Kiki?"

The girl ignored her, opening up the pantry and pulling out three yellow mugs that she set on the table. She pried the lid off a striped ceramic jar and plunked tea bags in two of the mugs. Then, making little clicking sounds with her tongue, she took a carton of milk from the fridge and filled the third mug. After setting the carton in the middle of the table, she sat and stared at it. Quickly, she looked at Lila. "Do you take milk in your tea?"

"Yes."

"My mummy does too."

Lila couldn't help herself. Having Elisabeth back was still so fresh. *"Our."*

Kieran scrunched her nose.

"Our mummy. She's my mother too."

The moment Elisabeth sat down the kettle whistled, so Lila got up, wrapped a tea towel around the hot metal, carried it to the table, and filled two of the mugs with hot water.

Kieran jumped up to pour the milk, then held up the milk carton and waggled it back and forth. "Empty."

Elisabeth said. "All right. Just be sure to rinse it out a few times. There's nothing worse than the smell of old milk."

Kieran dragged her stool to the sink. Just as she started to climb up, Elisabeth stopped her. "Just a minute, young lady. Finish that glass of milk so I know you didn't empty the carton on purpose."

Reluctantly, Kieran climbed down and drained the glass in one gulp, then went back to rinsing her carton, careful not to soak her shirtsleeves. After emptying it of water, she set it on the counter. "Will you play hide-and-seek with me, Delilah?"

"Umm . . ." Lila looked to her mother for assistance. The last thing she wanted was to waste precious mother-daughter moments playing with Kieran. But Elisabeth just laughed. "Kiki loves her hide-and-seek."

"Okay," said Lila, sipping from her tea. "You hide, I count."

"Promise you won't forget to come look for me? Mummy always forgets."

"Cross my heart. Now go. One. Two. Three . . ."

When Kieran left the room, Elisabeth's eyes flashed with the wiliness of a teenager whose parents had just left for an out-of-town weekend, and she nodded for Lila to follow her into the living room with her teacup. She wandered over to the open window and perched herself on the sill, setting down her cup, striking a match, and holding it to the end of a cigarette. Lila watch the tip burn red as Elisabeth inhaled deeply. "I never get a minute to myself." She exhaled out into the afternoon air. "I'm not complaining. I never complain, not after what I've been through."

Lila adored the moment. She and her mother, coconspirators, sharing confessions in the soft afternoon breeze. She reached for Elisabeth's cigarettes and raised one brow.

"You smoke?" Elisabeth's expression was one more of pleasure than surprise.

"Only on special occasions."

Her mother grinned, holding the match while her daughter sucked on the filter. Lila blew clumsy smoke rings through the screen, watching them break apart, hover unsteadily a moment, then vanish.

"Remember my sister? Your auntie Kathleen? And her sons, Jeremy and Clayton?"

Lila nodded.

"They've e-mailed letters for you. I think those kids missed you almost as much as I did. They're all planning to come out here in a couple of months. We'll have a bit of a reunion. Grandma, of course, is gone. But my brother Trevor and his new wife will come. And one of my aunts. You're finally going to have family."

"Wow."

"My one wish was that my mother would live to see you again. But I like to think she's looking down now, cheering and waving." Elisabeth hugged one knee to her chest, her bare foot propped on the ledge revealing toes painted a sultry red. The inside ledge was blackened with small burn marks. "Actually, knowing Mum, she'd be waving to the police, pointing out the way to your father's house."

A hornet landed on the screen and, feelers searching, crawled over to the edge where the dirty aluminum frame met the mortar surrounding the window. After feeling his way along the edge, he located a slender gap and tucked himself inside. Moments later, two smaller hornets emerged and flew away. When Victor and Lila had moved into the cabin, there'd been a huge wasp nest under the eaves.

They'd discovered it only when wasps started flying out of one corner where the wall didn't quite meet the ceiling. Victor had come home with four cans of insect spray and, come dusk, when he figured they'd all be inside the nest, Victor emptied them into the attic. The chemical stench had been so bad, they'd had to camp on the back deck for two nights.

"Aw, baby. I can see I've upset you." Elisabeth slid off the sill and took Lila's shoulders in her arms, pulling her tight. "Forgive me. But I believe in justice."

"It's not enough to have me back? I mean, you won in the end. You're the good guy; he's, well . . . He's not looking so good these days."

"Okay. No more of that talk, I promise. We'll deal with it when you're ready. You will be ready, won't you?"

Lila shrugged. "Soon."

"I'm beginning to think I'm ready to confront him. Face-to-face."

Like the police being called, this was inevitable. And no matter how much Lila didn't want to be there when it happened, she would be. With the tension of twelve years to ratchet up the emotions, anything could happen. The only way she could guarantee no bloodshed would be to park herself squarely between her parents with milk and cookies.

"Can you arrange it?'

Here was Elisabeth needing her. Just like at the restaurant when her mother asked her to watch Kieran. Lila rolled this request around in her mouth a bit, savored the precious metal taste of it, before answering. Here was Lila, the remover of robes, the wrecker of cars, the doodler of boots. Queenlike, she need only pick a date, pass it around amongst potential attendees, and all would be there. If she cared to, she could moderate. Set a few ground rules. Dad sits here, in his recliner by the window. Mum sits in the good dining-room chair, the only one whose seat bottom doesn't have any runs in it. Soft music—from *The Big Chill* soundtrack—should thump all sexy and reminiscent from the old speakers. It would be cinematic, this meeting of the parents. Rife with tension, but quirky and adorable at the same time.

Because of her artistic manipulation, because of her understanding that great stories had even greater resolutions with problems being solved, but not too solved, the confrontation would end with a glorious meal. Characters on the floor, barefoot, arms draped over knees in front of dirty plates and uncorked bottles of Shiraz. Laughing through tears. No one would mind the paper cups they drank from, or that Lila was underage—only that this crazy family had found a new way to be.

"Yes," Lila said with a sniff. "I can arrange it."

Kieran stomped into the room, tiny fists pressed into her sides, a look of fury on her face. She pointed at Lila. "This Delilah Blue person forgot all about me."

Lila jumped up. "I'm sorry! Let's try again."

"No."

"This time I'll stay focused, I swear." She turned back to Elisabeth. "Do you mind . . . Mum?"

Elisabeth's face broke into a smile so wide she began to cry. She took a moment to fan her face and sigh before saying, "Oh, Delilah Blue. You've just given me the gift of a lifetime."

Lila grinned, turned to follow Kieran into the kitchen. Kieran checked to make sure her sister was behind her before turning her nose in the air. "It's too late to play now.

I have to make my lunch for school and finish with my milk carton."

"Yeah, what's up with that?"

"Amanda Iaello." Kieran shook out any remaining drips and wrapped her carton in the tea towel. "This was very hard to find."

"What?"

She held it up for Lila to see. The girl on the milk carton. "Missing: Amanda Iaello. Age: eleven. Height: five-foot-one. Weight: ninety-six pounds. Last seen wearing a yellow dress and sneakers." She looked up at Lila. "There are only two milk companies in California that still put kids on cartons, so we have to shop at certain stores."

Lila looked at Elisabeth, who had just padded into the room. "She's keeping that?"

Her mother shrugged. "Show Delilah your friends, Kiki."

Kieran motioned for her sister to follow. The room itself was nothing special. Pale green walls with a vinyl blind. Worn-out carpeting. Sprayed stucco ceiling. No baseboards to speak of. Single bed dressed with sheets undoubtedly made of 100 percent cotton, and two rows of stuffed animals. But on the wall beside the bed was a huge corkboard nearly covered in the faces of missing children cut from milk cartons. Out of four rows of faces, some smiling, some not, two were x-ed out.

Michael William Lee.

Christiana del Toro.

Steff Johnston.

Lindie Suzanne Wyatt-Kress. X.

Joanna Vicenze.

Marsha Elena Jane Gillott.

Frederick and Jackson Burroughs.

Delilah Blue Lovett. X.

It was the most heartbreaking display imaginable for a child. Lila sat on the foot of the bed and stared at the wall. "Jesus, Kieran. Look at them all."

"Forty-three. Minus two."

"Lindie was found too?"

Kieran nodded sadly.

"Alive?"

The child turned away to adjust the blind. "No."

"Why do you do this, Kieran?"

She ignored the question and climbed across her plush toys to point to an empty spot on the board. "This is where I'm going to put Amanda."

Lila reached out and poked her sister playfully in the side. "Ever think of collecting stamps instead?"

The child looked at her as if she'd suggested sleeping on the roof. "What would I want with a bunch of stupid stamps?"

September 16, 1996

It was just over a week after Delilah drank the backwash at the cowboy bar back in Toronto. The house was strangely quiet, nothing but the dryer whirring and ticking from her mother's studio at the back of the house. She began to wonder if racing down the street ahead of the other kids after school had been such a good idea. She despised being alone in the house, especially today. Something creaked in the next room.

"Mum?" she whispered, hardly daring to breathe. She reached for a fire poker, held it up like a sword, and tiptoed toward the kitchen. "Mummy?"

Footsteps. Then a sharp clatter, followed by Elisabeth rounding the corner and nearly tripping over her. "My word, you scared me to death!" shrieked her mother, clutching her chest. "What are you doing, sneaking around with a fire poker? Planning to murder someone?"

"No. I was just . . ."

"You should feel my heart pounding."

"It was Stranger Danger Day at school."

"Ah." Elisabeth pried the poker out of Delilah's hand and set it back against the fireplace. "I can see they frightened you kids to pieces."

Delilah rubbed soot on her jeans.

"Well? What did they tell you?"

She held the pamphlet behind her back. It had been big news at school, but here? She wasn't sure. "Last week they made us all do drawings of strangers," she padded into the kitchen behind her mother and pulled a chocolate cookie out of the tin on the counter. Perching herself on her knees on top of a red vinyl chair, she bit into her cookie, sending crumbs chattering across the table. "It was for this art contest. The best drawing wins and gets on the cover of the stranger booklet. Today they passed out the books and guess whose drawing was on the cover?"

"Whose?" said Elisabeth, eying her daughter with a sly smile.

"Mine!" Delilah held up her winning cover art: an exquisitely detailed rendering of a green monster in a trench coat. Crimped hairs sprung from sinewy legs, polyps and moles decorated sausage fingers, claws stabbed through the toes of great black galoshes. His nose resembled a tent unwisely perched on

top of a precipice, and all four coat pockets bulged with gadgetry an ill-intended stranger might consider fundamental: candy, skipping rope, squirming puppies, smiling princess dolls. Skulking behind the monster was an unmarked van, its side door yawning open like a hungry mouth.

"This is wonderful. They actually picked your drawing?"

"Yup."

"And the teacher didn't help you with it?"

"Nope. Not one bit. I gave my stranger regular ears because Mr. Meade said strangers might look like everyday people." Delilah held her breath as her mother studied it. It was her best drawing ever, she was fairly certain. When Mrs. Bonet, the principal, made the announcement that she'd won, she'd said the winner was "South Toronto Public School's premier artist, Delilah Lovett."

"You really are a very talented girl. I hope you told them your mother is an artist?"

"Um." She scratched the side of her nose. Her mother didn't actually sell her work. Delilah wasn't sure it qualified as a job. "I don't know. I might have forgot."

Elisabeth jerked back, staring at her daughter as if she no longer recognized her. "It would have been the first thing out of my mouth if I were you. Shows you come by your talent honestly. Plus I would think you'd be proud."

"I am. I'm going to tell them tomorrow."

"No. Don't. Telling them tomorrow would be weird. Like I told you to say it."

"You didn't. I'll say you didn't."

"That would be worse."

"Do you like it?" It didn't really matter what a second grader thought, or the principal. The only opinion she really cared about was the one she was about to hear.

"Let's see." Elisabeth sat beside her daughter at the kitchen table where a cup of tea and a cigarette awaited. "Your artwork is certainly advanced. Adult even." She took a thoughtful drag, blew the smoke toward the open window beside her, then pointed toward the outside of the monster's calves. "But if you look at this, the peroneus longus muscle here, there are slight flaws."

Delilah felt the smile slide off her face. No one at school had mentioned flaws.

"You see how you've shaded the outside edge of the muscle? That's fine—you're learning how to make things round, how to give them dimension. But your figure has one foot flexed. One day, when you know more about the body's structure, you'll understand that this muscle here should be bulging because it's at work—it's actually pulling the foot upward. We need our shading to reflect this effort. But you don't need to worry about that yet." She turned to her daughter, who hid clenched fists. "I'm sorry, sweetheart. Did I upset you?"

"No."

Elisabeth rubbed her arm. "It's called constructive criticism, sweetie. That's when someone gives you an honest evaluation. One you can really learn from. And that's far more valuable than empty praise, believe me. You're old enough to understand, aren't you?"

Delilah nodded, watching as her mother opened up the booklet and began flipping through the pages, sipping her tea and commenting on various bits of stranger advice. Asking questions. Delilah wasn't really listening, busy as she was chewing on the inside of her cheek and swallowing the blood pooling on her tongue, wondering how on earth a mother could know so much about monster muscles. And whether it wasn't just a little bit possible for monster muscles to behave differently from human muscles.

Delilah swung her feet from the kitchen chair, letting them hit the table legs in the same beat as the ticktock of the wall clock above her mother's head.

"There's some decent advice in this booklet," said Elisabeth. "Most of it is over the top, but it does say we should come up with a secret code for you, one that only we know. So if anyone tries to pick you up from school, you'll know you're only allowed to go if they know your code."

"I don't get it," said Delilah.

Elisabeth reached behind her to the windowsill and stubbed out her cigarette, waving the smoke out the window. "Like if I were to send a friend to pick you up, you'd know it was okay to leave with that person if she had your secret code. It would mean I gave it to her. Should we pick one? Come on, it'll be fun."

"Okay." Delilah glanced around the room. "Cookie."

"Too boring."

"How about windowsill? Or clock?"

Elisabeth pulled Delilah onto her lap. "I think it should be more special. More distinctive." She tapped the calendar hanging beside the phone. It was a glossy, oversize calendar featuring French Impressionist paintings. September's masterpiece was Paul Cézanne's Three Bathers, *depicting a group of female nudes in a landscape the artist painted in 1875. "Cézanne," said Elisabeth. "No, let's make it two artists. My two favorites. Your secret code will be Monet and Cézanne."*

Delilah slid off Elisabeth's lap and crinkled her nose, unsure. "Monie and Cézanne?"

"Mon-et and Cézanne." She stood up and dumped her tea in the sink. "So we're all set then. Delilah Blue Lovett, what is your top secret code?"

Delilah snatched up her stranger booklet and, holding it under the table, tore off the cover and crinkled it into a ball.

"Sweetheart, what's your secret code?"

She stuffed the crumpled drawing under her leg.

"Monie and Cézanne."

Elisabeth laughed and ran her hand over her daughter's forehead. "That's okay. You'll get it with a little practice." She pulled a pizza from the freezer and set it on the counter with a clunk. "Just remember—don't tell a soul, not even your father. Monet and Cézanne will be our little secret. It'll keep you where you belong. With me."

Twenty-Two

It was mid-October, three days before Lila's portfolio was due. Adam had removed his black glasses for the occasion, left them dangling in the pocket of his shirt—which Lila had not permitted him to take off in spite of his willingness to bare his chest in the middle of Willett Greens, a miniature neighborhood green space that consisted of a couple of benches, a trash can, a water fountain that didn't work, and a rusted swing set. She had, however, allowed his sleeves to be pushed up, providing full exposure of surprisingly brawny forearms. Adam stood on the grass, shaded by a large oak tree, with bare feet spread apart and hands held low, in front of his hips, fingers splayed open to show white palms.

"I've been thinking about your situation," he said over the sound of a car backfiring on the street behind her.

Perched on a collapsible stool, she balanced the art board between her knees and sharpened a pencil with her Swiss Army knife. "You have, have you?"

"You know, with your mom. And your dad. What he did."

"She wants to call in the police. I keep stalling her because he won't tell me what went on. But she won't wait forever, you know? And I do get that." She over-sharpened, breaking off the tip, and started all over again.

"Maybe he's not answering you because he's trying to spare you."

"I don't think so."

"You have proceed carefully. You have to ask yourself if you really want to know what went down." He reached up to swat an insect from his face. "I mean, if I were raped by a pack of French-Alpine goats as an infant, I don't think I need to know."

"I'm pretty certain I wasn't raped by any French-Alpine goats."

He shrugged and said in a high-pitched voice, "Okay."

"What's that supposed to mean?"

"Just that it's your life. Your head in the sand."

"Actually, the head in the sand would be yours. I would be operating with full disclosure. I would know all about the goats. Anyway, I've set up a family meeting. She's coming to the house. They're going to talk. Or scream and yell and pull out knives. But no matter what happens, it's good. I'm going to find out what happened."

"That's major. Are you nervous?"

"Not bad."

"I'd be nervous."

"Yeah, well. Both of them will be there, explaining everything. Even if they fight, as far as I'm concerned, it can only help."

"Sounds like a good time." Whistling softly, he allowed his eyes to follow a couple of kids racing toward the fountain while their nannies followed with plastic wagons.

"Right now the whole thing's so confusing. I mean, you think you know your life. It might suck, but at least you recognize it. Then . . ." Dropping the board to the grass, she leaned her elbows onto her knees. "I can't draw today. This scholarship thing, who am I kidding? It's not going to happen."

He didn't break his pose. "It's my fault. Forget the goats. As far as I know, there is no documented case of gang rape by Alpine goats, at least not in North America. So you're good there."

She allowed herself a smile.

"So here's what you do. If you want this piece of art to really sing, and I believe you do, you want to zero in on the soul in my pose."

"Okay. Go on."

"Figure out where the enchantment lies."

Lila picked up her board, tilted her head and stared at it, trying to ascertain whether she'd shaded properly beneath the brow bones. They didn't look right. When she was finished with the highlight, she set the board on the grass and stood back. Scowling, she dropped back onto her stool. "I'm not seeing it today. I don't know what's wrong with me."

"You're thinking I should remove my pants aren't you? Right here in the park."

"I am *not* thinking about your pants."

Starting to unbuckle, he said, "I'll do it. In the name of your future."

"No! Do not drop your pants in the park!" She started to laugh. "There are children."

He unzipped, grinning and swaying his hips. "Don't think I won't—"

"Adam? Is that you?" a female voice called from behind Lila.

She spun around to see a tall woman with short blond hair being ruffled by the wind. She wore slim pants and a girlish blouse, with expensive-looking tan sandals. Pushing her sunglasses up onto her head, she revealed enormous brown eyes that tilted up at the corners. Eyelashes so long they could have been, but likely weren't, fake. A guy walked up to her, laid his arm over her shoulder.

Adam's face flushed red. "Nikki. Hey. How're you doing?"

She nodded, looked at the guy. "I'm good. We're good." Nikki turned to Lila with raised brows. "I'm sorry, have we met?"

"This is Lila. Lila, Nikki."

When Nikki greeted her, Lila tried to reciprocate but her words came out as silence. Who could speak when confronted by such a whole person. Lila had never encountered someone who exuded such wholeness in her life. Nikki was an oasis to the mirage that was Lila.

Adam looked at Nikki's friend. "Bruce, right? Or is it Brice?"

Bruce or Brice was not impressed. He puffed up his mint green–striped chest. "It's Bruce."

"Right. Right." Adam quickly zipped and buckled, embarrassed. "This wasn't what it looked like. I was just posing and started goofing around." When neither Bruce nor Nikki spoke, Adam cleared his throat. "Lila's putting together a portfolio for a scholarship and, well, you remember, Nik. Sometimes the work doesn't come and you need a distraction. It's not a thing like accounting or whatever. Where the numbers are numbers, and whatever just blew apart in your life they're still going to be the same crappy numbers and you just add them up. Art takes advantage when you're down. Doesn't cooperate and then you *really* feel like shit. Some people say it's therapeutic—and it can be, don't get me wrong—but other times it just kicks you in the groin—"

"Right. I bet." Nikki stepped backward as if Adam might be contagious. "We're actually headed to lunch. Meeting some friends and Bruce only has an hour." She looked at Lila and shot her a sweet smile. "Good luck with the scholarship."

"Thanks."

"Bye, Adam."

"Bye, Nik. Good to see you. No, awesome to see you!" As the couple walked back toward the sidewalk, unhurried, he called out, "Good-bye, Bruce."

As soon as they were gone, Adam crumpled to the ground and buried his face in his hands. "Did you hear me? I think I used the word 'groin.' In my whole life I've never used the word 'groin.' I babbled like a total idiot."

"Not an idiot." She crawled nearer. "A fool maybe. Or a dork. But not an idiot."

"What she must think of me. She must be congratulating herself on the breakup."

Lila pushed hair from his face. "She looked hungry. She's probably just thinking of a big garden salad with some crusty bread."

"I thought I'd be cool when I first saw her, but then she took off the sunglasses and those eyes." He sat up. "Those are incredible eyes—are they not incredible eyes?"

"They are."

"That's what I'm saying."

"But incredible eyes are everywhere. Show me a sensual mouth, then we'll talk striking beauty."

He started nodding, slightly at first, then more emphatically. "Yes. You're right. The mouth is where it's at. And her mouth is really nothing special, is it? Just a mouth. Two lips."

"A garage for her teeth. That's all."

"Right. A garage." He picked at the grass, rolled it in his hands, and tossed it on her boots. "Thanks. Do you want me to get naked now?"

"No." She climbed to her feet. "I think we're done for today."

Twenty-Three

Lichty's back was to the door. He was arguing with someone on the phone, leaning against the plate-glass window while staring down at his shoes. "Yes. Yes. We've been through all this. Those dates don't work for me. I'll be in Chicago at the end of January."

Lila stood in the hall clutching her portfolio, uncertain what to do. Today was the day to turn in her scholarship application. October was an odd time of year to be considered. Then again, Lichty was an odd guy. He likely made his own rules. But he'd been firm when he told her October 16. By five o'clock. One minute later, he'd said, and her application would be nullified.

"No. Impossible," he said into the phone. "You'll have to change the dates on your end."

It was five to five.

"I can't leave Chicago early; the event is in my honor. You know, this is exactly what happened last year when I let your people make the arrangements."

She cleared her throat, hoping to get his attention. He stood up taller, but now stared out the window. In vain, she glanced around the room as if she might come upon a large box labeled OFF-SEASON SCHOLARSHIP SUBMISSIONS HERE. Of course there was no such bin.

Four minutes to five.

"No. I'm immovable on this. You'll have to get dates from my assistant." There was a long pause, followed by Lichty thumping his fist on the glass. "No. No. No. No. I don't think you're hearing what I'm saying. End of January is out. Period. Do I have to repeat my entire three-week itinerary to you?"

No. Please don't, thought Lila. Repeating your entire three-week itinerary will blow my entire education.

Three minutes to five.

This was ridiculous. He never said anything about handing it in to him in person. She tiptoed in and went to place her portfolio and the envelope containing her application papers on his desk. But she knocked his lamp as she leaned close and Lichty spun around. With a dour expression on his face, he covered the receiver. "Office hours ended at four, Miss Mack."

She set the materials on top of the papers on his desk and whispered, "My scholarship application. And portfolio."

Into the phone, he barked, "Well then put Lionel on the phone. I don't have time to deal with this nonsense." Crooking the telephone between ear and shoulder, he peeked inside her portfolio, pulled out each of her five pieces and looked at them, one by one. With no change in expression, he slipped them back in and shouted, "Don't think they won't be hearing about this from me! I plan to head over there the moment I leave."

When Lila didn't move, he covered the phone again. "Are you waiting for some sort of gold star, Miss Mack?"

"No, I—"

"Off you go then."

Twenty-Four

His ex-wife was on her way over. Of course Victor's actions would lead to this day. He wasn't so far gone he couldn't see that. On this Wednesday, this twenty-second day of October, whatever remained of Victor's reign as Noble Father would end. He could never compete with Long Lost Mother. Ravishing Mother. Left-behind Mother.

It was the start of the finish. After working so hard to prevent it, after running his daughter to the farthest edge of the continent and hiding her away, he was finally going to lose his girl. He knew how it looked. Elisabeth appeared wholly good. Victor appeared wholly bad. It didn't take a genius to know whom the child would choose. Anyway, you take away a parent and the child's going to idealize her. Simple as that. Then tell that child the other parent manufactured the loss. Well.

There was another time, nine years back, when he'd almost lost her. Lila, about eleven or twelve, had been invited to camp on Lake Havasu in Arizona with a new girl from school and her parents. They were to sleep in a pop-up trailer and cook hot dogs over an open fire, maybe even water-ski behind the family's speedboat. As much as Victor wanted Lila to have a friend, it was out of the question. Lila and this other girl, tucked in sleeping bags on a tiny bunk, would stare through the overhead screen at a sky filled with the kind of stars you cannot see in Los Angeles where, with the exception of a complete power failure, the lights never really go out. It was a charged atmosphere that would create imagined intimacy. Turn a casual friend into a trusted confidante.

Secrets could be told.

Victor couldn't risk it. He'd told Lila no.

Maybe it was the strain of a tough school year. Maybe it was because Mother's Day had just passed. But Lila had taken it hard. She'd refused to speak to her father for three days. Then, on a Thursday morning, after the camping weekend had already passed, Victor had padded into her room to wake her up for school and found her bed empty.

A quick search of the cabin, shed, and property revealed Lila was gone. He'd been unable to breathe, his entire being consumed with panic. Had to sit down with a paper bag pressed over his mouth to stop the tingling in his fingertips. It was the one and only time since the move that he lost his composure and did the unthinkable:

Victor Mack called the police.

The LAPD scoured the neighborhood. Informed train stations, bus stations, LAX. All of this while Victor tried not to die of fright for his daughter. Never, not once in the five hours she was gone, did Victor fear for his own freedom. It was quite possibly the most unselfish three hundred minutes of his life.

Just before noon, he got a phone call. A red-haired, big-eyed, eleven-year-old girl wearing scribbled Converse running shoes was sitting on a Greyhound bus destined for Toronto via Las Vegas, Chicago, and Detroit. She refused to give the police officers her name. Refused to get off the bus, the police officer on the phone said, so could Victor please hurry? Schedules were being disrupted. By the time Victor arrived to find Lila in the very back seat of the bus, she was fast asleep, her arms wrapped around the tiny plush Snoopy Elisabeth picked up in the gift shop at the Hospital for Sick Children back home.

Trust Elisabeth to know best how to soothe her child after an injury. Trust Elisabeth to come out of any catastrophe smelling like the sweeter parent.

Now he sat on his bed in fresh boxers and a T-shirt, the sleeves of which no longer strained against his biceps. Lost in his own underwear. Either the shirt had stretched or he had shrunk—didn't really matter which. Meant the same damned thing: He didn't fill out his own life anymore. There was no growing bigger, no building himself up, not at his age. He didn't have the testosterone; he didn't have the energy. He didn't have the presence of mind some days to even remember if he'd exercised or just crawled out of bed. He supposed he could ask his daughter to help him keep track, but that seemed a bit much, given the circumstances. He would have to be content with innards that rattled around loose, like leftovers in a paper bag.

In a way, his current condition of broken man, or man

breaking apart before his own eyes, made him feel better. He still felt guilty, no mistaking it, but offering himself up to Elisabeth as a weathered replica of his former self was proof of justice partially served, was it not? It wasn't prison, and wouldn't likely bring about forgiveness, but if you took your neighbor's lawn mower and kept it for a few years, the neighbor would be quicker to forgive if the blades had sliced off a few of your toes.

So if Elisabeth felt vindicated, it was a good thing. If she was thrilled to see him looking wasted and useless, well, she deserved that one small pleasure. She would chalk it up to karma, if she still believed in that sort of thing.

He stood up and put his body through its morning stretches, almost certain he had not yet indulged in them today, while something pattered on the roof. Rain? Squirrels? Once his regimen was complete, he padded into the bathroom to shower and shave, taking extra care with himself. Toothbrush, Q-tip, Listerine, deodorant.

He poked through his medicine cabinet and pulled out a dusty bottle of Paco Rabanne. Ancient, maybe even from the days before Lila was born. He cracked open the lid and dabbed the thickened cologne on his neck, and, for good measure, under his arms.

Satisfied with his toilette, he padded into his room to dress. From inside his closet he heard the muffled rap on the front door. The squeaky hellos. The silence of an uncomfortable hug followed by the expected comments about the clouds that had darkened an hour or so earlier. Victor could imagine the vague tension in the hallway. Elisabeth's eyes darting nervously about. Looking for Victor. Looking for a kitchen knife. Not necessarily in that order.

The sounds trailed off as the ladies moved toward the living room.

He turned his attention back to his closet. His frail body aside, vanity dictated he look his best. Choose something unfrayed and crisp. His fingers wandered across the hangers and stopped on his leading-man suit. Victor smiled as he pulled it out and laid it on the bed. He slipped on a light blue shirt and climbed into the suit.

Silver was his color. Gen had always said so.

He zipped the pants, but when he tried to fasten the waistband, he realized they weren't going to button. Clearly, what he'd lost in his upper body, he'd gained in the middle. He slipped on a belt to keep them from opening up and dropping to his ankles, then pulled on his jacket.

From the kitchen came the sounds of the fridge opening and closing, glass clunking down on the table. Such a good girl, that Lila. Playing hostess. Poor kid must feel sick.

There had been very little conversation between them in recent days. Other than "Well?" and "I'm sorry, Mouse," communication had been limited to grocery lists and laundry instructions and banal observations about the level of canine vocalizations next door.

It had never been his intention to hurt his daughter so. His single-minded goal of keeping Lila alive had nudged all other concerns into the ditch. Making sure her soul remained uncrushed had, wrongly, been as low on his list of priorities as what brand of conditioner might best prevent split ends. Yet crushing her was precisely what he had done.

And he'd had no bloody choice.

Staring at himself in the mirror, he smoothed his shirt

over his belly. Satisfied he looked if not physically fit, at least mentally fit, he took a deep breath and entered the hallway. The voices grew louder as he approached. Not ten steps ahead of him lay the confrontation of a lifetime.

He felt his breathing grow shallow again. He slowed his step, leaned against the wall, his heart pounding so fast he thought it might come through his shirt. And the hall—why was it so shadowy? Ever since his mind had begun acting up, shadows seemed to follow him. Why was it so dim? Was it not daytime? And if not, why was the light not on? And, more important, how did one turn on this particular light? The fixture was all the way up on the ceiling. "Shitcrap place for a light!" he roared.

"Dad? We're in here."

Peering into the dim living room, he saw the back of a stranger's head. Darkish hair. Hands that fluttered as she spoke. Could it be Gen?

No. Not here. She wasn't in his home, just like she wasn't in his neighbors' yard.

Still. Smoothing his beard, he started toward the room. God, how he'd missed her. It had been . . . too damned long was what it had been. He tried to stop his grin from taking over his entire face.

It couldn't be.

The dark hair turned and he caught sight of the profile. The upturned nose and small chin. This wasn't Gen at all. It appeared to be—impossible—his ex-wife. Elisabeth. He felt his heart race again and crept back into the hall.

He couldn't think right away why Elisabeth was to be feared. Only that he feared her.

He reached for the keys and slipped out the front door. As he thrust the car into reverse, he looked back at the house to see his daughter's face at the kitchen window, sweet and shocked and, yes, crushed.

SEPTEMBER 19, 1996

Victor threw the covers off his shoulders and glanced at the digital clock perched on top of a stack of magazines beside his bed. Four o'clock. It was no use trying to sleep now. Renovations on the house next door had continued until well after dark, and the incessant hammering, sawing, and shouting continued to reverberate in Victor's head. After swinging his legs over the side of the bed, he paused to let his blood pressure adjust. He'd once heard about a man who stood up too quickly getting out of bed; the quick change in altitude caused his blood pressure to drop, bringing on a temporary blackout that resulted in him hitting his head on the iron bedpost on the way down. The fellow suffered countless complications and his mind was never the same afterward.

Victor couldn't afford to lose his mind just now.

After a quick trip to the bathroom in sleep-rumpled linen pajamas, then to his closet to wrap himself in a terry-cloth robe, he wandered into the living room and turned on the television, flicking from one infomercial to the next. Eventually he settled on a black-and-white movie, pulled a small quilt over his legs and leaned back on the sofa. With any luck, the film would force his mind to focus and settle. Maybe enough so that he could catch an hour of sleep.

He sunk deeper into the cushions and stared at the television. A commercial came on showing a couple strapping their toddler into the backseat of a car, then buckling up themselves. As the father pulled into traffic, they both lit up cigarettes while the child stared out the window. Billows of smoke morphed into animated hands, snaking into the backseat, wrapping long, hazy fingerlike tendrils around the child's body. Then an antismoking logo and a phone number flashed against a black screen.

He tried to stop the image before it crystallized—if he allowed the picture of the Cabbagetown rooftop to form, even for a fraction of a second, he'd be forced to get in the car and drive downtown to convince himself that Elisabeth or one of her stoner friends hadn't fallen asleep with a lit cigarette or joint. Counting backward from one hundred, he managed to fight it off. A small triumph; one only he and his therapist would appreciate. He lowered the volume of the TV, pleased with his resolve, and let his eyes fall shut.

Then, somewhere outside, a chorus of muffled wails pierced the night. Sharp and close at first, unmistakably the siren of fire engines. Ambulances. He sat up and listened. As the wails grew more and more faint, it became clear they were traveling southbound on Bayview. They could be headed anywhere, of course, and would probably turn off the extension long before they reached the deep bowl of a park at River Street, turned right on Gerrard. Wound their way through the one-way streets of Cabbagetown to the sleepy windows of Sackville Street.

But when it came to his daughter, probably wasn't good enough. Fully aware he was behaving irrationally, Victor pulled himself upright, slipped his feet into shoes, and reached for his keys.

Twenty-Five

The walk from kitchen window back to living room—where her mother waited—was a long one. If, after learning what Victor did to her, Lila had had a moment of believing that her father had kidnapped her out of some sort of misguided sense of necessity, it vanished along with the rear chrome bumper of the Datsun as it careened away from the cabin. Agreeing to meet with Elisabeth, then bolting, was truly her father's most despicable act. Showed zero compassion, even less remorse, and an absolute lack of understanding of the gravity of what he'd done.

She followed the brick road back to the living room, back to where Elisabeth sat on the sofa, her shaking hands wrapped around a clay mug Lila had made in fourth-grade art class. When Lila had pulled it from the kitchen cupboard, Elisabeth had teared up, turned it over in her hands, asked if she could keep it. She'd insisted upon drinking chilled Zinfandel in it while she waited for Victor to emerge. She looked up as Lila entered the room. "I was just staring out at the hill here. It's just like the psychic said. That you were facing directly into a mountain. That there was one big window, but other rooms had little natural light. Like an animal's lair." She looked around the room. "It's all here, everything she said. The stone fireplace, the uneven floors, all this wood. Spooky to think how accurate she was."

"I've got something to—"

"She also said I'd had a tough life. That I would have to work harder than most people to have what I was meant to have."

"You mean me? And Kieran?"

"Not really. I think Amelia meant nice things. That I was meant to have them, but circumstances—like your father—got in the way. Not that I mind about material objects." She laughed into her mug. "No. Now that I have you, I'm the richest woman in the world. Now if your father would just get in here, we can get this thing over with. I'm not sure my stomach will hold out; I'm so nervous."

"Mum."

"My sister, now she had it easy. Married a pediatrician who came from money. There was never any question about going out to work to support the family. Right from the start, she had her babies and played tennis. Wore diamond studs and shopped at Chanel. Sometimes I wonder how different my life would have been if I'd been the one to marry well."

Lila said, "About Dad . . ."

"I might have been a very famous artist. Did you know I once sold a painting to Edgar Sherman? He's like Donald Trump in Canada. He said to me, 'Ms. Lovett'—that was what he called me—'I'm going to make you a very successful woman.' So I waited, certain he was going to the press or something. But nothing ever happened. I always worried he soured on my work after living with it a while." She eyed Lila hopefully.

"No way it was that. People have great intentions and then get busy."

"He would be a very busy man."

"I'm sure. If he really is like Trump."

"He is! Look him up if you don't believe me. One of the richest men in Canada. Owns nearly the whole country."

"I totally believe you. Listen, Mum. Dad just took off."

Elisabeth stared at her, mouth agape. "He left? You mean just now?"

Lila nodded. "Just now. I'm sorry."

Without a word, her mother stood up, circled the room several times as if in a trance. When she passed by the window for the third time, her mouth flattened into a thin line and she hurled Lila's little green mug into the fireplace.

Twenty-Six

A male model got an erection yesterday. Tristan Brandeis, an L.A. Arts ballet major who picked up extra cash by allowing the lesser forms of life in the art department to interpret his beautiful physique.

There he was, facing Lichty's Thursday-night acrylics class, seniors only, heels pressed to the baseboard, the wall rope snaked around his wrists so he could let his body fall forward forty-five degrees as if he were flying. Or rising up from the grit on the floor. His muscular face turned up to the heavens. Or the acoustic tiles, depending upon your religious bent. The weight of his body pulled the rope so tight that his hands were swollen. He'd cut off circulation, but the pose was only to be for twenty minutes, so he probably figured he could handle it. But what took the stance into legendary status was that, before the students arrived at the south studio, in honor of Halloween next week, he'd painted his entire body, face, even his bald head silver.

The students loved the paint. And the pose—such a delicious juxtaposition of looming threat with utter vulnerability, all immortalized in metal like a lobby fountain in Las Vegas. What a challenge! From the right angle it would have looked as if he had no arms and his feet were growing right out of his shimmering hipbones. The first ten minutes were silent, so frenzied and intent were the artists upon capturing the essence of this magnificent glittering beast who had burst through the crack where floor met baseboard.

Then it happened.

Some people thought it the model's love of his own form—who, after all, would deem themselves worthy of basting their own parts in liquid metal? One girl thought it was the breeze coming in from the open window at the back of the class. Another said he'd been dateless too long. Lila herself wondered about the metallic paint, perhaps it prevented oxygen from getting to his pores and what happened was simply a sign his body was in distress, reaching and clawing for O^2. But whatever the reason, aeration, self-adoration, or dermal suffocation, at about the eleven-minute mark, Tristan's great silver phallus—at first leggy and unsure, helmeted and apologetic—rose up from beneath his flawless belly.

En pointe.

It stood proud, as Tristan dangled like a magnificent hood ornament.

Two or three students left the class, offended. Others stayed, choosing to ignore the uninvited guest. One older man—widely known for preferring to sketch nude females—crumpled up his drawing and turned himself backward, choosing to draw the vent on the wall behind him rather than the confirmation of what he'd long suspected: that any man who chose to drop his clothes in public, silver phallus or not, wasn't a man at all.

If Tristan was troubled by this occurrence, or embarrassed by it, it didn't show. Neither a wince nor a quiver crossed his beautiful face.

It was Lichty who surprised Lila most of all. He told his students that this assignment was now worth a full 20 percent of their term mark. Said they could interpret the pose any way they wished, but their decision would affect their grade. When Tristan had finished his pose—both poses—he'd thrown on his robe and made a dash for the changing area behind the curtain. All models were aware of the potential repercussions in the case of impromptu erections. Models who inadvertently succumbed were not only mortified, but depending upon the professor, were sometimes asked not to return.

Lichty had waited for him. Once Tristan reappeared, fully clothed and hopefully headed for a shower somewhere, Lichty told both him and the class that becoming aroused was a natural part of modeling nude and such things had happened to models since the beginning of art itself. Then he told Tristan he'd be in contact with his booking agent to secure him for regular sessions because his focus, under extreme duress, was worthy of an Oscar.

Lila walked into the changing stall and dropped her bag, immediately pulling off her top. Today was to be different than any other class. She'd never posed longer than forty minutes at a time—not without a short break. And some days she struck five-minute poses while the class did quick sketches. Those days were the best. She was able to stretch for a few seconds while rearranging herself, thereby increasing blood flow to strained body parts.

Today was Lichty's infamous Three Pencil Class. By three pencils, he meant three hours. Artists loved it; models dreaded it. Two of his life drawing classes—one freshman, one junior—were coming together for one marathon session. They said it was the ultimate seal of approval from Lichty. There were only two models he'd ever used for this once-a-year session: the legendary Yaffa Street from Marin County and her local protégée, Mei Sing.

Today it would be Lila Mack. Most days, Lichty allowed her to construct her own stance, but this time was different. This time he had parameters. She was to wind her limbs and ooze both sensuality and strength. Youth and exhaustion.

This time was different in another way. Lila had agreed to do the class on one condition: that she have a heater. A forty-minute session was one thing. She would not pose for three hours in frigid air. It hardly seemed possible but the studio had grown colder since the weather had changed, and three hours without moving meant almost zero blood flow to twisted body parts. Surprisingly, he'd agreed. But when she walked around the class looking for it, there didn't seem to be a heater in sight.

She wandered over to his desk. "I'd like to set up the heater before I pose. Shivering will start me out cramped."

He slipped a piece of paper into a file folder. "No heater today, I'm afraid."

"But you said—"

"Nina Previn needed it for room three-oh-five. You'll pose without it."

She'd never have agreed to three hours without a heater. She looked at him levelly. "That's going to be a problem."

He looked at up at her and grinned sweetly. "It might be a problem in someone else's room, but not in mine. Not for anyone who wants to continue to work in my studio. It's a privilege to pose for my Three Pencil Class. And every model knows it."

Of course. Because everything in her life had to come with a "but." Hey—your mother's back in your life. But guess what? She comes bearing missing child posters with your face on them. And that father you've adored and trusted all these years? Brimming with Basenji facts, but don't get on a plane with him!

It was wrong to talk back to Lichty. It didn't take a genius to recognize that. But she couldn't help herself. "So Brandeis can have an erection and keep working, but I'm finished unless I work in the snow?"

"Tristan Brandeis is a pro. And he didn't start out by lying to me about his experience."

"You think I lied?"

He unfolded himself, dusted off his thighs, and walked into the changing stall. When he emerged, the brown robe dangled from his finger. "You wore this on the first day, did you not?"

"Sure."

"Do me a favor." He passed it to her. "Smell it."

"I'm not—"

"Smell it."

She held it close to her nose and sniffed, grimacing.

He grabbed it back and tossed it into the changing stall. "No one who has modeled even once pulls on the studio robe." He glanced down at Lila's robe. "Because studio robes rarely get washed."

She looked around the room, her eyes settling on a scuff mark on the floor. "Do you want me to leave?"

"No, Miss Mack. I don't want you to leave. I'd very much like you to stay."

Something about his tone—it implied something else. As if he had news for her but wasn't sure if he was at liberty to say. "Wait. Do you know something about the scholarship? Have they given you their answer?"

"They have not. It has only been a week." He clapped his hands, turning to the class. "Prepare to draw, people. Model, assume your pose." When she didn't move he barked, "Now!"

She'd tried poses where she leaned against the wall and intertwined her arms, flexing her wrists outward. But she didn't feel this was powerful enough—it promoted flexibility but offered no contractions, no polarity between muscles at work and those at rest. And you had to consider the time frame: 180 minutes. It would be a lifetime if she chose the wrong pose. Ultimately, she'd decided upon sitting with one foot tucked in close, the other leg crossed over the bent knee. One wrist rested on the top knee, hand dangling with delicate fingers. The other hand would be held out behind her, supporting her weight while she thrust her chin in the air, stretching the muscles in her neck. She settled her body into the pose, pushing her skeleton into its own grooves to ensure she could hold it for three full hours. Or pencils.

From across the room, Adam smiled, gave her the thumbs up on her pose.

She tried to focus on the wall beyond his head. Already, her neck was beginning to cramp, sending threads of pain down behind her right shoulder blade. She glanced at the clock. They were barely ten minutes into the pose. One foot was nearly numb and her entire torso had tensed to counterbalance her uptilted head. Her shoulders started to shake. Only 170 minutes to go.

IT WAS JUST about the two-and-a-half-hour mark when she realized her neck was injured. She'd held her head tipped back, as if watching a kite, for far longer than the trapezius muscles would tolerate. When Lichty turned off Earth, Wind & Fire's "Fantasy" and declared the class to be finished, Lila had had to reach behind her skull and gingerly guide it back into place, so locked was her upper body. She disentangled her limbs and sat forward, allowing her chin to droop down to her collarbone and stretch the muscles that roared so loudly up the back of her neck. Standing was out of the question until she could find a way to carry her head. Once she balanced it on top of her shoulders with one hand on the back of her neck, she slid her robe over her shoulders and hobbled toward the changing stall.

She yanked the curtain shut behind her and pulled on panties and skirt. T-shirt and cardigan. Socks. Boots. Beloved, adored boots. God, her neck pained. Emergency-room pain. She stood still, relishing the warmth thick cotton brought to her body, and kneaded the bulges in her neck. As she massaged, a glint of gold on the floor by her feet caught her eye. She kicked her dropped robe aside to see a chunky bracelet winking up at her.

Her first instinct was to pull open the curtain and ask the students if anyone had lost a bracelet. Or maybe just say a piece of jewelry in case several acquisitive hands shot up at once. Probably not a great idea. She should just turn it in to Lichty. Or the office even. If someone lost a piece of jewelry this special, they'd go straight to the office.

That's what she'd do. Stop at the office on the first floor on her way home. Or after the emergency room, depending on her neck.

The thing is, no one had used this studio in a few days. One of the sinks had been leaking, and the room had been closed to students. So whoever lost it did so the week prior.

She yanked back the curtain to find Adam waiting on the other side. "Hey."

"Hey."

Fidgety and nervous, he pointed across the room. "Did you even see that guy at the back? Spent, like, twenty-five percent of his time highlighting your, you know . . ." He motioned toward her hips. "Your lady parts."

Lila slid the bracelet into her pocket, secretly pleased with his possessiveness. "It's kind of the drill around here."

"Seemingly." He nodded, pulling at his nose. "Seemingly. If he'd kept it to even fifteen percent, I could see it. But you stretch it out much longer and, man. If you're uncomfortable, I can drive you home."

She hoisted her bag over one shoulder. "I'm okay. But thanks for watching out. Are we still on for later? I warn you, when I model in private, I expect to be paid in pizza."

"Right. That." He winced as if about to deliver bad news. "I sort of have to cancel. Postpone."

"Why? Assignment?"

"Actually, you're not going to believe this. Nikki called."

"Really?"

"She wants to talk. Wants to go out tonight."

She stared at him, dumbfounded that a) Adam's senseless yammering hadn't turned Nikki off the other day, and b) her own stomach had just lurched so violently the pain in her neck vanished. Thinking back to their tête-à-tête on his front porch, the way his forehead felt, warm and solid and real, pressed into hers. She tried to sound thrilled for him. "Hey. Adam, that's great. It's what you've wanted, right?"

He shrugged. "We'll just be talking. Two people making sounds with their mouths."

Hopefully that was all they'd be doing with their mouths.

"I'm sorry. Maybe tomorrow?"

"Maybe," she said. "I'll have to check."

He stood there smiling like a fool.

"Congratulations, Adam. Seriously."

WANDERING INTO THE office, fingering the cool metal in her front pocket, Lila let the silky rope slide between her fingers. An office secretary smiled at her. "May I help you, dear?"

"Yes. I was just wondering if anyone had reported any missing jewelry. In the last few days."

"Nothing valuable, as far as I know. Let me check with the others."

She disappeared down a darkened hallway. After a few moments, she returned. "No, we have no reports of anything valuable having gone missing. Have you found something you'd like to turn in?"

Somewhere between the second and first floors, maybe on the landing halfway down, Lila had changed her mind about the bracelet. It might have been the way the pain from her lengthy pose had scrabbled up to her brain and inserted its fingers firmly in the gray matter and started to squeeze. Or the fact that she still hadn't stopped shivering. But she suspected it was something else entirely. Someone else entirely.

Nikki and her ability to control her life. Adam's life.

Whoever owned this bracelet didn't even care enough to search for it. There were a lot of moneyed kids swanning around this campus; the bracelet could belong to someone who just didn't care. Or someone who wanted to get rid of it.

On the other hand, there were people who had done without for far too long. There were people for whom nothing went right. Like her mother. And she never complained. Just marched on and tried to do the best for the people around her. Seeing the look on Elisabeth's face when Victor took off down the street was too much to bear. How much could one woman take? How much could Lila take?

It was two weeks until Elisabeth's birthday. And while this bracelet—once Lila had it resized, had the clasp fixed, had it polished—might not make up for twelve years of pain, it might just make her mother feel a little bit special. As if, just this once, life wasn't fighting back.

"No. I have nothing to turn in."

Twenty-Seven

As the child stared into the cooler, a buzzing fluorescent light flashed on and off overhead. Never had anyone spent more time choosing a cold beverage than Kieran. It had been ten minutes and the fan inside the refrigerated unit was blowing arctic air on Lila's bare legs, amplifying the shortsightedness of wearing shorts out on a cool night in late October. When Lila reached for a plastic bottle of chocolate milk, individual size, Kieran tilted her face away. "No. I want white."

"Okay, this." Lila handed her a carton of white milk.

"Too small."

Lila pointed toward a quart of low-fat milk. "There's this, but I warn you, you won't be able to finish it. And once the straw falls inside, you can poke around with your tongue forever but you'll never get it out."

Having had her evening plans with Adam fall through and with nothing better to do than imagine Nikki and her pale nipples standing at the door to the sunroom, Lila had jumped on the chance to watch Kieran when Elisabeth called to say she was tied up at a late meeting. After confirming with her mother that this meeting was not taking place at the police station, Lila hopped in the 240Z and knocked on the babysitter's door, across from Elisabeth's. When a male voice called, "Enter," she did just that.

Inside, the room was dated: matching tartan love seat and sofa. Chunky floor lamps with attached wooden tables. Braided rag rug on the floor. Coffee table with large round doilies marching across the center; when Lila looked closer, hand-rolled cigarettes scattered on the doilies. Ashtrays overflowing with butts everywhere. An old pizza box on the floor. It was no place for a child.

Lazing on the long sofa was a tall, loosely muscled man of about twenty-five with a diamond stud in one ear. He wore paint-stained chinos and nothing else. One hand was doing a cavity search of a bag of organic pretzels and the other squeezed a can of beer. Broken pretzels that hadn't made it into his mouth lay strewn on his flat stomach, while rolling papers and a tiny foil package rested on a pillow. Reluctantly, he looked up from the TV.

"Hey," he said.

To his left, with her blouse and cardigan buttoned right to the chin, sitting on the edge of the seat cushion beside him with knees and ankles pressed together and hands clasped primly on her skirt, with a pained expression on her face, sat Kieran. She jumped up when she saw her sister. "Delilah!"

The man introduced himself as Finn. With Kieran hanging on to her leg, Lila politely inquired as to the whereabouts of the sitter. After draining what was left of his Schlitz Malt Liquor and wiping a grain of sea salt from his beard, he informed Lila he was not only Kieran's sitter, but the landlord as well.

Lila tried to hide her shock. "You own this house?"

He scratched himself. "Technically my parents own it, but it's mine to live in, profit from, whatever. Gives me a little income to support my work." The wave of his arm directed her gaze behind the sofa to a makeshift studio with tarps pinned to the walls and a sculpture in progress: wire mesh forming the shape of a reclined woman, with only the lower torso finished in some sort of sculpting medium. From the looks of things, the project had been neglected for some time. The clay seemed to have cracked and dried from the sun streaming in the window, and the floor was littered in crumpled takeout bags, empty wine bottles, dirty glasses.

Stepping closer, Finn looked Lila up and down. "So you're Elisabeth's other daughter?"

"Lila. Kieran and I have to be someplace." She grabbed Kieran's backpack and pulled her toward the door, then stopped. "Sorry. Do I owe you anything?"

"Naw. Your mother pays me good. Don't you worry, doll."

Lila frowned, unsure what he meant by this. Elisabeth paid half rent, plus the guy was babysitting—how was this considered good? Her eyes drifted back to the unfinished sculpture. If Elisabeth was nude modeling for this guy, she didn't want to know. Hypocritical, maybe, but what daughter wanted to picture her mother lying on her back with her thighs in the air, spread wide with Finn's face in between? And if Elisabeth was doing more than modeling with a man who could practically be her son, Lila didn't think she wanted to know about that either.

It was time to go. She said her good-byes and ushered Kieran out to the car. Kieran, however, took one look at the lack of backseat and in her gravelly voice informed Lila that there were laws about front seats and children under twelve not sitting in them because of death by air-bag deployment. She only deigned to climb in once Lila convinced her "air bag" wasn't even a phrase when the 240Z was manufactured, therefore no laws would be broken.

They'd gone for burgers and milkshakes. Stopped at the bookstore. Now the child was thirsty.

Kieran looked at the carton and shook her head. "I don't want low fat."

Lila grabbed another and turned to go. "Fine. Let's get out of here. I'm freezing."

"I don't want that one."

"Come on, Kieran. You're not going to tell me you drink whole milk. No one in L.A. drinks whole milk. It might even be . . ." she leaned closer and whispered, "illegal."

"Not funny. Anyway, I don't want whole milk." She stood on her tiptoes and reached for a large carton of nonfat. Chocolate.

"But you said you didn't want chocolate. You said white."

"I don't care what flavor." Kieran pointed at all the choices Lila had offered up. "Those ones don't have kids on them." She moved closer to her sister to show her the side of the carton. "Zachary John Miller. Last seen wearing a blue softball uniform."

Lila tucked the milk under one arm, took the girl's hand, and shuffled toward the cash register. "My God, Kieran.

I don't know which one of us is more screwed up, me or you."

Her phone buzzed from inside her pocket and she flipped it open. Adam. "Hey, how's it going?"

He blew his nose. "Not good."

"Aren't you with Nikki?"

In the background she heard a heavy thundering sound. "She left. I'm . . . I don't know what I am. A mess."

"I'm on my way. You're at home?"

He let out a long groan, then, "At the beach."

IT WAS DARK by the time Kieran and Lila stepped onto the sand in Santa Monica. At Kieran's insistence, they'd removed their shoes, and the sand was cold and damp beneath their feet, like sugar that had been stored in the freezer. To their left, the famous pier sat neglected. It was, after all, nine-forty-five on a Friday night and barely sixty degrees. Even tourists trying to capitalize on off-season rates weren't intrepid enough to venture out into the wet, fishy-smelling ocean air.

"This is definitely not good," scolded Kieran as she trudged across the sandy parking lot, her unopened milk carton in hand. "I'm usually asleep by now. Into bed at eight, read for half an hour, write in my diary for fifteen minutes, then lights out at eight-forty-five."

"Is that Mum's rule?"

Kieran looked as if she'd just been asked if she lives beneath the dock on weeknights. "That's *my* rule. There was a study; if schoolchildren don't get eleven hours of sleep, their focus in class suffers. It's a fact."

"I'm sure it is. But it's okay to break out and do something wild every now and again."

"That's not what the scientists say."

"It's what I say. It's never hurt me." Kieran grunted loud enough that Lila stopped. "What's that supposed to mean."

Kieran looked into the wind, squinting. "Nothing."

"You can tell me."

"Just . . . you're a nude model. So I think I'll stick with the scientists."

They waded through the sand toward a small campfire about halfway to the shoreline, where the waves crashed onto the beach. As they drew closer, ocean spray misting their faces, they could see Adam lying on his back beside a wicker basket and a bottle of red wine. From deep within his being came a low-pitched groan.

Lila dropped to the sand beside him. "Are you okay?"

Only his eyes moved. "If breathing qualifies me as okay, then yes. For now. But don't get comfortable. It could all change without warning." He turned his head to stare at Kieran, who now cradled her milk like a baby. "You brought a child to my wake?"

"I'm Kieran Scarlett Lovett-Moore. But Scarlett has two T's, so it's complicated. Also it's bedtime."

He raised himself up on one elbow. "I know. I'm disruptive like that. If you had any sense, you'd make a break for it."

Kieran pretended not to glance back toward the parking lot. With a resigned sigh, she dropped to her knees on the unzipped sleeping bag and shivered. Lila leaned down to move a wicker basket full of crusty bread and cheese, wrapped one end of the cowboy-spackled flannel around her sister's shoulders, then poured herself a glass of wine.

"Okay, what happened? The date didn't go well?"

"Turns out it wasn't a date."

Kieran plucked a few rose petals off the sleeping bag. "Looks like a date. *More* than a date."

"That's what Nikki said." Still supine, he reached for the wine bottle and swigged. Wine dribbled across his cheek. "Turns out this wasn't a getting-back-together kind of event. More of a let's-itemize-all-that-is-wrong-with-Adam kind of affair." He let out another weak groan. "Turned out to be a rather lengthy catalog."

"The rose petals were a mistake," said Kieran, crinkling her nose. "Too *Days of Our Lives.*"

"Wait," said Lila. "I don't understand. Why come here and rip up your ex-boyfriend two months after the fact?"

He rolled his eyes. "It was for my own good, don't you know? Because after she saw me, us, in the park the other day, she felt inspired—no, obligated!—to swoop in and fix all that is broken in Adam Harding."

"In her defense"—Lila tried not to smile—"you were trying to get naked in a public place. I mean, there are laws in place to control people like you."

Kieran let out a disapproving sound, like the scrape of a chair.

"You're not helping, Lila," Adam said. "I'm wounded here. I need empathy, not ridicule. I blew it the other day. I went on and on like a complete moron. And there was Bruce-Brice all quiet and respectable with his mint green stripes. And do you know what I almost did earlier? I nearly canceled New York. I figured Nikki and I were going to work out, so why go, you know?"

Lila watched the way the shadows from the fire changed the look of his face. One moment handsome, the next moment hollowed out. Driftwood snapped and sparked in the flames. "I guess. Depending on why you're going."

"Don't analyze me. You won't like what you see."

She sat back on her heels. "The view's not so terrible from here."

Another grunt from Kieran.

Adam glanced at Lila sideways, amused. "Did I just get a compliment from Lichty's favorite model?"

"Don't get all full of yourself. It is pretty dark."

"You know what would make me feel better right now?"

"Not sure I want to hear this, but okay. What?"

"Painting. You, in my studio, lit only by moonlight. You know I need a model for the designer."

A huge wave crashed on the beach. Lila stared at him. She did have a new pose she'd been working on. It wouldn't be a bad thing to try it out on Adam before class.

"I asked Nikki," he said. "She turned me down flat. You know what she said?"

"Shut up about her."

"What?"

"If you stop talking about Nikki, I'll do it."

A crooked smile inched across Adam's face. "Seriously? You're not playing with me?"

Kieran, who had started crawling around collecting tiny stones, got up on her knees and made a face. "You're going to strip in front of Adam, Delilah Blue?"

"Delilah Blue?" Adam repeated. "That's your full name?"

"Hey, any teasing and suddenly I'm busy tonight."

"No teasing. I like it. It suits you. Delilah Blue. Woohoo."

"Gross," said Kieran. "This night could not get any

worse." In the blackened distance, from about a mile up the shoreline, two close-set lights bobbed and danced across the sand, headed straight toward their fire. She stood up and pushed white strands from her face, watching the lights. "What's that?"

Adam jumped up. "That, sweet Kieran, is a sign of our night getting worse." He began scooping handfuls of sand over the fire, coughing and sputtering when smoke billowed in his face. "It's the cops."

"Kieran, start running." Lila threw things into the basket. "Go straight to the car."

Kieran's eyes nearly popped out of her head as she scrambled to her feet and wrapped herself in the sleeping bag. "I have to run from the police? Are we criminals?"

"Kind of." Adam watched as flames still licked their way through the grit and sand. "We need water." He caught sight of Kieran's milk. "Can we use that?"

"That's Zachary John Miller!"

The police jeep was down on the flat sand by the water's edge now, gaining speed. "*Please*, Kieran."

Scowling, she handed it over and watched, begging Adam to be careful with Zachary John's face as he doused the fire with nonfat milk. Finally, the flame died out, replaced by billows of hissing gray smoke.

Adam and Lila threw remaining bits of food and trash into the basket and started to run. "Hurry, Kieran!" When she stood frozen in the smoke, Lila ran back and took her by the hand, pulled her toward the car. "What are you waiting for? Do you want to get caught?"

Kieran allowed herself to be led, feet dragging through the sand. Finally, as the jeep pulled up to the fire and a cop climbed out and started to shine his flashlight around in the dark, she broke into a run, shouting at her sister's back, "Next time I listen to the scientists!"

AFTER INSTALLING KIERAN in bed, watching her wish sweet dreams to her wall of lost friends, and bidding good night to Elisabeth, who had been dozing on the sofa in front of an old movie, Lila picked her way through Adam's backyard and stood on the steps, watched him set up an oversized H-frame easel in the corner, facing her. He motioned for her to step onto the fresh roll of unstretched canvas in front of the French doors, which were flung open. "Right there."

She did what he said without comment.

When she'd offered to pose, she hadn't anticipated feeling quite this nervous, or this exhilarated. It was one thing stripping down in class where things were official and she received a paycheck. Stripping down for Adam at eleven-thirty at night in his studio-cum-bedroom was something very different.

He walked over to his easel and picked up a brush. "Anytime you're ready, Miss Delilah Blue."

She started to unbutton her jean skirt, then stopped. "Can we lose the lights?"

He flipped a switch and the room went black, save for the glow of the moon filtered through the trees.

Emboldened only slightly by the velvety darkness, fully aware of his eyes following her every move, Lila regretted not bringing her robe. Dropping the robe would have made things more workmanlike. Peeling off her clothing made it sexual. She debated asking him to step out of the room but decided against it on the grounds that it would call unnecessary attention to the charged atmosphere.

"Are you sure you want to do this?" he asked.

"Yes."

And then there was silence. Too much silence, soft and loaded. She should have thought to suggest music, if only to cover the sounds of her undressing.

Her fingers moved along her waistband and found the buttons. She shimmied out of her skirt and kicked it away. Then, standing in a shaft of filtered light, she turned away from him, took hold of the hem of her sweater and paused for a few moments before pulling it over her head. It landed on the floor with a delicate thud.

Her hands moved up to cover her breasts.

After a quick glance back to assure herself Adam was still parked at the easel, she stepped out of her panties, one arm still shielding her chest.

She should turn around.

If she were in class, she would spin around now. Drop her hands and move into a pose. Any pose. Tonight it felt impossible. As much as she wanted to, she couldn't turn and face Adam. Staring into the backyard, she said, her voice shrill in the quiet room, "I was thinking I'd lie down on the floor. With my back to you."

"Okay."

She squatted, lowered herself down, and settled on her side, propped up on one elbow, the other arm resting on her waist. "Like this?"

He waited, then cleared his throat. "Almost."

She listened to him shuffle around a bit, then pad across the tarp. Looking up, she found him standing over her in his boxers, jeans in one hand. Her heart started to thump, with fear and excitement. Was this it? Did he want to make love? More important, did she?

He bent down, but instead of leaning over to kiss her, touch her, or make any sort of romantic gesture, he carefully draped his jeans over her lower hip, arranged the denim into pleasing folds, and walked back to his canvas. "Now tilt your face up. That's right. And turn your head slightly toward me. Just a bit." When she did, he said, "Good. Let your hair fall down your back a bit."

She leaned back slightly and shook her head. "Okay?"

"Perfect. You're perfect." His husky voice trailed off, replaced with the sound of bristles stroking taut canvas.

Twenty-Eight

It was the last Friday in October and Victor felt like a boy again. He hadn't woken up this way. He'd opened his eyes groggy from a heavy sleep. In fact, from the way his left arm had gone numb and rubbery, he might not have rolled over the whole night through. As he'd lain there, trying to work feeling back into his deadened limb, he'd been vaguely aware of something exciting he had planned.

Then it came to him and he smiled.

Marching along Sunset, he ignored all the commuters honking, the shopkeepers polishing windows, the waitresses setting up tables. He strolled through herds of oncoming joggers and young mothers in high-heeled sandals pushing toddlers in strollers built for off-road adventure. Victor, after all, had just as real a destination for his morning as anyone else.

The day had come. He was going buy himself a dog. No longer would he be alone. For all that had fallen apart in his life, he would have just one tiny being who believed him to be without flaw.

Not half a block down, he came upon the pet shop. The very one where he'd been denied his multicolored puppy with the spotted tail and the alpha attitude. And the tongue that lapped against Victor's bearded chin.

It was Friday. Manager's day off. That male clerk's day off too; he'd double-checked by phone yesterday.

There was the window. The pen. For a moment, he became anxious the pups might have been sold. His little friend might be gone. But as he drew near, he smiled. The fluffy, multicolored pups were right there—fewer, though; there were only three left—napping in a pile in the corner, his alpha pup on top.

Victor peered through the open doorway to see no sign of the young fellow who'd destroyed his previous attempt. The store was empty but for a meek-looking college-aged girl who stood on a stepstool and sprinkled brownish flakes into an aquarium. A parrot screeched from beside the counter, and one side of the room hummed with filters.

This time Victor was prepared. He cleared his throat. "The puppies that are in the window. What breed are they?"

She snapped her tin of fish food closed and stepped down onto the floor, smiling. Her nametag read DIANE. "They're Maltipoos."

Victor nodded. "That's what I thought."

"Are you looking for a puppy?"

"I am." He wandered over to the pen in the window. As if sensing Victor's presence, his pup looked up and yawned,

"No thank you." Victor made his way toward the door nd stopped, turned around. "You'll take extra good care of 'rankie will you?"

She nodded. "You bet. And if you check back in a few weeks, we may have a line on another Maltipoo litter."

"That won't be necessary." Victor stepped outside again, his ears stopped up with the roar of traffic, eyes pained from the brilliance of the morning. That was that. Good. Now he could forget about the pup—Frankie—and move on.

There was a coffee shop on the corner, one with a fenced-off courtyard that ambled along the side street. He'd been stopping by for a coffee and bagel several times each week since he was fired. Place was fairly typical, packed with office workers on their lunch breaks, young mothers with infants, people out walking their dogs. Today, other than the table in the far corner, where two suited men shared a scone and argued over a stack of papers in the sun, the rest of the patio was nicely sheltered by green umbrellas and nicely devoid of people. He walked inside to pick up his coffee and bagel—poppy seed, lightly toasted—asked for a side packet of cream cheese, and carried his treat back outside where he set it all on the table farthest from the two men as possible.

There was a scuffle in the doorway. Raised voices while three young ladies—dressed, in Victor's opinion, in not nearly enough clothing—argued with someone inside, someone who was insisting they vacate. One of the girls, the tall one with blond hair tied up in a messy ponytail, had a dog in her arms. A curly-tailed, taupe-and-black dog with a mashed-in face and eyes bulging on the sides of its head. A pug, if Victor could trust his fair-weather memory.

A employee emerged and moved toward the patio,

curling his tiny tongue. Once he saw Victor, he c
over his siblings and stumbled to the side, waggir
and asking to be lifted up.

Victor reached down and brought the dog to h
thrilled when the tongue lapped against his neck. T
had grown to almost twice its former size and was a
deal heavier. "You're very careful about who you sell
pups to, I presume?"

"Oh, yes. But this area is filled with dog lovers, so
usually don't have too many problems."

"This one's my favorite."

"He's a real imp, that one. I call him Frankie. I've bee
threatening to buy that one myself if he doesn't sell. I'd buy
him today if I had the cash."

Frankie. The dog stopped licking for a moment and stared into Victor's eyes, smiling and panting, wiggling and wagging.

"If you'd like to get to know him a bit, there's a playroom at the back of the store where you can set him down."

He stared through a window at the play area, and a distressing thought hit him like a basketball to the chest. Buying a dog right now was short-sighted. Not only that, but incredibly selfish. How had he missed this? Had he become that lonely since Elisabeth and the past had entered their lives? That desperate?

Buying a puppy ran contra to his plan. He chided himself for his lack of focus.

Victor allowed the dog to nuzzle into his collar a moment, then rubbed him behind his tiny ears and handed him over to Diane. "No thank you. I just came to say good-bye."

She looked surprised. "Okay. No problem. Did you want to see another dog?"

pointing to Victor's right, where a stainless-steel bowl filled with water was chained to the iron fence. "See? Just tie her right here."

"You expect me to just leave her outside by herself?"

Victor didn't look up. Just sipped his coffee, nibbled on his bagel.

The employee shrugged her apology. "Café rules. Sorry. But we'll serve you quick and you can eat out here with your dog."

"It's cold out. I want to sit inside. With my dog."

"So sorry."

The girl sniffed. "Starbucks wouldn't do this to me. The manager there even keeps dog cookies for me behind the counter."

"I know. The rule sucks. But there's nothing I can do."

As the girl's friends examined the doggy area, Victor chewed and watched a small bird hop along the black iron fence that surrounded the patio. The two men from the back table got up to leave, sidling between Victor and the girls before heading off toward a parked SUV. The pug had been placed on the ground and appeared worried, what with her panting and pacing. The bug eyes took in the surrounding scene and finally settled on Victor and his toasted bagel. Ah. Here was something that caught the beast's attention. She licked her lips, then packed her tongue away as she moved closer to Victor.

It pleased him, this being wanted. Even by a creature that looked as if her eyes were sliding down the sides of her face. Victor patted his mouth with a napkin before he spoke. "I'll watch your dog."

The girl turned around, noticing Victor for the first time. "Excuse me?"

"I said I'll watch your dog." He motioned toward his breakfast. "She can keep me company while I finish my coffee."

She sighed and glanced at her friends, who nodded and started inside the coffee shop.

"You don't mind?"

"Not a bit."

Victor watched as she wound the fancy green leash through the dirty rungs of the iron fence, then blew the pug a kiss before disappearing inside. The dog had lost interest in Victor now that her owner had vanished, and took to investigating the shiny water dish.

Victor drained his coffee cup, folded what remained of his bagel into his mouth, and stood up. After a good stretch and a satisfied smack to his belly, he walked over to the black iron trash receptacle and pushed his paper plate through the flap. He turned to find the pug looking up at him, pig tail wagging excitedly, little raisin face opening into a smile. When Victor didn't react, the dog wandered close, raised herself up on tiny drumsticks, and rested one paw on his pant leg.

HE STARED UP at the sky and tried to determine whether the tree that shaded the dog pen would keep the shade for the rest of the day. The ancient oak hung over the trampled grass like a great prehistoric creature, and Victor determined the sun wouldn't bake the ground directly beneath until long after four o'clock. Besides, the day seemed in no danger of heating up too much. He tested out the corner posts by giving each a good shove and, satisfied the enclosure was sturdy, he stared down inside it and smiled at the mashed-up face that looked back at him. The pug spun in a circle and yipped her reproach.

"You settle down now. Might not be as fancy a home as you're used to, but you're not in any danger."

He looked around, proud of himself. Stealing a dog had been a brilliant move on his part. A few people might get ruffled in the short-term, but no one winds up hurt in the end.

Victor realized he was hungry again. It had been a long walk home. He spun around to find his daughter staring at him, open-mouthed.

"What are you doing?"

"I know. It's a huge responsibility and I should have discussed this with you first. But an opportunity came up and—well, you see that squishy little raisin face. How was I supposed to resist? Happy early birthday, Mouse."

"You bought me a dog?"

"Isn't she a cute one?"

"Dad, I'm not a little kid you can distract with puppies or candy."

"Not meant to be a distraction. Just a small household change that should bring us both a bit of joy."

"There's no way we can handle a dog right now."

"I'll do the dirty work, I don't mind a bit."

"You can't handle it either. The walking, the feeding, the training. Keeping it out of reach of coyotes. It's a nice gesture, Dad, but we have to return it."

He glanced down at the pug, who grinned and panted and looked up at them both as if they were the most beautiful creatures on earth. Leaning over the pen, Victor waggled his fingers and allowed the dog to lick them. "We can't."

"Please. Just call the place where you got the dog and tell them I'll drop it off in the morning."

He searched his mind. The dog, here, now, was a good thing. That much he knew. And he was the reason the dog was here. Yet, how it had happened had vanished. The pet store flashed in his consciousness, but he'd left there without a dog. "I don't know, Mouse. I can't think where she came from . . ." He fiddled with his tie, loosened it. Undid the top buttons of his shirt. Damn this sticky mind. "It'll come to me. It will. It's this sludge; it fills my head. This stinking, reeking like mother-fucking shitface sludge."

"Dad, we have to do something. You're scaring me."

"I have my own plan."

"Plan? Your mind isn't functioning all that well. If there's a plan, I think I should be involved."

"I can't think of it right now, Mouse, but I have a feeling the plan is all about you. All about my girl."

September 20, 1996

Delilah was standing at the counter, spreading peanut butter onto a slice of Wonder bread when her mother slammed down the phone. Elisabeth ran her hands through her hair. "Dratted sitter," she said. "Canceled again."

Delilah walked her sandwich and glass of milk over to the table and sat down.

"I'll fail my midterm if I miss another art class." Elisabeth lit a cigarette and crossed the room to the window, tugging it open and perching herself, barefoot in paint-spattered leggings and undershirt, on the ledge. She stared outside and, with a barely perceptible wobble of her head, exhaled. "I don't know

what I was thinking, enrolling in night school as a single parent. Thirty-one years old and still working on my BFA. Remember this, Delilah. Marry someone with money. Don't get all starry-eyed over someone having a good year in sales. Those bonus checks aren't a sure thing. If you want an easy life, marry a man who comes from money. One who has a nice fat bank account."

Delilah wasn't too sure what was desirable about a fat bank account and wasn't interested enough to inquire. "Okay."

"They say money doesn't buy happiness, but let me tell you, it buys you nice things. You want to marry smart. A husband with money means you'll never have to go out and work. You can, but you don't have to. See the difference?"

Delilah nodded.

"That was my mistake. I didn't marry smart."

"If you didn't marry Daddy, you wouldn't have had me," Delilah pointed out, her cheeks smeared with peanut butter.

Elisabeth smiled. "You'd still have found your way to me. You might not have looked exactly the same. You might have been shorter or taller, or a boy, but you were definitely meant for me."

Delilah thought about the possibility of being born a boy. "Disgusting."

"But you'd have had a father who was able to support his family properly."

"Why don't you call him?" Delilah asked. "I can go stay at his house."

"Friday's not his night. You go to his house Saturdays, sleep over until Sunday."

"I want to go today. Dad builds a tent in his living room for me to camp." Right away she regretted the confession. Hearing that Victor was exciting enough to build indoor tents could backfire. "No booze, I promise."

"What kind of life is this?" Elisabeth said, stabbing out her

cigarette. She picked up the phone and started to dial. "Victor? It's Elisabeth. I need a favor . . ."

Delilah listened while her mother ranted again about the sitter and the situation Victor left her in, before announcing she needed child care. "Delilah is to be home no later than ten tomorrow morning," she warned. "One minute, one half *minute later, and the judge will hear about it on Tuesday."*

She hung up the phone and looked at her conniving daughter. "Well? What are you waiting for? Go get packed for your father's."

"Should I bring my bath toys?" Delilah asked.

"Don't bother, baby." Elisabeth gathered her daughter's silky hair into a loose ponytail. "It's just one night."

Twenty-Nine

Ransom Park. In the history of parks, it was quite possibly the worst name ever conjured up. Called to mind untraceable phone calls, bundles of unmarked bills, and—the irony was not lost on Lila—kidnappers.

A metal fence, knee high to an adult, chest high to a toddler, had the same white sign dangling every six feet or so, on both the inside and the outside of the fence: NO ADULTS UNLESS ACCOMPANIED BY CHILDREN. When Kieran caught sight of it, she'd announced that no one need worry. She'd keep an eye out for unattended adults.

Lila and Elisabeth sat side by side on a swell of grass in the sun while Kieran, dressed like a sixty-four-year-old spinster in thick tights and wool skirt, put her hands on her hips and stared across the grass at the wading pool, where a few children with rolled-up jeans were racing through the water. Another two girls were perched at the water's edge trying to float a paper boat. "Why didn't you tell me there was a pool? I don't have the right clothes."

"I didn't *know,* Kiki," said Elisabeth. "Just peel off your tights and dip your toes in like the other kids. It doesn't matter if you get splashed a little."

Kieran shook her head solemnly and sighed. It was clear that part of her was desperate to be a kid, but she didn't know how. "It's not even warm enough for wading pools. Those kids don't know anything."

Elisabeth leaned forward and fussed with Kieran's bangs. "You know I don't like it when you wear that hair band. It's too severe for your face." She sat back and assessed the child.

"Look, Kieran," said Lila, pointing toward the pool. "There's a boy wearing his sneakers in the water even."

"I hope he has another pair, because those are *not* going to be dry for school tomorrow."

"Then you should hang here with us." Lila shrugged and leaned back on her elbows. "We're going to talk about world politics and the depletion of the ozone."

Kieran huffed in annoyance. "Does this mean you're going to smoke?"

Elisabeth looked at Lila and laughed. "It's like living with a prison guard." She patted Kieran's leg. "Hardly at all. Now run off and play like the other kids. Try to make a friend."

Kieran scowled, then stomped down the little hill toward the pool with her arms folded across her chest. Once at the water's edge, two girls ran past and splashed her, causing Kieran to jump back, indignant, and kick at the water as payback.

When Elisabeth had suggested an afternoon at the park with Kieran, Lila hadn't been interested. But it turned out to be the perfect place to have her mother all to herself. Her little sister was now too busy policing the other kids to steal away any of Elisabeth's attention.

"Mum, I'm worried about Kieran."

"She's fine. Just a bit uptight."

"This fascination with lost children. It's not healthy."

"Kids have bizarre interests. I find it best to allow it and let them tire of it on their own. If I forbid the milk cartons flat-out, it'll only feed her obsession. You were obsessed with the foil wrappers from cigarette packages when you were young. Used to go through the garbage trying to find empty packages. I didn't stop that."

"I was peeling it to make a silver ball. That's different."

"You know what I think? I think now that you're in Kieran's life, she'll start to focus on what is here. Not what is missing."

"Maybe. But what about that Finn guy who babysits her?"

"What? Finn is a wonderful human being. He's gifted, you know. Once he comes out of his slump, he'll be a very famous artist."

"His place is littered with hash and rolling papers and empty bottles. That's no place for a child."

"The creative process is different for everyone. Honestly, Delilah. Your father raised you to make terrible judgments about people. Finn is just lovely. He's been very good to me."

Lila debated asking if they were dating. She wasn't sure she could handle the answer.

Elisabeth lit a cigarette, then stretched back on her

elbows in the grass. She was underdressed in a T-shirt and orange batik wrap skirt that exposed far too much tanned thigh as she crossed one leg over the other, twirling her foot. "I just got these shoes."

"Nice."

"Really? You don't think they're flashy? All that beading?"

"No. They're bold."

"Are you sure? The saleswoman was pushy. But they make my ankles look slim, don't you think?"

Lila nodded.

"It was such fun, picking you up from school again," Elisabeth said, rolling onto her side, closer to Lila. "Must have felt a bit like kindergarten to you, though."

Lila had been mortified. This time Elisabeth hadn't waited in the parking lot, but came right up to the class. A braless woman in a pale T-shirt knocking at the door and wandering inside the studio to lean against the sinks as if there were a sign out on the street—hand drawn by Lichty, with no hard edges—that announced the need for a studio audience. When Lichty asked if he could help Elisabeth, she'd pointed at Lila and announced she was just picking up her daughter. Lichty's face had turned toward Lila's and crumpled into a delighted smile, before he announced, "Miss Mack. Your mommy is here."

The last five minutes of class had been torture. Not only were the students distracted by the maternal presence, but standing nude in front of her mother made Lila feel vulgar and ashamed. The damaged slut of a daughter, in spite of the obvious pride on Elisabeth's face.

"No. It was fine that you came." Lila shifted her mother's

cloth purse from beside her knees and put on a fake smile. "A happy surprise."

"It's a nice, bright studio."

"Yeah. But cold."

"Does your teacher ever bring in outside experts? You know, professionals?"

"Umm . . . I don't know. Not yet, anyway."

"You should tell him your mother is a painter. Tell him I'm from Canada. I bet he'd be interested to bring in a foreign influence, don't you? It would be fascinating for those sheltered kids to see what's going on in other parts of the globe. Let them know Los Angeles isn't the be all and end all of the art world."

"I don't think anyone around here thinks that."

"Thank heavens."

"Have you ever taught before?"

"I taught at a private art school for a few months after I finally completed my degree. Just as a substitute. Never what I wanted to teach, which was Nature in Oil. Kathleen Digby seemed to have cornered the market on that class, what with her ridiculous field trips to the Butterfly Conservatory. Poor students had to haul all their supplies to Cambridge on a Greyhound bus in the middle of February and get special permission to set up after hours. Do you know how long it takes for oil paints to dry? If I see another smudged monarch butterfly rendering in the lobby of that building, I'll pull out my own fingernails."

"I love painting in oil. Even the smell."

"You have to ventilate, you know. That smell isn't healthy."

Lila felt a little gush of warmth in her chest. This was

what her life had been missing. The grim warnings about obscure things that could kill you from someone invested in keeping you very much alive. Her father's lack of concern for air flow in the laundry room where she painted was absolute. While he may have been cognizant of many other perils, as far as she knew he'd never given her inhalation of art-related toxins the slightest thought. It was a miracle she'd made it this far.

"Anyway, ask your teacher. I could make time."

"I'll ask but I doubt he does that kind of thing."

"What about the scholarship?"

"No word yet."

Elisabeth watched Kieran by the water for a moment. "Is this man even any good? You don't want to waste your time in a class if you aren't even learning."

"No, he's good. He's a Lichtenstein, you know."

Elisabeth raised her eyebrows.

"A second or third cousin. He's teaching us . . . them . . . to draw as adults, not as children. Actually quoted some great researcher—I forget who—"

"Whom."

Lila glanced sideways at Elisabeth. "Whom. Anyway, it was a great quote. When a child was asked how he drew, what went through his head, the boy said, 'First I think. Then I draw my think.'" Lila laughed, tucking flyaway hairs behind her ears. "I really like that. To me, it says so much about not letting our preconceptions get in the way of our work, of what is actually in front of us. It's best just to stop thinking. It'll only get you into trouble, you know?"

Elisabeth pulled a bottle of mineral water from her purse and drank, observing her daughter, tightening her lips and nodding. If Lila had ever believed herself to look more like her mother with her dyed locks, it ended this moment. Seeing Elisabeth's spiral curls, winking and sparking with ribbons of gold, silver, cinnamon, and wheat, she knew she was wrong. Her own hair was flat, lifeless in comparison. Elisabeth set one hand on top of Lila's and said, "You should try not to pepper your language with so many questions, sweetheart. You don't need to seek the other person's approval when you speak. If you project confidence, you'll feel confident."

A gush of cool wind blew in Lila's face. She busied herself with collecting her hair into a ponytail using a rubber band she'd had around her wrist, then reached up to tug on her lower lip. She couldn't argue with this. It was a terrible habit, a needy habit. There was something wrong with her. When she spoke, her voice was thinner. "I think it's time we talk about Dad."

"Still no explanation?"

"I don't know that it's ever coming. Because if he ever changes his mind, it might be too late. He probably won't remember. His behavior is getting more erratic by the week. He refused a job interview. He came home with a dog and had no idea where he got it. Plus he left when you came over."

"Taking off was definitely not a case of forgetting. You do know that, don't you?"

"Maybe. It's just so weird. And he won't go to a doctor."

Elisabeth pulled her close and rested her chin on Lila's head. "It's not easy for you. You love him and now you find out he's someone else." She smoothed the hair away from Lila's face. "I wish I could go back and change it all. Forget me. Just for you."

Tears trickled down Lila's cheeks.

Elisabeth felt them and pulled Lila upright. "Oh, sweetie, I know it hurts to discuss this."

"No, it's not that. It's just that everything's so messed up, and I know the whole business with the police is just hovering there, about to happen, and I can't do anything about it." She looked at Elisabeth. "And I'm not trying to make you feel guilty. I get why you need to do it. God knows I'd do the same if I were you. But . . ."

"I should tell you I've spoken to the police."

Lila felt her stomach drop. "You said you'd wait."

"Don't panic. I didn't release your father's name. I just wanted to find out what would happen once I gave them the go ahead. So I can be prepared as far as you're concerned. Now that I know the procedure, I don't want you to witness it."

"Tell me."

"Sweetheart, you really don't want the details . . ."

"I do. He's my father. I need to know."

Elisabeth rolled her tongue around in her mouth as if prolonging the taste of her cigarette. "Okay, but only because I think too much has been kept from you already. After I file the report, a warrant is issued. Then the officers will head up to the house and arrest your father—you might have to help us by telling us when he might be home."

"They wouldn't handcuff him, would they?"

"Not unless he resists."

Pick the wrong moment and Victor was capable of anything: cussing, insulting, fleeing. "Go on."

"Then they bring him into the station and fingerprint him. Take his mug shot. That sort of thing. Does your father have a lawyer?"

"You can't do this yet, Mum. You promised you'd wait until I'm ready."

"I'm waiting, baby, but the fact is you may never be ready."

"I will. I swear. But with waiting to hear about the scholarship and him bringing me dogs and not having answers, I just can't take it yet."

"Okay. But soon."

"Soon. I promise."

Her mother kissed her forehead. "Now let's not talk about it any more today, okay? We're meant to be enjoying a nice, lazy afternoon."

Kieran came running up and perched herself on her knees at their feet. Elisabeth reached behind her and ground out her cigarette in the earth like a child fearful of being caught by a parent, but Kieran was too agitated to notice. She pointed across the park to where a few people sat on benches by the play equipment. "That lady looks weird."

Tall, big-boned, it seemed unlikely this was a lady, in spite of the girlish attire of minidresss, flip-flops, and cardigan. He had a smile the shape of a peanut frozen on his clean-shaven face as he watched over the sandbox area with daisy wicker purse perched on huge hairless knees.

It seemed Ransom had failed here as well. All the effort put into those stern metal signs, the deliberate placement so they could be seen from any place in the park, so easily ignored by potential pedophiles. Lila tried not to stare. "It's a man."

Elisabeth looked again. "You think?"

"Look at those feet. They're size eleven, maybe twelve. And there's stubble on his face. Maybe we should call the police."

"What for?" said Elisabeth. "So far the man's only crime

is his fashion sense. He's just an old queen, probably hanging out with his grandchild."

Lila got up on her knees and shielded her eyes from the sun. "Does he even have a child here? If he doesn't we should definitely call the police."

Kieran narrowed her eyes. "He wants to kidnap someone, I bet."

"Don't you worry about it, Kieran," said Lila. "We'll keep an eye on him. Just play on this side of the pond and he won't be anywhere near you."

"Isn't it time to leave yet?" the child whined. "I want to go."

"Soon," said Elisabeth.

"I want to go now."

"Ten minutes. Then we go. I promise," said Elisabeth. Once Kieran shuffled off, clearly miserable, Elisabeth grinned. "Not often you hear that. A child begging to leave the playground."

Kieran wandered down toward the stucco shack that housed the changing rooms. She seemed to be studying the walls. Perhaps spying on a caterpillar attempting to climb up the rough plaster. Then again, this was Kieran. She could very well have been inspecting for structural soundness.

It was heartbreaking, Kieran's inability to be a kid. Lila didn't know what was worse, having your childhood hijacked without your knowledge or having never had one at all.

Elisabeth sighed. "Sometimes I wonder if I was born under a dying star."

"That's crazy. You have so much going for you."

"I'm forty-three. I could have really done something with my life, you know? And now it's so late." She pushed errant curls off her face and pointed. "See those lines between my brows? My forehead will never be smooth again. I worry I look old."

Lila didn't answer right away, busy as she was trying to flick away an ant making its way up her boot.

"I do, don't I?"

"What? No. I just have this bug on me."

"It's all right. You can say it. I'm past my prime."

"Not at all. You're beautiful."

"Soon I'll be at that stage in life when men no longer look at me. Not that I even want a man right now, but still. It will be a shock when it's gone. The only real mercy is my vision is going too. So I won't see them not seeing me."

Lila laughed.

"I'm modeling for Finn. Did you see that sculpture in his dining room?"

"I wondered if it was you."

Elisabeth nodded. "Though I just did it the one time. Then he got into his slump."

"Is that what he meant when he said you already pay him enough for the babysitting?"

"What a house to manage at his age, don't you think? He'll inherit the place one day. Sometimes I imagine what the place would be like if it were converted back to a single-family dwelling. I've always wanted to have an old mansion like that . . ."

"Mum, he's really young."

"Don't worry, sweetie. I do realize he doesn't see me that way. It's a waste of time to dream, and yet I always do." She laughed miserably and looked at Lila. "Do you want to hear something ridiculous? Since I was fourteen, I've wanted a thick gold necklace. Nothing fancy, just a chunky piece of jewelry I could wear with everything—T-shirts, dresses. Something I would never take off. A trademark piece. My best friend had one and, I don't know, that wish just stayed with me."

The bracelet. Lila had to force herself not to smile.

Kieran was now inspecting the doorway to the girls' change room, and Lila and Elisabeth went silent as they watched the man get up, dust off his skirted lap, and wander over to the door. He stood under the roof overhang for a moment before self-consciously rooting through his purse.

Lila said, "This can't be good."

"He might just be waiting for his child to come out of the restroom," said Elisabeth.

When Kieran didn't move away, Lila stood up. "Call 911."

"Seriously?"

Lila ran toward the change room, watching as the man closed his purse, looked around, then wandered over to Kieran. Just as he bent down to speak to her, Lila pushed her way between them and picked up her sister, twisting her body to position the young girl behind her. Out of the corner of her eye, she saw Elisabeth on the phone, looking toward the street sign, giving directions.

The man smiled and tried to veer around Lila and head into the change room, but Lila stepped to the side and blocked his entrance. "You need to have a child to go in there."

He smiled nervously and tried to squeeze past her. When he spoke his voice was high-pitched. "Excuse me. I need to use the facilities."

"Show me your child or I scream bloody freaking murder."

He seemed to lose his nerve, his eyes darted around, and he stepped backward. One hand touched his brow in distress, and he turned and sashayed toward an old Schwinn bike leaning on the fence. A lady's bike. Lila watched as he dropped his pretty handbag into a wire basket strapped to the handlebars, swung a leg over like he was mounting a stallion, and pedaled off down the side street.

It wasn't until he'd disappeared that it struck her. His bike had had a child seat on the back. He'd come with no child.

Had he been planning to leave with one?

She set Kieran down and gripped her shoulders. "He could have taken you, Kieran. Do you realize that? Do you know how devastated Mum would be? And me?"

Kieran said nothing. Just stared into her big sister's eyes as if seeing straight back to the day Lila went missing.

Elisabeth jogged up, breathless and barefoot. "Police are on their way." She blew hair out of her face, looking around and panting. "They thanked me for calling."

Thirty

The dog had proven to be good for Victor. Dogs need a certain predictability in their lives, and Lila was fairly sure her father was providing it. Up at seven for a short walk followed by breakfast on the back deck, a short game of fetch in the yard, and an hour in the playpen. Light snack at lunchtime, then a short pee and a long nap in Victor's room.

While it might not compare to the career Victor had once had, the canine demands had meant he was having a good week. Only one forgetful episode involving his keys. No wandering too far. No repeating himself.

Of course there had been no mention of the past. Victor wasn't offering and Lila wasn't willing to upset the present state of balance by bringing it up.

It was November. The morning of Adam's art meeting and the first time she'd seen him since taking off her clothes in his studio. While nothing had happened, everything had happened. The feel of his eyes on her skin had left her barely able to breathe, and the thought of seeing him again had had her tossing in her bed every night since.

The question was—had he felt it too?

She had nothing to show this designer, as Lichty had neither returned her artwork nor breathed a word about her scholarship chances. It was okay. She'd give up selling all her work to the designer for a shot at an education.

Adam asked her to come anyway, for emotional support, he'd said on the phone.

With a napkin-wrapped fried egg sandwich in one hand, Lila set her coffee mug on the passenger seat of the Datsun and leaned over to lower her purse onto the floor, accidentally tipping the travel mug and soaking the seat.

Damn. She set her breakfast on the floor of the hatch area behind her and, leaving the door open, ran back to the house for a towel.

When she returned, she heard her phone ringing from her bag on the floor. She dropped into the driver's seat, threw the towel on the spilled coffee, and reached for the phone in her purse, stopping when she realized the atmosphere in the car had changed. It felt warm, close, as if it were about to rain. Stranger still, was the scent of dirt, dander. Animal.

A low grumble came from behind her seat and she spun around to see a coyote's face staring back at her.

Slash was in the car.

She froze, stunned by the very fact of him. She'd never been so close to a coyote and in broad daylight. His good ear pricked forward like a great velvet dish while the ragged ear listed sideways. The bottom of his tawny snout was pure white, impossibly clean, unstained by garbage, compost, or bloodied neighborhood vermin. Most stunning of all, the eyes. Irises as pale gold as the pupils were black. With an expression of utter curiosity, but mixed with something else. A look Lila couldn't quite grasp right away. Fear, maybe. Or resignation.

She fought her instinct to reach out and stroke his muzzle.

The sandwich lay between them; Slash was well aware of it. His yellow eyes darted from her to his prize and back again. Then he dropped down and took the edge of the bread in his front teeth, inching it back between his front legs.

It was the best time to bolt, while he was worrying about his meal. She scrambled out of the car and ran to the front end, slapped her palms against the hood to scare him off. The car wiggled beneath her hands and the coyote streaked out her door, egg sandwich between his teeth, and across to the neighbors' yard. She stared at the spot in the bushes where he disappeared, watching the branches shiver in his wake. Shocking, his willingness to climb into a car and remain so calm when she dropped into her seat. Other than his concern about breakfast, he'd been completely unruffled by her presence, even with her body essentially cornering him in the back. She thought about Corinne Angel raising orphaned wolf pups in her Arizona kitchen and wondered—what becomes of an animal released into the wild after months and months of living on a bed of ragged towels in a warm kitchen?

ADAM WAS WAITING for her outside the building, leaning against a concrete planter and rubbing his jaw. He stood when he saw her.

She scanned his face for clues, but he seemed to be all business. His voice. Maybe his voice would reveal more. Throwing his arms in the air, he squeaked, "Where have you been? We were supposed to be up there six minutes ago."

So much for sexual tension and pent-up desires. He might as well have been talking to his sister. "Sharing my breakfast. Where's your work?"

"I had it delivered. Wouldn't fit in the car." He squinted up at the sun and started to pace. "Why's it so freaking sunny today? It was supposed to rain. Jesus, I hate L.A. I can't wait to leave."

"What's with you? You have to calm down."

"You brought nothing? No word about the scholarship?"

"No."

"That's terrible. Lichty's blowing a huge opportunity for you here."

"It's okay. The scholarship matters more."

"Yeah, but you won't be able to come to New York if you get it. Think what you're passing up."

Her eyes traveled from his battered, thrift-store desert boots up past his paint-spattered jeans and lumberjack shirt, to the red spot on his neck where he'd nicked himself shaving. She pulled a tissue from her bag and dabbed at the cut. "A girl can't have it all."

"I don't know why I listened to her. No, I do. She said I look like a cult member when I take the other."

"What are you talking about?"

"My sister. She convinced me to take DayQuil." He reached for her fingers and pressed them to his neck. "Time my pulse. See if it's the same as yours."

She prodded the skin around his throat. "I can't even find it."

"What are you saying?" He started breathing fast and shallow. "Of course I have a pulse. You think I don't have a pulse?"

"You have a pulse," she said, louder. "I just can't find it. Pull it together, Adam."

"I can't do this. Tell them I'm sick."

She took him by the shoulder and led him inside the lobby. "No one's sick. We're going straight up there and you can stay perfectly silent. Let me do all the talking. We'll say you lost your voice."

He stopped her from getting on the elevator. Slithered one hand beneath her hair to rest it on the back of her neck and grinned, his eyes scanning her face. "Delilah Blue?"

A jolt shot through her. "Yes?"

"Hi. Just hi."

THE DESIGNER STOOD face to cheek with Lila's nearly naked and glowing bottom, then reached up to touch the faint stain that was the birthmark on her upper hip. If Lila had ever imagined being touched by another female, she could not have conjured up a more unlikely participant. Norma Reeves was less than five feet tall, all boxy torso, banged mahogany bob, and cat's-eye glasses with blue-tinted lenses. She wore silver lipstick and a black unitard under a pleated pastel mini that looked as if it had been peeled off the underside of a muffin. As much as Adam's nude of Lila, titled *Nude with Denim,* fascinated Norma, she seemed to have no idea the model stood right next to her.

There was something both sensuous and ordinary about this particular nighttime nude. Adam's talent was obvious in the intense shadows, the lines of Lila's body, and the luminosity of her skin in the milky moonlight that trickled through the windows, but it was more than that. The true mastery was more commercial, in the way he'd positioned the pair of faded jeans across the curve of her hip. Perfect for a denim designer.

Norma hadn't spoken to them except to nod a silent hello. Adam and Lila had been ushered by an assistant into a boardroom with leather walls lined with several nudes. The assistant had offered them espresso, which Adam wisely refused, and they'd waited for the great Ms. Reeves herself to arrive. When she had, she'd walked straight over to the artwork, pausing for three or four minutes in front of each. Adam's pieces weren't the only pieces being considered, Norma's assistant had made that perfectly clear. He was just one of about five artists invited to submit works, and probably the only student.

At the far end of the room, a monster-size wall clock ticked with all the drama of a bomb. Other than the sound of Adam trying to slow his own heartbeat, the room was completely silent.

Five more minutes of silence and it was over. Norma turned away from Lila's lunar-lit bottom and marched toward the door. Just before she vanished, she called back, "I'll have the one titled *Nude with Denim*. Tell my assistant to cut you a check."

Thirty-One

There he was, marching across campus, his stinger leading the way past the water fountain and toward the parking garage. Lila, on her way to a third-year sculpting class where she would re-create the same pose she'd been holding for five classes straight now, broke into a run. It was mid-November. It had been more than three weeks since she'd turned in her pieces. Part of her didn't want to ask—why hurry bad news? But mostly she could no longer take the waiting. Wondering.

Just as he was about to step out of the sunlight and into the darkness of the garage, she called out, "Lichty!"

If he heard her, he didn't react, disappearing into the three-story structure. She followed him up the stairs, which smelled faintly of urine and beer, calling his name and blinking hard to adjust to the dim light. There was no sign of him on the second floor, so she raced up to the third and saw him climbing into a little yellow Beetle.

"Lichty, wait!"

The car sputtered to life and started to back out of the narrow spot. It was about to speed past her when she jumped in front of it, holding up her hands and shouting, "Stop!"

The car skidded to a stop and Lichty poked his head out the window. "A very good way to get yourself killed, Miss Mack."

"Sorry." She struggled to catch her breath. "It's just that it's Friday, and I couldn't stand the thought of going through the weekend without knowing."

He nodded, shifting the car into park. "The scholarship."

"The scholarship. Yes. You said it would take three weeks and it's been longer."

"If you'll stop by my office on Monday, I'll give you back your pieces."

"So that means you've made a decision."

He let out a long sigh. "In the end, we all felt the same way. I showed them the spider drawing and we all agreed the four other pieces lack the focus and clarity of that one. It's almost as if it wasn't done by the same person . . ."

It wasn't, she wanted to say. It was done by the girl who hadn't yet been kidnapped, hadn't yet learned her life was total bullshit. "They were. I swear, I did all of them."

"I believe you. But the others suffered from a certain lack of sureness. A lack of confidence and artistic sense of 'this is who I am.' "

"Yeah, but . . ."

"Don't get me wrong. We all felt you showed promise. But you're just not ready yet. Maybe you'll try again next year. Right now, you need to solidify a few things, develop your sense of groundedness. Some consistency. I need to know, from one quick glance at your work, the truth about who you are."

Her eyes grew hot and she fought to keep her bottom lip from giving away her emotions. "I'm not sure I'll ever figure that out."

He looked at her, his face unsympathetic. "That, Miss Mack, is a terrible shame." The yellow car thumped into gear and sped away.

Thirty-Two

Lila slammed the cupboard door shut. When it bounced open again and struck her in the chin, she grabbed the plastic knob and shut the door again, as hard as she could, again and again and again until the tiny red knob broke off in her hand. She threw it into the sink and leaned over the counter to focus on her breath, still herself, before she tore apart the entire kitchen.

"What is going on in there, Mouse?"

She didn't answer. Just closed her eyes, turned her face to the ceiling, and tried to wipe Lichty's words out of her memory. *A terrible shame.* She'd wanted the scholarship. She'd ached for it. And she'd known she'd be upset if she was turned down. What she hadn't counted on was this feeling of absolute nothingness. Of spinning somewhere in space without any sense of where she'd been or where she was headed.

It had been raining all morning. The incessant drumming against the roof, and dampness within the cabin, and grayness outside, had only added to her misery.

"Mouse?" She heard the rhythmic shuffling of his bedroom slippers against the bricks with the *clickety-click* patter of tiny canine toenails. *Clickety-swish. Clickety-swish.* Then Victor's voice at the doorway. "What was all that banging?"

"Nothing, okay? It was nothing."

"Didn't sound like nothing."

"Yeah, well. It is what it is."

"What's that supposed to mean?"

She spun around. "I don't really know. Because around here, nothing seems to be anything. Have you noticed? Whatever happens just happens. Nothing is explained. And whoever gets knocked down is supposed to get up, wipe their ass, and gallop on as usual."

Victor looked confused. "But that's not true at all. I've told you things were complicated back then. I've asked you to trust me when I say I did what I had to do."

She slid down to the floor and thumped her head against the cabinet behind her.

He picked up the dog. "Enough of that now. You're scaring the dog."

"And why do you call her the dog? Why don't you give her a name? Or, wait, give her one, then just go and change it on her. Just so she doesn't get too settled."

"It was a nickname. Lots of people have them. Wasn't as if I started calling you Heather or Emily." Victor slid into a chair and reached for the vinyl placemat in front of him. He held it up like a menu. "Could you get me a pastrami sandwich, my dear? With pickles on the side, if we're not out. And if you don't mind, pour a bit of that kibble into the dog's bowl."

She stared at him, incredulous. Nothing about this situation had affected him. He still expected his wretched victim to tend to his every need. And feed the dog without a name. She reached for the kibble and dumped it into the bowl on the floor next to the oven, then pulled open the fridge and rummaged around in search of pastrami, finally locating it beneath a package of spinach tortillas.

Something about the little deli bag looking up all unperturbed got to her. She grabbed it, along with a loaf of bread, and slammed it on the table.

"You know what? Make your own damned lunch." She reached for her keys and her purse. "And, by the way, that dog food you bought isn't even the right kind for your dog. It's for seniors. And she's clearly not a senior."

"Oh dear," he said. "I hadn't realized . . ."

"I'm going out." She stormed out the door and into the rain, started up the front steps, slowing as she neared the top, turning her face into the drizzle.

Damn him for looking so helpless.

She marched back down and into the house. Without removing her wet boots, she walked into the kitchen, where her father sat staring at the door, just as she'd left him. She picked up the meat and the bread, pulled the pickle jar from the fridge, then set about making his lunch. "You always put on too much mustard," she said as she cleaved the sandwich in half, rainwater pooling beneath her feet. "Makes the bread all soggy."

AN HOUR AND a half later and it was a different day. The skies had cleared, the sun was sucking up the puddles on the roads, and staff at sidewalk restaurants wiped down tables and chairs in hopes that the people filing out of cars and buildings might stop in, help make up for the morning's lost profits.

Kieran—as she ambled along beside Lila in her usual puritanical uniform—insisted upon holding the dog's green leash. The leash was long, the child was short, the dog was friendly, all of which added up to an animal who was able to race on ahead, hoist himself up on bare female calves, and mushroom his face up between the knees of every girl who happened by.

"Let me hold him, Kieran," said Lila, tugging the pug back. "He's being lewd."

She shook her head and growled. "You said I could hold him all the way until there, so I'm holding him all the way until there."

"And the leash is soaked. You're dragging it through puddles of slop."

"*Slop*." Kieran shook her head in disapproval. "You're so dramatic."

Elisabeth had an appointment with Finn. No doubt to lie naked on her back among the debris in Finn's work space. Lila couldn't stop the image of Finn drunkenly crawling across the floor and rubbing clay-stained hands all over Elisabeth. More upsetting than this was Lila's growing hunch that Elisabeth was reading way too much into the exchanges.

Lila had insisted Kieran spend the day with her. She had nothing special planned, just an afternoon filled with errands. First stop was the jeweler who had resized the bracelet.

"So do you dress like an executive every single day of

your life?" Lila asked Kieran as they tied the dog to a bicycle rack outside the store.

"Only if I need to feel grown-up."

"Huh. Does that happen a lot?"

Kieran sighed, as if her sweater weighed twenty pounds and her back were buckling from her managerial duties. "Almost all the time."

"Bummer."

Kieran examined Lila's clothing. "Why do you dress like that?"

Lila looked down at Victor's oversize sweatshirt—the gray one she'd cut the arms out of and made into a dress—bare thighs, and kneesocks with ever-present doodled boots. "I don't know. I'm artsy, I guess."

Kieran stopped and considered her sister's outfit more carefully. "Always big and baggy on top. And then bare legs. Like look at me but don't look at me."

Lila was too shocked, too annoyed, to answer right away. A bus roared past, sending a fine spray of puddle water toward them. They darted to the side, but not before Lila's boots got spotted, which only irritated her further. "You think that's how people see me?"

Kieran pursed her lips together and mulled this over. "How should I know? I'm not even eight."

Inside the store, the child was dumbstruck in the face of jewels set against black cloth, and the way they sparked and winked beneath halogen spotlights. She pulled away from Lila and hopped from case to case, drooling over the gold, platinum, and diamonds. As the shop assistant took Lila's ticket and headed off to the back to locate the resized, re-clasped bracelet, the owner invited Kieran behind the counter and encouraged her to drape her neck in finery.

Even Lila had to admit the girl looked cute, gobbed as she was with pearls and chains, her prim blouse rumpled by extravagance.

"Can you take my picture, Lila?" Kieran asked as she admired herself in the mirrored wall.

Lila pulled out her phone and snapped a few times as Kieran crinkled her nose and grinned. Kieran was a natural, posing for the camera as if she'd been doing it all her life. There were poses sitting on a stool, sitting cross-legged on the floor. Hands on hips with feet planted apart. Modeling must be in the genes. But when she caught Lila grinning from behind the camera, she stiffened up. "I'm done now. Can we print one for me?"

"Maybe when we get home."

"Can we go home now?"

The owner waved toward the open door behind him. "I don't mind printing it out for her. Just send it to me from your phone." He gave her his e-mail address, disappeared for a minute or two, and returned with a warm sheet of paper. "Here you are, Missy. Pretty in pearls."

Kieran thanked him and, as he disappeared with Lila's debit card, stared at her image, her cheeks flushed pink with pride. "Lila, can we play hide-and-seek?"

"Not here."

"Please."

The jeweler came back to say Lila's debit card didn't work and did she have an alternate method of paying. She dug through her bag for rumpled bills and change at the bottom.

"Please." Kieran tugged at Lila's sweatshirt. "Play with me."

"How much did you say?" Lila asked the man.

"Thirty-five dollars, fourteen cents. That's with our November discount."

Kieran tugged at her belt. "Do a long count. A hundred."

"No. There's nowhere to hide here anyway."

"You're lucky," said the jeweler, slipping the box into a paper bag. He summoned a quiet burp and released it into his hand. "Discount ends tomorrow."

She counted out $35.14, watched the man recount the money, and then scooped up the paper bag. When she got to the door, she turned around, looked for her sister. Kieran was nowhere to be seen. "Kieran? Time to go buy dog food."

A tall cardboard sign fell over to reveal Kieran sitting cross-legged, elbows resting on angry knees, photo of herself on her lap. "You didn't even *pretend* to look for me. You didn't even know I was gone!"

THE WALK TO the pet store had been quiet. Kieran hadn't been able to take her eyes off her photo. After she tripped over a curb, got tangled—twice—in the dog's leash, and walked straight into a baby stroller, Lila had threatened to take the photo away. But Kieran threatened to shout out that Lila wasn't her mother and was abducting her, so Lila took the dog leash in one hand and Kieran's elbow in the other.

You could smell the pet shop before you could see it. A whiff of Riverdale Farm back in Toronto, complete with twenty-five-cent pellets and goat fur and dung-packed hooves, wafted toward them from the open door. Kieran parked herself beside the window full of dachshund puppies—a tempting vista for any child—and informed

Lila she could pick out the dog food on her own because she wanted to examine her picture.

"Come in. We'll play hide-and-seek in here while I shop. This time I'll look for you. I promise."

Kieran sat cross-legged on the sidewalk and placed the photo on her lap. "I'm not falling for that."

"Seriously. I'll even count to one-fifty."

The twitch of her mouth revealed the count of 150 tempted the child, but Kieran pushed her nose in the air. "No."

"One-seventy-five and you get to pick the dog cookies."

"Two hundred and you choose your own stupid cookies."

"Two hundred it is." Lila started inside with Kieran and the dog on her heels, but stopped to allow Kieran to stuff the photo in her purse. As she waited, a poster tacked to the door caught her eye. The poster flapped in the breeze of a passing bus. STOLEN DOG, it read in thick black marker strokes. Under the ominous headline was a full-color photo of a pug. And not just any pug. A pug with a serrated green collar. A pug with a matching lime green leash. A pug that could very well be squirming right now in Kieran's arms.

The poster said the dog's name was Sammi. Barely daring to breathe the name, Lila whispered, "Sammi?" Sure enough, the dog looked up. Squirmed. Yipped.

Victor had stolen a dog. A *dog.*

A tall, ponytailed man of about thirty, with a gold hoop earring and the tattoo of a winged horse on one arm, emerged from the back of the store, wiping his hands as if he'd been eating lunch. He smiled. "Turned out to be a nice day after all."

"I'm ready to hide now, Lila," Kieran sang, setting

Sammi on the tile floor, then pushing up her sleeves. "You have to count to two hundred like you promised."

"What's your pup's name?" said the man.

They had to exit fast, before the clerk made the connection and called the police. Kieran had dropped to the floor to inspect a stack of cartons for crevices. "Kieran, we're going."

"But you said—"

"Now." She grabbed the child's arm, scooped up the dog, and ran back to the car.

SEPTEMBER 20, 1996

Victor peered through the flaps of the nylon pup tent pitched on his living-room rug and listened to his daughter's breathing, soft and relaxed, as she lay strewn across the pillows and duvets she'd dragged inside. God, he loved when she was with him. Since she'd arrived, he'd washed the smoke out of her clothes, had her shower and change into fresh pajamas, and fed her ready-made beef stew he'd picked up from his local market and heated up until steaming. Fortification, perhaps. As if any effort he made on this overnight, these fifteen hours he had with his girl, could steel her for what she might face later.

He hadn't heard from Graham all day. The judge had been assigned, that much was certain, but Graham had been curiously silent. Victor had tried to convince himself it was a good sign. That Graham was so relaxed, so confident of their chances, he didn't feel the need to call.

He padded into the dining room and stood in front of the sideboard his parents left him, along with the antique table and eight battered leather chairs, before they died—his mother after what seemed like a lifelong battle with Alzheimer's, his father of a broken heart. He wrapped his fingers around the wooden knobs of the center drawer and paused.

Drastic. Crazed. Unheard of. It was what his mother, in her better days, would say of Victor's preparations. Illegal, his military father would say. But neither of them had ever met with what Victor faced four days before his hearing. They'd never had to contemplate, even for a moment, losing the right to watch the way their child's eyelashes flutter in her sleep. Or to hear the sweet, unselfconscious whisperings between her Barbie dolls as she lay on his living-room floor, unaware anyone was listening.

Before he could pull open the drawer, the phone rang, and Victor hurried into the kitchen to pick up before it woke Delilah.

"Yes?" he whispered.

"It's me," said Graham. "Sorry I didn't call earlier. Kelly dragged me all over town to look at new office space. Apparently, we don't have enough square footage to accommodate—"

"Who'd we get?"

"What?"

"The judge. That's why you're calling, right? Did we get the right judge? That older woman?"

Graham was silent for a moment. Then he exhaled slowly. "We didn't. We got Henry Schiff. Midforties and recently divorced and, even more recently, dropped twenty pounds and started training for Ironman competitions. But that's not the reason I'm calling."

"I'm waiting."

"Before I left the office, I heard from Elisabeth's lawyer. Why the hell didn't you tell me about Delilah drinking alcohol at some bar?"

"It was nothing. I swear to God. She picked up someone's

dirty glass—a nearly empty glass—and downed it on a bet with another kid. Why do I have to explain this to you? She saw a pool of disgusting backwash and figured she could shock a few people. How was she to know there was rum in it? Looked like Coke to her."

"Jesus Christ."

"Oh come on, Graham. You can explain away this one. It could have happened to anyone."

"It's the kind of thing you mention to your lawyer when you're about to go before a judge to ask for more access."

"I figured . . . I don't know what I figured. I was hoping it would go away."

"Well, it didn't and it won't. Anyway, I know Elisabeth's lawyer. We articled together at Torys. He didn't have to, but he gave me the heads up."

Victor felt his heart hammer against his chest. "The heads up about what?"

"It's the law, Victor. He had no choice."

"No choice about what?"

"Once Elisabeth told him it was Delilah's second episode of drinking, he was bound by the law to report it."

"To whom?"

"Children's Aid."

Victor was silent. He could hear the sound of Delilah snoring softly in the next room. "You there, Vic?"

"I'm here."

"Buddy, I hate to be the one to tell you. You're going to be investigated."

Back in the dining room, Victor fought to control his breathing.

Children's Aid. Investigating him.

This hearing was always going to be a he said/she said affair. It would be Elisabeth's word against his. And all he had was his reputation as a father. Now—with an investigation under way—his reputation looked dubious, if not fully sullied. And then there was the larger issue. The issue that drove Victor to fight for custody of Delilah in the first place.

The accident that damned near killed her.

When Elisabeth laid her fingers across her bare throat and let them trail down her open-necked shirt, exuding sensuality, professing her absolute innocence, which parent would this newly single judge believe? Sure as hell not the one being investigated by Children's Aid.

Sweat dribbled down Victor's collar; his hands shook. His old Boy Scout motto rang in his head, Always Be Prepared. *He and Graham used to laugh about it. About preparing themselves for alien invasions, for alligators in sewers, for when sparrows attack. They envisioned themselves after the apocalypse, sitting in the middle of the ice rink at city hall in their Boy Scout uniforms—sashes decorated with badges for every possible accomplishment—surrounded by the lifeless bodies of the unprepared.*

No smiling today. He opened the drawer and felt around beneath the stack of folded, pressed linen napkins. Pulled out a fat manila envelope and dumped its contents.

Laid out on the sideboard was a well-padded bankbook, as well as new passports, new birth certificates, one-way airline tickets—two of each—along with one vital sheet of paper: a permission letter from his ex-wife. Forged.

Victor's only shot at a life worth living.

Thirty-Three

The girl's name was Hilary Cooper, and her shorts were so short that Lila could see the pale half-moon of the underside of her buttocks. She looked away as she followed Hilary and Mr. Cooper up the steps from the cabin to the road. It hadn't gone well. The only thing that had prevented Mr. Cooper from calling in the police, animal control, and the Department of Fish and Game, he'd said, was that he had to catch a flight to London that night and didn't have time for all the follow-up. But Lila should consider herself warned: Her father was a dangerous man.

Mr. Cooper said, "Thinks he's above the law, stealing a dog. Man's capable of just about anything."

She couldn't help herself. "Tell me about it."

In spite of the afternoon's warmth, Hilary had the pug swaddled in a fleecy white blanket with silky fringe. Sammi stared at Lila and grinned, tiny tongue darting in and out contentedly.

"Missed my golf game. Missed a breakfast meeting," Mr. Cooper ranted. "Idiot dog's been more trouble than it's worth." When Hilary shot her father an aggrieved look, he added, "Daddy's just tense, sweetheart."

"I'm really sorry," Lila repeated for the hundredth time.

Mr. Cooper circled the hood of the convertible BMW and paused at the wheel well, inspecting the paint. "What's this?"

No. Please, no.

"Where did this scratch come from?"

Lila looked back to see Victor's face dart behind the kitchen curtains. He did it—he actually scratched up a car this time. Followed through with his written threats and moved right into vandalism.

"It goes all the way . . ." Mr. Cooper followed the gauge to the taillights, around the rear end, and back up the right side of the car. "All the way around the car!" He looked up and down the street, then at the 240Z as if he might be able to wrestle up a class-action suit. But the 240Z was, of course, pristine.

Lila started to apologize. "I'm really sorry. If you get an estimate, we'll pay for any—"

"Hilary?" Mr. Cooper boomed. "Have you been driving my car?"

Lila was about to explain, but thought better of it. The man was already livid. Learning Victor trashed his paint job might send him raging down to the house again.

"Shut up and drive, Dad," Hilary said, climbing into

the passenger seat and arranging the dog in a patent leather carrier. "I have my bikini wax in twenty."

Mr. Cooper shook his head and trotted around the car, slapping his keys against his palm. "Nightmare of a day."

"I'm so sorry for your trouble. Please know we took good care of your dog. Of Sammi."

Hilary peered over the tops of her sunglasses, reached a slender arm over the car door, and gave Lila the finger. Then the car sped away, washing Lila's feet in dust.

Slowly, Lila turned around to see Keith Angel leaning on a tree at the road's edge, his mouth hanging open in disbelief.

Or, quite possibly, satisfaction.

She marched past him and down to the house. Shoved open the screen door, stomped into the kitchen, and pulled out a phone book, flipping through it so fast the pages tore. Victor peered over her shoulder. "Who are you calling, Mouse?"

She reached for a pen and scrawled a number on the back of an envelope. "A doctor."

"For whom?"

"For you."

"That won't be necessary."

She laughed angrily. "Oh, yes it will."

"I have an appointment booked already."

She stood up straight, shocked. "You booked an appointment?"

"I did."

"With an actual doctor?"

"That's right." Victor pulled his shirt away from his wrist and looked at his watch. "I'm due there in twenty-five minutes—that pale pink building away over by the pharmacy."

Lila reached for her keys and started for the door. "Get in the car. I'll drive you."

IF HIS DAUGHTER was surprised he didn't fight for the privilege of driving, she didn't show it. The poor girl probably hadn't recovered from the shock of his canine caper. It was okay. She'd soon know all she needed to know. With any luck it would soothe her. Not fully. Never fully.

After leaning over the center console, he patted her knee, said, "I'm doing this for you, my dear," then hauled his guilty bones up and out of the car, across the empty sidewalk, and through the revolving doors of the Goodhew Medical Arts Building.

It was true. Nearly 100 percent true.

September 21, 1996

Victor hunched in the little plastic tub chair at Pearson International Airport, certain his pounding heart was casting reverberations down the adjoining seats in his row. He pressed a hand to his knee to stop the nervous bouncing, then set his Styrofoam cup on the floor behind his feet, unable to tolerate airport coffee on top of the guilt and fear already churning in his gut.

It wasn't that he had imagined abducting his own child and smuggling her out of the country would be emotionally uncomplicated, but, deep in his heart, he never really believed following through with his just-in-case plan would be necessary. Preparation had been intense—six full weeks of planning. There were no how-to guides on paternal abduction. He'd had to consider every possible glitch that could arise—and what did a former Boy Scout know about skipping town with his daughter?

If there were a merit badge awarded for the act, surely he'd earned it. He'd emptied bank accounts, dropped hints around the office as to whom would be a good replacement should he suddenly get hit by a train, risked his life picking up fake IDs from a nail salon with a hidden back room that locked from the inside, and studied different states to determine where a single father and his shell-shocked daughter might best remain anonymous. The activity, the busyness, had kept him astonishingly calm.

Until now.

Every flight attendant and sanitation worker who cast a glance in his direction while going about their business caused him a gush of stomach acid. Every time Delilah looked up from her sketchpad, he thought he might drop dead from guilt for what he was about to do to her. To her mother.

He couldn't go through with it.

It wasn't too late. He hadn't yet done anything wrong.

He would gather her up, explain that the trip had to be canceled, quell the girl's tears with ice-cream sundaes and one last trip to Toys "R" Us before Children's Aid knocked on his front door. It was barely seven A.M.*, and there wasn't a chance in hell Elisabeth was even awake yet, let alone wondering where her daughter was.*

It would be so easy to undo everything.

Delilah's head sunk down onto Victor's arm. Soft. Heavy. Sweet. He looked at her, curled up in the seat beside him, her face puffy with lack of sleep, sparkly fairy wings strapped to her back. "Can we go back and get my new bike?"

Victor stiffened, a prickly feeling spreading through his chest. No. Elisabeth wouldn't have. The doctors had been clear after the accident. No jumping, no running. No skipping, no skateboards. No bikes. Not for a full six months. Another hit to the head could be devastating.

He tried to sound casual when he spoke. Tried to sound as if the lives of all three of them didn't depend on the child's answer. "Your mother got you a bike?"

Delilah yawned into her hand and closed her eyes. "Mm-hmm."

"When?"

"Last week."

It was all he needed to know.

A garbled voice announced over the loudspeakers that flight 764 was ready to board. Passengers in business class were to move toward the gate, as well as anyone with small children or limited mobility. People in the seats around them began to rise, gather their bags, move toward the gate where a flight attendant checked their tickets.

Victor stood up and pulled his daughter to her feet. "Time to go, Mouse."

"Wait. I forgot about my secret code." People picked their way past them and their toppled carry-on bags, until no one remained in the row. "It's the rule," said Delilah, refusing to budge. She looked up at Victor. "We have to call Mum. She told me not to go anywhere with anyone unless they say my secret code. It's from Stranger Danger Day."

"Delilah, I'm your father. Secret codes are for strangers, not people who love you."

Delilah folded her arms across her chest, chin tilted upward. "I can't get on the plane unless Mum says I can give you my code. We have to call her."

"We're not—"

"I WANT TO CALL MY MOTHER AND YOU CAN'T STOP ME!"

All around them, heads snapped around. Couples mumbled to each other. An airline employee frowned. Victor had no choice. He couldn't afford to make a scene.

Red-faced and fumbling, Victor pulled his phone from his jacket pocket and dialed. As Delilah snatched it, holding it to her ear for all to see, he slung their bags over his shoulder and got ready to dart onto the plane once Elisabeth caught wind of what was going on.

"Hello?" Victor could hear Elisabeth's sleepy voice.

"Mummy! I'm on Dad's cell phone."

"I can barely hear you, Delilah. Speak louder."

"Daddy's taking me to Disneyworld. That's in Florida."

The line filled with static. Elisabeth said something, but Victor couldn't make out what, exactly. "I get to miss school on Monday."

More static. Then, "No! Delilah, you wait there. I'm coming right now . . ."

Delilah covered the receiver and looked at Victor, crinkling up her nose. "I think she wants to come."

Victor, sweating, pacing, rubbing his temples, shook his head and pointed to the shrinking lineup of passengers, most of whom had disappeared onto the boarding ramp. "We have to go, Delilah. Now. The plane is boarding."

"He says you can't come. But we'll be home soon. Can I tell him my code?"

"Delilah?" More crackling, then, "Delilah? Daddy does not have your code—" and the line went dead.

Victor stuffed his phone back into his bag. It was now or never. Final boarding calls were being announced. And Elisabeth would be on the phone with 911 at this very moment. Police would storm the airport, armed with descriptions. And from the looks of things, he and Delilah were the only bearded father and fairy-winged daughter in the vicinity. Victor forced a relaxed smile. "Well, young lady? Shall we go?"

"She said you don't have the code . . ."

It wasn't the time to argue with Delilah. She was antagonistic and would fight for the sake of the fight. He decided upon a different tactic.

"Well, then. I forbid you to tell me the code. It is top secret and I am never allowed to know. It would be terribly wrong for you to tell me. Much worse than drinking backwash for money."

The corner of her mouth twitched.

"I assure you, I do not want to know that code."

Her little chest heaved up and down with all the possibilities. Such power lay at her feet. The disobedience. The lawlessness. It was too much for her. A smile spread across her face, nearly reaching all the way to her bent wings. She shouted, "Monie and Cézanne!"

Looking through the tiny oval window at the mouth of the runway, as the engines rumbled with the might necessary to heave the great aircraft into the sky, he could feel the city waking up and stretching. The millions of people going about their lazy morning rituals, showering, shaving, maybe scanning the Globe and Mail *over their first cup of coffee.*

Then he thought of Elisabeth. There would be no coffee, no paper for her. By now, twenty-three minutes after her daughter called to say good-bye, she would be panic-stricken, unsure what this unplanned, unapproved weekend trip would mean.

The plane lurched forward, nudging the passengers back

against their seats. As it lumbered along the runway, the engines let out a mighty roar and picked up speed. The plane lifted off the tarmac, and Victor watched the ground hurl itself farther and farther away. He whispered toward the vanishing city, "I'm sorry, Elisabeth."

Thirty-Four

The day had started out rough. Lila had woken to find Victor gone. He'd been quiet since his visit to the doctor a few days prior, though he'd insisted nothing conclusive had come from the appointment. Just a series of tests and an assurance the office would call him with results within a couple of weeks. A quick tally of his footwear revealed his bedroom slippers had disappeared with him. So had the baby blue pajamas he'd worn to bed. She'd checked the property, the neighbors' properties, and was about to get in the car when she'd stopped, sensing he might be close by. She wandered to the end of the street where there was a path carved through a precipice, almost completely obscured by half-dead bracken. It was the route the local children used as a shortcut to the elementary school. She followed it, ducking under branches in spots, and, sure enough, there he was.

Sitting on a smooth flat rock in the clearing where the more rebellious sixth graders used to sneak cigarettes.

His back was to her, but even in his baggy pajamas she could see he was tense, sitting on his hands the way he was, rocking back and forth as if trying not to vomit. Shoulders hunched, he looked around him, chattering nervously to an audience that didn't exist.

As she moved closer, she could make out his words. "Articulated skeleton, miniature and life-size. Latex tourniquet in three fashion colors. Adhesive bandages in flexform fabric . . ."

An inventory of products available through RoyalCrest Medical Distributors. For no one in particular. Keeping him calm, she supposed. She started toward him then stopped. There, in the bushes, relaxed as could be, lay Slash, panting contentedly and staring at Victor. It wasn't until the animal saw Lila that he stood up, then dropped forward into a stretch, and trotted off into the trees.

It hardly seemed possible. The old dog had been watching out for Victor? Coyote as hero—just like the myths said. Stunned, she stared at the place Slash had lain and mouthed the words "Thank you."

If it hadn't been her mother's birthday, she wouldn't have left Victor alone. But by the time they arrived home, he had settled down and seemed more himself. Lila locked the doors, hid the car keys, and climbed into the Toyota with her mother and Kieran.

Elisabeth wanted to celebrate her birthday at Disneyland. A day at the "Happiest Place on Earth" with her two girls. Lila wasn't sure what was more dizzying—the hordes of blond people speaking a language she guessed was Swedish or maybe German, the pastel-colored shops that looked as if they were made of cookie dough and peppermint icing, or the impeccably clean asphalt on Disney's Main Street. They had been inside the theme park a full hour before Lila spied a piece of trash, and even then, a cast member came by to sweep it up before Lila could confirm it wasn't just a fallen scarf.

Now Kieran stopped in front of a pretty little building with scalloped trim. Her cotton candy drooped sideways as she stared at the sign, which read DISNEYLAND BABY CARE CENTER. "What's that? They keep babies in there?"

Lila smiled. "You change their diapers in there. Also, it's a place kids go if they get lost."

Kieran lit up. "You mean Zachary John Miller? Christiana del Toro? Joanna Vicenze? Frederick and Jackson Burroughs . . . ?"

"No." Lila stopped her. "Sadly, those kids have much worse trouble than getting lost for a few minutes at Disneyland."

"If only it were that simple. If only every parent whose baby has gone missing could come to this little cottage and find them. God." Elisabeth reached out to stroke her older daughter's cheek. "How different life would have been for me."

"Actually, if you'd come at the right moment, that Saturday, you'd have found me here."

Elisabeth stood still, only her hair twisting in the soft wind. Her eyes traveled over the hut. "You were right here. In this little house." She sunk down onto a bench. "If only I'd known."

"We came here straight from the airport. Later, when it was getting dark, I ran off to find the bathroom and got lost in the crowd. A Disney employee brought me here to wait."

"So while I was calling the police, crying and screaming and throwing up, here you were."

"Trying to call my mother."

Her lips parted like a dying fish desperate for oxygen.

* * *

The Baby Care Center on Main Street had seemed surprisingly small, even to an eight-year-old. She'd waited on a wicker chair, swinging her legs as she watched a mother and infant step outside and rush into the crowd. Delilah slipped off her new Disney sunhat and dropped it onto the floor.

An employee sat down beside her. The woman didn't appear to be much older than a teenager, with her peachy lip gloss, tanned face, and long brown hair pulled into a ponytail. Her breath smelled like cherry cough drops. "Hi there, honey. What's your name?"

"Delilah Lovett."

She showed her teeth. "Nice. You can call me Janice. Can you tell me who brought you to the park today? Was it your mom?"

Delilah shook her head. "My dad."

"Does your dad have a cell phone, by any chance?"

"He used to. But he threw it in the garbage."

She laughed. "I sometimes feel like doing that with mine. Well I can assure you, your father is probably looking for you right now. And the first cast member he approaches will tell Daddy to come straight here, so you're going to be just fine." She shook Lila's knee to show her just how fine she would be. "Does that sound good?"

"Do you think we could call my mum in Toronto? My stomach's sore and she knows the right medicine."

Janice thought for a moment. "I don't know. That's Canada, right? Long distance. Let me just ask someone."

After a little while, an older man poked his head into the room and said his name was Richard. He considered the phone call for a moment, then shook his head. "I have no problem with making the call. But here we have her father, poor soul, who's taken his daughter on the trip of a lifetime and lost her. Won't go over too well at home. Let's give the guy a break, see if he doesn't show in a few more minutes. Might prevent a whole lot of trouble for him." He left the room.

Victor was taking too long to come. The blackened waters of the river flashed in Delilah's mind. Her father was probably panicking at that moment, certain that she fell in and drowned. In his frenzy, he probably forgot she was a great swimmer, that if she did fall in, she'd only paddle around and climb right back out again, stand on the riverbank, and ask him if he could buy her a dry sweatshirt.

"Please can I call my mum now?" Delilah asked.

Janice looked around to make sure Richard was gone, then leaned close. "Okay. Come and we'll call your mother and tell her we have you. Safe and sound."

Delilah leaped off her seat and followed. Janice motioned for her to sit down in another chair in another room. This chair leaned back with you and spun. Delilah whirled around with excitement until Janice pulled a phone onto Delilah's lap and put the receiver in her hand. She pressed it to her ear and started to dial.

Just then, Richard appeared, a big grin on his face. "Guess who's here?" He stepped aside to reveal her father standing in the doorway. Victor rushed forward and scooped her up, pressing his daughter into his chest so hard she could barely breathe.

"Don't ever wander away from Daddy," he said into Delilah's ear. "Promise me you'll never, ever leave Daddy again. Not even for a second."

The phone dropped to the floor with a clatter.

As Richard led them to the door, Janice called out, "Wait!" She stood behind her desk with one hand over the phone receiver. Could Elisabeth be on the phone? Delilah wriggled out of her father's arms and tore back into the other room.

But Janice just smiled. "Y'all will want to go straight toward Sleeping Beauty's Castle to see the fireworks."

* * *

Now Elisabeth shaded her eyes from the sun, her caramel skin blanched with emotion. "So close."

"So close."

Kieran was growing bored with all the memories. She leaned against Lila and whimpered, "I heard there are black widows in California. Are they here?"

"People live here their whole lives and don't see a black widow," Elisabeth said. "I've been here a few times in my life—before either of you were born—and I've never seen one."

"They're more poisonous than a rattlesnake," said Kieran. "I saw it on TV." She rubbed her eyes with the heels of her sticky hands. What was left of her cotton candy dropped to the ground. "I want to go home."

"Home?" said Elisabeth, scooping up the candy and stuffing it into the plastic bag she held. "We've barely been here an hour. Who wants to go over to Tom Sawyer Island?"

THE REST OF the day passed in a blur of arachnid-laced misery. Every ride or attraction seemed to be the perfect hiding place for a deadly spider. Pirates of the Caribbean, Tarzan's Treehouse, the Jungle Cruise, Thunder Mountain. Kieran couldn't enjoy any of them, so busy was she trying to ensure a deadly spider wouldn't scuttle across her bare toes.

By the time they got out of the Haunted Mansion, it was dusk and Kieran was exhausted. They waited in a long line for food, then Lila and Kieran trailed behind their mother toward a table that was being emptied of a group of giggling preteens wearing Mickey ears.

Kieran bit into her burger and looked around, her gaze resting on the T-shirt of a brawny young man at the next table. On his back, just below the strawberry blond curls at the base of his neck, was a small red maple leaf. "Look. Canada."

Elisabeth smiled. "It's what Canadians do, you know. Wear the flag when they're traveling. So people will treat them well." She leaned over to tap the man on the shoulder.

"Mum, leave him," said Lila. "He's trying to eat his dinner."

Too late. The man turned around and, when asked if he was from Canada, he nodded, his mouth full. "Toronto."

"Really? We are too!" said Elizabeth.

His plumpish female companion, sunburned and cheery, leaned across the table to shake Elisabeth's hand. As she did so, Lila noticed she also wore the flag shirt. "I'm Kate. And this is Tony. Or Doc Brock, as his patients say."

Elisabeth introduced herself and her daughters, her smile trapping the tip of her tongue between her teeth, her fingers caressing her jawbone, when she discovered Tony worked out of St. Michael's Hospital, a stone's throw from Cabbagetown. Kate and Tony, recently married, had just moved to the Danforth area, to a funky row house in Greektown. After a brief conversation about the sunshine in Los Angeles, the frigid late-autumn air back home, and the ups and downs of converting to American dollars, all talk turned Disney.

"Have you been on the teacups?" asked Kate, short brown hair blowing back from her round face. "That's where we're headed next. Though I haven't been since I was a kid. You should try them."

"No way," said Lila. "I'm not a fan of spinning."

"Kate's a big talker." Tony pointed at his wife with a French fry. "She'll never get on the teacups when she sees how fast they twirl. And I'm not sure I should sit next to her if she does."

"How about this, funnyman?" said Kate. "I go on tea-cups with you and you agree to Space Mountain."

He waved his hand above his food. "I'm not getting flung around in the dark after this meal. No way."

"Then we may have reached an impasse," said Kate.

"Kieran is dying to go on the teacups, aren't you, doll?" said Elisabeth.

Kieran nodded. "With my sister."

The couple broke into a collective "aww" at this, but Lila put a stop to it. "Sorry, Kieran. I've been on it once and vowed never to do it again."

When Kieran crossed her arms and slumped in her seat, Elisabeth slapped the table. "I have an idea. Why don't you go on it with Tony after we eat? Delilah and I will take Kate and meet the two of you at Sleeping Beauty's Castle. Right at the gates. Then we can all watch the fireworks together." She leaned over and nudged her suntanned shoulder against Tony's, her hair trailing across his arm as she sat straight again, giggling. "We'll make an evening of it."

Tony took a moment to consider this. He pushed his hands through his curly hair and looked at his wife. "I suppose that could work. What do you think, Kate?"

"Then it's all set," said Elisabeth, not giving Kate a chance to reply. "That teacup line might even be long enough that we big girls can sit over a glass of Chardonnay, if we can find a place that serves in here. And don't you worry, Tony, we'll bring you a nice cold beer."

"Mum," Lila whispered.

"I'm so glad we bumped into you. Like kismet." Elisabeth winked at Tony, seemingly unaware of Kate, who was no longer smiling.

It wasn't because Kate was reaching for her jacket. Nor was it Kieran's obvious displeasure at being handed off to Tony. It was Elisabeth and her willingness to dump her youngest child with a stranger because he had a red leaf the size of an animal cookie on his shirt and an MD license in his wallet. "That's okay, Mum," Lila said. "I'll take Kieran on the teacups."

"But that's silly. Tony is headed there anyway. And if you'd rather, you and Kate can go on Space Mountain. I don't mind waiting."

But Kate was already getting up, tugging on Tony's sleeve. He stood up, guzzling the remainder of his soda under Kate's stern glare. "You know," he said, "we might not head over there just yet. Probably best if we part ways right here. Really nice meeting all of you, though."

Of course, thought Lila. Not only was it weird to be trusted with a stranger's child, but Elisabeth had been presumptuous and manipulative and downright flirtatious.

"Okay then," Elisabeth said. "Lovely to meet you."

Kate and Tony mumbled good-byes and hurried away.

"Did you see the rock on her finger?" said Elisabeth, tucking away her burger. "Definitely pays to marry a doctor."

KIERAN FELL ASLEEP halfway through her meal, her head resting on Lila's beaded handbag, whitish hair fluttering in the soft evening breeze. Inside the toppled purse, being fondled by strands of hair, was a turquoise box with a tiny silver bow.

"What's that?" Elisabeth grinned mischievously and looked at Lila, her mouth dropping open into a big smile. "Is that for me? For my birthday?"

"Maybe we should wait." Lila slid her bag off the table, in no mood to be doling out gifts. "Open it at home."

"Are you kidding? I could never wait that long!" Her mother pulled out the box and set it on her lap. "You know what the last present you gave me was?"

Lila shook her head.

"A painted wall plaque with your handprint in it for Mother's Day. It's hanging in my bedroom. You signed the back LOVE, DELILAH, MAY 1996. Do you remember?"

"Kind of. I'm not sure."

Elisabeth undid the ribbon and tore into the little package as excited as a child. She held up the turquoise box and pried off the lid. Her eyes flashed when she saw the bracelet. "Oh, sweetheart, it's beautiful."

"Try it on. See if it fits."

"This must have cost a fortune."

She shrugged. "Not really. I got lucky."

Elisabeth slipped it on to her wrist and held it up to the lights shining down from the ceiling. "You remembered my story?" She reached out and smoothed Lila's hair. "It's not a necklace, but still. I love it. I won't take it off for anything in the world."

Thirty-Five

They were surrounded by undressed Lilas. Lila birthmark, blistered heel, and left breast slightly smaller than right. Under that, Lila gluteus maximus, deltoid, latissimus dorsi. Lila knuckles, beneath that lay Lila underneath, Lila proximal phalanx, Lila humerus right and left, Lila sacrum. Behind those, more twisted together, less visible to the naked eye, was a tangle of fallopian tubes, esophagus, and perforated soul. All captured for eternity in graphite, ink, oil, acrylic, and, yes, even Magic Marker.

When she'd been alone with Adam, the long, escapist art sessions had seemed anything but raunchy. They'd been tiny jewels, these afternoons, just the two of them. But now, standing in his studio, introducing her mother to him while surrounded by wall-to-wall evidence of their closeness, the sweetness was flattened somehow. Lila wished she'd thought to introduce them at a Starbucks. A gas station. Anywhere but here.

"Nice," Elisabeth suppressed a smile as she assessed a delicate graphite rendering of her daughter's breast and shoulder.

Lila remembered this one well. It was drawn on a rainy afternoon, and Adam had set up his stool closer than usual. So close she could smell his toothpaste, his lemony shampoo. She'd been able to study him as he worked, the way he chewed on the inside of one cheek when he was focused. It was the first time she'd wanted to kiss him. She might have too, but Adam's sister had come home with a new rug for the living room and needed them to bring it in from the car. Once the furniture had been moved and the rug positioned and the beer poured, the moment was gone.

The electricity of that afternoon wasn't lost on Elisabeth. She looked at Lila and arched her brow.

"Nothing like a wash of natural light for painting skin, hmm?"

Lila nodded. "I thought you'd appreciate his talent."

Elisabeth looked him over. She was dressed in a teal sundress, one that gathered tight across the bust and tied at the shoulder with spaghettini straps, one of which had slipped clear down to the crook of her arm. Elisabeth did nothing to adjust it. "I do."

If Elisabeth weren't her mother, if she were anyone else, Lila would have sworn she was flirting. But it was impossible. Her mother was at least twenty years older than Adam, plus he was her daughter's . . . something. Friend, at the very least.

"You're a wonderful artist, Adam," Elisabeth purred, letting her fingers trail along the bottom of a canvas.

He tripped over a pile of rags and righted himself, his cheeks beet red. Though, knowing Adam, he was blushing out of self-consciousness rather than flattery. "Thank you."

There was a thump from the front of the house and a young voice called, "Mummy?"

"Back here, sweet pea," called Elisabeth.

"Wait," said Lila. "Kieran was in the car?"

"Napping. She was up until two last night so I didn't want to wake her when we pulled up." When Lila showed her surprise, Elisabeth explained, "I had Finn and a few of the other neighbors over. Kieran gets overexcited and can't sleep."

"Or it was noisy," mumbled Lila.

"What's that?"

"Nothing. Just I can't sleep when it's noisy."

"Doesn't bother me. Then again, I always keep those little earplugs in my bedside table."

Before Lila could ask if she keeps those for Kieran, her sister raced into the sunporch and her eyes bulged. "Whoa!" She spun around in a slow circle, taking in her sister's naked body.

"Mum," Lila scolded. "This is a bit much."

"Nonsense. Children should be surrounded by art without the constraints of censorship. Isn't it wonderful, Kieran?"

"Come on. I'm her big sister. It's different."

Kieran blinked at a drawing of Lila's bare hip and tried not to appear too shocked.

Adam sat on a stool, whacked a dry paintbrush against his thigh. "Did Lila tell you I sold a painting of her? To a fashion designer."

"Well," said Elisabeth. "Very impressive to be selling before you graduate. Delilah, did you hear that?"

"I was there."

"You haven't heard the best part," said Adam, tapping Lila now with the brush. "I met with the designer again today. It involves you. She's using *Nude with Denim* in her new ad campaign. Your portrait will be on billboards across the country. Times Square even."

"Seriously?"

"Delilah Blue," Elisabeth said, cupping her daughter's cheeks in her hands. "You'll be famous."

Lila pulled away.

There had been a student exhibition earlier in the week. Thursday night at the Mommesin Gallery. Seeing as only L.A. Arts student pieces were shown, there'd been quite a few nudes of Lila. There were poses she was proud of, poses that made her shoulders or neck hurt just to think of them. Some of the students had beautifully interpreted what she offered—captured the ribs rippling beneath the latissimus dorsi in her scapula rotation pose as Lila had intended. Others missed the challenge presented in the bulging deltoid, the protruding trapezius, the angled scapula, and simply drew a coquettish girl with one hand at her head, the other at her hip, as if she were posturing for an incoming ship full of sailors.

Certainly there were nudes other than Lila, glittering under the halogen spotlights. At least six, maybe seven other models' sternomastoids and mandibles looked down upon her. But their poses lacked something hers didn't. A certain vulgarity. An ugliness that was fresh and dirty, almost animal. There was no point to being attractive as an art model. To make yourself sexy was to miss the point.

She looked up to see Adam staring at her, and quickly averted her eyes.

The thing was, no one in the crowd had noticed Lila the person. No one realized the breasts on the walls were living, breathing, and walking around the room in search of a glass of champagne.

It was the artist who was celebrated, never the subject. Even if Lila was hanging in the Louvre or lolling across the gutter of *New York* magazine, her identity would be unknown.

"Mum, we should go," said Lila. "We've invaded Adam long enough."

As they approached the door, the bell rang. Adam pulled it open to be greeted by none other than Lichty himself. He stood in the shadows of the porch, looking outlandish in a polo shirt and plaid golf shorts. "I'm in a bit of a hurry. Just need to pick up those Modern Art History papers if you have them ready."

"Perfect timing," Adam said. "Look who I'm just releasing into the wild." He opened the door wider to reveal Lila and her family. If Lichty had wondered how close she'd become to Adam, he hadn't let on before and he didn't let on now. He nodded to Lila and stared at Elisabeth a bit too long, probably re-savoring the terrible moment she'd come by to pick up Lila after class.

Adam disappeared into the next room to dig up Lichty's papers while Elisabeth wiggled her way closer to the door. She leaned against the wall and smiled at Lichty. He said, "Looks like something of a party."

"Should be." Elisabeth nodded toward Lila. "Every day is a celebration to me now. I haven't seen Lila since she was eight years old."

"Well," said Lichty. "This *is* a special. Were you off somewhere working?"

"No. I was right there at home," said Elisabeth. "My ex-husband kidnapped her and I only just found her a couple of months ago."

His had been an innocent question, intended to do nothing more than help pass the itchy, crawly, post-scholarship-denial minutes until Adam returned. Lichty's eyes flicked over Lila, then darted away, embarrassed. Horrified. He hadn't counted on seeing right through Lila's clothes, not here at the door without any studio lights to make things official. He didn't count on seeing through her Nice 'n Easy roots to the dirty-blond stems sprouting beneath. It was too much at three-seventeen on a weekday, with traffic whizzing past and sparrows hopping beneath the bushes looking for crumbs. He rubbed his neck and glanced toward his Beetle, mumbled, "I should wait in the car. I have a few calls to make."

The look of discomfort on the man's face made Lila bristle. She wanted to pin him to the welcome mat and scrape off his eyebrows with a palette knife.

Elisabeth continued as if nothing happened. "I suppose my daughter has told you I've taught art up in Toronto."

"She hasn't actually."

"I'm sure you've heard of it. Bromley Kerr. Great school."

He nodded out of politeness. "Sounds like a fine place."

"I really just substitute, but I find it's the subs who are the ones who are able to offer the freshest viewpoints." Her other spaghettini strap fell down. "Since we're out there in the real—"

"Pardon me," he said, suddenly fascinated with her wrist. "Your bracelet."

"You like it?"

"Looks very familiar. Where did you get it?"

"My beautiful daughter gave it to me for my birthday." Elisabeth reached out to touch Lila's elbow.

Lichty turned to stare hard at Lila. "You gave it to her?"

No.

No.

No.

Lichty meeting Elisabeth should never have happened. "It's not what you think. I checked at—"

"I don't know what you're playing at, Miss Mack."

Elisabeth interrupted. "It's Lovett now. Mack is just a name her father dreamed up. Not even legal."

"It's my bracelet."

Lichty's bracelet? In the model's stall? Why hadn't she considered that? What was wrong with her? She tried to answer but had no idea what to say.

Elisabeth laughed, haughty in her anger. "You, sir, are incorrect."

"Am I? Let's examine this, shall we? My partner gave me a bracelet. It had a loose clasp. It fell off my wrist. I've been looking for it for weeks, and now here it is on the wrist of my model's mother."

"Are you accusing my daughter?"

"Mum . . ."

A packet of papers floated over Lila's shoulder and forced themselves into Lichty's hand. Adam's face appeared as he wrapped his arms across Lila's and Elisabeth's shoulders and gave them both a squeeze. He looked from Lila to Lichty. "What'd I miss?"

ADAM'S STUDIO WAS strangely bright. There was a full moon and without curtains or shutters, the light fanned out across the drop cloth like shards of glass. She and Adam had been sitting on the floor for hours, leaned up against the wall, taking turns sucking red wine from a box.

Adam wiped his mouth with the back of his hand. "You don't know you'll be fired. How could he after what he just heard about you."

"Like I'd dare show my face."

Adam fell silent. Just gazed at their shoes and tapped her foot with his.

"It's not as if I even liked modeling. The guy never adjusts the air conditioning. Never brings in the heater. I swear, eventually my neck would have been permanently wrecked. It still hurts from the Three Pencil Class. Being an art model is way harder than it looks."

"I know."

"Plus the floor is never swept. There must be a decade's worth of skin follicles and grit in that changing stall. And don't get me started on the robe. Is it so freaking hard to bring it home for the weekend and drop it into the wash?"

"Sometimes I can smell it while I'm cleaning brushes at the sink." Adam allowed his hand to reach over and squeeze her leg. "Modeling is a total grunt job. So why are you so upset? You're worse than after getting turned down for the scholarship."

Her first instinct was to pull her leg away. Instead, she lifted the wine box to her face and drank. Wine dribbled down onto her T-shirt and she made no move to do anything about it. "I don't know." She looked down at his hand. It wasn't the typical elegant hand you'd imagine on an artist. Adam's hand was wide and sturdy. Mapped with veins and power. Competence. Maybe it was the wine, maybe it was the day, but suddenly, that hand seemed the most fascinating object in her world and she didn't know how she'd missed it. She wanted to touch it, kiss it, feel the fingertips against her skin.

She set the wine box on the floor. "Is your offer still open?"

"Which?"

"New York. I think I want to come."

"Seriously?" He sat up taller and looked at her. "I'd love it. I've been thinking, you know, about your home life. You need to get away from it for a while. Just let the dust settle. But I'm planning to bump up my move date. My cousin's leaving in December now, and I've applied for a transfer to NYU."

"You won't get that by December."

"So I'll take a few months off and finish my degree next year. In the meantime I'll be working. *We'll* be working."

"We'll get one of those booths, like you said. Set up on Prince Street."

"We'll hang out at the MoMA and the Frick."

"I'll get new cowboy boots. New York cowboy boots!"

"We'll polish the cat."

"She'll be our model. *Nude Sleeping on Counter. Nude Watching Birds. Nude with Dead Mouse.*"

"It's New York. *Nude with Dead* Rat."

She hugged herself. "How many bedrooms?"

He hesitated, pushed his glasses up his nose, then wrapped his arms around his knees. "It's more of a studio."

She looked around the room, her eyes resting on his unmade bed over by the far wall. White sheets, blue duvet balled up and dangling off the end.

"I'll sleep on the floor." He grinned. "Like the gentleman you know me to be."

She flipped her hair over one shoulder and moved closer, setting her hand on his shoulder and tracing the seam of his T-shirt. "About that . . ."

He waited, barely breathing.

"Your previous offer. I think it had something to do with removing your pants."

He started to get up. "You want to draw me? Or paint me, maybe?"

She pulled him back down. Reached her arm around his neck, touched her lips to his earlobe, and took in his scent. After a moment, she heard herself whisper, "No."

Thirty-Six

It was a mistake. She knew before waking up, before opening her eyes even. Before looking up through the skylight to see the faint purple brightness of a drizzly day sprinkled across the treetops out back.

There was too much of him. As if his flesh had fused, through heat and exertion and perspiration, to her own and threatened to hold her there, mashed into the dirty drop cloth forever. All she felt was the need to run. From the weight of his bare leg draped across her thighs. The hairy arm flung across her abdomen. The damp T-shirt bunched beneath her elbow. His hot breath stroked her neck like a fever, and the stubble on his chin stung her naked shoulder like hundreds of tiny insects.

Another someday come and gone. When she'd imagined losing her virginity, she'd filtered out her own aversion to human touch. There she was in her reveries, stroking and being stroked, caressing and being caressed, like some kind of slippery and practiced nymphomaniac. Sure, sex with Adam had been lovely while it lasted, momentous even, but how long was one meant to endure the touching? The aftersex was like a bad bout of the chicken pox, an itch you suffered to avoid pockmarks.

It was becoming a pattern. The somedays of her life would teach her not to look forward to anything. Because life is passive aggressive. Once it finally gets off its ass and allows you a wish fulfilled, that wish will come with a heavy price. You want your mother? She'll come with a kidnapping on the side. Sorry, no substitutions to the order. Menu items are unchangeable. In other words, someday will cost you your future dreams.

Very slowly, careful not to wake him, she slipped out from under his sweaty limbs and hunted for her clothes. Jean shorts in the corner. Panties and sweater on the stool. Socks . . . Forget socks—she could do without them. She slid her feet into boots, then pictured him alone, sad, two days from now when he came across her cable knit knee-highs. But hunting through the mess of strewn artwork and clothing was too risky. He might wake up. Instead, she mouthed "good-bye" and stole out into the feeble daylight.

IT HAD RAINED hard during the night. She'd heard it once or twice as she lay pinned beneath Adam's limbs. It made walking across the wet slope in the hills behind her house a challenge. More than once, she skidded down onto her hip and wound up covered in mud. The dampness, however, made it the perfect morning for a cigarette.

So stupid. Everyone knew better than to have sex with a

close friend. Things would turn ugly now. She could never again look at him without imagining that terrible, claustrophobic moment of waking up covered in his never-ending parts.

She should have thought ahead. Lost her virginity with one of those arrogant, immature males from school. The kind your mother—should you have grown up with one—warned you about when you hit puberty.

Adam was different. Lila's taking off would wound him, especially after Nikki. The thought of it, the guilt, propelled her frantic pace through what was becoming an annoying, prickly, on-again, off-again drizzle.

After rounding a corner, she stopped. There was a smallish coyote in the clearing up ahead.

With fur much blonder than Slash's, this animal—though sodden—was delicate. A female. She just lay there, right out in the open, light rain pattering against her big ears. Panting, staring out at nothing in particular.

Lila dipped her cigarette butt in a puddle, squeezed the water out of it, and slid it into her pocket, then crawled up the slope and crouched behind a cluster of bushes. More movement. Sure enough, Slash, just upslope, walking through the scrub with a dead animal in his mouth. Something small and dark. A groundhog maybe.

The female jumped up to greet him, her body curled in submission, her tail tucked low as she reached up to kiss his face and fuss over him. He ignored her attentions, continuing across the incline to a crevice in the rocky hillside where he set his tiny prize on the ground.

Slash yipped and circled his offering. A smaller, darker coyote emerged from the den, pausing at the entry to sniff the air, look around. This coyote's blackish snout was even more refined, petite. Another female, Lila guessed. Maybe younger. She moved toward Slash, her tail low as well, shimmied into him, and nosed his chest. Slash was having none of this emotional nonsense and neither was the first female, who rushed at her and drove her to the sidelines. The jealous wife.

The alpha female nosed the den and backed right out to make way for pups—one, two, then three, four, five. Not squat and tubby, these youngsters. More leggy and pubescent and awkward. They leaped all over Slash, nipping at his bad ear, his tail. One pup was more businesslike and started poking at the dead rodent, dragging it closer to his mother as if to ask her to cut his meat.

Lila watched Slash sit back, satisfied. He made no move toward the food himself, but seemed content to watch his offspring dig in. As the mother helped them tear the kill apart, the patriarch began to groom himself.

She'd been wrong about Slash. He was not the bloodthirsty killer she'd thought. He was nothing but a father, doing what was necessary for his brood.

The darker female—a kindly aunt perhaps, or a youngster from a past litter—kept her distance from the other two adults, from the pups and their dinner, lurking as she was in the brush nearby. When the pups had eaten their fill and seemed to be looking around for more, Slash and his wife made eye contact with this female before trotting off into the fog. Now the female's role became clear. She allowed the pups to tumble around in the grass, but when one of the youngsters started to follow his parents, she rounded him back up and ushered them all into the den.

Lila backed out of the bushes as silently as she could—not wishing to give the sitter cause for alarm—and pointed herself back toward the cabin.

Thirty-Seven

Later that morning, Victor hung up the kitchen phone and sunk into a chair. That was that. He had his answer and, in spite of having suspected it for some time, the finality of it knocked the bluster out of him. The nurse hadn't come out and said as much—the patient never received such news over the phone. She'd called to ask him to come back to see Dr. Barrow. They'd made the appointment. Only what happened next absolved him of the need to show up. The woman dropped the telephone receiver as she tried to hang up, and said to someone nearby, "No, it was Victor Mack. Early-onset Alzheimer's."

Diagnosis by fumble.

He sat with it for a bit, horrified, validated, relieved. Some sort of justice, he supposed. He could just hear Fate up there, laughing its pimply ass off. As terrible as it was to hear it said out loud, it was what he had hoped for. Mightn't thrill the next man, but the next man had likely led a more dignified life and had every right to hope for more.

Anyway, as he'd told himself for a couple of months now, it was all for Lila. Or damned near all. As long as he could keep it together long enough to follow through with his plan.

Enough for one day. He was tired. Needed a nap. He stood up and steadied himself using the back of the chair. He'd gotten clumsy lately. Bumped into things, tripped over a magazine on the living-room floor. It made navigating his own house a frightening endeavor.

Standing there, swaying side to side, he tried to think why he'd gotten up. He'd been headed someplace. A place of his own choosing, none of that sense of dread he'd been having surrounded it.

He heard a noise from the cellar. Lila. He'd feel better if he were close to Lila. After wandering out the door and around the house, he found her dressed in a navy sweater and jeans, bare feet, pulling clothes from the machine. Though he couldn't remember if this machine was meant to wet the clothes or dry them.

She looked up. "I heard the phone. Was that the doctor?"

Her face, such a sweet young face, was paler than usual. "I don't recall the phone ringing. Likely that dog next door."

Slinging a laundry basket onto her hip, she stared at him. "I wonder why these tests are taking so long. Maybe your file got misplaced. We should call them."

"That won't be necessary. They said the tests would take a bit of time. We don't want to be nudniks."

"You want lunch?" When he nodded, she motioned toward the machines. "Switch that last load, will you? I'll heat us some soup."

He watched her leave and felt his pulse quicken. "Where will you be?"

"The kitchen."

Not wishing to upset her, he turned to the closest machine and opened the lid. Wet clothes lay twisted and wound together in a basin rather like a centrifuge. He shouted into the air vent overhead, "You still in the kitchen up there?"

"Yes," she hollered. "I told you I'm making soup. Chicken noodle sound okay?"

"That will be fine." Trying to calm his nerves, he began to pull clothes out of the machine and drop them, wet, into a cotton-lined wicker basket. Each piece fell with a sloppy *thunk*, spattering the floor with drips and drops. Didn't seem to make much sense, as no one could wear such nasty sopping garments.

The sound of footsteps, then Lila's face in the doorway. "What's that—" Tipping her head to one side, she watched what he was doing. "No. Dad, no." She threw the clothes, piece by piece, into the other machine and spun a few dials. He watched her move around the cellar, so sure. Strong. Able. Still willing to feed him and care for him after all she knew. What did she do to deserve such a father? When she was done, she stared at him, hands on her narrow hips. "I want you to give me the phone number of that doctor you saw, okay? I'd like to talk to him."

"I've never claimed to be perfect. Not once." It wasn't an apology. Just a fact.

"What?"

"Did I ever tell you there's a window company called Shattered Glass? They called us earlier. I'll have to tell Gen. She gets such a kick out of that kind of thing."

"Why don't you go upstairs and lie down, Dad. I'll bring you your soup once it's ready."

LILA WHEELED THE bike out of the shed and laid it on the grass. It had been Elisabeth's idea to get the child a bicycle for her birthday next weekend, but neither she nor Lila had much in the way of extra cash, so when Lila had seen this little blue bike at a garage sale down the street for thirty dollars, she'd bought it. It was a boy's bike, but she didn't think Kieran would mind. In all honesty, she didn't think her sister would ride it—not unless she could strap a basket to it and use it to haul home cartons of friends for her wall.

The bicycle hadn't been well cared for. But Lila was hoping a bit of oil would work some life back into the rusty chain and that a lick of paint would revive the scratched frame.

She'd gone to him. Lichty. Offered—even though her mother refused to part with it—to give his bracelet back. But even if she had been able to pry it out of Elisabeth's clutch, it was too late. Lichty's attentive partner had replaced it with something finer. A thick twisted rope of tricolored gold that winked at her the entire time she stood at Lichty's desk. She'd explained having found the bracelet on the ground. She'd admitted she was wrong not to turn it in, but still. Mr. Lichtenstein had stood up, pointed toward the clock, and asked would she mind clearing out before his seniors started to arrive and got excited that she might be their model.

Strangely, the loss of her stealth art education bothered

her less than the loss of Lichty's barbed voice in her life. His words had a sting, but his sarcasm was real and true. It didn't tear you down because you understood, as he criticized your rib cage or the turn of your ankle, that this was a man whose aim was to build professionals, not bolster himself.

As she left his studio, she couldn't help but look back. Instead of turning to the stack of charcoal drawings he'd been evaluating when she'd walked in, he was staring out the window, his face stilled by an expression that seemed, more than boredom or disappointment, to closely resemble despair.

Now she popped the lid off the oil can and dripped it along the chain, continuing to soak it until the pedals turned smoothly. It was far too small for her, but she couldn't resist. It had been years since she'd ridden a bike—Victor had always been against it—so she removed her sweater, tied it around her neck and pedaled around, all giant knees and elbows, on the grass. It wasn't until she'd fallen onto her side and scraped her elbow that she noticed Victor watching her from the porch, sipping from a cup of coffee.

She got back on and waved, calling out, "Look, no hands," as she wobbled along the bumpy ground past the front steps. When she turned to ride back, she saw her father drop to the steps, his hands covering his forehead.

"Dad!" She ditched the bike and raced across the property to find him breathing hard. His eyes had a wild, faraway look to them and he stared at her as if he had no idea who she was. On the porch beside him, his coffee mug lay broken, coffee with cream trickling toward his pant leg. "What's wrong? Are you sick? Is it your heart?"

He shook his head, still fighting for breath.

"Should I call 911?"

"No . . . I'm just muddled up. I'm not sure. I thought I saw my daughter, but that's not possible."

"It's me, Dad. Lila."

"No, my Delilah is dead." His face crumpled in pain.

She took him by the shoulders. "Dad. It's okay. I'm Delilah and I'm not dead. Do you hear me?"

The world in front of him grew nightmarishly large as he listened to the words coming out this young woman's mouth. He couldn't comprehend. The bike, the sun coming through the tree just so, the smell of spilled coffee: It was all very obvious to him what day it was. He started to speak.

June 6, 1996

It would be three months before he would take her.

He was at the open window of his second-floor office on Bloor Street, staring down through the lacy, impulsive branches of the locust tree on the sidewalk at the heavyset girl from the jewelry shop below. She was juggling a key ring, a cigarette, an overstuffed purse, and a tray of four large coffees for her coworkers, and in her attempt to open the door, the tray toppled to her feet, sending paper cups, lids, and hot brown liquid all over the tiled stoop. The smell of coffee drifted all the way up to Victor's window.

Gabrielle was her name. Victor knew this because she'd helped him pick out a necklace for Elisabeth a few months back in the hopes of rekindling his dying marriage. His wife had wanted a thick, gold necklace. Had spoken about it for years, but the sort of piece she described cost thousands of dollars. Victor could never afford it, not after buying the house in Cabbagetown and supporting his wife and daughter. But that year, pharmaceutical sales had been strong. His bonus had been twice what it was the year prior, and Victor was determined to give Elisabeth what she'd coveted nearly her entire life.

"Take this one," Gabrielle had said, holding up a white gold necklace, fourteen inches long with a smooth, flat chain that clinked softly as it moved. Polished to such a sheen that it reflected light around the room in jagged rainbow shards. "It's our newest link," Gabrielle explained. "Just in from Europe. Your wife will love it."

Elisabeth had been so excited upon seeing the black Yorkville Jewels box, she could barely pry off the lid. But, once she pulled out the chain and held it up to the light, she made no attempt to hide her revulsion. "Silver? You finally buy me jewelry and you pick silver?"

"It isn't silver, Elisabeth. It's white gold. And the clasp is engraved with your initials."

She dropped it back into the box and replaced the lid. "Looks like silver to me. Everyone will think it's silver."

"Who cares what anyone thinks?"

"After nine years—nine goddamn years—this is how well you know me?"

When he'd tried to take it back the next day, Gabrielle explained they had a policy. No returns on engraved goods. Victor had given it to Ross Chapnick from accounting, whose wife adored the white gold so much she was happy to ignore the E.L. on the clasp.

Now, staring down at the spilled coffee and the frazzled Gabrielle, Victor moved away from the window to run down the steps and help her get inside. But his intercom buzzed. "Victor, grab line one. Something's happened . . ."

Victor ran through the wide sliding doors of the emergency room entrance, the side entrance, of Toronto's Hospital for Sick Children, his heart hammering so hard, so fast, he wondered if he'd live long enough to even find her. Inside, the mood in the waiting room—decorated with cutout butterflies and posters warning parents of dangerous symptoms to watch for while their loved ones waited to be seen—was remarkably quiet, almost amiable compared to how Victor felt. A mother fed a fussing baby as she watched a triage nurse position a thermometer in the child's ear. A man wheeled his teenage daughter past, her hair strewn across her face and her arm cradled in a sling fashioned from a sweatshirt. Younger families seemed to have settled in for a long wait, watching their little ones—most of whom appeared far too energetic to require a visit to the hospital—play with blocks or sit, eyes fixed, on the cartoon playing on overhead monitors.

The banality of it, the normality, was surreal. Victor seemed to float as he raced past the lineup of people, some of whom informed him he needed to take a number and wait in the row of plastic chairs facing the nurses' area. Victor burst into triage and took hold of a doorway for balance. "Delilah Lovett. Where is she?"

The nurse, a bony young redhead with a high ponytail and ultrashort bangs, looked up as if unsure what to say.

Victor repeated himself. "Delilah Lovett. I'm her father."

"You beat the ambulance," she said, forming her words too carefully. "They just radioed; they're pulling in now." She took his arm and pulled him to the side of her desk. "You just stay with me."

A flurry of loud voices rang out in the entryway. Two female paramedics appeared, clearing the way for a stretcher. Victor recognized Delilah's tangled blond hair but not the white tape pressing her forehead onto the board. Nor the plastic neck brace.

He rushed toward the stretcher as paramedics moved to hold him back.

People in hospital scrubs and white coats blocked him as they continued through a set of double doors and down a winding yellow corridor. Doctors, nurses spoke, but their words were gibberish to Victor. A stethoscope fell to the floor. It dawned on him they'd been standing by these doors when he'd run through them.

They were waiting for Delilah.

He trotted alongside the stretcher and grabbed the side rail. For the first time, he caught a glimpse of her face. Her forehead and temple were cut, covered in dried blood, dirt, gravel. She strained against the tape holding her head down, eyes closed, murmuring. Blankets covered her to the chin.

"She had an accident," said a firefighter as they rushed down a long hallway. "Something about a bike. A jump on the driveway. She's been in and out of consciousness. We've stabilized her neck and back, just precautionary."

"How bad—is she going to be okay?" asked Victor.

"She spoke a bit when awake, asked for you. Knew your phone number even."

"Who was with her? Where's her mother?"

"She was with a neighbor. There'd been a sitter apparently, but he'd gone . . ."

Friend of Elisabeth's. Probably stoned out of his mind, Victor thought.

"Talking's a very good sign," explained a nurse. "Oftentimes these things look a lot worse than they are."

On cue, Delilah opened her eyes. Blinking furiously, she strained to lift her head. "I'm stuck. And I can't see anything. Why is it dark? I can't see!"

Without a word, doctors, nurses, paramedics took hold of the stretcher and broke into a run.

The stretcher barreled through swinging doors and into a huge operating room—more of an arena—that read STUEBBEN FAMILY TRAUMA CENTER *on the door. Victor tried to move closer, at one point got close enough to hold Delilah's hand, but frantic doctors inadvertently butted him out of the way in an effort to yank down overhead lights, pull off the tape holding her head still. So many people, some doctors, some nurses, some—who knew? There had to be fifteen to twenty people bustling around his girl.*

Delilah began to thrash around again, swearing as if possessed, shrieking, "Turn on the lights! What are you people doing? I want the lights!" A nurse instructed several others to hold down her limbs as she sliced the child's jeans from ankle to waist.

A woman nearby tapped his arm. She barely came up to Victor's chest, so tiny as she was. She wore a dark skirt and sweater, dark hose and sensible shoes. Her graying hair cut short and permed. A stiff cap perched on her head like a caregiver from another era.

She handed Victor a pair of fairy wings—part of a Halloween costume from years past, now mangled and flattened and smeared with blood. "She was wearing these."

He took the wings and held them close. A glint of gold caught Victor's eye. A thin cross dangled from the woman's neck. He looked back up at her cap, chilled. "You're not a nurse."

She moved closer. Placed an impossibly small hand on his upper arm. "I'm the hospital chaplain. I've been assigned to you."

Victor shook his head.

"I'm here to make you more comfortable. Make sure you're okay."

The floor rushed up at him and he realized his knees had buckled. There was only one reason they would assign a chaplain. "She is going to be fine. I don't need a chaplain."

"Mr. Lovett, they're prepping your daughter for emergency brain surgery."

"I'm Dr. Heller." The pediatrician's hair was thick, nearly as white as his lab coat. His face, even with its burgeoning early-summer tan, was surprisingly unlined, only a faint softening of his skin belied his age, which Victor guessed to be around sixty. Eyebrows hooded his eyes, shadowing them in kindness. Behind him, Delilah was still conscious, combative. As quickly as nurses set up IVs, she yanked them out of her hand.

"We're going to do a CT scan right away," said the doctor. "We can't begin to treat her until we know what's going on in terms of possible trauma to the brain." He turned and motioned toward the scene around the stretcher. "She's a fighter. As difficult as it makes our jobs, it's something we like to encounter."

"Why can't she see?"

He didn't answer. "We need her to keep still. We're going to administer a drug that will essentially paralyze her."

Victor rubbed his forehead. "I don't understand—like an anesthetic?"

"Sort of. This particular drug will quiet her nervous system. Slow some of her organ functions. Her lungs may cease to function. A nurse will do her breathing for her with a manual pump."

"Her heart?"

"Her heart will beat just fine."

"But if I stay by her side," said Victor. "Surely I can keep her calm for the length of time it takes for the scan. I'll talk to her . . ."

"She's volatile. Reactive. Her behavior isn't voluntary, which is why we need to act quickly. Please."

A nurse approached with a clipboard. The doctor handed it to Victor. "We'll need you to sign."

Victor squeezed the wings. A piece of broken wire pierced his palm. "So there are risks to this . . . this paralyzing her?"

"The release is standard procedure."

Victor couldn't read the release form, his eyes swimming as they were. It was too much to take in. The accident. Being kept back from her. The chaplain who wouldn't stop staring at him with that sympathetic smile. And now they needed his okay to take away her ability to breathe? Victor's knees liquefied and he slumped into a chair behind him.

What if her breathing never returned? If she never woke up? What if the nurse with the pump suffered a stroke on the way to the scan and no one reacted quickly enough? The whole thing sounded medieval—breathing for her with a hand pump. With the stroke of a pen, Victor could be signing away her life, his own right along with it. Her behavior, other than this loss of sight, was a good sign. The doctor had said that himself. She was conscious. And who was this doctor, this total stranger, to say that Victor couldn't calm his daughter long enough for the x-ray?

On the form, the words "accidental death" caught his eye. Jesus Christ, why was this happening?

Shouting from the other side of the room. "Dr. Heller, we're losing consciousness again."

Dr. Heller's body turned, but his eyes didn't leave Victor's face. "We have to move quickly. Every second counts . . ."

Victor signed the paper.

Seconds later, they were jogging down the hall again, Victor directly behind the nurse who held a large black rubber ball over Delilah's chest. Keeping her alive by squeezing in regular intervals. This woman, nearly six feet tall, with her wildly patterned scrubs, long French braids, and fat pink pen hanging from a string around her neck, was all that stood between his daughter's life and death. Victor willed the nurse not to trip, sneeze, lose her rhythm in any way. Should a natural disaster strike, right there in the brightly lit halls of the hospital, this stick-thin nurse, with all the power in the world, would be the only one, aside from his girl, whom Victor would save.

The smiley buttons on her scrubs clicked together, chattering above the sleeping face as she moved, their merriness unappreciated by her patient, whose eyelids had been fastened shut with transparent tape.

For protection, Dr. Heller had explained. Just for protection.

The only light in the hospital room came from a sliver of moon that hung so low in the sky, it appeared to be pulling back the curtains and peeking through the window. The calm, the quiet, the relief, of being in this room, this tiny recovery room, wrapped itself around Victor like a down jacket.

It had nearly killed him. Waiting for the outcome of the CT scan. Imagining Delilah slipping away from her little body with no one who loved her by her side. How long had it been? An hour? Maybe more, until they came for him. By that time he'd convinced himself it was over. The very best scenario was his daughter was blind. The worst . . . too horrific to contemplate.

When Dr. Heller finally came into the dim parents' waiting area, his face had been tired. Stern. Victor hadn't been able to stand, so sure was he that his world was about to collapse. But then the doctor smiled and said she was fine. Her sight was back.

The scan had showed a slight brain bleed, a subdural hematoma, just beneath the skull, that would not require surgery. There would be strict limits for physical activity the next six months—no skateboards, no bikes, no skiing or skating. Nothing involving jumping—no trampolines or pogo sticks or leaping on beds. No gym at school, no boating, no swings. There might be dizziness, nausea, and confusion. With any luck, the doctor said, she won't even remember it happened.

Delilah stirred in her sleep, tucked into the nook of his arm, then settled into a quiet slumber. Glowing monitors behind her bed beeped rhythmically, almost soothingly; fat bags of intravenous fluids dangled from poles; wires and tubes leading down to their unconscious beneficiary, some piercing the flesh on the back of her hand, others snaking under her green gown, attaching themselves to her body.

Her face. Impossibly oblivious, impossibly pale. Angry red patches, swollen, skinned, groused from her forehead, her nose, her cheekbone. A bruise was already forming under her left eye. Victor settled back against the pillows and wrapped himself around her, careful not to jostle the hardwiring. He kissed her cheek, the right side.

God, he was tired.

Just as he started drifting off, a sound.

He opened his eyes to find she'd awoken. There, inches from his own, her blue eyes blinked, looked around. He started to laugh, blink back tears.

"What happened? Where am I?" she asked.

"You're with me, Mouse. You're with your dad."

Delilah let sleep take over again.

The gods have given us a gift, Elisabeth, he would say. This time. We have to treat this tiny person with more care. No smoking around her. No leaving her with strangers. Next time, Elisabeth. Next time, who knew?

His speech wasn't to be. His ex-wife was already marching into the room, a policewoman behind her. Elisabeth was shaking mad. Spitting mad. Sweating, flushing, sputtering mad.

"How could you?" she said, standing to the side of the door so the policewoman could hear, see. "You bastard. You were supposed to pick her up."

Victor was stunned. "Yes, at five. This happened much earlier, three-thirty . . ."

"We agreed you'd get her at three. None of this would have happened if you were remotely dependable."

It was what Elisabeth did. Bent the facts to suit herself. "Me? You left her with that stoner again, didn't you? That trust-fund loser that calls himself an artist."

"Ian's a good person. Don't you knock him." For the first time, her eyes lighted on Victor's daughter. Their daughter. She rushed to Delilah's bedside, kissed her all over her face, all over her gashes, slashes, and bruises.

The policewoman was busy taking notes. Every once in a while, she glanced up at Victor, then scribbled some more.

"I trusted you," Elisabeth said to Victor. "How could you not show up, you garbage excuse for a father—"

"Keep your voice down," Victor said, nodding toward Delilah, who had fallen asleep again. "We'll discuss this later."

"He didn't show," she said to the police officer. "So typical."

"It isn't true. Elisabeth has a tendency to bend stories—"

"How did you find out?" asked Elisabeth.

"Delilah gave them my number. She was lucid at first, walking around and asking for—"

"And you didn't even have the decency to call me," Elisabeth spat. "I had to find out from the neighbor."

"How was I to know this responsible friend of yours, this Ian, didn't stick around and wait for the ambulance! Left her with a neighbor."

"Don't you start on Ian. You're the one who went AWOL!"

she shouted loud enough to wake up Delilah. The child curled in a ball and began to sob. "Get out," said Elisabeth, stroking her daughter's head. "Now!"

"But . . ."

The policewoman stopped her note-taking and came closer. "I think it's best," she said to Victor, "if you come with me. Let's let the family get settled—"

"The family?" he said, raising his voice for the first time. "I'm her father."

She stepped into the room and took his arm. "If you'll come down the hall, I'd like to ask you a few questions." Victor stared at Delilah, who stared back while her mother piled extra flannel sheets on top of her. "Please, sir."

Victor blew Delilah a kiss and followed the officer out of the room, his daughter's wrecked wings in his hand.

Thirty-Eight

Lila sat in the gloom of her father's bedroom, cross-legged at the foot of his bed. His sleep was so deep she leaned closer to check his breathing. The story, the memory, had exhausted him. Every now and then she kissed his forehead, the back of his cool hand.

Lila was calmed to the core. The truth about her father remained unchanged. He was, and always would be, the man she grew up believing him to be. The man willing to move the sun and the moon for the sake of his girl. Sure, he moved the sun too close and scorched the moon in the process. He wasn't perfect. He was a criminal. But the man wasn't evil.

Interesting too that his long-term memory was largely undisturbed. Though, she'd researched enough about Alzheimer's in the past months to know the past was usually the last thing to go.

What struck her after he'd finished his story, however, and she'd thought very little of it at the time, was that her mother had bought her another bike. Not three months after the accident, which—the doctor was right—Lila did not remember. They'd been on Yonge Street, passing the huge Canadian Tire store, so white and red and out of place in charming, upscale Rosedale. There in the parking lot, with lavender streamers waving from the handlebars, was a white girl's bicycle with a purple racing stripe along the frame.

If she'd known, if her parents had told her about the accident and explained she was not to ride a bike until the following spring, if they'd revealed where on earth her own bike had gone, Lila wouldn't have begged. She wouldn't have crossed her arms, dropped down to the hot pavement, right there in the stream of Torontonians flowing in and out of the store, and announced she wanted that bike more than anything else on earth.

Then Elisabeth, being Elisabeth, wouldn't have pulled out her wallet and said, "Then you'll have it. No child should be without a bike."

Elisabeth and her hippie parenting.

It was against the hospital's orders. Victor, being Victor, was far too paranoid to let her risk another fall. Maybe he'd planned it, maybe he'd snapped, but he grabbed Lila and fled.

He thought he was saving her life.

Who knew? Maybe he had.

Elisabeth was the last parent on earth likely to follow through on stringent rules when it came to child safety. She could see that. Elisabeth had always been the child herself, far more likely to plop her daughter on a bed and tell her to see how high she could jump than to set her in front of the TV in the name of cerebral immobility.

Elisabeth and Kieran were due over any minute. The plan had been that Elisabeth and Victor have a bit of face time, then Elisabeth leave Kieran with Lila for a sleepover while she gave herself some time to recover from the trauma of confronting him. Whether she'd be recovering in Finn's uninspired arms was anyone's guess.

The meeting between the parents couldn't happen. Not now. Victor was in a delicate state, needed this rest, and Lila wasn't about to let anyone make it worse for him. She checked the clock again.

Thirty-Nine

Kieran's suitcase was not what you'd expect. First of all, it weighed enough that she might have had a cadaver stuffed inside. Second, it was shiny gold and covered in the letter G. G's on the handle, G's on the pocket, and big brassy G's as zipper pulls. The sort of thing an aging diva might wheel through LAX while wearing sunglasses and metallic baseball cap to create the impression she wanted to travel undetected.

When she caught Lila staring at it, Kieran made a face. "Mummy bought it." The child stood at the top of the walkway with the suitcase and surveyed the grounds. It had stopped raining and the yard looked especially green, all wet and dripping in the bourgeoning sunlight. Still, the child was unimpressed. "The pool doesn't look so clean."

"It isn't. More of a pond, really. I still float in it. Or I used to. Now I wade in it."

Kieran had wandered down to the yard. She stopped in front of the weathered green shed, then looked up to her sister at the road's edge. "How do you get your car in here? It's way far down."

"It's not a garage. Just a shed. Where we put the garbage cans and rakes and stuff."

Elisabeth had climbed out of her car and started down the steps. Lila had tried to get hold of her mother before she headed over, but it had been too late. "Go inside and explore, sweetie," Elisabeth called. "It's like a haunted barn or something. If I were a child, I'd make it my magical playhouse. Find a special corner inside and spy on everyone outside."

"I used to do that. But now it's pretty ramshackle," said Lila. "There are boards with rusty nails poking out; there might even be a hornets' nest under the eaves. I've seen some action in the far corner."

"See, that's what's wrong with the world today. Children aren't allowed to be children. No one grows up anymore having used their imagination. They're all sitting on their computers living a virtual life because of all that 'might' go wrong. Look at you—people thought I was permissive because I let you roam around the neighborhood. But it wasn't a stranger who destroyed our lives, was it?"

Lila closed her eyes for a moment and willed herself not to jump to her father's defense. Now, in front of Kieran, wasn't the time. Instead, she tucked her blowing hair down the back of her sweater and moved closer. "The bike's in there, Mum. She'll find it."

Elisabeth raised her brows and smiled. Nodded and feigned zipping her lips and throwing away the key.

Turned out it didn't matter. Kieran eyed the rusted hinges and the missing planks of wood and turned up her nose. Instead of considering the magic or the hornets, she sighed and started toward the house, disappeared inside.

"Mum," said Lila. "I tried to call you. It's not a good time for you to meet with Dad. I'm happy to watch Kieran, but you guys can't have it out today. He's sleeping now."

"No problem. I don't mind waiting for a bit." Elisabeth smiled sweetly.

"You can come in, but I can guarantee he'll be out for another couple of hours. He's sleeping more and more in the day."

"Okay. Let him sleep." Her mother was unusually accommodating. Lila hadn't expected it. Elisabeth took in the view, her face dreamy. "You know, this place is starting to grow on me. Has a certain eccentric sort of Los Angeles charm, don't you think? And the location is divine. I was just reading that these properties go for millions. Even if they're"—she sniffed and looked around—"not kept up."

Elisabeth's approval irked Lila.

"I want you to live with me, sweetheart."

Lila looked up. "You mean move into your place? It's a two bedroom."

"I don't have much time left here. What I'd really like is for you to come with me. Let's all go home for Christmas."

"But Dad—he can't be here alone. He's not well."

"Delilah. It's time to stop thinking about your father."

To stop herself from reacting, Lila reached into the mailbox to pull out a handful of bills and a folded flyer. A notice from the neighborhood committee announced that the coyote with the torn ear was suspected of helping himself to a few local cats. Residents were warned to keep an eye on small children and pets for the time being, and rest assured, the committee was seeking assistance in dealing with the coyote threat and expected a swift and effective resolution to the problem.

Slash, like Victor, was doomed.

Forty

The house was quiet. Soft feminine voices could be heard from the back room, where Lila had likely stationed her mother and the little girl while he slept. Victor padded into the bathroom to relieve himself, unwilling to attract attention by flushing. He had to move quickly, before one of them wandered into the kitchen in search of a snack.

Sixty seconds later, he was up on the street. Clearing out of the house had been easy. The only thing he'd taken was his wallet and his doctor's phone number scrawled on a scrap of paper. Victor stood under the unlit streetlamp and looked back at the house, his heart thumping from his dash up the hill.

The cab's engine rattled and banged, and the driver opened the passenger-side window. Victor could smell garlic on the man's breath. "You coming or what?"

Victor cast a final look toward his castle, his land, the daughter who waited inside. Took one last peek at his car and frowned when he noticed the neighbors' white Prius was parked too close again, after three separate warnings, *written* warnings, that Victor had taken great care to compose. Moving nearer, he bent over and noticed another chalky ding in the side of his car, precisely where the hybrid's door had swung open too wide. Again. He tried to wipe off the smudge, but it was paint from the Prius's door. Jesus Christ.

The buzz of chatter from the cabbie's radio, then, "Come on, man. I don't got all day. You called me for five and it's twenty past."

Victor ignored the man. He searched his pockets for keys and came up with nothing but his metal sunglasses. They would have to do. Holding them folded, temple edge out, he walked around the Prius and gouged the paint from nose to tail, around the back and up to the front grille again. That would teach them.

"What the . . . ?" The cabbie looked shocked. "You crazy?"

Victor climbed into the backseat, pulled the sunglasses on, and barked, "I'm not paying for a psychiatric evaluation. I'm paying you to take me to thirteen-fifty-eight North Wilcox Avenue."

ELISABETH SLIPPED INTO the kitchen, where she refilled her mug with hot tea, then reached for the milk. She looked up when Lila came into the room. "Well, I suppose you're right. That father of yours is going to sleep all afternoon. You're sure you don't mind Kieran staying?"

"Not at all. I promised her we'd play hide-and-seek. Dad'll be up soon anyway. Best if you go."

Her mother rooted through the drawer for a teaspoon and stirred the milk into her tea. She set the spoon on the table and drank. "I've put up with so much from that man."

"He's not himself, Mum."

"You know what? It doesn't matter. I was positive he'd be a no-show today."

"Then why set this all up?"

Elisabeth pulled on her sunglasses. "It was a test. If he spoke to me, apologized, it might have swayed me a little. But if he took the coward's way out, if he avoided seeing me, it would make my decision simple."

Lila knew the answer but had to ask. "What decision?"

She downed the rest of her tea and scooped up her purse. "Sweetheart, I'm meeting my lawyer at the police station. No more waiting. I'm having your father arrested. Today."

Forty-One

Just like that, Elisabeth was gone.

It wasn't so surprising, what her mother had planned. What left-behind parent wouldn't do the same thing? Her ex-husband had committed a terrible crime. To her, to any parent victimized in this way, a crime that was unforgivable. It was right that he pay and that Elisabeth receive some sort of closure for what she suffered.

So why did Lila feel like throwing up?

Kieran wandered into the kitchen. "I'm bored. Can we play hide-and-seek now?"

"It's not a good time, Kier."

"But I'm bored."

"There are markers in my room. Paper, too, under the bed. You can bring it all in here and draw me a picture."

"I don't want to."

"Then go check my dad's room. He should be waking up any minute now."

"I did already."

"And? Is he up?"

Kieran wound her arm through the chair back and tipped her head sideways. "He's not even there."

Lila stood up and marched out of the room. "That's not possible. Of course he's there."

Kieran, energized by her discovery taking on such unexpected importance, bounced along behind her. "Nope. He's not."

With the rest of the house being empty, Victor not being in his room was a very real cause for concern, especially after his lapse into the past earlier in the day. Lila flew through his room, his bathroom. Sure enough, he was gone. Stupidly, she stared at his rumpled sheets. "This isn't good, Kieran. My dad's not well."

"I once had an earache."

Lila shook her head, trying to think of where he might go. She heard loud voices from up somewhere nearby, on the street maybe, and glanced out the window to assure herself Victor hadn't taken the car. The Datsun's grille stared down at her, which meant he was on foot.

"I had to take banana-flavored medicine."

"Can you just please not say anything for a second? I'm trying to think if I should call nine-one-one or if he's just out for a short walk."

"How do you call nine-one-one?"

Lila looked at her, annoyed. "Take a guess."

"Are you devatsated about your dad?"

"It's devastated, and where did you learn that word?"

"You said it at the park. If I got abducted. Did you like

the color of your Find Delilah Web site? Did you like all that red? I didn't."

"Seriously, Kieran. I need a few minutes here. Go. Go do anything else but talk to me for a bit."

The girl sunk down into the chair and picked at the table's edge. In her usual severe attire, she looked even more morose. Perhaps quietly contemplating how best to handle the situation. What would yield the more desirable result—continue to badger her big sister until she agrees to a game of hide-and-seek, or go plunk down in front of the TV all by her lonesome and wait things out? But at the same time, Kieran appeared far too young to make such a premeditated decision and might just resort to that old childhood standby—tears. As if inhabiting the body of a seventy-year-old woman, Kieran pulled herself to her feet and said maybe she'd like some art supplies after all. Some scissors. Markers.

"That's a good idea," said Lila. "Do a little arts and crafts." Lila gave her the safest pair she could find—a pair of blunt-ended fingernail scissors—a near-empty roll of masking tape, and a tin of colored Sharpies, and watched her sister trot out of the room.

Forty-Two

Victor hauled himself out of the cab, dropped his overnight bag onto the sidewalk, and pulled a handful of bills from his wallet. The fare said $17.50. He stared at the bills in his palm, trying to make sense of the math, then crumpled them into a ball and dropped them into the passenger seat. "Ah, take the whole bunch of it. I don't need it where I'm going."

He shuffled across the sidewalk in the dense shade of the trees lining the front of the redbrick building. Birds chattered at him from the smooth, mottled gray branches as he made his way past the dirty silver letters of the sign.

LOS ANGELES POLICE DEPARTMENT.

HOLLYWOOD STATION.

Inside, he marched up to the first desk he saw, slapped his bag on top of it, and said, "Put down the stapler, honey. You're going to want to lock me the fuck up."

Forty-Three

She'd checked the entire house twice. She'd checked behind shower curtains, inside large closets, and behind the big armchair in the living room. Idiotic. It wasn't as if the man was playing hide-and-seek and would jump out once she called "Ollie Ollie oxen free."

The phone rang from the kitchen and Lila rushed to pick it up. When the female voice on the other end announced it was 911 calling, Lila felt her chest tighten.

"What happened to him?"

"To whom, ma'am?"

"My father. You're calling about my father."

"No, ma'am. We received a silent nine-one-one call from your address. Did you call for assistance?"

"No. No one called nine-one-one."

"Someone did. Could it be the father you mentioned? Could he be in trouble?"

"He's not here. I've been thinking of calling you, but no, he didn't use the phone. Can I report to you if he's gone missing?"

"For how long?"

"I don't know. An hour. Maybe a bit more. He's fifty-three, but he sometimes lapses into memory loss."

"How often does he have these lapses?"

"Not often. Not every day. But he had a bad morning. He's gray-haired, has a short beard, is probably dressed in a shirt and tie and—"

"Let's give it another half hour, honey. If you haven't heard from him by then, call us and we'll send out a car. But you're sure no one called for help? Is there anyone else in the house?"

Kieran's question rang through her mind. *How do you call 911?*

"KIERAN?" LILA MARCHED from room to room, furious. It was something a toddler would do—call 911 as a joke. A seven-year-old—nearly eight—should definitely know better.

"Kieran?" Following the same route she'd taken not three minutes earlier, Lila searched the house. "Are you hiding?"

The girl was nowhere to be found. Damn her hide-and-seek. As if no one had anything better to do than drop everything whenever the whim struck that little blond head.

"Kieran, you come out right this minute, you hear me? This is not funny!" Loud voices rang from up on the street again. Ignoring them, she checked the bedrooms one last time, this time peeking under beds. When she got to her own room, she got down on all fours to check behind the dusty boxes and stacks of art paper. No giggling child underneath. As she climbed to her feet, she noticed the nail scissors splayed open on the bottom bunk just waiting to pierce the flesh of the next person who plopped down for a rest. She set them on the night table and, for the first time, noticed the carton of milk.

Of course.

It was why Kieran wanted art supplies: to add another face to her growing collection.

Angry at Kieran, angrier still at her mother for encouraging this macabre hobby, she snatched up the empty carton.

This one wasn't cut apart at all. This one had a four-color photo of a child taped on one side. At the top, carefully printed in black marker, was the word MISSING on torn masking tape. Beneath it was,

NAME: KIERAN SCARLETT LOVETT-MOORE.

AGE: 7–9/10.

And sure enough, the child fixed to the carton, the child under the word MISSING, was a smiling Kieran, draped in strand after strand of necklaces from the jeweler down on Sunset.

"KIERAN!"

AFTER CHECKING EVERY inch of the property, Lila pulled open the shed door. It wasn't likely Kieran would have dared enter; she'd seemed fairly repulsed by it earlier in the day. The door croaked its annoyance and Lila poked her head inside. It was dark, but missing planks allowed a few dusty shards of light to crack into the blackness, allowing her to see there was nothing inside but the broken lawnmower and a few unused rakes and shovels. A freshly oiled child's bike.

She slammed the door.

More loud voices from up on the street. Kieran maybe. Or Victor. Or both.

Lila raced up steps two at a time to find no sign of her sister. Instead, she found herself staring face-to-face with Keith Angel, red-faced and spitting mad. He took one look at her and waved toward his Prius. His deeply scratched, heavily keyed Prius.

"That crazy-ass father of yours! He thinks he can mess with me? Thinks he can go around hacking up my property?" The guy pulled a golf club out of his backseat and whacked it against his palm. Lila saw the deeply etched line wrapped around his car and took a step back, unsure what he might do.

"Keith, stop," said Corinne, trying to pull the five iron from his hand. "Remember *you* manage your anger—it doesn't manage you."

"Shut up, Corinne." He stormed the 240Z, raising his club in the air and bringing it down square on the rear bumper with a crash.

"Don't!" said Lila. "We'll pay for your damage. Don't do this."

"Crazy old prick!"

"Please stop!"

"With his pompous-ass notes!" Whack.

Crack.

Smash.

Pieces of Victor's shattered taillights pelted Lila's shins. He hacked and sliced until the rear bumper broke loose and the back windshield shattered. With his wife hanging from his arm, he cracked off the license plate.

Finally, sweating and heaving with exertion, he gave in to his wife's pleading. She took him in her arms and held him a moment, murmured something in his ear, and started to guide him back toward the house. After three or four steps, he spun around, roared like a plane about to take off, and ran at the car one last time, this time hoofing the tail end with his foot.

A clunk.

The sound of gravel.

The car shifted, creeped forward an inch or two in the shattered glass, then paused before crawling forward again. Toward the road's edge. Toward the front yard. With the back bumper dragging in the dirt, the car started to roll.

It had popped out of gear.

Because of her terrible driving, the car was now creeping toward the ridge. There was no barrier. Nothing to stop it from going over.

She lunged at the door handle. Locked. She slapped her pockets. Empty. She'd dropped the keys onto the porch railing earlier.

There was no way to prevent what was going to happen.

Lila looked down at the shed below. Her mother's voice rang in her mind: *Make it your magical playhouse, Kieran.* Lila's own shush. *Her bike's inside.*

But she'd checked the little shack. There'd been no sign of Kieran.

Lila watched the front grille creep closer to the edge. The car was going over. Right over the cliff. Onto the shed.

When Lila was younger, smaller, she used to climb up to the rafters of the shed. The walls didn't quite meet the roof and it left a nice gap and made her perch the most perfect place to spy on whoever might be wandering about in the yard.

The perfect hiding place for a little sister who might be feeling ignored.

Because she'd grown up with a missing sibling.

And watched people hunt.

Saw posters being made.

She became obsessed with missing children.

So much so, she became one herself. A child on the back of a milk carton.

Lila bolted down the steps.

Tearing into the shed, Lila looked up and saw the blackened outline of a figure crouched on a fat beam. Frantic, she screeched for her sister, pulled her down into her arms. She pressed Kieran to her chest, stumbling out into the daylight as bits of debris pelted the cedar rooftop from the cliff's edge above.

Just as the girls tumbled onto the solid steps of the cabin porch, the nose of the car started to tilt downward. Dirt and rocks careened downhill in miniature avalanches as the tires rolled over the edge, spinning uselessly in the air. For a moment the car teetered there and seemed as if it might hold, but with a mighty groan, with the Angels looking on, horrified, the 240Z tipped over the slope and smashed down onto the little green shed.

They watched as a huge cloud of dust and debris mushroomed up the hill, billowed outward toward them. Scrambling, coughing, they both ran to the far end of the porch and squatted down again to gawk at the flattened shed, the mangled car, the spinning wheels.

Lila pulled Kieran onto her lap. "What were you thinking, Kieran?" she whispered, pressing her face into the dust-covered softness of the child's neck. "What on earth were you thinking?"

Kieran didn't speak.

Lila hugged her hard, holding her until she squirmed to get away. "You wanted to be a milk carton kid?"

Kieran grew still. For the first time since Lila met her, she looked like the child she was. "People miss them. Everybody looks for them."

"That's what this is about? Because we forget to look for you?"

"Mummy talked about you all the time. Every night we sat on my bed and asked the universe to find you."

"Not because I was loved more than you. Just because the whole thing was terrible and sad and Mummy missed me. Kieran Scarlett, you are adored. Don't you know that?"

The girl tugged on her bangs and Lila reached up to stop her. "I love your bangs off your face. And I love your school uniform that isn't a school uniform. I love that you care about all these lost children and quote scientists so you can get to bed on time. If you were gone, a part of me—a *huge* part of me—would die. Is that what you want?"

Silence.

"Do you need any more proof than me risking death to save you?"

Kieran stared at the crumpled car, upside down with steam leaking from its great belly. "Delilah?"

"Yes?"

"How come you never call me Kiki like Mummy does?"

"Doesn't really seem like you like it."

She rested her head on Lila's shoulder and tapped her small fingers on her sister's neck. "I don't."

Forty-Four

The neighbors, the firefighters, and the police stood around staring at the morass, while plaid-shirted men with heavy chains in their hands made grand plans to extricate the demolished vehicle. It was more commotion and intrusion than Lila could take just then. She hadn't thought they'd tow the car up and away so fast. You'd have thought, with such a mess of twisted metal and such a difficult slope to impede rescue, the city would have let the car sit a few days. But damaged gas tanks were nothing if not persnickety, and the Hollywood Hills were nothing if not flammable, so specialized towing operators were busy chaining up the Datsun to haul it up and out of the front yard.

Elisabeth was back. Lila hadn't asked how it went at the lawyer's office. At this point she didn't really care.

"I can't believe no one was hurt," gushed Elisabeth as

the three of them sat cross-legged on the porch. "It's a miracle. Plain and simple."

"Delilah saved me," Kieran bragged from where she was twirling in the grass, holding a long twisted stick like a wand, granting wishes to the clover heads, the bumblebees, the dead leaves.

Lila watched her sister. Kieran might not have been abducted, but she was every bit as needy and insecure as Lila. With Elisabeth, a child could never just be a child. To protect herself from a mother who was still a child herself, that child either becomes a wild thing, bold and feral and impulsive, the sort of being you'd imagine being found at the side of the road, the kind of child like Delilah Blue Lovett, who chugs rum-laced backwash in bars and throws herself down in parking lots and begs for fancy bicycles that would—just days later—wind up getting her abducted. And grows up to strip bare for an invisible degree, scribble on her shoes, and steal bracelets.

Or that child hurtles straight toward her adult self, like Kieran. She becomes her own little parent, the exact opposite of her mother. She takes no risks at all, unless it is to prove she's worth risking everything for.

Either way, the outcome was the same. Both girls lost out on childhood. Elisabeth lived it for them.

A meaty cop with mirrored sunglasses and a rusty goatee wandered over to where Elisabeth and Lila stood on the verandah. He grinned at Kieran.

"You're one lucky lady."

Elisabeth pulled the child onto her lap. "And I'm one lucky mother."

"Would have been a terrible day for this city if it weren't for her big sister. You have two very special daughters."

A smile was in order, but Lila didn't have the energy.

"That I do," said Elisabeth, reaching out for Lila's hand.

"All right." He looked at Lila. "The removal crew has everything under control. You've given your statement, so I'm going to head next door. Get their story. Like I said, I would recommend you press charges. It's never good when people become vigilantes. You'll let me know?"

"I will. Later, when I can think straight." She was starting to sound like her father.

"I'm off then. Everything seems okay here for a bit."

No, Lila wanted to say.

Nothing is okay here.

Instead, she said, "My father has been having episodes of dementia. He's been out wandering for I don't know how long. Maybe two hours. Maybe more." The cop took down Victor's description and the house phone number, told her to stay at the house to wait for information, and walked up to the road promising to notify all officers in the area.

Elisabeth let out a quick sigh. "Doesn't that just figure. Just when I make all my arrangements and the police are set to arrive, he isn't here. Trust Victor Lovett to screw this up for me too."

Forty-Five

Kieran stood on the vinyl chair and leaned over the kitchen sink, wincing and complaining as Lila rinsed shampoo out of her hair and wrung it out with a dish towel. "You're pulling it, Delilah!"

"It was full of cobwebs."

She pulled her head to the side, her eyes wide with fear. "Black widows in my hair?!"

"Just dust and stuff. Hold still. We're almost done."

Elisabeth ignored this scene and moved the length of the room, opening cupboard doors and slamming them shut until she reached the cupboard next to the fridge where the cans and boxes of pasta were kept. "I need a little nibble. Something with protein." She pulled out a can of Campbell's Chunky soup and set it on the counter. "Where do you keep the can opener?"

"Second drawer."

"You're ripping out my hair!"

"Just stay still and it'll be over quicker."

"I don't see it in here." Elisabeth rooted through the jumble of scissors, extra keys, unraveled twine, and breath mints. "I can't believe he lives like this."

"At the back. The red plastic thing next to the garlic press."

Elisabeth found it and set about attaching it to the lid of the can. "The lawyer was appalled that your father was able to get away with this for so long. He said even though things have changed, there's still this belief that an abducted child isn't in real danger if she's with a parent. Makes for a whole lot of foot dragging and red tape, he said." She repositioned the can opener and tried to puncture the lid. "But the worst part is what it does to the left-behind parent. Which was no surprise to me, that's for certain. There's nothing more devastating you can do to a person. It's the parent left waiting and wondering who suffers the most."

Lila didn't look up. "It's also the child."

"What?"

"Nothing."

Elisabeth slammed the can down on the tiles. "This can opener isn't even sharp enough to bite into the metal."

It had been just under two hours and still no word from the police about Victor and his whereabouts. He'd been gone at least three hours now. He could be down on Sunset, lapping up cappuccinos at a cozy café. Then again, he could be lying in a ditch someplace, injured, confused, waiting for help.

Elisabeth realigned the can opener and attempted to pierce the lid from a new angle. "I've been meaning to tell you, I spoke to your teacher the other day. That Lichtenstein person."

Lila spun around, her hands dripping wet and covered in conditioner. "You called Lichty? Why? There's no arguing for the scholarship. Or my job."

"Nothing to do with you." Elisabeth raised her brows in reprimand. "I went into his studio to ask him to schedule me in, like we discussed. It would be good for his students, and quite frankly I need the money. Finn's become something else. Started dating this young girl, spends all his time with her. Not only that but he raised my rent. I tell you, I never thought he was so talented. He's dreaming if he thinks he's going to make it in anything other than property management."

Lila wasn't listening. The thought of Lichty at the paint-splattered sinks listening, incredulous, as the woman wearing his bracelet sashayed in to ask him for a favor, even without the slightest chance of Lila seeing him again, ever, in her entire life—it was beyond mortifying. "Mum. There are other art programs in this city."

Elisabeth rolled her eyes, still fussing with the can. "That was pretty much your teacher's reply. Said he was 'all booked up.' Which is fine. I don't need a place like L.A. Arts—such a pompous name. Who's even heard of it? I'll try UCLA, I think. They probably attract a much higher caliber of student anyway. And if they say no, well, I guess I'll book our tickets home." She banged the can onto the counter again. "This can opener is a piece of junk." She opened the cupboard under the sink and hurled it into the trash can.

Lila stared at the way the plastic bag had crumpled over, unprepared for such force, then reached in and pulled the little red can opener out again, so irritated she could barely speak. She stood upright and stared at Elisabeth. "Did you ever think I might happen to love this thing?" Lila opened the can in one motion and handed it to her mother.

"Well." Elisabeth paused for a moment, confused, then laughed and poured the soup into a pot on the stove. "I guess I know what not to get you for Christmas." When Lila didn't answer, she added, "I'm sure your dad just went for a long walk. He's probably spying on the house, waiting for me to leave so he can come home and watch TV."

The phone rang and Lila jumped for it, her hands dripping water all over the floor. "Yes?"

"It's Detective Jorgen, LAPD. Is this Lila?"

"Did you find him? Is he hurt?"

"You are Lila Mack?"

"Yes, yes. Where's my father? Is he okay?"

"He's . . . Well, I think you'd better come down to the station and see for yourself."

Forty-Six

Lila pressed her face between the dirty iron bars and watched him, sitting in profile, forearms resting on thighs, staring at the opposite wall with no more concern than if the bus he was waiting for were running a few minutes late. Beside him was a stainless-steel toilet with no seat and a graffitied message: JANKOWITZ CAN SUCK MY DICK. Victor's jaw muscle balled up and relaxed, balled up and relaxed, as he chewed contentedly on a piece of gum. Funny. She'd never known her father to chew gum before.

Even though he'd turned himself in, the sergeant had explained, they couldn't release him. Not until they could get him before a judge at an arraignment hearing. Of course, judges weren't like plumbers. You couldn't offer them double-time to work Sundays. Victor would have to wait until Monday morning.

It was Saturday night.

"Dad."

He looked up, smiled. "Mouse."

"I'd have come earlier but—"

"I'm never coming to this place again. The food's just terrible. Do you know they served me egg salad? I haven't eaten egg salad in thirty years. I told the waiter to shove it up his ass."

"You're in the police station, Mister. And if you talk like that they may not feed you at all."

He looked around his cell, his gaze resting at the gaping mouth of the toilet beside him. "Well, the place is disgusting."

"You didn't have to do this. You weren't coherent when you turned yourself in. I'll call a lawyer."

He shook his head.

"We'll get you out. I don't even know if Mum will follow through. Maybe I can convince her to drop the charges."

"Your mother tried to turn me in?"

"Don't worry, you beat her to it."

He set his hands on his belly, pleased. "Good. And don't you go calling any lawyers. I knew exactly what I was doing when I checked in."

"You're in a holding cell at a police station, Dad. You're not at the Chateau Marmont."

"Don't tell me where I am!"

"And they'll put you in real jail."

"They won't put a sorry old crust of bread like me in regular jail. I've taken certain steps."

"What steps?"

He tried to suppress a grin. "I'm not out of my head just yet. Headed there, but just managed to squeak in a little something to protect myself. There are special places for the likes of me. My doctor confirmed it."

So it was true. The Alzheimer's. It shouldn't have hit her so hard. She knew. She *knew*. But doctors confirming it took her breath away.

Her chest ached for him. For her. He was slipping further and further away. And even if they managed to slow the disease's progression, sooner or later his physical self would be all she'd have left.

Then, far too young, he would be gone.

She cleared her throat. "So it's true? It's Alzheimer's?"

"Seems they can't get a definitive diagnosis until I'm dead, but yes, all signs point toward it. Strangely enough, it isn't connected to your grandma. I don't have the familial gene, which means you should be okay."

"Dad."

"Plus you take much better care of yourself than I did myself."

"I don't care about me right now."

"Well, I do, Mouse. I definitely do."

"And this is the reason you finally got yourself tested? So you could get diagnosed and put into some kind of psych lockdown?"

"It's the reason I did a few things that might have seemed . . . out of the ordinary. Couldn't afford to take any chances."

"What's that supposed to mean? You faked this memory loss?"

"No, no. But I might have amped things up a bit once or twice. So I appear sufficiently far along. Stealing that little dog was never really going to hurt anyone. I took excellent care of her, did I not?"

She was nearly too stunned to speak. "You stole her

on purpose? What about the Prius? And the pug owner's car?"

He pushed his hair off his forehead, confused. After a few moments, he grunted. "If I touched that hippie bastard's car, he damned well deserved it. The way he parks—like he owns the whole canyon!"

"Oh God . . ."

"Believe me, I plan to pay."

"You think it's going to be much better than prison? It's going to be terrible to be locked up—and you'll still be locked up. Let me call a lawyer and explain. There were extenuating circumstances . . ."

"I will not be fighting anything. Can't undo what I did, but I do plan to repent."

"Do you understand what that means? It might not be jail, but you won't be able to change your mind. You'd be living there for a long time. Maybe forever—I don't know."

He stretched his arms behind his head, leaned back against the dirty wall. "Sounds about right."

She heard footsteps behind her and turned to see the balding guard had returned. "I'm sorry, miss. It's time to go."

Lila nodded, then pushed her face through the bars. "Dad? I have to leave now." When he didn't react, she said, "You're sleeping here tonight. I'll come check on you in the morning."

He stood and unzipped his fly, turning to face the lidless toilet.

"Okay!" Lila spun around. "You have a good night, Dad."

The sound of an urgent stream hitting smooth metal followed by a contented sigh. "Nighty-night, Mouse."

Tears pricked her eyes as she followed the guard out into the main office. "You'll take good care of him?"

He smiled. "We will."

"Sometimes he has trouble sleeping. You know, if it's noisy."

"Can't control the noise on a Saturday night in here, miss. That's our busiest night."

"With the dementia, if he doesn't sleep, it can get worse. I just don't want him to wake up in the morning—all disoriented—and panic, you know? He might forget this afternoon ever happened."

"I'll tell you what. If it looks like he's having trouble, I have a white-noise machine in my bedroom. I live nearby. I don't mind popping home on my dinner break to pick it up."

For the first time in memory, Lila reached out to another adult and hugged him.

ON THE WAY home, Lila pulled the rental car into the parking lot of the drugstore on La Cienega, wandered inside, and located the hair product aisle. Her fingers trailed along the boxes, across the perfect faces of contented models, and stopped when she came to a woman with dirty-blond waves.

She couldn't get out of the store and get up to the cabin fast enough. If she had to spend one more day as a coppery redhead, she'd cut off all her hair. Lila marched toward the door with the package of hair dye in hand, slapped down a ten-dollar bill for the confused cashier, and left.

Forty-Seven

Lila couldn't say what made her sit up at dawn and look about her room from the unfamiliar vantage point of the lower bunk. Or what made her pull on jeans, Wellies, and an oatmeal sweater, wake up her sister, bundle her up, and sneak out into the steely light of a morning that was still only made of skittering birds and dew.

It was an adventure, she told the sleepy Kieran, who'd been loathe to appear outdoors without the dignity of her pleated skirt. It was the change in Lila's appearance, the return to her natural dark blond, that made Kieran sit up. The younger girl, who had gone to bed with one sister and woken up with another, was content to head out onto the trails as siblings who now looked astonishingly alike, and insisted upon bundling herself in jeans and a shrunken sweater of Lila's to match.

Ditching the uniform, if only this once, had to be a good sign.

We're going out for breakfast, Lila told her. Granola bars and water at the tippy top of the city with the sun creeping up their backs to warm their hair. They slipped out the door to find Elisabeth, zipped up in a windbreaker, squatting on the steps and enjoying a coffee and cigarette.

"Mummy!" Kieran ran across the porch and wrapped herself around their mother.

"Sweetie." Elisabeth's eyes widened when Lila sat down next to her. "Delilah. Your hair."

"Time for a change."

Elisabeth ran her fingers through it, enthralled. "You look like my girl again. My beautiful girl."

Lila stood up, irritated by her mother's touch. She'd slept very little. Kieran made for a sweaty, thrashing top-bunk mate. But squirming aside, Lila had lain awake for hours trying to decide what to do about Elisabeth. It was too late for Lila, but Kieran still had a shot at childhood. "We were just heading out for a hike. Can you do rough terrain in those shoes?"

Elisabeth looked down at her slip-ons and laughed. "Anything for my children." She stood up and dusted off her sunny skirt. "Where are we headed?"

Lila reached for Kieran's hand. "Any ideas, Kieran Scarlett?"

Turned out the child was plenty nimble, leaping from rock to rock, stick to stick, in Lila's old rain boots. As they traversed the back of a shaded rise and worked their way up to where the tips of the grass were tinged with morning, Lila purposely slowed to allow Kieran to run ahead.

"Mum. We need to talk."

Elisabeth slipped her arm through Lila's. "Sounds yummy."

"This is serious."

"Now you're making me nervous."

"It's too late for me. I don't even want to talk about that, other than to say I get it now."

"Get what?"

"The whole Dad taking me and everything. Mum, he was scared. Doesn't make it right, but he did what he thought he had to do." She looked at her mother. "I know about the accident. The bike."

Kieran came racing back along the path and handed them each a purple wildflower. She giggled and raced off again.

"This is so good for her," said Elisabeth. "Nice fresh air. Early-morning exercise."

"Mum, I know about you accusing him."

Elisabeth walked along in silence, then reached into her pocket and lit a cigarette. "It's funny. Just last night I was thinking about the accident."

"What happened, exactly? I know I was on my bike . . ."

"Of course, I wasn't there. But it seems you were playing around on the driveway. Went over a jump or something, typical kid stuff. Anyway, I figured out that that moment changed my entire life. If that moment had been different, none of this would have happened."

"Maybe. Maybe not."

"I also made a decision not to dwell on the past anymore. What's done is done. Justice is finally being served, no matter who went to the police first. Much healthier for all of us to look forward. Stay positive."

"Looking forward is what we need to discuss. For Kieran."

"Kieran?"

"She's young. She needs more order. She needs to feel secure enough to be a child. It's why she's trying so hard to be grown up. She wants attention from the adults around her—and, believe me, I'm just as guilty for ignoring her."

"You're saying I ignore Kieran?"

"I'm saying she doesn't feel protected. Look at the way she grew up, surrounded by the overwhelming issue of me. The feeling that life isn't safe. Then you're so ready to trust her to any stranger who seems kind of cool or has a few bucks."

"I am very careful about who is around Kieran."

"That Finn guy? Come on, Mum."

Elisabeth began to nod, her eyes narrowing in the angled sunlight. "I see what's happened here. Your father's poisoned you. Delilah, listen to me: It is vital to trust the good in people. To never give in to this paranoia the media feed us. That sort of fear is the end of community. There is love all around us, do you see that? And look—the person who kidnapped you wasn't a stranger or one of my friends. It was your own father."

Lila kept walking. She'd had enough of her mother's moral stance. It was hugely flawed and only served to magnetize what Lila already knew: neither of her parents was what they appeared.

"I have never left Kieran in any danger. Not for a second."

"Mum."

Elisabeth waved her hand, turned away. "No. I spend a lifetime trying to find you and this is how you treat me?"

"This is about what's best for Kieran. Nothing more."

"Now you're saying I'm not what's best?"

"Mum."

"I am a good mother. Nobody can tell me I don't love my girls." Her chest heaved up and down now.

Why did Elisabeth have to be so delicate? So frail? Surely it would have been easier to confront a woman with big wide shoulders and a commanding bosom. But Elisabeth, she was nothing but a kid herself. This mother, whom Lila had dreamed about all these years—had imagined into a near-mythical being made of nothing but breast milk and kisses and squishy maternal selflessness, whose only flaw was the odd fleck of paint beneath her fingernails—was in reality a self-absorbed child, cunning and insecure and too bewitching for her own good. And, right now, on the verge of tears.

Up ahead, Kieran stood on a small rise and pointed up a crest, her face agape with horror. "Look, a wolf."

Lila left Elisabeth and jogged closer. It wasn't a wolf; it was Slash, lying on his side in a small clearing, exhausted, wild-eyed, and panting in the morning light.

"I know that animal." She started to crawl up through the grass.

Elisabeth called, "Come back here, Delilah! That thing could have rabies."

But Lila was already scrabbling up the slope. As she got closer, she could see the glint of metal around his thick ruff. Snare. A camouflaged loop of wire placed level with a coyote's head. Typically, animals walked into it unknowingly. It was a savage, archaic method of trapping, not only indiscriminate in terms of catching a particular coyote, but could easily trap a family dog or young deer. Death by snare was a slow, agonizing death.

"Please, baby. That's a vicious animal. It's trapped for a reason."

One of Slash's paws was wrapped around the wire, inadvertently forcing the noose around his neck even tighter. She approached carefully, inching closer slowly enough that she could dart out of reach if Slash got testy. He didn't. His sides heaved up and down as he watched her approach.

When she was within a couple of feet, she stopped and dropped down low, murmuring, "It's okay, boy. Easy now."

It was clear he was too injured, too exhausted, to attack, so she crawled close and unwound the wire from his foreleg. This left a little slack in the wire, hopefully enough to free him without moving him closer. First she let him sniff her hand, then stroked his shoulder, his head, behind his ear. There was no reaction whatsoever, so she let her fingers travel up the wire into the bloodied fur around his neck where she began to work it loose and cradled his head while she slipped the wire off. He was free.

"Delilah, he'll kill us all!"

No surprise, Slash didn't budge.

Lila looked back at Kieran, pointed to the water bottle in her hand. Kieran tossed it. Using one hand as a spout, she poured a trickle of water between the coyote's teeth. He didn't react, just let the water pass through his mouth and pool in the dirt beneath his snout.

She continued to dribble water between his teeth until she saw his throat contract. He'd swallowed. It was a good sign. Slowly, sparingly, she offered him water until he was able to lift his head off the ground and lap from her hand, his tongue impossibly soft and gentle. He paused for a moment, looking around and panting, before struggling to his feet. He chanced one more drink, threw her a look that might have said thank you but probably said, "You're one of them," and wandered unsteadily into the vegetation.

Beautiful creature. Free for now.

Whether he was raised in a kitchen or a canyon, whether he mistook the local cats for prey or limited his meals to mice and ground squirrels, it was Slash's all-knowing admirers, people like the Angels, who'd offered him a taste of what it meant to hang with the humans. It meant a full belly. And way too much trust to keep a safe distance.

There was no turning back for Slash. Anyone who'd lived in Rykert Canyon for any length of time had heard it before: A fed coyote is a dead coyote.

Lila returned to where her mother stood, helpless, shrunken, wringing her hands.

It was time for someone in this threesome to step up and be the adult.

Lila needed it. Elisabeth needed it. And God knows Kieran needed it.

"I thought that beast would kill you. All this time without you and then you'd just be ripped to pieces right before my eyes. It all seemed to fit. I was never meant for the good life."

Lila wrapped her arms around her mother and smoothed her unruly curls while Elisabeth held herself stiff and aggrieved. After a few moments, the woman softened, loosened, allowed her body to conform to the hug. "It's okay, Mum. I know how much you love us. And how hard it's been for you."

"It was. No one can imagine how hard."

"I know."

"And not everyone understood. Some people thought, 'At least she's with her father.' Like it was bad but not as devastating as it could've been. But it was! It was every bit as terrible."

Lila held her tighter. "It's over now, Mum. It's over."

"I missed your entire childhood."

"I know."

"All those birthdays and holidays."

"We're going to look forward, right? Just like you said."

Elisabeth pulled a tissue from her pocket and dabbed her eyes. After drinking in a few deep breaths, she began nodding her head as if to calm herself. "Right. We'll look forward. It's the only thing to do."

She let Lila take her arm and they resumed walking. Ahead of them, Kieran hopped on one foot until her boot fell off, then stepped back into it and hopped again, blissfully unaware of the gravel and dead grass stuck to her sock.

"Still, I'm not going to be able to stay on here much longer," said Elisabeth. "The rent is just too much. I just . . . I really don't want to go home. Not unless you come with us."

"I won't leave Dad."

Elisabeth shielded her eyes from the sun and looked at her. "You always belonged to him, didn't you?"

Lila watched her flick her cigarette onto the ground, allowed her mother to step ahead on the path before she stamped it into the dirt, then slipped it into her pocket. When she caught up, she wove her arm through Elisabeth's. "I have an idea."

Forty-Eight

Monday and Victor's hearing came and went. Lila was there, sitting directly behind him, willing him to stay lucid long enough not to cuss out the judge. Before walking into the courtroom, the lawyer Lila hired told them there would be one of two outcomes. Victor could be released pending trial, which was a distinct possibility because he wasn't a huge flight risk—though Elisabeth, Lila had thought to herself, might have had a different opinion of this. The other outcome was that Victor could be admitted to a psychiatric facility on consent pending the trial, whereupon he planned to plead guilty.

Victor's desire was clear. Sitting across the polished wood table in room 17B of the courthouse, he told the lawyer, polite as anything, he'd like to check into the facility after lunch, if it could possibly be arranged. Please and thank you.

Turned out the judge agreed. Said Victor, given his condition, would probably be safer there than at home without a trained health-care worker. Victor had nodded his approval, kissed his daughter on the cheek, and presented his wrists to the bailiff for handcuffing, mildly disappointed when the bailiff announced he wouldn't be shackled for the journey.

LILA HADN'T KNOWN what to expect from a psychiatric institution largely dedicated to locking down criminals. Mint green walls and windows facing birdfeeders and special nooks dedicated to knitting, perhaps. Actually, no knitting. The needles were too sharp. Rug braiding and checkers? Maybe even guards with smiley stickers on their badges? Fairfax Institute wasn't like that. Stern but functional. The decor was spare—with linoleum floors and ugly couches centered around an enormous TV. But the hallways were painted the soft pink of the inside of a conch shell, and just like with the shell, if you listened hard, you could hear the pound of the Santa Monica surf.

No wonder Victor had insisted upon this place.

His room was small. Whitewashed cement lined the lower parts of the walls, with a gray-blue paint above. The décor here was spartan as well: iron bed and nightstand in one corner, speckled white floor, laminate reading table flanked by two tired armchairs. Overhead lighting. He sat in the armchair by the window wearing the taupe shirt and pants you might see on a zookeeper. The look on his face was unexpected too. He looked peaceful. Content. Had atonement softened him?

"Your mother all settled in?"

Victor had endorsed Lila's idea immediately. Not only

did it offer him a shot at giving something back to Elisabeth, but he'd actually been calmed by the knowledge that Lila would be surrounded by family.

To Lila, the move meant much more. Like the small dark coyote in the hills, Lila would step in as unofficial, unasked-for guardian of her sister. At no time would the girl be offered up to a couple of tourists at an amusement park, or left to amuse herself among empty beer bottles.

"Mum's settled, yes. And she's surprisingly thankful to you. She's selling the Cabbagetown house now, so she'll have a bit of a nest egg, not having to use it for another place."

"She take my room like I said?"

"I told her to sleep on the other side of your bed. Seemed fitting."

He nodded his approval.

"Kieran shares with me."

Confusion crosses his face. "Kieran?"

"My sister, Dad. Mum's other daughter. I've told you about her."

He thought about this for a moment. Then asked, "Is your mother all settled in?"

"Yes. She is."

"You give her my room, Mouse?"

She should have grown used to it by now, but she hadn't. Every time he got disoriented, it made her ache. "I did, Mister."

This seemed to please him.

A nurse came in with a tray dotted with paper cups, and announced it was pill time. He flat-out refused. Told her to send in someone else. She frowned, shot a disapproving glance at Lila, and left the room.

When she was gone, Victor pulled a sealed envelope

from his pocket. He handed it to Lila and pretended not to watch as she tore it open. After she'd scanned his words, she looked up. "Seriously?"

"Seriously."

"You were dead against it. Now you'll fund it?"

"I've been thinking—and I do maintain a modicum of reasoning up in this rotting melon on top of my shoulders. You're not your mother. Down there in the cellar working day and night—your mother never did that. Spent most of her time lazing around with these artsy characters she started bringing home. So for you, this art school thing—it might just turn out differently. As long as you stop destroying every damned thing you make."

She leaned forward to hug him, but he swatted her gesture away. "Now, now. Don't get all sappy or I'll think about it harder and have to ground you."

"Good luck with that, Mister," she said. "I'm nearly twenty-one."

"I'm nearly fifty-four, and as you can see . . ." He got up and walked toward the window, unsnapped a lock and pushed it open a few inches. The frame clanked against an iron barrier painted the same seashell pink as the lobby walls. ". . . . being grounded is always a possibility."

"Dad . . ."

He held up his hand. "No. I asked for this. No regrets here."

A male nurse wearing chocolate brown scrubs came in with the tray. Victor waved him away before he got halfway across the room. "No pills from you, either," he roared. "Doesn't anybody around here listen?"

Lila reprimanded him. Told him if he was too bossy, they might ship him off to prison. He smiled, completely unconcerned, and Lila informed him he was a crotchety old bugger. He smiled wider.

"I've been wondering. Why didn't you tell me earlier?"

He stood to adjust his hair in the brass mirror.

"Didn't you feel me hating you? And idealizing her?"

"I did."

"Then why?"

Settling himself in his chair, he cleared his throat and looked at his daughter. "She's still your mother."

Even in the face of that terrible accusation, he'd been unwilling to tarnish Elisabeth as a parent. Lila leaned over him, held down his arms, and forced a kiss to his cheek.

The door swung open and a third nurse walked in with a tray. She placed it on the counter and brought a paper cup and a glass of water to where they sat. A pretty woman, with short brown hair, tiny marshmallow nose, plump lips and cheeks. "I hear you're causing trouble again." With mock sternness, she handed him his pills.

"Me? Never." Victor tossed the contents of the cup into his mouth.

She set about fluffing the pillow behind him and laying a throw across his lap.

"There you go. Can't have my favorite patient getting chilly knees, can I?"

Victor blushed fiercely and reached out to pat her hand.

"You're still an old rascal." As she stood up straight, Lila noticed her nametag said GENEVIEVE. She looked at Lila. "You must be Victor's daughter. Lila, is it? I've been hearing about you since you moved out here, what? A dozen years ago?" She held out her hand, which Lila shook, confused. "I'm Gen."

Gen.

"Your dad never could get enough of this place."

Gen.

She wasn't made up. She'd really been deserving of donuts.

"It's kind of nice to have him here full time. We'll take extra good care of Victor, I can promise you that."

Victor reached out to pinch her arm and she playfully swatted him away. When Gen walked out of the room, Victor sat back in his chair, closed his eyes, and smiled.

The old trickster—Lila could practically see his black-tipped tail twitching.

Some things never changed. Victor Mack always got his girl.

Forty-Nine

After dinner she took the bus over to South Pomona. Went straight around the back of the bungalow, snaking her way through massive hydrangea bushes with thick waxy leaves and glowing flower heads so huge they could have been human heads nodding as she passed. It wasn't fully dusk, but the lights in his studio were already on, spilling into the dense shade of the yard.

As always, the glass doors stood wide open. Through them, she could see Adam, bent over, piling handful after handful of paint tubes into a carton.

She stepped inside and leaned against the doorframe where she watched for a moment.

"If you want to come, it's too late," he said, not looking up. "I didn't book you a seat."

"That's not why I'm here. It's just . . . it's possible I've been a bitch."

He looked up, his expression unsympathetic. "You think?"

"I'm sorry. I've been . . ." She wandered in and perched on a stool. "You know."

"I do."

He sealed up the box, then placed a stack of drawings on a huge, badly cut piece of cardboard, before sandwiching the artwork with more cardboard that appeared to be cut with a plastic knife. She watched while he taped up the edges, then brought out the kraft paper and started to wrap it up like a gift.

"I'm sorry about the magazine thing," he said. "Who could have predicted all that?"

There'd been an article in *Vanity Fair* about Norma Reeves and her ad campaign of painted nudes and very little denim. Specifically about Lila's buttocks. Rumors had been flying around that it was Keira Knightley's posterior, but her camp had denied it. Adam had been not only named as the artist, but Norma had been asked to reveal his model's identity. Adam had refused to name Lila.

So she'd made it into *Vanity Fair* after all, ironically, with absolute anonymity. But the speculation had passed as quickly as it began, and nude models everywhere could now return to their usual and preferred state of elegant obscurity.

"Doesn't matter. Not your fault," she said, looking around the room. "I thought you weren't leaving until after Christmas break."

"Nikki's getting married."

"No."

"I found out online. She posted a moment-by-moment recap of her engagement night. From a single white rose to a table by the window at Bellini's, to crème caramel, to two carats—marquise-cut diamond set in platinum."

Lila grunted. "Classy. And intimate."

"Yeah. Her, him, and all three hundred and fifty-eight of her closest followers."

They were silent for a moment while he scrawled New York addresses on his packages. The marker, which appeared to have no lid, went dry, and he had to dig through a desk drawer for another.

"So you're really going."

"This time next week, I'll be outta here."

"You're sure you're going?"

He sat back on his knees and blinked at her, then pulled his NyQuil from his pocket and tossed it into an open box. "Kind of looks that way."

She walked around the room, peering into boxes, stepping over packing supplies, leaning over to inspect the remains of a takeout burger. After crinkling her nose, she wandered back over to where he sat and stared at him.

"Actually it doesn't. It looks an awful lot like you're running to New York, not going. There's a difference."

Standing abruptly, he left the room, returning with an unzipped duffel bag bursting with clothing. A shoe fell out onto the floor. "That's your opinion. You're allowed one."

"Thank you."

"Anyway, you'd be the expert on running. You're so ready to bolt, you wear short shorts no matter what the weather. God forbid a pair of pants should slow you down. Not that I'm bitter." He bent over to dump a basket of folded laundry into the bag, his shirt riding up his back, revealing the waistband of blue plaid boxers. The same ones he was wearing the night they were together. A girl doesn't forget the first pair of underwear she tugs down a guy's thighs.

Suddenly, she wanted to touch his legs again. Feel their solidity and warmth pressed against her. To feel him all over her—his hands, his mouth, his arms—needing her like he had that night.

She could go. Elisabeth and Kieran were all set up at the cabin. She could make arrangements for appropriate after-school care for her sister, throw a few things in a bag, and escape what remained of her life. Start fresh with Adam. Come up with a hip artist's name, maybe even start wearing long pants. Wake up next to Adam and, instead of feeling suffocated by his feelings for her, take a deep breath and luxuriate in them.

Would he still have her? "Adam . . ."

He turned around and pointed. "Grab that little vinyl case behind you, would you, Nik?"

Nik.

She tossed him the black case.

"Sorry. It was her case. Her name was on my brain . . ."

"Yeah. That's the trouble, isn't it?"

"You've got it wrong. I'm over her."

Lila laughed and turned around.

"It isn't her, Lila. It isn't Nikki I'm running from . . ."

But she was already out the doors, marching down the steps into the yard.

"It wasn't Nikki who left so fast she forgot her socks!"

"Good-bye, Adam."

Fifty

It was warm for mid-January, even for Los Angeles. Lila put down her art bag, tugged off her jean jacket, and tied it around her waist—she had two and a half hours free until she needed to pick up Kieran at school. She pulled a slip of paper from her pocket and checked the numbers on the buildings. Halfway up the block, she came to a one-story building, adobe style, with buttery clay exterior and a wooden door with oversize hinges in rusted iron. A small sign, oval with hand-painted letters, to the right said, THE ARTISTS' SPACE. She pushed blond strands from her face and wandered inside.

It wasn't fancy. Just a foyer with a vending machine sorely in need of refilling; a metal coat rack, unused but for two or three light jackets; and a huge open space dotted with stools and easels. At the far end, a counter with a steel coffee pot, mismatched mugs, and a carton of milk. She'd found this group through a classified ad in the *L.A. Times*. Just a bunch of art lovers who funded a tiny school through car washes and garage sales and private donations. Prominent local artists stopped by, sometimes to speak, other times to draw or paint. Models were paid from a hat that was passed around the studio at the end of a session.

A fifty-something man, red-faced with a wide nose, stood at the door and nodded to regulars, checked the roster for names of the newcomers. Lila approached him. "Hi. I spoke to you on the phone?"

He looked at his list. "What's your name?"

She'd made a decision. Mack was no longer. Neither was Lovett. She wasn't either one of those people anymore. It would take some time to figure out who she was. For now, she was just the daughter of a man who loved her more than his own freedom and a mother who had suffered more than any parent ever should. She was the sister of an eight-year-old in desperate need of a childhood. For now, that was enough.

Still, the man with the clipboard wanted an answer.

"It's Delilah. Delilah Blue."

"Righto. Here you are, Miss Blue." He pointed toward the room. "Welcome. Feel free to get yourself set up. We start in fifteen minutes. Glad to have you on board."

She poked her head inside. About twenty or more adults were standing, sitting, unpacking, sharing a laugh with someone nearby. Portfolio in hand, she crossed the room and set her case down next to a stool by the front window. She unzipped her case and pulled out her blue silk robe. After slipping into the bathroom to change, she returned to the little red carpet square by the window and looked out.

She smiled. There. Across the street, above a flower shop, was Adam's painting. In billboard form. A reclined nude looking up, copper hair tumbling down her back, a pair of faded jeans draped across her hip.

Nude with jeans.

Naked and anonymous, bare and concealed.

There were worse things to be.

The man from the foyer nodded for her to begin, and Delilah stepped onto the carpet where sun poured in from a skylight directly overhead and dropped her robe. But before she assumed her pose, she reached into her bag and pulled out a pair of bent, child-size fairy wings. After reshaping the wire framing—still lavender, but missing some of their sparkle, drowsy from a lifetime of Lila's dreams—she slipped her arms through the satin straps. She planted her feet, hugged herself with arms crossed, rested her chin on her right hand and shoulder, and gazed out above the heads of the artists. Then came the best sound of all. The creaking, squeaking, crunchy-cold snow sound of sharpened pencil on paper.

For now, the feel of their eyes on her skin, on her wings, was all she could handle. Art school could wait. Not forever, but long enough to settle Kieran into her classroom at Rykert Public School and for all of them to get used to the new taste of their lives. For now, this seemed just right.

There. At the back. A latecomer walked in.

Lichty.

Their eyes met and she stopped breathing for a moment, unsure what to do. Leave maybe. Before he announced to the class that they were sketching a thief.

No.

I'm here, she thought. Enough with the running, the

hiding. Truth is, I'm here now. Drenched in sunshine, this is me.

Delilah shot him a glance that said this is my pose. Deal with it.

Lichty stared at her for a moment, listening. Then he lowered himself onto a stool, closed his eyes for a moment and nodded as if saying, "Okay."

He pulled out a pad and started to draw.

ONCE IT WAS over, the students put down their pencils and looked around the room, blinking as if lost and finally found. Smiling, sighing, stretching backs taut with ninety minutes of concentration. A few packed up to make a quick exit; others were more inclined to linger, chat, compare sketches.

Delilah rubbed her neck and shook out her arms. The stillness, the focus, had been just what she'd needed. She'd missed it. And she'd made a decision. Still unclothed, still winged, she folded down to the floor and reached into her bag. Pulled out her phone. Dialed.

A click.

The roar of New York traffic.

His voice. "Hello?"

"Come home."

Acknowledgments

Much appreciation goes out to people I could not have done without. Camilla Fox, wildlife consultant and director of Project Coyote, for educating me about coyote behavior and the predicament of urban wildlife. Jytte Lokvig for Alzheimer's accuracy. Viola Spolin for creating a hillside home I loved enough to wrap a story around. Carol and Aretha Sills for preserving and sharing it. Harold Cohen for legal clarification. Dr. Gary Shapero and Dr. Jeffrey Werger for medical accuracy and Kerry Lewis for teaching me to love L.A. from beneath the Hollywood sign at midnight—I am happy to have lived through it. Jessica Keener, Ricki Miller, Patry Francis, John Lindsay, Jennifer Kolari, and Danielle Younge-Ullman for early reads. Dr. Karen Sharf for Alzheimer's information and Lachlan Mackinnon Bleackley for vintage car details and raising me in the back of a

240Z in the first place. Patricia Gill for launching my love of art. The fabulous folks at Hidden Valley for putting up with the obsessive writer over in Bernie's old place. The gem of a book *The Undressed Art* by Peter Steinhart for insights into the psychology of drawing and nude modeling. Hope Ryden's *God's Dog*, Marc Bekoff's *The Emotional Lives of Animals* for coyote habits.

At HarperPerennial, words cannot do justice to my brilliant editor, Jeanette Perez. Jeanette, you have the wisdom and insight of ten editors, plus two. Carrie Kania, my publisher, who offers the kind of in-house enthusiasm and support every writer dreams of. Amy Vreeland and Nancy Tan for the most thorough copyedits.

At HarperCollins Canada, Iris Tupholme for continuing to publish my books. Jennifer Lambert for her most excellent editorial eye. Leo MacDonald for dazzling marketing and being the man I can always count on bumping into in New York. Alex Schulz for stepping in with enthusiasm and a fabulous British accent. Melissa Zilberberg for tireless publicity.

At Goldberg McDuffie, my publicist, the elegant and persistent Grace McQuade. At United Talent Agency, my film agent, Kassie Evashevski, and her assistant Dana Borowitz. At Writers House, the literary agent with the mostest, Daniel Lazar, who has stayed on this roller coaster without screaming to get off or throwing up even once. Seriously, you are THE best agent a writer could wish for. His witty assistant, Stephen Barr, who sometimes sends me money. Also at Writers House, Maja Nikolic and Angharad Kowal.

As always, my most patient family, who put up with my craziness and absolute lack of domestic skill: Steve, Max, and Lucas.

Insights,
Interviews
& More . . .

About the author

About the book

Read on

About the author

Tish Cohen
Helmets Excluded

I've never claimed to have had a typical upbringing. Nor did I want one. My older sister (Pamela), two younger brothers (Lachlan and Michael), and I grew up in Montreal, where snow banks dwarfed even the tallest of fathers, our grandfather swore he wrestled the alligators that graced his shoes, and our mother lined us up in the kitchen to watch as she offered the unsuspecting babysitter whipped goat's milk disguised as a chocolate shake. Our father, in an effort to coax my sister and me to behave, told us tales of his "other" daughter—a sickeningly mawkish puritan called Tishpam. We never met the phantom creature, but that didn't stop Pam and me from hating her priggish little guts.

It was a time when seatbelts were superfluous, drinkers were drivers, and nearly every house wept cigarette smoke when the windows were flung open in spring. While my mother drove a respectful Cutlass Supreme station wagon that accommodated us just fine, our dad was more sporty. He rode a BMW motorcycle and drove a 1973 Datsun 240Z, a two-seater with a flat hatchback area.

"It was a time when seatbelts were superfluous, drinkers were drivers, and nearly every house wept cigarette smoke when the windows were flung open in spring."

To go out with Dad was an adventure in staying alive. If it was Daddy and you time, you strapped on the sparkly red passenger helmet that weighed more than your next youngest sibling, wrapped your arms around Dad's waist, and, as he guided the bike through traffic on the

TransCanada highway, clamped your eyes shut and apologized to God for never having stepped inside a church.

If it was an outing rich with kids, and Mum was out in the big car, you raced like hell to the driveway shouting "Shotgun!" to the losers on your tail. It was a matter of simple arithmetic. There were two seats in the 240Z and Dad was likely to claim the driver's side. Typically my sister got to the car first, which left the rest of us to open the hatchback, climb inside, and lay supine, our skinny brown arms touching as we lined ourselves up side like little pieces of chalk. Our feet faced forward, of course—otherwise one sudden stop could have rammed our heads into the seat backs, wrenching our necks—which left our trusting faces to stare up at the sky. Our view? Overhead wires, stoplights, seagulls. Cloud after cloud, but mostly the relentless sun. Punchbuggy was less about spotting Volkswagen Beetles and more about the odd passing airplane. And boy did we punch.

Nighttime was different. Typically we were tired, often we were in pajamas, and none of us minded staring up at the indigo sky to wonder at the stars, or watch raindrops or snowflakes hurl down at us like confetti.

Was my childhood happy? Sure. Happy, complicated, lonely. It made me who I am and because of that, I wouldn't change too much about it. My parents eventually divorced and I was brought up by my father, who might have raised me in a way that was unusual, but he ▸

Meet Tish Cohen

Peter Gaffney

TISH COHEN is the author of *Town House*, which was short-listed for the Commonwealth Writers' Prize for Best First Book (Canada and Caribbean region) and is in development to be a feature film, and *Inside Out Girl*, which has also been optioned for film. She also writes a series of children's books, collectively titled the Zoe Lama. Cohen lives in Toronto.

believed in me. Every day I was told I could do anything I wanted in life. That's a message every kid needs to hear.

Years ago my dad, who was living in California with none of his kids nearby, needed surgery for a herniated disc. Not a life-threatening problem but one that had to be dealt with. He was in terrible pain leading up to the surgery, and doctors had made it clear he would need a great deal of care during the two-week period post-op. Our parents had both been robust and self-sufficient until this time and now we were all faced with caring for a temporarily incapacitated parent. One of us had to go—it wasn't an easy choice as two of us had young kids in school and insane careers, one had just had a new baby, and hauling children into Dad's town house wasn't going to help the poor man rest. In the end, Michael, being young and single, with the more moveable career, went.

For all of us, it was an awakening. While Dad recovered from the operation with ease and both parents are still relatively healthy, it made us all quite cognizant of what awaits. Our parents will grow old and our roles will change. We will be caring for them the way they once cared for us. Helmets excluded.

It brought up an interesting issue for me. It's easy to imagine how a child who was doted on—even in an offbeat way—as a youngster would handle caring for an aging parent. But what about the child who was wronged? How would a

“Every day I was told I could do anything I wanted in life. That's a message every kid needs to hear.”

grown child feel toward the vulnerable parent if that parent had seriously done them harm? How would that person cope with the parent needing them? How torn this child would be? Love, hate, allegiance, vexation—which emotion would win out?

It seemed a fascinating start to a novel.

> "Love, hate, allegiance, vexation—which emotion would win out?"

A Life in Books

Favorite little-known novel?

I loved *Me & Emma* by Elizabeth Flock—no one I know seems to have read it, but it was a poignant story about the resilience and terrifying vulnerability of children.

Favorite bookshop?

Book Soup in West Hollywood

Best film based on a novel?

Rebecca

Best short story you've ever read?

"The Lovely Leave" by Dorothy Parker

Any authors you'd like to have dinner with?

Jane Austen, Alan Hollinghurst, and Joan Didion

Favorite little-known children's novel?

I don't know how little known it is, but I adored *The Railway Children* by Edith Nesbit. When I mention it to people, no one seems to remember it.

Books on your nightstand?

Bleak House by Charles Dickens
Lying on the Couch by Irvin D. Yalom

My Latest Grievance by Elinor Lipman
On Chesil Beach by Ian McEwan (a reread)
The Creative Habit by Twyla Tharp (a reread)
American Pastoral by Philip Roth
The Namesake by Jhumpa Lahiri
Must Love Dogs by Claire Cook
Atonement by Ian McEwan (which is coffee stained from the last time I read it)

All-time favorite literary character?

John Irving's Owen Meany

Book you wished you'd written?

This changes by the day. Today I would say *Atonement* by Ian McEwan. One of the most perfect novels on earth, in my opinion.

> So when my German shepherd peed on my unframed business degree while I was at work, I took it as more than proof that my puppy was developing a severe case of separation anxiety. I took it as a sign from the universe that the direction I'd been headed was wrong, wrong, wrong.

Tish Cohen
Skinned

I WAS TWENTY-TWO and looking for myself. I'd recently peeled off my newly minted business-major skin—turned out the square shouldered suits and power briefcase weren't all that necessary for the receptionist job I secured after the life insurance gig and before manning an art gallery. So when my German shepherd peed on my unframed business degree while I was at work, I took it as more than proof that my puppy was developing a severe case of separation anxiety. I took it as a sign from the universe that the direction I'd been headed was wrong, wrong, wrong.

The business world was just not that into me. Not a huge tragedy. I wasn't all that into it either. The discovery meant I'd wasted a few years, but I was young. Naïve. I figured I had plenty of selves to try out yet. The self du jour was about as far from business major as it could be. I'd always loved to draw—I would try life as an artist. Not just a girl who spends every spare minute drawing only to stash the evidence under her bed, but an actual artist.

I kept my reception job by day with the plan to attend art college by night. The eve of my first class, I headed into the restroom at work to slip on my new uniform of Levi's, black T-shirt, and unlaced Doc Martens. I pulled on the black fisherman's cap I bought in Greece—so tight it dented my forehead—hauled my enormous black portfolio out from behind the photocopy machine at work, and hopped on the subway with no small amount of conceit, fairly certain my fellow passengers were eying me with respect and, dare I say, envy. It was clear, after all, that I was a person who knew herself.

My life drawing class was in a converted mansion and the coincidence of me being a lover of old buildings did not escape me. Another sign from the universe—this time telling me I was on the right path. The portfolio full of thick white paper and unused graphite pencils bumped against my legs as I climbed the stone steps, hoping my rolled-up, office-appropriate trousers and sweater set weren't poking out of my army backpack and giving me away. Inside, the halls were thick with the tang of eraser shavings and the wet dog smell of good paintbrushes.

With the exception of the balding man with the Bolivian sweater, the students in my class were mostly younger than I was. Hipper, too. I doubted any of them had gotten sidetracked for four years to study economics and I doubted any had agonized about the costume they would wear to class that evening. I hunted for a free stool and removed my cap.

Before class started, a youngish male walked in, bored and barefoot and wearing a navy robe. Dark hair clung to his forehead like overcooked rotini and he had the beard of an Airedale who had just pulled his snout from a bowl of water. I blinked at him for a moment, confused by his state of undress. Of course—idiotic of me—he was our model. And in a moment he would be ▸

“Before class started a youngish male walked in . . . I blinked at him for a moment, confused by his state of undress. Of course—idiotic of me—he was our model. And in a moment he would be naked. Which I could handle. Totally.”

Tish Cohen *(continued)*

naked. Which I could handle. Totally. I'd been expecting a female for some reason, but a male would do fine. And it was a relief that he wasn't beautiful, I decided. Less pressure that way. Less embarrassment.

Our model chatted easily with the other students and I wondered about him. Was he a student here, doing this for extra credit? Or was he some guy who rents a room above the sandwich shop next door, who saw this as an easy way to bring in the bucks he needs for a new futon? Maybe he did it for the art—maybe he was that dedicated to this community I so badly wanted to join.

When the professor announced it was time to get started and introduced Hunter, our model, I congratulated myself on the seat I had chosen. Hunter was settling himself on a chair in the center of the class. He faced away from me, saving me from having to draw his everything. It would give me a chance to observe the other students, see how they handled his clandestine bits. Were we meant to render them in detail? Or was it a mere suggestion of his manhood we were meant to get on paper—more of a respectful little smudge? I would peek at other people's work when class ended, so I wouldn't embarrass myself next time.

Then it happened. Hunter shifted in his seat. Swung both knees in my direction, hooked one elbow over the chair back, and leaned back as if he were waiting for a bus. Slowly, unceremoniously, his knees dropped

“He faced away from me, saving me from having to draw his everything. . . . Were we meant to render his bits in detail? Or was it a mere suggestion of his manhood we were meant to get on paper—more of a respectful little smudge?”

open. I was face to face with his penis, lying like a slab of unrefrigerated kielbasa atop its nest of matted hair and startled testicles.

Not that I looked.

It was a lot to take in right away. I mean, it wasn't fifty minutes prior that I'd been removing a jammed profit and loss statement from the photocopier at work and now I sat staring at the very possibly unwashed pocket contents of a total stranger.

"It was a lot to take in right away. I mean, it wasn't fifty minutes prior that I'd been removing a jammed profit and loss statement from the photocopier at work and now I sat staring at the very possibly unwashed pocket contents of a total stranger."

Okay maybe I looked. A little.

My alarm troubled me. It called into question my commitment to my new self—my true self. What kind of artist goes into circulatory shock at the sight of what amounts to just another prop in a figure drawing class?

The professor wound his way through the class as we sketched, pausing to offer critiques and compliments. Every so often he would interrupt the class to make a certain point. By the time he made his way over to me, much of Hunter's person was down on my paper. All that was left, other than highlighting where the harsh studio lights bounced off his skin, was sketching in his genitals. I tried to do this quickly, breezily—a slash here, a curve there—lest anyone think I was overly engaged with the task.

A shadow fell over my work.

The professor stood behind me. Determined not to buckle under observation, I embarked upon my lewd and wholly mortifying shading of Hunter's shaft. I willed the professor to ▸

Tish Cohen *(continued)*

move on to another student, but he didn't budge, didn't speak. I started to sweat. What if I was the only student to have drawn this area in minute detail? What if everyone else just roughed it all in?

There was no undoing it. As long as the man watched, I had to continue. Up-down, up-down went my pencil—I could see my hand shake as I worked. Why did the deepest shadows have to fall on the model's groin? And why hadn't I chosen a darker pencil? More important, did I look like an artist or a fool? I scrubbed on. Finally, the professor spoke.

"Easy there."

Feeling smaller than my now snapped pencil, I looked up. The man, who may or may not have been suppressing a smile, gave me a nod and moved on.

I would go on to draw and paint many nude models, none of which unglued me like the first. But did I ever truly fit into my artist's skin? Years later, after attending a second art school—this one for old world paint techniques, frescoes and European plasters—I would be paid to paint using walls, ceilings, and furniture as canvas. But I don't think I really achieved that artist-as-self status, even as a writer, that I tried so hard to portray until the day I stopped trying to portray it. Stopped caring what someone on the subway or someone behind my shoulder might think of me. Because when you discover your true skin you don't want to find it's dented by a fisherman's cap.

"Because when you discover your true skin you don't want to find it's dented by a fisherman's cap."

Author's Picks
Favorite Female Characters in Literature

Emma by Jane Austen

Emma Woodhouse is perhaps the greatest heroine of all time. She's complex, pretentious, opinionated, and meddling. In other words, charmingly human. If she wants something badly enough, Emma is fully capable of imagining her wish to be true; and if what she deems best for others *happens* to benefit her own situation, well, it's a coincidence she'd rather we ignore. And just when her wicked little ego has us completely smitten, she shows herself to be capable of self-examination, honesty, and remorse. Who but Jane Austen could accomplish all this in one pretentious young lady?

Anne of Green Gables
by Lucy Maud Montgomery

This book didn't survive my childhood. There is a point, apparently, where paper simply gives up. Each time I read this novel, I *was* Anne Shirley. I pulled cows out of neighbor's gardens, ogled Gilbert Blythe, giggled with Diana Barry, and despised that my red hair dictated that I couldn't wear red. Or maybe it was pink. Whatever. I even had a winter hat with thick braids for ties and loved the way Anne's braids swished against my cheeks when I tossed my head. I still carry with me a love for the name Anne, but only when spelled with an e. ▸

To Kill a Mockingbird by Harper Lee

Scout Finch is the ultimate tomboy, a feisty little six-year-old who rubs the penniless (and lunchless) Walter Cunningham's nose in the dirt because sticking up for him meant getting her hand smacked with a ruler the first day of school. In spite of her lack of mercy for those she defends, she has a heart big enough to feel for the very teacher who punished her. Too smart for her own good, Scout suffers no illusions. She knows the jingle in her brother's pocket means only one thing. He had to be paid to walk her to school.

The World According to Garp by John Irving

Jenny Fields, T. S. Garp's mother, is to be loved for her extremism, her passion for the Ellen Jamesians, and most of all, her deep-rooted suspicion that lust is the source of all evil. It is this very suspicion that drives her, when ready to have a child, to impregnate herself by having sex with a wounded but perpetually aroused gunner who is dying backwards—by returning to a fetal state. Once born, her young son's well-being drives her every life decision, even compelling her to attend classes to ensure they're worthy of her Garp's time. Jenny Fields is as powerful as they come.

Rebecca by Daphne du Maurier

The unnamed narrator of *Rebecca* has a vulnerability that captivates from the first page. Plucked from her position as traveling companion to a nightmarish society woman, the reader can do nothing but cheer for the future wife of widower Maxim de Winter. But happiness evades her. Manderley, Maxim's colossal and renowned estate, is still haunted by the aura of his "perfect" deceased wife, Rebecca. I don't know that any character has ever given me more worry or strain than the timid and self-doubting young Mrs. de Winter.

Have You Read?
More from Tish Cohen

TOWN HOUSE

Jack Madigan is, by many accounts, blessed. He can still effortlessly turn a pretty head. And thanks to his legendary rock star father, he lives an enviable existence in a once-glorious, now-crumbling Boston town house with his teenage son, Harlan. But there is one tiny drawback: Jack is an agoraphobe. As long as his dad's admittedly dwindling royalties keep rolling in, Jack's condition isn't a problem. But then the money runs out . . . and all hell breaks lose.

The bank is foreclosing. Jack's ex is threatening to take Harlan to California. And Lucinda, the little girl next door, won't stay out of his kitchen . . . or his life. To save his sanity, Jack's path is clear, albeit impossible—he must outwit the bank's adorably determined real estate agent, win back his house, keep his son at home, and, finally, with Lucinda's help, find a way back to the world outside his door.

"For someone who can't leave the house, Jack Madigan is a heck of a guy. *Town House* is everything you could ask for in a novel: touching, wry, bewitching, eccentric, and riveting to the end. I love this book and eagerly await Tish Cohen's next." —Sara Gruen, *New York Times* bestselling author of *Water for Elephants*

Have You Read? *(continued)*

INSIDE OUT GIRL

Rachel Berman is extra careful about *everything*. An overprotective single mother of two, she is acutely aware of the statistical dangers lurking around every corner—which makes her snap decision to aid a stranded motorist wholly uncharacteristic. Len Bean is stuck on the shoulder with Olivia, his relentlessly curious, learning disabled ten-year-old daughter. To the chagrin of Rachel's children, who are about to be linked to the most mocked girl in school, Rachel and Len begin dating. And when Len receives terrible news, little Olivia needs a hero more than ever.

But the world refuses to be predictable. When personal crisis profoundly alters Rachel's relationship with a wild, very special little girl, this perfectionist mother finds herself drawn into a mystery from her past and toward a new appreciation for her own children's perfect lives.

"There is not one single wrong note in this story of crisis and courage. It drives home the truth we ignore to survive: Each of us is a secret, especially to ourselves."
—Jacquelyn Mitchard, bestselling author of *The Deep End of the Ocean* and *Cage of Stars*